EVERY OTHER GIFT

EVER

EVERY OTHER GIFT

by
NAOMI JACOB

THE BOOK CLUB
121 CHARING CROSS ROAD
LONDON, W.C.2

To my friend
TREVOR ST. CLAIR HARRISON

PRINTED IN GREAT BRITAIN BY PAGE & THOMAS, LTD., CHESHAM,
AND BOUND BY NOVELLO & CO. LTD., LONDON

BOOK ONE

CHAPTER ONE

THE story began, properly speaking, in Bradford, where William Henry Hostley ran a bakery, while his wife, Mary Elizabeth, known usually as Mary Lizzie Hostley, attended to the shop. He was a bright, bustling kind of man with reddish hair and hands which were always covered with freckles, though he rarely saw the sunshine, being shut up in his bakery all day. She was what is called in Yorkshire 'a bonnie woman', which meant that, while she could not have been called a beauty, she had something about her that was attractive and pleasing. She had a great memory for faces and names, and in Bradford people like their names to be remembered. So Mary Lizzie's "Noo, Mrs. Smithson, w'at can Ah do fer you this mornin'?" or "My word, boot it's a longish time while Ah saw you, Mrs. Powers. Not bin poorly, Ah hope?" were appreciated by her customers. For children she had always the same greeting, "Noo, luv, w'at is it?" and usually a boiled sweet to pop into their mouths before they left the shop.

Both Mary Lizzie and her husband were regular theatre-goers, and it was arranged that the shop was shut for a half-day to coincide with the matinées at Leeds. On one occasion they visited a celebrated Panorama, which was then causing much attention, but they came away disappointed, William Henry giving it as his opinion that, "Shadders, Muther—nay, Ah dean't want ter sit and watch shadders, no matter 'ow clever they may be. Gie me flesh and blood!"

He was lucky with the 'horses', though he never attended a race-meeting, except Doncaster, in his life, and made his selections in the most haphazard fashion. But what turned the tide so that it flowed strongly in favour of the Hostleys was—the bun! For months William Henry had been working on 't' boon', much in the spirit that a scientific chemist might work on some new and important discovery. Again and again he would bring the latest experiment to Mary Lizzie, and hold it out saying, " 'Ow d'yer find it, luv?" Gravely she would weigh it in her plump hand, carefully break off a small piece, eat it, and deliver her verdict.

"Ah doot as it's not reit yet, William Henry. Mind yer, it's a

5

good boon as boons goa, but—nay, tha mun have anuther goa, lad."

It was when their daughter Charlotte was about twelve that he came, treading heavily, for he was a big man and putting on weight, and entering the overcrowded, comfortable sitting-room, sat down in his own easy chair, panting a little.

"Muther, Ah've done it! Take a luke."

There lay the bun, in fact there lay two buns; light as feathers, covered with a glossy dressing of some kind, the kind of bun which children—and their elders—dream of as the perfect article. Mary Lizzie examined them; Charlotte pushed forward, pale with excitement.

William Henry said, "Well?"

"Hold on a bit," she returned, and breaking off a small piece, tasted it. "Tha's done it, our Daddy, tha's done it reit enoof this time."

"Aye," he agreed. "Lottie, taste a bit, luv. Penny each, seven fer sixpence. Pay?" in answer to his wife's look. "Pay 'and ower fist! It's mixin' as does it, an' Ah'll tak' particklar care as not a livin' soul mixes but me!"

Three days later there was an announcement in Hostley's window—"Something new! Hostley's famous buns! Light as feathers. Penny each." Mary Lizzie, leaning forward over the counter, said to her customers, "Why, Mr. Hostley's been workin' on this boon fer Ah can't tell 'ow long. He knew w'at 'e wanted, an' as you know ondly the best can satisfy him. Six-penn'orth? Thank you, Mrs. Fisson, an' Ah know you'll like 'em."

Within a week everyone knew of Hostley Buns; even the gentry, driving in behind splendid horses, ordered their coach-men to stop and "get some of Hostley's buns." Orders were placed; people knew that if they were not there early Mary Lizzie would shake her head regretfully and say:

"Nay, Ah'm proper vexed, but we're sold out! There's anuther batch in now . . . boot Ah doot as they're all ordered. Nay, Ah'm sorry."

Then William Henry began to experiment on the Hostley Pie! "Only a limited number for sale, orders taken. Price varies according to size." A girl was installed to take orders, the shop next door was taken for the sale of pies and buns alone; ruthlessly William Henry cut down 'lines'.

"Ah'm makin' noa mower rock caakes. Folks can mak' em at home. Ah'll keep on little Queen cakes, an' parkins and congress tarts, bread and teacakes. That wi't' boons and pies is enoof."

6

Then Charlotte, grown tall for thirteen and graceful, even though she was leggy like a young colt, announced that she wished to 'go on the stage'.

Mary Lizzie cried, "Nay, our Lottie, what will you saay next!"

Lottie persisted, "But I want to do that, Muther, an' nowt else."

Her mother turned to William Henry "Daddy, saay something to 'er!"

There was something Jove-like about his complete calm. Mary Lizzie had never felt such admiration for him. He spoke at length, slowly, and with considerable weight. He said that if Lottie really was set on the stage they had probably themselves to blame, they had taken her to the theatre for years every week, she had listened to opera, burlesque, to melodrama and the like, and he admitted that he had noticed that she was trying to 'speak well put on'.

Lottie blushed and said eagerly, "Did you reely notice it, Daddy?"

"Ah notice moast things, my lass. Mind, it's a hard life, an' if soa be as yer muther an' me hadn't made a goodish bit o' brass, Ah'd niver gie it anuther thought. Well, we 'ave! You mun be trained, Lottie; no use of goin' ter start wi' no knowledge, all 'arf baked like. A year it 'ul tak'. Singing, dancing, de-port-ment an' soa on and soa forth. Ah shall mak' all enquiries. If you work, well and good; if you doan't work, then you mun goa inter t' business wi' yer muther and me."

When, later, Mary Lizzie said, "Boot, Daddy, think on the temptations! Think of the lives some o' these folks lead! Ah'd break my heart if aught happened our Lottie," he answered: "If our Lottie's bent that road, she'll find it soon enoof, whether she's on t'stage or walkin' down Manningham Lane."

So Lottie studied for a year, and learnt everything that her teachers could impart; she sucked up knowledge of her 'business' as a sponge takes up water. She developed, and although still young, promised to be a 'fine figure of a woman'. She appeared in the chorus of pantomime, later she played second girl, and later still the part of principal girl was given to her. When pantomime ended she toured the provinces with musical plays such as *My friend the Duke* and *Sweet Mignonette* with great success. At twenty-three she was very much mistress of herself, she had assurance, and her smile won the hearts of her audiences. Various men asked her to marry them, others asked that she would accept their protection, usually because they had stout and very admirable but uninteresting wives living in large and over-decorated villas. Lottie cared nothing for any of them.

She was playing principal girl in *Jack and the Beanstalk* when her father died. She had been over the previous week-end, and had told him that he 'luked proper dowly', and that it was time he stopped bothering about with his old buns and pies and took a rest.

William Henry, his eyes twinkling, said, "Naay, dean't talk daft, luv. Whatever'd Bradford do wi'oot my boons and pies, choose how?"

Three days later he died, and Mary Lizzie sent for Lottie. The pantomime had only one more week to run, and Lottie announced to the manager that she was 'packing up'. He expostulated; she refused to listen to his arguments.

"Lottie, you can't do it!"

"Ah can—you watch me!"

"I shall sue you, my girl."

"Sue away. Ah shan't stop you."

"There'll be no pantomime for you next year!"

"Who says I want pantomime next year—not me!"

"Your salary will be stopped; you know that, eh?"

"Of course Ah know it. What d'you think Ah am—daft?"

Lottie left, and her place was taken by Miss Florrie Finnimore who made a tolerable success. Back in Bradford, Lottie found her mother inconsolable. She had adored her William Henry, and the prospect of life without him was terrible. Now she sat in the rather stuffy sitting-room, stout, with—it seemed to Lottie—all her comeliness washed away by her tears. She refused to eat, only taking cups of strong tea at short intervals.

"Is panto ovver, luv?" she asked Lottie.

"It's over, Muther—s'far as I'm concerned, any road."

"Then you'll be able to stop wi' me a bit, won't you?"

"Don't you fash yourself, I'm stopping. I shan't leave you, ducky."

"Naay, Ah'm reit gled at that—reit gled."

During the days that followed her father's funeral Lottie Hostley did some hard thinking. Her mother had changed; it was as if someone had breathed on the mirror of her mind, clouding it. Not that she was 'daft', but she seemed incapable of making decisions. It was evident to her daughter that Mary Lizzie Hostley would never be able to run the business. She would never settle down to travelling with Lottie from town to town, she wanted a home of her own, somewhere where she could take roots. William Henry had left money; the amount had surprised Lottie by its immensity. Nearly nine thousand pounds, and all made out of buns and pies and the like! But what to do with it? Lottie frowned over the problem, and, finally, leaving her mother in the care of Maude Phillips, the head assistant, who 'lived in', she walked down to the local music-hall, and sent in her card to the manager.

She had known Alfred Tuller for many years; as a child she had appeared in dances with other small girls with the object of obtaining money for charity. She had later appeared to give her own turn at a benefit organized for some artiste. Tuller liked her; indeed, on several occasions he had hinted pretty plainly that his regard for her was heavily tinged with sentiment.

"Get along, Alfred," she had retorted. "With that bonnie wife of yours, and four children! You've got a cheek, you have!"

He asked her now to come into his office, and as he sat watching her and thinking how attractive she looked in her deep mourning, she stared about her and wondered how anyone could tolerate such a dirty, dusty place, or ever hope to find anything among the heaps of papers which were scattered around.

"What a dog-hole, Alfred; eh—I couldn't stand it."

He replied gloomily, "The dressing-rooms are pretty nearly as bad."

She shrugged her fine shoulders. "The old idea—anything will do for the pros, the people who bring the public in!"

"I can't do anything about it, Lottie."

"The rooms we have to stay in on tour! One decent place and twenty that are filthy. Landladies who can't cook, and won't clean! Poof!"

Tuller rose and went to a small cupboard and produced a bottle of whisky and two tumblers, saying over his shoulder, "You'll take a spot, Lottie?"

"Are those glasses clean?" she demanded. "They don't look clean to me."

He held one up to the light and squinted at it doubtfully. "I think they are. They're supposed to be washed every morning, when they do the office."

"If they wash 'em as well as they 'do' the office," she retorted, "small wonder they look so mucky. Give them to me."

She carried them to the small washstand which stood in the corner, and with much 'T'ch, t'ch'-ing, and suppressed exclamations of disgust, washed them. "There—now you can give me a drink without my endangering my life, Alfred."

She sipped her drink, then said suddenly, "You've given me an idea, Alfred, with your dirty old office and dirty old glasses. I came here to get advice, well, you've given it. I shall let rooms to pros!"

"Here?"

"No, somewhere bigger. Manchester or Liverpool, somewhere where there are several music-halls, a couple of theatres, and an opera-house. What's the word I want . . . somewhere where Ah'll have scope! I'm working Manchester the week after next, I'll begin to look round. Thanks for your help, Alfred."

He sat watching her, a heavy man who had once been good-looking, wearing a shabby dinner-jacket suit, with a carnation which was certainly past its prime in his buttonhole.

"But the business? You'd leave the business?"

"Tell you the truth, I've had about enough of the business. I've not done badly, but I shall never do any better nor what I've done up to now. I'm not the stuff as stars are made of. I don't like sleeping with men—not unless I think I'm in love with them at the time—I don't like being pawed about, and—oh, I've had enoof of it, choose how. Then there's muther, she can't live alone, she can't come traipsing round the country with me! Nay, I've got it all worked out. . . . Whoa, Emma! That's me! Nothing 'ul stop me. Good night, Alfred, and thanks for your help. Get that office of yours cleaned, or I'll come and clean it for you one day!"

Lottie went to Manchester and after the first house on Monday asked her old friend, Josh Mander, the stage manager, to come into her dressing-room for a drink. She had known him for years, and he had asked her several times to marry him; she had always refused, but they remained fast friends, and Mander made no attempt to conceal his admiration for her.

She gave him what she called 'a nice liqueur of Bass', which was one of her small stock jokes, and immediately plunged into details of the plan which she had evolved since her visit to Bradford.

"My poor dad left nine thousand, Josh, all made out of buns and pies, mark you! Muther can't carry on the business, that's quite clear to me. Not that she's gone actually queer in her head, bless her, but she seems a bit dull, if you know what I mean? I shall sell the place, the goodwill; and the recipes for the buns and pies are worth a good bit, I reckon. Dad always kept the recipe in his safe, and not a soul ever did any mixing but himself. I've told you all that so's you can get the general lay-out."

Josh, a solidly built man, with a heavy dark moustache of which he took the greatest possible care, nodded gravely, wiped the moustache with a very clean blue-bordered handkerchief, said, "Aye, I've gotten the idea, Lottie. Go on wi' the tale."

"I'm getting out of the business."

"Is that so? You'll be missed, my dear."

"Not me! I'd rather leave the business before it leaves me, choose how. I want to open a place and let rooms to pros. Rooms, mind you, that will be *rooms*—not pigstys. I want to give 'em meals that they'll enjoy. I only want the best, the cream of the profession. I'll charge sufficient, but I'll give them their money's worth. I b'lieve that Manchester's the place. What do you say, Josh? Somewhere just off of the Oxford Road. I'll buy—not rent. Any ideas?"

Again Josh nodded, and in answer to her unspoken question as she held out her hand for his glass, said, "Thanks, I don't mind if I do. Aye, I've plenty of ideas. Not too small a place—they don't pay. I've an idea as there might be a place in Robey Street, or Stratton Street. Biggish places, well built, bit of garden in front, bigger bit at the back. Have a scout round in the morning, Lottie. Get the keys of anything you fancy, and if I can be of any use in giving you advice, I'll be glad to come round wi' you in the afternoon. Nothink like striking while the iron's hot. Well, I must be off. Thanks for the beers, they did me a power of good."

The next afternoon Lottie Hostley, looking very trim and neat, accompanied by Josh Mander, inspected a house in Stratton Street, off the Oxford Road, which she declared fulfilled all her ideas and expectations.

"Three sets—dining-room, drawing-room, and that smaller sitting-room, that takes up three of the bedrooms. I don't want any 'combined chats' in my house! No more do I want aspidistras in the windows. I want anuther bathroom, modern range in the kitchen, better sink—I must have a deep sink, can't abide those shallow things. I'll have anuther 'double-you' I don't hold with having folks hammering on the door like they do when there's only one in the place. What d'you say, Josh?"

"I say that I reckon you've got something pretty good, Lottie. Redecorated nicely, the various improvements as you've mentioned put in, an' I'll bet there won't be a nicer place in the whole city of Manchester."

"Never mind city of Manchester," she retorted, "there'll be no nicer place in all the provinces, my lad."

For the rest of the week Lottie worked without ceasing. She saw the lawyers, she interviewed decorators, plumbers, chose wallpapers, carpets, curtains. On the Saturday morning she signed the cheque for the purchase of the house and returned to Bradford a very satisfied and contented young woman.

Josh came to see her off at the station on the Sunday morning, and, as he stood by the open window of her carriage, said, "Lottie, I suppose you'd not consider takin' me on as a partner in this house business?"

"You mean will I marry you? Nay, lad, let me get things straightened out before I start thinking of anything like that."

Gently persistent, he said, "Then when you're settled, d'you mean as you might think about it, luv?"

"I'm making no promises, Josh. I like you as much as any man I know. I can't say fairer than that, can I?"

He smoothed his moustache. "I s'pose I'll have to be content. I'll ask you again, Lottie, later. Till then, I'll hope for the best."

The following week Lottie sold the shop, and premises attached. She bargained hard, sold at an excellent price, and in addition sold the recipes of William Henry Hostley's Famous Buns and Meat Pies. The sum which these realized surprised even Lottie herself, and when she announced the sum to her mother and gave her all the details of the new venture, it was surprising how Mary Lizzie's general outlook on life changed. Ever since the death of her husband she had taken little or no interest in anything; now she became interested, and excited.

"My word, our Lottie, you've gotten a right headpiece, I must say. How proud your poor dad 'ud be of you! Ah think maybe it's a good job we'll be moving; Bradford holds over many memories fer me. There's one thing, our Lottie, as I can do—that's cook! I'll lay as your lodgers 'ul be well satisfied with the meals as I'll cook fer them! Nay, I'm longing to come over to Manchester an' see this lovely house!"

Lottie wrote at length to her agent, explaining her changed circumstances, and directing him to cancel any dates which were still to be played. As she was not a star of the first—or even second—magnitude this presented little or no difficulty, and within a month she had removed to Manchester, taking her mother and the furniture with her.

Nowhere does news travel faster than in the legitimate and variety professions. Josh Mander recommended Number Seven

Stratton Street to the 'bill-toppers'. Herbert Campbell told Dan Leno that he would never stay in a hotel in Manchester again after spending a week at Mrs. Hostley's. Lovely Maggie Duggan told Bessie Wentworth that it was worth going to Manchester if only to taste Mrs. Hostley's meat pies. Mrs. Kendal, doing a short tour of *The Elder Miss Blossom*, stated frequently that "not only are Mrs. Hostley's rooms furnished in excellent taste, their cleanliness nothing short of perfection, but the cooking is completely admirable. I can recommend them most highly." 'Mrs. Hostley's' was to take its place among the famous theatrical rooms, in that all-too-short list which included Gertie Dillon, Sophia and Hannah Ogbourne, Mrs. Hunter and possibly half a dozen more admirable 'landladies'.

The fact that the house was always spoken of as 'Mrs. Hostley's' was Lottie's idea, she felt that to be at least the nominal head of the venture gave her mother additional interest. Her health had improved, she moved energetically, cooked beautifully, and presented her bills—made out by Lottie—on Sunday mornings with considerable dignity.

Josh was always a tower of strength, he was 'handy about the house'; there were no small repairs which he could not—and did not—tackle. Lottie used to watch his capable hands with their strong blunt fingers and broad palms with something like admiration as he worked.

"You're a handy lad to have about the place, Josh."

"Why not have me about the place for good, Lottie?"

She laughed. "I've a good mind to, lad."

He laid down the screwdriver and came to where she stood.

"You mean it?" he asked. "Lottie, I'll swear that no lass shall have a better husband. I'll be good to you. Eh, you've made me happier nor I ever thought to be. Give me a kiss, my dear, an' we'll go and tell your muther."

They were married quietly. Josh continued to work at the Majestic Palace of Varieties. The rooms were never empty. Lottie had bookings for more than twelve months in advance; only when each pantomime season ended she insisted upon keeping them vacant for two weeks in order that the place might have what Yorkshire housewives know as a 'thorough clean'.

She had been married nearly two years when she told Josh that she was going to have a baby. His eyes filled with tears, for under all his solidity he was intensely sentimental.

"Nay," she expostulated, "that's no way to take the news—to cry about it! Aren't you pleased?"

"I'm that pleased," he said shakily, "that I don't know what to say. It's what I've longed for. Give me a kiss, luv, and we'll go and tell your muther."

Lottie laughed, "Tell my muther! No need to—she knew before I knew myself! No call to tell her; she told me, if it comes to that."

The child was born and named Jenny. Her mother refused to consider the name 'Jane', she hated it, and so Jenny Mander was introduced to all the stars of the legitimate and variety stage. She was a pretty child, well behaved and never allowed to be obtrusive or precocious.

When Jenny was twelve years old and her mother the shady side of thirty, Mary Lizzie died. She had been cooking as usual, and was still smiling over the recollection of young Bransby Williams' delight at her pie of blackberries which she told him, in Yorkshire, were known as 'bumilkites'. The name had amused him, and he had promptly made up a rhyme introducing the word.

She returned to the big, spacious kitchen beaming happily. "Yon's a lad," she told Lottie. "Mind you, when you see him on t' stage you'd never think he was able to laugh his head off at a Yorkshire word. Fair roared, he did!" She sat down in the armchair which was reserved for her exclusive use, and said, "Eh, my lass, I'm tired. I doubt as I'm getting old. It's a good job as you've learned yourself to cook, for I doubt I'll not be a lot of use much longer."

Lottie replied smartly, "Nay, Muther, don't talk so daft. You'll see me and Josh out, if I know anything."

"Happen," Mary Lizzie answered, "but I doubt it." A few minutes later she said that she thought she'd away to her bed. Lottie went up with her, saw her into bed, came down for the usual glass of weak whisky and water, which her mother always took. On her return to the bedroom Mary Lizzie was lying back on her pillows breathing rapidly. Lottie, alarmed, offered her the whisky and water; she sipped it, and said, "Nay, I'm tired to death!"

"Stay in bed in t'morning," Lottie advised. "We can manage all right. Have a good rest, Muther."

"Stay i' bed!" her mother repeated, "an' me promised Mr. Williams one of my steak-and-kidney pies! An' Mr. Randall one of my chicken *ong casserole* what he's so fond of! Nay . . . I'll be up and about."

Two hours later Lottie went into her room; it was obvious that her mother was gravely ill.

Lottie called for Josh, saying, "Josh, muther's really poorly. Run for the doctor. Get moving, lad."

The doctor, kind and ineffective, arrived; he made clicking noises with his tongue, felt for his patient's pulse, advised 'a little stimulant' and promised to call in the morning. When Lottie demanded, "Aye, but what *is* it? What's ailing her?" he replied with the quiet assurance of complete medical ignorance, "Ah, Mrs. Mander, if I gave you the correct medical terms how much wiser would you be? I shall prepare a tonic for your mother. Among other things she is distinctly run down. Good night. I shall be round early in the morning."

Lottie returned to her mother, who greeted her with the words, "Say what you like, yon doctor's a soft piece. Sitha, Lottie, keep them two recipes for buns and pies under your own hat. Don't let anyone else do the mixing. Half the pros in England are talking about our buns and pies. 'Keep the name—Mrs. Hostley'. They know it, they like it. Now I'm going to sleep."

And go to sleep she did, and never woke again in this world. When Lottie went in about six in the morning Mary Lizzie was dead. She looked very peaceful, and utterly content. Lottie, heartbroken though she was, told Bransby Williams, "It's no use, Mr. Williams, you've got your work to do, and it behoves me to do mine. Josh is down seeing the undertaker now. This house will go on just the same. It's my 'public', same as what audiences are yours and Mr. Randall's. Muther promised you a steak-and-kidney pie—you'll get it. Mr. Randall 'ul get his chicken *ong casserole*. That nice little Miss Gitana will get just what she ordered yesterday. Thank you for your sympathy, I appreciate it, but the work's going on! Muther 'ud be the first to understand."

So Lottie took over the cooking and did it as efficiently as Mary Lizzie had done. She got two strapping girls from Pudsey, who regarded the work of the house as 'nobbut play', and 'Mrs. Hostley's' went on as before.

Jenny confided to Eugene Stratton, who liked the child and encouraged her to talk to him about her wishes and ambitions, that she wanted to 'go on the stage'.

'Gene said, "Why, honey, d'you want to be an actress?"

"No, Mr. Stratton, I want to be like you—a dancer."

"You mean that? It's not just a kinder dream? Dancing's hard work. Means giving up quite a heap of things. Practice morning, afternoon and night. You're certain sure you want to be a dancer? If you do, be a good dancer, honey. A bad dancer is just an offence against God. That's a terrible thing to be."

She shook her head. "No, I want to be a good dancer. I don't care how hard I work, Mr. Stratton."

He said, "Sweetie, I'll do all I can."

That evening, after the performance, he sat in Lottie's kitchen and talked about Jenny. He painted no rosy picture, he stressed the hard work, the demands made upon the human body, but he insisted that if the child's heart was set upon being a dancer, they were fortunate in that she could go for tuition to the great John Tiller in Withy Grove and be trained magnificently, and sent out into the world as a first-rate artiste.

"For," he said, "John will never tol-er-ate the second best. Unless his dancers are in the first class, they just aren't in any class of his."

So Jenny Mander at twelve went to John Tiller, and was trained, and instructed, had her heart broken five times a week, suffered despair and then splendid moments of elation. She knew what it was to feel that her feet could never dance a single step again; she knew what it meant to feel that she was skimming like a swallow, only to be brought heavily to earth by the statement of her instructress that her imitation of an elephant was admirable.

At fourteen she emerged—trained. She was too old to be sent out with the 'Manchester Mites', but she was given a place in the celebrated 'Sunshine Girls', and later graduated into the famous Tiller Troupe.

Her mother and her kindly stolid father were disturbed at the idea of her touring the Continent, dancing in such places as the Folies Bergères, or the great music-halls in Berlin, Vienna and Milan. They visited the school, where Mrs. John Tiller granted them an interview. This dynamic woman, with her incisive manner and tremendous energy, told them, "Our girls are *looked* after. We don't stand any nonsense. They have a matron with them. If they can't behave they can—get out. If that kind of thing suits them—well, it doesn't suit either me or my husband. If your girl's a good girl, she'll be all right. If she's not, then you'll have her home very quickly."

Josh said, "Mrs. Tiller, I've been at the Majestic for years; my wife's been on the stage. We know your girls are the top of the tree. That's where we want our Jenny to get to. I'm satisfied, if my dear wife is. What'd'you say, Lottie?"

Lottie said, "I went on the stage, Mrs. Tiller. My dad never tried to stop me. I don't want to stop our Jenny. I only want to know that in so far as a girl can be kept right—and I believe if they want to go wrong nowt 'ul stop them—she will be, so far as is possible. Right, our Jenny comes to you! Thank you for giving us your time as you have done."

So young Jenny went off on her first tour; the troupe visited Paris, where night after night they were acclaimed and applauded. To Vienna, Berlin, Milan, Budapest, Geneva, Genoa, and even to Alexandria. She loved touring, loved the change of scene and climate. She was startlingly pretty, with bright fair hair, small and very neat features, blue intelligent eyes, and feet which literally flew over the stage.

Lottie, in Manchester, waited for her letters, her postcards and the small gifts which she sent from time to time. She thrilled with pleasure when some famous artiste asked, "Where's your pretty little girl, Mrs. Mander?" and was willing to abandon her work to tell of Jenny's doings and success. It was with pride she would tell Josh, as they sat over their late supper, "Fancy, Josh, Miss Lloyd asked where our Jenny'd got to! Said what a nice little girl she was, so well-behaved. Nice, eh?" or "What d'you think? Miss Ford wanted to know where Jenny was. Spoke so nicely about her. Said if she was on the same bill as the troupe she'd have a word with Jenny, and ask her to tea. Makes you feel proud, doesn't it?" To which Josh invariably replied, "She's all right, is our Jenny."

Then came the news that Jenny, who had been working at Genoa, had fallen on the stage, where some previous act had used real flowers and left a petal lying where the Tiller Troupe danced. She had broken her ankle and was in hospital. The matron was doing everything possible to ensure that she had the best possible treatment, but it was doubtful if she would be able to dance again.

Josh, who never swore unless deeply and profoundly moved, said, "That *is* a b——, that is!" Lottie in her distress forgot to say, as she always did, "That 'ul do, Josh, you know I hate language," and wept bitterly.

That week Harry Fragson was staying in the house, and Lottie went to him in her distress.

"Mr. Fragson, you've been abroad; neither me nor Josh ever has. Our girl's ill in Genoa—that's somewhere in Italy, if the map is right. Could I get to her? I'm worried sick."

Harry Fragson, proverbially kind-hearted, told her all she needed to know. He worked out routes and trains, he gave advice, and, most important of all, he assured her that Italians were kindly and that they liked the English.

Lottie, feeling that she was flinging herself out of the world she knew into one which was completely unknown, departed for Genoa. The two girls from Pudsey assured her that they 'could manage all right', and suggested that their aunt, Mrs. Formly, of Manningham, might be imported to do the cooking in Lottie's absence.

"Mind yer, missus, she's a 'igh-class cook, is Aunt Formly. Goes out to cook for dinner parties for swells, weddings an' such-like."

Exhausted, frightened to death despite the fact that she put a bold and brave face on everything, Lottie arrived in Genoa. The Troupe had left for Vienna, and she made her way to the hospital almost trembling with apprehension. To find that it was staffed by nuns added to her fears. She was no church-goer, but she had been taught that Catholics never lost an opportunity of trying—by any means, possible or apparently impossible—to convert all with whom they came in contact.

As she was escorted along the seemingly endless corridor by a small, bustling nun, who kept beaming at her and repeating, "*Va bene! Va bene!*" she thought, 'They're half daft. They could learn to speak English if they liked. They just want to be awkward!'

She entered the ward, and saw, seated by Jenny's bed, the most beautiful young man she had ever imagined. He was slim and above medium height. His hair was dark and waved a little, and when he turned at her approach she saw that his eyes were dark, large and very gentle.

Jenny cried, "Muther! It's my muther! Alfredo, this is my muther come to see me. Give me a cuddle, Mummy darling. Eh, this is luvely!"

Later the young man took his leave; his English was halting but understandable. He bowed over Lottie's hand in a manner which she stigmatized as 'right outlandish'.

"Who's he, luv?" she asked Jenny.

"He was on the bill with us when I had my accident, Muther. Oh, he has been kind, so's his muther and father. His name's Alfredo Menetti. He's an acrobat and wire-walker. He's so sweet, and—darling, don't be cross, he wants me to marry him. He's joining Trumelli's Circus, and I shan't be able to dance again. I could just assist him in the act. It's the finest circus in the world. They're booked for years ahead. Alfredo gets a huge salary. He's right at the top. Mummy, say you and dad won't mind. Please, say it, darling. I do love him so—and he loves me."

18

Lottie drew a deep breath. "Why," she said, "this is a right do, this is."

CHAPTER TWO

THE following day Lottie interviewed Alfredo Menetti. She had questioned her daughter, and had sent a telegram to Josh saying:

Jenny in love with Italian nice looking acrobat wirewalker do you think all right Lottie.

To which he replied:

Your judgment good enough if you approve.

Menetti called at her hotel in the evening and dined with her. She found him modest and well mannered; his English might not be perfect but she could understand him, and he apparently understood her. Dinner over, she ordered coffee and said, "Now, let's get down to business, Mr. Menetti."

He smiled engagingly and said, "Pleaze?"

She said, rather more loudly, "I say, let's get things talked over. You want to marry our Jenny, eh?"

His smile widened. "Yes, eef you pleaze, signora."

"You really love her? It's not just a fancy you've taken to her?"

"I loff her, signora. Ver' much. Wiz my w'old heairt. Wit her all ver' good; wizout her—nossing! I truly spik to you. No more *poverina* possible to dance!" He sighed gustily. "Wiz me no dance, only in act, pass to me sings lika—how you say—*falsoletto*?"

Lottie said, "Nay, lad, how'd I know? Props—would that be it?"

Menetti said, "How is zis—prrops, pleaze?"

"Eh, this is getting beyond me! Never mind, it's something she hands to you. Have you enough money to keep her properly? She's been used to the best, mind."

He nodded energetically. "Plenty money! Of bills always Menetti is top name, big letters. I hev fine caravan, leetle travelling 'ouse. All hev admiration for eet. De lusso is my caravan. Much paint, also gold paint. One day I take you to see eet. Trumelli best circus in the world—everywhere goes Trumelli. America, Australia, Africa Sud, Spain, France—all the world wishes to see Trumelli."

"What kind of salary do you get?"

The beautiful young Italian stared at her, wrinkling his forehead, making a desperate effort to understand this well-dressed, still-very-attractive English woman. He thought how strange it

19

was that so few English understood any language but their own, then remembered that they were a rich and powerful people, with possessions all over the face of the globe, and that they had grown accustomed to finding people in all parts of the world who spoke their language. Lottie was conscious of a rising sense of irritation. Here she was trying to talk to this good-looking young man who wished to marry her daughter, and, she decided, 'making a poor job of it all'.

She repeated her question, "What kind of salary d'you get?" Then falling back on pantomime, and the only Italian phrase she had learned, she flicked her open palm with her first finger as if counting money and said loudly and firmly, "*Quanter coster?*"

The effect was electrical. Menetti threw back his head and laughed with complete abandon and amusement, crying, "*Brava, signora, ma bravissima!* Monie—eh? 'Ow mooch money I get, no? In America in dollar American t'ree 'undred all weeks. Now wiz Trumelli I get me more, for I am ver' better and get same as t'ree 'undred an' fifty dollar. Same in Italy, Germany, all places but in lire, franc, mark, etcetera. Much saved, for me ver' careful man. Not smoke moch, not drink moch, womens—no, no! I not like."

Lottie beamed her approval. She found that she liked this young man, with his rather oversmart clothes and a tie which would have made Manchester blink its eyes by reason of its brilliance. She felt that he was honest and kindly; he did not resent her questions, and his smile came very readily. The rather gloomy lounge of the hotel seemed to have suddenly become lighter, and more friendly.

She thought, 'By gum, if this lad and our Jenny have any bairns I'll lay they'll be beauties', and with that thought came another which made her face grave once more. She leaned forward and tapped Menetti with her finger on the knee.

"Look," she said, "what about religion? Our Jenny's been brought up Church of England. Mind you, we're not what you might call church-goers, but we've never had any dealings with the Catholic Church."

He stared at her blankly; she felt that if he said 'Pleaze' again she would scream; he frowned, then said, "Church, oh yes. Jennee is Protestant, no? I am Christian man. Jennee is pleazed to be made Christian lady."

"Catholic, eh?"

"Yes, pleaze, Catholic."

"Why, I'm sure I don't know what Josh 'ul say. That's her

father, Josh Mander. We'll have to talk it over. I don't know that I like this changing religions much."

Agreeably Menetti said, still smiling, "No? Yes. All right. We shall talk. I am good man; Jennee is also good. It shall be ver' good for all."

She returned to England, having visited the father and mother of Menetti in their home. They were kindly, simple people, who obviously adored their son, their only child. They kept a pleasant and exquisitely clean restaurant, and lived in the flat above it. While she realized that they were not rich people, yet the furnishings and general atmosphere told her that they were comfortably off. Neither of them spoke a word of English, and conversation was carried on by Alfredo acting as interpreter.

'Though I bet he understands a lot less than what he lets on', Lottie thought.

Their hospitality was unbounded; later she told Josh that she never sat down to a meal where there was so much to eat, "and mind you, if you refused a dish—there were dozens of them, Josh —they looked that hurt you felt that you'd given them a smack in the face." In the dining-room hung a large coloured oleograph of an elderly gentleman dressed in white with a white skull-cap on his head. His hand was raised, and his face wore a large and expansive smile. She looked at it several times, until Alfredo, noticing her eyes turning again and again to the picture, said, "Signora, zees ees the great Pope, Leo the Thirteenth. See 'ow 'e gives blessings to all. Ver' fine man, much loved always."

Lottie nodded. "Looks a kind old gentleman, any road."

Alfredo said, "Oh yes."

His mother clasped her hands, and in mime did her best to denote that Leo XIII was an individual worthy of admiration and affection. Lottie smiled back at her, saying, "That's right—*si, si, si.*"

Back in Manchester she and Josh sat far into the night while she told him of her impressions. He listened in silence, only rising at intervals to pour out another glass of beer.

"Mind, Josh, it's romantic. They were on the same bill in Rome and seemingly this young man—a right lovely young man, mind—just fell head over ears with our Jenny. He told me so. Couldn't get her out of his head. They went about together, seeing places, like where the Pope lives and so on, and then she went on to Genoa. That's where his family live. Nice little restaurant, John, clean as a new pin. He had a week out, went home and saw our Jenny at the music-hall. Went in front every single night. He was there when she fell and broke her poor ankle. He visited her in hospital—all the nurses are nuns, and I must say they seem very kind. Jenny speaks of them most highly. Well, the long and short of it is, after getting your telegram I gave our consent.

"When Jenny can leave hospital, she'll stay with his father and mother until she can travel home. They'll be married here. I insisted on that. Seemingly money's no hindrance. Alfredo—we'd call it Alfred—will come over with his cousin, Carlo Benzoni, to be best man. I'm a bit worried about this changing her religion, but she seems happy enough about it, so—there it is!"

Josh said, "Nay, luv, I'd not worry overmuch, there's plenty of folks honestly believe it's the right religion. I've heard arguments about it. George Mozart's one, that lovely Cressie Leonard's another. T'proof of the pudding's in the eating, an' when I find an artiste who's kind and polite, considerate and good at their job, and hear they're Papists—well, there's no doubt something in it. Don't worry."

"Aye, I'll try not to, Josh."

Jenny came home, walking with a very elaborate stick, a parting present from Alfredo. Her engagement ring was equally elaborate, and the presents showered upon her by her future husband's family were almost astonishing in their value and elegance.

Alfredo followed with his cousin Carlo Benzoni three weeks later. He had been refurnishing the caravan, and pronounced it to be a miracle of beauty and luxury.

"Ver' large," he told Lottie, "a sleep place and also a place to live. Wonderful also is a leetle small bat'-room. Oh, eet is a splendid caravan. Jennee and I ver' much 'appy. One day you see, signora."

She said, "Seems queer to me, our Jenny living in a caravan like some gypsy girl. I only hope she won't find it cramping and stuffy."

Alfredo smiled; "Pleaze? W'at ees zis crampling and stoffie?"

The wedding, as even Lottie admitted, was a great success. The two girls from Pudsey with the help of Aunt Formly worked wonders. The artistes living at Mrs. Hostley's at the time were most amiable, they allowed their rooms to be used for the wedding breakfast and reception, and took their meals at the Midland Hotel—where Lottie insisted upon paying the bills.

With considerable difficulty Alfredo and his cousin were

persuaded not to appear in full evening dress, but in the conventional English ceremonial clothes. Josh, suitably grave, looked like a stage earl in one of John Lawson's sketches in a frock-coat of impressive length; Lottie, in purple silk, wept throughout the ceremony; and Jenny looked, as everyone said, 'a proper little beauty'. Paul Cinquavalli, the word's great juggler, Miss Florrie Ford and Mr. Wilkie Bard attended the ceremony, the last-named making a speech at the breakfast which was acclaimed to be a masterpiece of wit and kindly sentiment.

The bride and bridegroom left for London, *en route* for Dover and Calais. Josh clasped Alfredo's hand so that the young man winced with pain, saying, "You see that you're good to her, or I'll break your neck for you, mind that!"

To which Alfredo, who had possibly understood three words of this impulsive speech, replied, "Always good. I not mind. Pleaze, good-bye, signor."

Lottie clasped him to her well-corseted bosom, began to cry again, then recovering—because you never knew if the photographers were not 'on the prowl'—said, "I believe you're a good lad, Fred. Take care of her. *Var beney. Viver.*"

They were blissfully happy. Alfredo had no inhibitions and Jenny was sufficiently unconventional not to mind her husband holding her hand in public and murmuring affectionate phrases in Italian irrespective as to whether other people present understood or not. They went direct to Milan, where Trumelli's great circus was refitting for their long prospective tour which would finally take them all through Europe.

Jenny Menetti never forgot her first sight of their caravan. It was all that Alfredo had promised and more. A miracle of ingenuity and compactness. She was like a child with a new doll's-house. She explored everything, opening cupboards, testing the spring of the cleverly contrived bunks, marvelling at the completeness of the arrangements for cooking, for storing china, for storing food. Then insisting that Alfredo should walk round and round the caravan to admire with her the beauty of the shining paint and gold scroll-work.

Her Italian was fairly fluent, though grammatically incorrect, and delighted Alfredo because she spoke it with a Yorkshire accent, which was a never-ending source of amusement to him.

"And, my heart's love, you are pleased with the home that your Alfredo has prepared for you?"

"I am delighted. It's lovely. Darling, we're going to be so terribly happy."

Once the great circus began to move, Jenny loved the life more every day. She enjoyed the long journeys from place to place, the steady, slow moving of the caravan drawn by its two fine horses. She was never tired of cleaning and polishing their caravan, of trying out new dishes, which Alfredo never failed to praise extravagantly. Gasparro Trumelli's caravans might be larger, furnished more elaborately, but they were never kept so spotlessly clean, so beautifully polished as the caravan of Alfredo Menetti.

The first halt was at Geneva, and there for the first time Jenny worked with her husband. He had ordered elaborate clothes for her in Milan, and when she stepped into the ring for the first time, doing numerous and quite unnecessary things such as shaking out handkerchiefs, settling the velvet cloth on the small table meticulously straight, the audience burst into applause. She looked so young, so well groomed, her hair shone with much brushing, and her clothes were so fresh and clean.

For a moment she felt a pang of regret. Why could she not dance for these people, and gain their applause not merely for her looks but for the work she could do? Then as Alfredo entered, magnificent in leotards as splendid as any worn by Paul Cinquavalli himself, her regret vanished. He came bounding into the ring, and Jenny's heart seemed to miss a beat at his sheer beauty. What did anything matter so long as she had this man for her husband?

He bowed to the audience, then to her, and lifting her hand to his lips, kissed it. Again the audience applauded, for the advance publicity for Trumelli's Circus had been good, and everyone knew that these two beautiful young people were recently married.

As Jenny watched Alfredo work she was amazed at the ease and sureness with which he moved; his muscles were like fine steel springs, his limbs fine and delicate yet strong and trained to fulfil every demand which he imposed upon them. She had seen many acrobats, people who were acclaimed as international artistes, but never one who worked as Menetti did. For the first time she watched him with an interest which was almost impersonal, and again and again found it difficult not to applaud, with the audience, at the end of some particularly difficult trick.

When he concluded the act with the flying trapeze she felt the tension which gripped the onlookers; even the magnificent ringmaster drew his breath sharply as Menetti flew through the air like a swallow, and grasped the bar of the stationary trapeze.

Jenny could have laughed from sheer delight at the grace of movement, the exactness of Alfredo's calculations, and the apparent ease with which he accomplished what he set out to do.

'They think that he might fall', her thoughts ran. 'How stupid; as if an artiste like Alfredo could fall!'

He was sitting now on the trapeze high above the ground, looking down and smiling as if he assured them that what might look like hard and dangerous work to them was merely glorious fun to him. The act was over, and the applause, Jenny thought, sounded like great waves breaking on a rocky shore. Alfredo slid down the guide-rope and stood beside her, holding her hand and making her bow to the audience as if she had actually contributed to the success of the act.

She tried to make him take his call alone, whispering, "But I've done nothing! It's not right!"

"You have done everything," he assured her; "to know that you are with me, watching me, makes my work so easy. Please bow to them, my loved one."

As they travelled farther north Alfredo insisted that the caravan must be laid up, and that Jenny and he would travel by train. They were staying in Hamburg when two things happened that affected them both very deeply. The first was that Jenny found to her delight that she was going to have a baby. Alfredo was almost wild with joy when she told him; if possible his devotion to her increased daily. He could not bear to be parted from her for an hour, and was never tired of making plans for the coming child.

"Shall we, darling Jenee, call her Genevra Maria? Maria for my mother, and Genevra—" he laughed—"for Geneva!"

"What about my mother and her name?"

"Carlotta, a very nice name; let her have three names all very beautiful!"

"Suppose that it's a boy?"

Alfredo shook his head. "No, I don't think we shall have a boy —not the first time. She will be like you, beautiful to look at, with a character to match her looks."

The second thing was a visit to their hotel by Trumelli. He was a huge man, heavy and moving slowly and ponderously. His big face was pallid, for he took little or no exercise and spent his days completely immersed in the business of running his circus. His relations with his artistes were conducted in a slightly aloof manner; he was polite but never particularly cordial. Alfredo and Jenny were the only two with whom Trumelli was in the least intimate. He liked and admired them both; probably the only other person connected with the circus that he liked was his head groom, a little Yorkshireman with rather bandy legs, and 'a way with t' 'osses'.

Gasparro Trumelli was regarded as a 'mystery man' by circus folk. The stories concerning him were legion. He was said to be the illegitimate son of an arch-duke, to be an escaped political prisoner, to have inherited a fortune from a millionaire father in America, and to have had for his mother an opera singer of tremendous beauty and incredible wealth.

The truth was less spectacular. Trumelli was the son of a fairly successful shopkeeper in Naples. At his death, when Gasparro was twenty, the shop was sold in order to form part of the site for a new luxury hotel. Trumelli left Naples for New York, and there, having previously worked in a livery stable in his native town, was taken on by Silas J. Hockett, owner of the greatest circus in the United States. He was young, strong and energetic, and Hockett watched him carefully. He mixed very little with the other grooms, he worked without ceasing, and before long Hockett gave him control of the horses. For five years Trumelli practically lived in the stables; at the end of that time Hockett sent for him and talked to him very frankly and intimately.

He was a tall, lean man, with a sallow complexion and sunken eyes. He had little education, and it was said that he could barely write his own name. His strength lay in the fact that he had an almost fantastic memory. No fact which he had learned, no statement which he had heard, no promise or contract made with him, were ever forgotten.

He sat chewing a cold cigar, his long legs stretched out before him, when Trumelli entered. He nodded to the Italian, and said:

"Siddown. I gotter talk to yer. You savvy enough ter onderstand me, eh?"

"I understand perfectly, sir."

"I'll say you're smart. You haven't forgot your Italian, eh?"

Trumelli smiled. "Like you, sir, I forget nothing."

"Right! You're Italian, I'm a good Amurican. I reckon somehow—God knows why—we two understand each other. Yes, sir, though I guess we ain't spoken for mor'n five minutes at one time in five years. Strange. Trumelli, I'm goin' to speak to you in com-plete confidence."

Trumelli answered, "Sir, have no fears."

Hockett permitted himself a momentary grin, a contortion of

his features which made him look like a good-tempered death's-head.

"I b'lieve you. I've never seen you open your mouth if you could keep it shut. Now, listen to me. I'm a sick man—a very sick man indeed. How long I've gotten I'd not like to say. I'm going to train you to run Hockett's. It's the finest show on the road, and that's the way it's gotter continue. When I shuffle off I'll see that you're all right. It won't be easy. I'm not the easiest feller in the world, but I b'lieve you can do it. What y'say?"

The rather dingy little room seemed to Trumelli to be charged with a strange mixture of tragedy and excitement. Here was his chance! He had no illusions or false modesty about his capabilities. He knew that he was astute, that he was able to make decisions quickly and calmly. He never allowed his personal likes and dislikes to affect his work and his plans. He had made a success of the magnificent horses which were the pride of Hockett's; he had kept his grooms 'on their toes', insisting that they should work as he demanded, not as they wished. His stables were always miracles of cleanliness and neatness, his horses' coats shone like satin. To take over the whole management of this circus was his opportunity; such a chance never happened twice in a lifetime.

He looked at Hockett, who sat motionless, chewing his cold cigar. His lean face with its hollow cheeks and sunken eyes was impassive. He looked terribly ill, and it was obvious to Trumelli that this interview was the result of some hard thinking, of observations made—in all probability—over a long period. He licked his lips, which were dry with excitement.

Hockett ejaculated, "Well? What d'you say?"

"First that I am grieved to know that you are ill——"

"I don't recollect askin' you your opinion about the state o' my health. What about Hockett's?"

"I shall be proud to work under your direction, sir. I shall try to do my best."

"Right! Get back to your work, an' I'll send for you later, when I've gotten things planned out a bit more."

Their association lasted for six years, during which time Hockett disappeared from time to time, entering some nursing-home, returning to the circus looking slightly more human. The benefit which he derived from these periodic visits was never more than temporary, and gradually he spent more and more time in nursing-homes and less and less with the circus.

His relations with Trumelli were never changed; he was always

27

impersonal, and at no time did their attitude towards each other alter. Hockett was always the master. Trumelli, despite the trust which was placed in him and his judgment, remained the very respectful servant.

Hockett rarely gave him any praise; at the most he would say, "I'm not given to makin' mistakes; I've not made one over you." He died in a private nursing-home in Chicago. Trumelli received a telephone message instructing him to report at the nursing-home the moment the show was over, as Mr. Hockett was gravely ill.

He replied that he would come immediately, but was told that Hockett was insistent that he must wait for the end of the show.

He found Hockett looking as if he were already dead. When Trumelli entered his employer said in a strange and rather terrible whisper to a doctor who was standing near, "Now, c'm on with that shot o' dope, I've work to do and not much time to do it."

He motioned to Trumelli to sit down while the doctor injected something into the arm which looked to be little more than bone.

"Takings good to-night?"

"Up hundred and ten on last night, sir."

"Good. Keep on as you are doing. Trumelli's Monster Circus. Late Hockett's. Certain deductions to be made. Legacies to old employees. Lawyer's gotten all instructions. Run it on the same lines. Don't try to make it anything but a circus. Horses, elephants. Good clowning. First-class acrobats. Not too many cats—darned nuisance those cats. Try Europe, there's money there. Watch your trainers. Mostly they're bastards. Well, s'long. It's been a pretty good partnership. Goo' night, Trumelli."

"Allow me to stay with you, sir."

"Not likely. I've mostly done things alone. I can do this alone."

Hockett died in the early hours of the morning, and Trumelli found himself the owner of the finest circus in America. Even after the deductions were made and legacies paid, he discovered that he was a rich man. He regretted Hockett, for although his active part in the management of the circus had for the past two years been only nominal, he had always been able to give advice which was invariably sound. Trumelli took his advice now, and in the spring of the following year he sailed for Europe, to add to the success and reputation of 'Trumelli's Monster Circus—late Hockett's'.

He grew more and more immersed in his circus; he was

ambitious, though he spoke of his ambitions to no one. His life was lonely, living as he did in a huge caravan, or in great hotels. He was reputed to be a millionaire, but when some misguided person put the question to him, "They tell me that you're a millionaire, Mr. Trumelli," his reply was, "What 'they tell' is usually damned lies. Any road, what the hell's it got to do with you?"

Now he came to see Alfredo and Jenny Menetti, lumbering into their stiffly furnished hotel sitting-room, and lowering his weight carefully on to an uncomfortable chair as if he feared that it might collapse with the strain.

Alfredo said, "This is a great very pleasure surprise, sir."

"Surprise, maybe; I'm not so sure of the pleasure. I'm going back to the States. Fixed it this morning. Now, Mrs. Menetti, just listen. Pin back both your ears, and you, too, Menetti. I've been scouting round. Things are going to happen in this continent."

"Happen? How do you mean, Mr. Trumelli?" Jenny asked.

He turned to her, and for a second his heavy, plain face looked almost fatherly.

"Look, you two are young, just married. Probably you'll start a fam'ly. I'm bettin' that Europe won't be a good place for mothers with young babies for a while. Things are growing to look pretty ugly. Better come along with the circus to the States, outer the reach of fighting and these stoopid things that happen when men get angry."

Alfredo, white-faced, his hands shaking a little, said, "Sounds lika you mean—a war?" He whispered the last words. Trumelli nodded.

"You said it."

"How soon a time shall we go?"

"I've got the two next weeks cancelled. I'm taking the elephants, horses, sending the cats to the Zoo here." He chuckled. "They think I'm being mighty generous! I'm takin' little Johnnie Watson for the horses. I'll take you two, and the clowns —Zippo and Zoppo. Maybe a dozen others. Then over there I'll refit. I wanter be off three weeks from now. Well, are you coming?"

Jenny sat biting her lip, while Alfredo watched her, his face drawn with anxiety. No one spoke for some minutes. To Alfredo the silence seemed to last for years. Trumelli did not move, but sat staring at Jenny.

At last she said, "I've got to go back to England, Mr. Trumelli. I must see my mum and dad. I'll not stay; we'll be back in time to move. You see, we have 'started a family'. I'd take risks, but I'm not going to have my baby take any. Maybe this will all blow over; if it does—well and good; if not then—well, we'll wait in America while it does. Is that all right for you?"

He grunted, "It's what I hoped you'd say, m'dear."

It was then that Alfredo beat on his chest with his open palms, and cried, "*Dio mio!* I 'ad forgot. Eef eet is a war, what if Italy fights——?"

Jenny said, "Fight who? Don't be daft, Freddo. What 'ud Italy fight for?"

He stared at her wildly. "Fight forr? 'Onour, *gloria*, *la patria*,"

She rose and laid her hand on his shoulder. "Now listen, Freddo, you wait until Italy does fight. Then if you feel it's right as you should go and get yourself killed—we'll talk about it again. Until then just keep calm, and be thankful as you've got work waiting for you. There, Mr. Trumelli, that's all settled."

They travelled to England, and in Manchester found Lottie and Josh waiting for them with a welcome that warmed their hearts, and caused the emotional Alfredo to look at them both with his beautiful eyes swimming with tears. The complete cleanliness of the Manchester house was a balm to Jenny, who had criticized every hotel in which they had stayed on the Continent adversely, comparing them all with her mother's home to their disadvantage.

On the night when they arrived they talked of the tour in America. Alfredo, after two of Josh Mander's whiskies-and-sodas, protested a little.

"But, Signora Mama, to me eff Italy shell enter the varr, vot is my pos-it-ion, pleaze? I am Italian, 'ave much love of my—vat you say?—countree. Eet is nec-essary I fight in 'err defence, no?"

Charlotte, who had allowed herself to lapse into broader Yorkshire than would have been permitted on the stage, said, "Sitha, lad, thee mind yersen. Who makes war? Not thee nor me nor Josh theer. There's men as have millions invested in munitions, arms, guns and lots else. They want t' brass on the reit side when they meet at Midland Hotel for their meetings, they want shareholders to be satisfied. They want to pay dividends. Is that right, Josh?"

Fingering his moustache, Josh nodded. "That's right, I'm convinced."

"Why do you have to go rushing out to fight? My God, yer don't even know what t' war's about! Someone kills an Archduke, and so boys have to be killed! Alfredo, it's all daft. No sense in it. You've got your job, and your wife and—please God —a bonnie bairn. Let that suffice. Any road, it's not started yet. I mind my muther telling me an old song. It was called 'Jeanette and Jeanot'. One line was, 'And let them as makes the quarrel be the only ones to fight'. It's true! Get yourselves off to America. Josh and me—we're old—or oldish. We don't matter, but you and my Jenny—you're young and hopeful, you're going to have luvly bairns. You're—you're—" she stumbled a little—"you're one of you Italian, the other English. It may be as you're the *Longtong Cordial* we're looking forward to."

She stopped speaking and looked from one to the other. At Alfredo, beautiful, slim, trained to a hair; at her daughter Jenny, whose own career had been cut short so tragically, but who had found happiness with this young man who so obviously adored her; and lastly at her husband—Josh Mander. He was growing elderly, he was not exciting, with his moustache which might have been carved out of mahogany, he was not in the least intellectual, but to her he was the finest friend and companion in the world.

At that moment Lottie Mander was a very frightened woman. She had heard of war and listened to the rumours, and she saw that in a short time the life and world she had known might be shattered. She did not view the prospect with great equanimity, but she had lived a good life, she had enjoyed almost every moment of it, and she had evolved a philosophy which enabled her to shrug her shoulders and say, "Whatever happens—life goes on."

Jenny and Alfredo stayed in Manchester for five days, during which time Lottie was able to have long and confidential talks with her daughter, to give her much obstetric advice—most of it complete rubbish—and to take her into Manchester to buy a complete outfit for the baby whose advent was not expected for at least six months.

They left to return to Hamburg. Lottie cried, but with a certain restraint; Josh fingered his moustache rather more than usual and cleared his throat very often. Alfredo threw himself on to Lottie's well-upholstered bosom and sobbed, *"Cara Mama, cara Mama,"* until Jenny said, "Nay, have done, luv. It's not the end of the world!"

Eight days later they sailed for America.

CHAPTER THREE

JENNY MENETTI always said, "Except that English lads were being killed and people suffering, the years of the war were the happiest I'd ever known—ever am likely to know, come to that."

She enjoyed the voyage out to the States, felt magnificently well, and was delighted that wherever he went, no matter with whom he talked, Alfredo was unfailingly popular. To her he was always the perfect husband and lover, he believed in her sound common sense in everything connected with business. With his dark eyes very grave and attentive, he would listen to all she said, nod his head in complete agreement when she said, "I want you to be wise for yourself, luv. It's all right holding out helping hands to all and sundry, but don't fall off of your own ladder doing it." Finally she ended, "There, I've said my say!"

Alfredo would change from a wise, attentive pupil, listening to a master, and become a cheerful smiling child angel. He would say, "Darrling, 'ow wonderful you arre!"

"Then I hope you'll mind all I say!"

"Darrling, I mind nossing that you say to me; 'ow could I?"

"I don't mean mind—not like—I mean mind which means 'think on'."

"Pleaze—t'ink on?"

Then Jenny would shout with laughing and assure him that either he must learn to speak decent English, or she must work harder at her Italian, because if they went on like this she'd probably murder him one day.

"It's all right while you say 'Pleaze', then I know that I've gotten you out of your depths, and you'll just sink!"

Still smiling, he would ask, " 'Dep'ts' and 'seenk'—pleaze?"

They stayed in New York until Trumelli had engaged new artistes, and interviewed agents. For the first time since they had worked for him they saw him as a man of tremendous energy. Whenever they met him he was just coming away from some interview, or just rushing off to keep some appointment. Invariably trotting behind the bulky figure came the little grey-haired Yorkshire groom, his short bandy legs fairly twinkling in their attempt to keep up with Trumelli's strides. Jenny and Alfredo lived comfortably in a small quiet hotel, making their rather tentative way to visit the places which they were assured they must see'. They were both anxious to improve their minds, so they visited picture galleries, and museums which, though neither admitted it to the other in so many words, bored them to extinction. One morning Alfredo rushed back to the hotel; he had been in conference with Trumelli, and returned in a state of frantic excitement.

"Life of my 'eairt! We hev been fools. We have walked for miles to see pictures—oh, so many oogly pictures—we hev' seen many dead rocks and bones of animals—darrling, 'ow tired we have become! Now Trumelli said zees morning, 'You have taka Jenny to the Metro-pol-itan, yes?' I say, 'Pleaze, Metro-pol-itan, what is?"

Jenny said, "I'd have laid any money that your old 'Pleaze' would have to make an entrance! Go on, luv."

"Yes. He says, 'You don't a know?' I reply, 'If I know, I don't a ask, no?' He smile an' tell me. Eet is an opera-house! Artistes come from all parts of the vorld, there to sing the music of Verdi, Rossini, Puccini—all Italians. I go to zees place. 'Pleaze to buy good tickeets for to-night?' They reply, 'You are a lucky feller— two 'ave been returned. Costa lotta monee.' I cry, 'No metter! La Signora Menetti is obliged to 'ear Italian opera!' To-night we go. You vill vear your beautiful clothes, and your Alfredo his *abito da sera!* Darrleeng, you are 'appy?"

Their prim little hotel sitting-room seemed to quiver with his excitement and enthusiasm. Jenny watched him smiling, thinking what a child he was with his impulses. This place, he said, was expensive. She knew what seats cost in opera-houses, they had one in Manchester. Except when Carl Rosa came the prices were no bigger than the theatres.

She said, "Sounds lovely, sweetheart. You'll have to tell me what it's all about. I've only seen two operas in my life—one when I was very little, called *Faust*, and the other some kind of a fairy tale. A man rode in on a swan, dressed in armour. I remember the swan got stuck. I laughed myself silly!"

Alfredo shook his head, "*Lohengrin*—German music. Alvays it 'gets stook'—lika zees swan, only it is in my t'roat zee music steeks."

"What's the name of this opera to-night?"

"Zee name is *Rigoletto*," he announced, pronouncing the word with a sudden burst and duplications of the first letter. "Verdi! Now I shell tell you the story. Ver' sad, but beautiful. Listen!"

Holding her hand in his, he recounted the story of the opera, and Jenny thought, as she did so often, how full and melodious his voice was, how varied his inflections, and how vivid his language. The story ended, and Alfredo demanded, his voice heavy with emotion—for, like all good story-tellers, he had been carried away with his theme—"Now, is eet not ver' beautiful?"

Jenny hesitated, then said, "Well, to tell you the truth, luv, you told the tale beautifully, it was lovely. But what a lot of bad folks. That Duke wanted a damned good hiding, and as for the girl—what's her name?—Gilda—well, I know what we'd have said about her if she'd been in the Tiller Troupe when I was! Never mind, Freddo, we'll go and see how it works out. It maybe sounds nicer with music."

That evening they visited the opera. Jenny wearing her best frock of pale blue silk, made in one of Manchester's well-known establishments, and Alfredo magnificent in a very waisted dinner jacket.

She surveyed him with satisfaction. "By gum, you look a treat."

"Also you, darrleeing, very much treat, my Jennee."

She admitted that Verdi's masterpiece did indeed 'sound nicer with music', that after all the Duke might be a 'bad gaston', but that he certainly was attractive. "Still," she added, "I don't believe that any young girl is all that innocent. If you ask me she got all *she* asked for! Still, it was luvly, and I heard one woman say to the chap who was with her, 'That's a handsome fellow', meaning you! D'you know what he said? He was one of those Little Johnnie Know-alls and he said, 'I fancy he's the new tenor, going to sing in *O Hello*'. Fancy that! Is *O Hello* an opera like this we've seen to-night?"

"Pleaze, I t'ink maybe he said, '*Ot'ello*', my Jennee."

She frowned. "Funny name; what's it about—this *O Tell O?*"

"A great Moor was named so."

"Moor? Oh, like those up by Alderley Edge, eh? Ought to be nice."

"Pleaze who is zeese Elderlee Hedge?"

Impulsively she kissed him. "Bless you, you're gormless but I luv you to death. Let's go to bed, I'm tired."

Then came the announcement that Trumelli was ready to go on the road, the circus was refitted, artistes engaged, a first-class band already rehearsing. Alfredo flung himself into a positive orgy of work, he invented new and dangerous tricks, he practised —it seemed to Jenny—morning, noon and night. He ordered two new and magnificent sets of leotards, and wished to have new gowns made for her. As usual her common sense prevailed.

"There's no sense in it, luv. In another couple of months I may not be able to work in the act. I won't go on if I feel embarrassed. I might manage another three months at a pinch, but I don't know, standing under those arcs—it's doubtful. They show up everything."

On the long journeys which they took he was tenderness itself to her, she was barely allowed to carry her own handbag. When they reached Arkansas she decided that she could not face those 'all-revealing' arcs any longer, and her place was taken in the act by a small boy, wearing a shining top hat with a cockade, an immaculate livery and boots with gleaming tops, complete in the manner of the 'tiger' of the '90's.

Trumelli approved, in his usual rather unenthusiastic fashion, saying, "For a time he's all right. He takes away some of the colour of the act. When it's over you'll come back, eh?"

"You bet I'll come back, Mr. Trumelli, even if I bring the twins on with me!"

The long tour with its seemingly endless journeys began to tire her. Alfredo was worried, and insisted upon her seeing the best doctor in every town they visited. The sight of his anxious face disturbed her, and she was in a fever lest his anxiety should affect his work. There were times when she realized that the war in Europe occupied his thoughts in addition to her own condition. To Jenny it all seemed too far away to be real. The British would win as they always had done, and even when she read of disasters on land and at sea she assured Alfredo, "Nay, it's nothing but a bit of a set-back. I'd not wonder if we were making it all up, just to make the Germans believe we're a lot weaker than what we really are. It 'ul take more than Germany to beat the English!"

They were making for New York; the tour had been an immense success and even Trumelli allowed himself to smile when he contemplated the profits they had made.

He told Jenny as she stood with him watching Alfredo's act one evening—Trumelli in his usual 'faultless evening dress', or what he imagined to be so, Jenny muffled in a long cloak—that they were going back to Europe the moment the war had ended. His contracts, he added, 'provisionally', were signed, and once more they would be back with their caravans, and he would engage a first-rate artiste to work 'the cats'.

Jenny shivered. "I hate those men who work the cats. Say what you like, Mr. Trumelli, they treat them damned badly. Nasty lot o' fellows. I never met an animal trainer that I liked."

She heard him sigh noisily, almost felt his huge, flabby frame heave with the expulsion of breath. He said, "That's all right. Maybe I think the same. I'm a tradesman. I sell what the public wants. If the public don't like the lines I stock, then I don't stock them. I gotter live. I gotter live up to Trumelli's being the best circus in the world, so I gotter have the best acts. Get me, Jenny?"

She shrugged. "Have it your own way. I'm glad that my Alfredo never wanted to take a monkey or something in his flying trapeze act. I'd have left him if he did. Never mind, Mr. Trumelli —oh, I'm going into the nursing-home to-morrow. Be nice, keep an eye on Freddo whilst I'm there. He *worries* so. It's bad for the act. Whew, it's an expensive business having a baby. What they charge here! In Manchester I'd have done it all for a quarter the price."

The act was ending, the little 'tiger' stood with his eyes glued on Menetti, holding his breath until the flying swing was accomplished, then relaxing visibly. The heavy scent of the tan reached them; the Liberty horses were standing ready for their entrance, the little bandy-legged Yorkshireman waiting to give his grooms the signal. The two clowns, dressed in white with red and blue 'pom-poms' and complete with their fantastic make-up, were lounging against one of the tent-poles of the near-by tent smoking and laughing. When one particularly low, rich chuckle reached Jenny, she thought, 'I bet that was a dirty one!' Once an elephant trumpeted, and she could picture the great animals waiting, swinging their trunks gently, their strange small, intelligent eyes fixed on the opening to the big tent into which they would follow the horses.

What a strange, complete world it was! None of the artistes made any new friends in the towns which they visited. She and Freddo asked the clowns to have dinner at long intervals. They were decent kindly men, inclined to melancholy. Zippo in particular loved to recite long passages from Dante—at least Freddo told her they were passages from Dante, but she only understood a word here and there. Now she heard the sudden burst of applause from an audience which had been too intent, too apprehensive to make a move before the last great trick was ended. She leaned forward, and there was her Freddo, glorious in purple leotards, slipping easily and smoothly down the guide-rope, leaping the last ten feet, landing lightly on the balls of his feet— bouncing like an indiarubber ball, she thought. He flung his arms wide, bowed to the audience, then turning to the little 'tiger' gave him an individual bow, in response to which the small boy touched the brim of his top hat with two fingers in the way that she had taught him.

She said, "It's a good act."

Trumelli replied, "In my op-in-ion the best in the world. He has no fears because he has com-plete knowledge." He touched her arm very lightly with two fingers and said, "Money. You don't have to worry. Freddo has only to tell me. I pay all. Glad to do it. I like you both so much. Good-night. Here comes your husband."

Menetti came bounding out of the ring in the same energetic fashion he had entered it twenty minutes previously. He sent one of his brilliant smiles flashing to Jenny, then darted back to take another bow in response to the continuous applause. He came rushing back; the little Yorkshireman snapped his fingers as the given signal, and, as Jenny and Menetti moved away, the splendid Liberty horses went cantering into the ring, their coats gleaming, their muscles moving like steel springs hidden beneath the finest satin.

Menetti slipped his arm round her and together they moved to the small tent which was his changing-room.

"How was I, pleaze?" he said, asking the question which is on the lips of every good performer no matter in which sphere he performs.

"Same as always," she told him. "I was talking to Trumelli. He says you're the best act—acrobatic—in the world."

Freddo said, " 'E ees too kind. The leetle Silass—what a name —is good too, no?"

She shrugged. "He does what I learned him to do."

The next morning she entered the nursing-home. Menetti came with her, his face grey with anxiety. She tried to cheer him, but his depression resisted all her efforts. His hands were shaking, and even when she said, "Luvey, pull yourself together. They'll think you're just back from a thick night!" he was too depressed to utter his usual 'Pleaze' and only said, "Me, I don't know zeese t'ick night."

He had been extravagant; her room was the best in the building; she was to have special nurses, every possible additional care. For the first time since their marriage Jenny watched him take charge of everything.

"I do not want," he said, with that particular emphasis on the word 'want' which Italians who do not speak English very easily invariably use, "I do not *want* monee to be saffed. Spend all. Only the Signora Menetti must hev alvays the best possible. 'Ere arre two telephone numbers; eff I am not at von, I am et see osser. If not von, try ozzer. I hev afternoon per-for-mance, it is neces-sary I go. Now for *un momento* ellow me al-one viz my vife. T'ank you."

As the door closed behind the nurse he turned to Jenny and took her in his arms. Never had she known such gentleness, such impassioned tenderness.

"My Jennee, you are all right, no?"

"I've felt better, luv."

"But not grreat pain yet, pleaze?"

She laughed. "You and your old 'pleaze'! I'm all right, luv." Very simply and naturally Alfredo took her hand and said, "Nice eff we togesser say small prayers, yes?" He knelt down by the high hospital bed and she knelt beside him. Like two rather frightened children, their hands met and clasped. In a low but very distinct voice he recited an 'Ave Maria', the 'Pater noster' and finally a 'Gloria'.

Listening, Jenny thought, 'It's a luvely voice. If he'd not been the best acrobat in the world he'd have been a grand actor. Funny, me—a Tiller girl born in Manchester—kneeling here with my husband saying prayers. It's nice. I'm glad he thought of it. Makes you feel kind of safe. O Holy Mary, I hope I give him a luvely baby. Please take care of us.'

Alfredo rose and very gently raised Jenny to her feet. He wiped his eyes, and said, "Now, darrling, it is necess-ary that I go. I must be in the rring in 'arf an 'our. I shell come beck. Now I ring for the *infermiera*. Eef she is not ver' good to you, I shell brring a great knife an' cut eire t'roat."

That night Trumelli watched him again, and gave his strange, fleeting smile. He thought, 'He's good, this fellow. He knows that his wife is in labour, they told him on the 'phone. He's not cutting a second of his act. I know that he's got a taxi waiting. He'll strip off like mad, but he'll do every minute of his act. Good lad.'

Alfredo slid down the guide-rope, sent his dazzling smile to the audience, bowed to the small Silas, rushed off and went past Trumelli without a sign that he had even seen him. One of the under-grooms acted as his dresser, and he thought that the acrobat was like a streak of lightning as he undressed, stepped under the shower and, towelling himself with vigour on an incredibly rough towel, began to resume his ordinary clothes. It seemed to the man that although Menetti dressed with incredible rapidity, he emerged looking even more meticulously dressed than ever. He even snatched up a carnation which stood in a glass on his dressing-table and put it in his button-hole.

The groom said, "That taxi's here. Sure I wish you all the best o' luck."

Menetti did not speak; he only nodded, then dashed from the tent and flung himself into the waiting taxicab.

He gave his orders to the taxi-driver, "Listen, ver' qvick. Ef the police gong you Menetti pays all. But drive lika as ef the devil was after you. I pay mooch monie."

The police did not gong them, and on arriving at the nursing-home Menetti gave the driver a sum of money which astonished him, and tore into the nursing-home.

A tall horse-faced woman, dressed entirely in white, came forward to meet him. He gasped out, "Menetti. *Come sta la Signora Menetti?*"

She eyed him coldly. "Please restrain yourself. Remember we have people here who are easily disturbed. Can't you speak English?"

He nodded his head violently; under the glare of the electric lights his forehead shone wet. "Yes, speak ver' good. Pleaze, my wife? 'Ow is she, madam?"

"Is she the lady with the Italian name? Oh, I thought so. If you will come into this room I will send and enquire."

He entered the prim little room, and as the door closed felt that he was trapped. He longed to fling the door open, and rush through the building calling 'Jennee' until he found her. He wiped his face, for the sweat was pouring down his cheeks, his hands felt wet and sticky, his heart was hammering against his ribs. He thought that he must suffocate unless someone came and let him out of this dreadful little room. He tried to say 'Hail Marys' but he knew that he was not capable of concentrating on the words, but that he was listening intently for any sound which might tell him someone was coming with news of Jenny. How long he waited he did not know, he ceased to pace restlessly up and down, and sat in a state bordering on collapse on one of the uncomfortable chairs, his hands hanging limp between his knees.

The door opened, and a man, very tall and thin, wearing a long white coat, entered. Alfredo tried to stand and found that his legs refused to support him. The tall man came forward and caught his arm.

"Sit down. Come, this won't do! Can't have more patients on our hands. You're Mr. Menetti? I've just left your wife and

39

daughter. They're fine, fine! Sit down, you can't see her for another few minutes. They're just making her comfortable. I'm going to get you a highball. Just stay there and cry if you want to. But she's fine, plucky little woman. I could do with a lot of patients like your little lady."

He went out and returned with a whisky-and-soda. "Drink it up. Say, stop crying! You'll upset your wife if you go to see her with red eyes and a shiny nose. There! That's better, eh? See, here's nurse to show you your daughter."

Menetti set down his empty glass, and turned to the woman who entered holding something in her arms. She smiled comfortably at him, and said:

"Now, what do you think of her? Close on eight pounds. There's a lovely baby for you!"

He stared at the small puckered face and wondered what anyone could find in it to call 'lovely'. He felt nothing but pity for the scarlet-faced little creature. How could this be what he and his beautiful Jenny had produced! It was incredible.

"She is so red," he said. "Pleaze, veel she alvays be so?"

The doctor laughed. "Say, you'd be red if you lived in the heat this little lady's lived in for the past nine months! She's a grand little girl, this one."

Alfredo smiled. "T'ank you, I am glad. Now may I see my wife, pleaze?"

"For five minutes, not a second longer. She wants to get to sleep, and you're all in yourself. Take him up, Nurse."

He walked on tip-toe to the side of Jenny's bed. If his daughter's appearance had disappointed him, his wife's loveliness had never seemed so evident. She looked tired, but she opened her eyes and said:

"Hello, luv. We done it, eh? Proper little Lancashire lass!"

He knelt beside the bed, and whispered, "I saw her. Lovely leetle *bambina*, but my Jennee is always the loveliest in the world. Zee doctor tell me—oh, how brave is this wife! I am so 'appy. Before, I was in desperation. Tears blinded me. I was so frightened. Now, alla is good. Dear, vonderful Jennee."

She chuckled softly. "Tears blinded you, eh? If you ask me it was the whisky you've had, you old soaker."

He said, "Soakaire, what is, pleaze?"

She answered, "I was waiting for that—the old 'pleaze'."

Then the nurse turned him out, and he walked out into the cold, clear night, feeling at peace with all the world. His wife was safe, he had been assured that his daughter was beautiful, he was

40

a success in his work, the whole future was rosy. Once the war was over they would all return to Europe, to England, to Italy. He thought nostalgically of Genoa, of the Galleria in Milan, of the Dolomites, and the good rough red wine, of the cheese, the *pasta*, purple figs and velvet-skinned peaches. Some day, perhaps, when he was too old to be an acrobat, he and Jenny would find a house on the shore of an Italian lake. They would live well and simply. Genevra would be the eldest of a family which should be noted in the district for their incredible beauty. Another girl perhaps and two or even three boys. Straight-limbed, with great intelligent eyes, and clear voices.

Jenny had once said, "I don't care how many bairns I have! We're both young and strong as horses; what's more, we're happy together. So let's have plenty of bairns, Freddo. Dash it! The whole world's waiting for more Menettis, and we'll give it them!"

He went the next day to see Jenny, bringing an armful of flowers, fruit, and a bottle of Asti Spumante which he had found in an Italian store. Very early that morning he had sought out Trumelli, and given him the news. Trumelli nodded, shook his hand and sent his love to Jenny.

He said, "See here, buying babies costs a damn' lot of money. Tell Jenny I'm putting this girl on the pay-roll right away. Her salary has been accumulating ever since you told me she was coming." He took out a roll of notes, licked his finger and began counting them rapidly. "Four dollars a week for eight months—Jenny didn't tell me for a month." He grinned. "Tell her being so cagey cost her sixteen dollars. There you are, Menetti, now get along and see her."

He was admitted to the nursing-home, and again met the woman with the horse-face. He beamed at her. "All is changed," he said, "last night—I suffered like peoples in Dante's *Inferno*, now I am in Heaven! Pleaze hev you seen my daughtaire? Last night the doctor say she is the most beautiful baby in the vorld. Do you know that she weights—eight pounds. Extraordinary, yes? Now I taka Asti Spumante an' my vife and me drink the 'ealth of t'is adorable baby."

She looked at him coldly. "You'll give no wine to your wife unless you have permission from her doctor, mind that, Mr. Menetti."

Alfredo laughed. "Ah, but you do not onderstand. The doctor is my good friend. Last night I drink vis 'eem, to-day he drink vis me an' my vife."

41

Warningly she said, "You'll get his permission or you leave that bottle down here!"

"Oh, yes, I get 'ees permiss-ion. Don't be afraid, missus."

To his great disappointment it was Jenny who flatly refused to drink his precious Asti.

"Get along, you big silly. I've got to think of the baby. Might make her properly upset. I won't risk it. Give nurse a glass, and ask the doctor to have one as well. He's somewhere about. Nurse 'ul get him. I'm going to tell him that he made you tiddley last night, mind! Coming here breathing whisky over your new-born child. What a horrible fellow!"

"I am not so weak in my 'ead so one drink makes me tiddilum."

She said, "Tiddley—not tiddleum!"

Jenny progressed quickly, and in a month she rejoined Trumelli's, engaging one of the clowns' wives to look after the baby when she was working in the act once more. The child was both good and beautiful; to Alfredo she was a living miracle, and he would stand and stare down at her in silence for long periods, alternately sighing with sheer happiness or smiling with intense pride.

"Look, Jennee," he cried, "our Genevra smiles at me!"

"Wind, luv; all babies smile when they have a touch of wind. She wants a spot of dill-water."

"Veend, what is eet?"

"Wind, old silly; what you call—*il vento*."

"Shell I send for a doctor?"

"Send for no one. She's as right as rain."

The tour continued; news came from Europe regarding the progress of the war; America entered it with the Allies against Germany. Alfredo was assailed from time to time with the conviction that it was his duty to return to his country and fight. While these attacks of conscience smote him he was acutely depressed and miserable, watching Genevra with sad eyes, assuring Jenny that he must go and tell Trumelli that his mind was made up and he must return to Italy.

Her robust individuality always reacted in the same way.

"Be practical, luv. You're a damned good acrobat. I should think as a soldier you'd be pretty bad. Anyway, you've earned your living in plenty of countries besides Italy, and you'll have to earn it when the war's over. How much could you earn if you came back without a leg, or an eye or a hand? I should have to wrap Genevra in a shawl and go out selling matches! We'd get fat on that, wouldn't we? They've got on so far without you; let them get on without you until the silly rotten business is finished."

Wrinkling his forehead, he would say, "But, my Jennee, eff alls said like that? No men at all would be fighting."

"And a damned good job, if you ask me," she retorted. "C'on, I've some spaghetti for supper, just the way you like it."

The Armistice was signed when they were playing Buffalo. Genevra was four years old, pretty as a picture, with fair hair and eyes which her father declared were blue as the waters of the Mediterranean. She had never been sick or sorry, and she was adored by all the people attached to the circus. She spoke a few Italian words which she had learnt from her father, but in the main her speech—such as it was—was that of Manchester, and she addressed Jenny as 'muther' and her father as 'our dad'.

She was an intelligent little girl, possessing great charm and individuality. To her the circus was the world, and she loved every inch of it. She attended every matinée and never tired of watching every act intently. When Jenny and Alfredo entered the ring she never failed to stand up in her seat, calling in her high piping voice:

"Muther—our Dad—it's me!"

In the February of 1919 Trumelli transported the circus to Europe. His dates were booked, his plans made with great conpleteness and thoroughness. Jenny told Genevra that she was going home to see her granny and grandpa in Manchester; the child asked, "Muther, what's Man-chester like?"

"It's grand, luv. Folk say it's mucky, but where muck is there's money. Mind that."

Jenny found both Lottie and Josh aged considerably, and at one time she wondered if she and Alfredo ought to leave the circus and come to Manchester to help with the running of 'Mrs. Hostley's', but when she mentioned it to Lottie the reply was both definite and prompt.

"Nay, whatever do you think there'd be for you both? Freddo's earning good money, you're seeing the world, you've him to think of as well as me and dad. Nay, maybe we're both a bit overdone; the war tried us, what with food tickets and such-like, as well as the anxiety; but we'll be ourselves i' no time. Your dad's not an old man, no more am I an old woman—fifty this year, and dad's four years older nor what I am. No, luv, when the time comes as we need help I'll let you know. Till then go work with that nice husband of yours."

So after a month's visit they packed and returned to rejoin the circus in Madrid. The caravan had been refurnished and re-painted, and to the small Genevra it seemed like something straight out of fairyland. For the next five years she came to know all the great cities of Europe; she remembered Milano as a place where she ate delicious ices, Rome as a great square where fountains played flinging up crystal jets of water to an incredible height. In Vienna she heard her mother say again and again, "Nay, those poor bairns, they make my heart ache—that's what wars do!" Lisbon smelt of orange flowers, and Madrid was hot, and she could not sleep well. Budapest she loved, and the lights on the water entranced her. Dresden had a fairy palace called the Swinger, and a great rolling river where barges swept slowly along. Paris had trees in the wide street where she was taken to walk, and wonderful cakes, and wildly driving taxicabs; Cannes was very light and the sea very blue. Dad said, "Like the eyes of my Genevra." And so it went on, a happy, care-free life, with the clown's wife, Mrs. Zoppo, teaching her to read about fat cats and big rats and mats and the rest, and to show her how to make curious things called 'pot-hooks', which were a means of learning to write in the future.

Twice her mother took her back to England, and she was petted and spoilt by her grandfather and grandmother. She thought Manchester a wonderful place, but she was always glad to rejoin the circus and to hear her father—whom she adored—cry, "Now all is good, for my Jennee and my darling *bambina* have come back to me."

CHAPTER FOUR

GENEVRA at nine years old was still the only child. Jenny said several times to Alfredo that she wished they 'were getting on with that family', but he only gave her one of his wide smiles and assured her that for himself he was ' 'appy viz the most beautiful wife and the most beautiful daughter in the vorld'.

Genevra, freed after two hours' lessons every morning, wandered over the great show-ground. She knew everyone, and was as much at home with the grooms as she was with the 'mahouts' who looked after the elephants. She loved to watch her father at his practice, and at the conclusion of every trick applauded vigorously with her small, energetic hands. She picked up a good deal of bad language, which she heard in the stables, not because the grooms wished to teach her but because they were so accustomed to her presence that they did not trouble to alter their usual mode of speech. Her mother might reprove her, but, as it was impossible to explain to the child what the offensive words meant, Jenny was at a loss how to effect a reform.

"Our Genevra, how many times have I told you not to use that bad word!"

Genevra, opening her blue eyes wide, would reply, "What is a bad word, Muther?"

"What you've just said, about Holst."

"I didn't say it; O'Reilly said it to Bill Triplet."

"Then there's no call for you to repeat it. It's a bad, wicked word."

"Why is it bad and wicked, Muther?"

Exasperated, Jenny would take refuge behind Alfredo's authority. "I shall tell your dad not to let you go into the stables if you're going to learn nasty talk. That's what I'll do."

Slanting her yellow head on one side, Genevra would ask, "Muther, what does it *mean?* If I knew an' it was really bad I'd not say it."

"It means—it means—something that's very nasty."

"But Holst is very nasty; I hate him. He's a bloody Hun! He killed O'Reilly's bruther. In t' war."

"And I won't have you say 'bloody', neither."

"Oh dear, what am I to say?"

"Talk nice like what other children do."

Holst, who had confided to Jenny that he was actually von Holst, and that he had been a high-ranking officer in the German Army, was the trainer of the new 'cats'. He was tall and fair, with broad shoulders and narrow hips. His waist was pronounced, and it was the opinion of the grooms that he "wears stays, I've 'eard 'em creak when 'e moves". His manners were perfect, and he professed an unbounded admiration for Menetti. He said to Jenny one day, when they met on the fair-ground in Padua, "Signora Menetti, how good is your husband! This a great artiste is. Tell me, he does not like me, what for is this? I like him so much."

She flushed, for Alfredo had made no secret of the fact that he, like his small daughter, disliked Holst. "Why, I don't know that he doesn't like you, Mr. Holst. To tell you the truth, we neither of us care about animal acts. We—well, we're old performers, an' we know that it isn't and can't be done by kindness like they try to stuff you up with."

"Kindness," he shrugged his shoulders. "I the use of the word

45

discipline prefer. Discipline is good for all, Mrs. Menetti. If I should be bad to my cats, my life in grave danger would be. They remember all that happens."

She stared at him, her eyes very clear and cold. "And isn't it?"

"Is not—what? My life in danger? Poof! That revolver I carry, the men waiting with iron rods, my whip! Surely you know that is part of the illusion we to create wish as showmen? The public like very much to watch acts which they believe to be dangerous; we are ready that illusion of danger to create. Why do they watch your husband? Is it because they admire his courage, his skill, the grace of his work? I reply—no. It is because they wish to see what happens if he falls. This is the old spirit of the Romans at gladiatorial spectacles. I tell you audiences are sadists, they wish for accidents."

"I tell you," she retorted, "you're talking a lot of poppy-cock!"

"I know my world," he replied with a certain arrogance; "I know the peoples of that world."

"Oh, you think you know a devil of a lot, I don't doubt."

"But indeed I do; I am not an animal trainer only; I a student of human nature am. I was educated in Heidelberg; I graduated with many honours. My family people of great culture are. My books and papers were destroyed in the war, my manuscripts also. Otherwise I would send to my father to tell him to send *Friedrich Holst on the Human Mind*. Also *Holst on Reactions to Fear*, and many more."

"You've had a busy time, writing books and learning to train 'cats'."

He smiled, showing very white even teeth. "To men of my race, always comes the desire to acquire knowledge and more knowledge. To us the knowledge is power."

"I'll lay your 'cats' wish you'd stuck to book-learning. Well, I must get on. I want to find our Genevra."

He said, "Also your beautiful little child does not much like poor Holst."

"Maybe not. Well, good morning."

He bowed from the waist, and left her to continue her search for Genevra. As he walked away he smiled. He was too clever for these people. They were so gullible; he could imagine Jenny telling Menetti all that he had said, recounting his literary attainments, his fine education.

His real name was Emile Bauer, and his father was an ironworker in Essen. He had run away from his very poor home when he was fourteen, and had never returned, indeed never wished to return. His father and mother might be dead, his brothers killed in the war, his sisters—mentally he shrugged his shoulders, dismissing them. He had been taken on by a lion-trainer called Holst, and when his employer was badly mauled by a lioness Bauer wrote out in German a will to which he added a well-forged signature of the dead Holst—for he died two days after the accident—stating that the lions and all other possessions were left to 'my brave assistant, Emile Bauer'.

The dead man was unmarried, no one appeared to contest the will, and Bauer took over the 'cats'. He changed his name to Holst, and when he wished to impress anyone stated confidentially that he was in reality von Holst. "Actually I Baron von Holst am. But," with a smile of mingled courage and sadness, "to a poor man what use are high-sounding names? One day, when happier times have come, I shall return to my beloved Fatherland, and try—with these two hands—the home of my ancestors to rebuild. Till that time," and he would give his formal bow, "believe that I am only Friedrich Holst, and at your service."

Holst acquired a small and not-too-well-bred fox terrier and prepared to begin his training in order that he might enliven the rather dreary spectacle of 'forest-bred lions' leaping through hoops and standing—with furious eyes—upon upturned tubs, while Holst uttered guttural and unintelligible orders.

It was unfortunate that one morning when he was engaged in training the dog to balance on one leg, Genevra pushed open the door of the room and stood transfixed, watching the lesson. She stood watching in silence, and Holst was too absorbed to pay any attention to her. Only when, to Genevra at least it seemed, the dog turned his appealing and tortured eyes towards her did Holst realize her presence.

He turned, furious, to see her standing there, and as she met his eyes she was galvanized into life. The beautiful ten-year-old child became a virago. She rushed forward and, reaching Holst, battered at whatever parts of his body she could reach with her clenched fists, pouring out a stream of obscenity which she had learned in the stables.

"You b——y Hun—oh, you bastard! Let 'im go! D'you hear, let 'im go! You b——y man, I'll tell me dad and me muther. Gie me yon dog, or I'll get O'Reilly to kill you. Gie me yon dog!"

Holst stood, his legs apart, staring down at her; his eyes were cold like glacier ice, his lips set into a hard line.

"How dare you come in here? You are everywhere, you little

beast. The grooms you may like, I—Holst—hate you. Take the damn' dog. He is no use to me anyway. A bad dog so I give him to a bad mistress. Go! I other dogs get. Take 'im or I shall him kill—und not quickly."

Genevra, her small face white, for no one had ever spoken so to her, licked her dry lips and said, "Take yon string off of his foot then, you bastard. I 'ope as you rot an' worms eat you. Stinkin' 'ound. C'm on, dog, I'll watch as no one gets you. I'll tell Mr. Trumelli, so I will."

It was curious that the huge German did not sweep the child from the tent; instead he stood watching her with narrowed eyes. Ten years against his thirty; her innocence against his knowledge, and—the child stood in the stronger position. He untied the thin rope from the dog's foot and flung him down. She sprang forward, and caught up the little shivering terrier. Holding him in her arms, smoothing his staring coat, she shouted her last defiance: "Get ter hell! I'll tell me dad. He'll paste you. C'm on, luv, I'll mind you, so will my muther." She turned to raise the flap of the tent and speaking over her shoulder, said, "Think on, I'll show you! So I will."

She told her mother that Holst had given her the dog, and when Jenny met him the following morning she thanked him, saying, "My word, that was kind of you, Mr. Holst. My Genevra is prop'ly set oop with that nice little dog you gave her. She's called him 'Haig' after a whisky they have in England. She's always longed for a little dog, but somehow my husband and I never got round to getting her one. Thank you very much. It was a kind thing to do."

Holst bowed. "Please, this nothing is."

Later Alfredo, who, while he had approved of the dog, experienced a slight spasm of jealousy that Holst, whom he hated, should have given him to Genevra, gave her a small marmoset.

Genevra had said nothing at the caravan. She had entered with the dog and when Jenny asked where she had found it, only said, "Yon Hun give it me. His name's Haig. I can keep him, Muther, can't I?"

Jenny was delighted; this might be the end of Alfredo's dislike for the lion-tamer and his for Alfredo. She beamed at her small daughter.

"Keep it, of course. Nice little dog. 'Haig', that's a whisky. Now I wonder where you found that name?"

Stolidly Genevra answered, "O'Reilly told me it was the name of—a good whisky."

When the marmoset was added to the family, Genevra was the happiest child in Europe. She was, despite her charm and intelligence, a careful little soul, and she devoted much time and attention to both animals. They were beautifully groomed and carefully fed, and their devotion to her was beyond question.

She was nearly twelve when Trumelli made his great announcement. The circus was to go to England! Not a very long tour, because England did not offer the same prices as the big Continental cities. Newcastle, Glasgow, Edinburgh, Leeds, Manchester and Birmingham, then—to wind up—London.

Alfredo was delighted; it had always been his ambition to work in England. This tour meant an extra week to be spent with Lottie and Josh. "Zee Inglese hev great taste. Me, I shell prepare a trick—not a trick boot somesings I do; t'ey will shout with delight. Listen—now I sving from moving trapeze to stationary. In zees new act I sving from moving trapeze to anuzzer moving one—end back again. T'ey vill go mad. T'ey cry '*Viva Menetti! Viva, viva!*' You, darrling Jennee, hev ver' lovely dresses, I hev new leotards. Genevra, my leetle angel, alls 'ave grand time, no?"

She said, "You bet, our Dad."

His success in England was spectacular. Various influential variety agents came to offer him contracts. Alfredo said the same to all of them.

"Pleaze, spik vis my vife. She compre'end all. I em not man-of-business. Chust acrobat. My vife ver' clever. I t'ink I stay viz my good friend, Mr. Trumelli, no?"

Jenny was adamant. "Very kind of you, sir, but my husband likes the life of a circus, and Trumelli's is the best in the world. Thanks all the same, but we'll stay where we are."

They protested that Menetti would be paid a tremendous salary. Jenny still shook her head.

"We're very happy where we are, thanking you just the same. It's a good act, and the life suits my husband and our little girl. No, I'd not even consider it. Good night, sir."

They opened in London, in a great fair-ground at Shepherd's Bush. The advertising was magnificent. Trumelli gave a luncheon to which were invited all the *élite* of London. And all the *élite* of London came. Photographs were taken and produced in the more exclusive of the weekly journals. 'The Countess of Marketbrough takes a cocktail with Trumelli', and 'Lady June Bellingford chats with Alfredo Menetti'. Jenny wore new dresses, which were just a little too elaborate, and Alfredo realized one of the ambitions of his life, to wear a morning coat and huge puffy Ascot tie with sponge-bag trousers.

Their first night was a triumph, and the Press could not have been more satisfied. Trumelli rubbed his hands and declared that their visit to England must be an annual affair, that it was worth all the money which the advertising and luncheon had cost. Houses were packed to capacity. Curiously Holst's lions were the least successful item in the show. He grumbled that he was at a disadvantage, that cages were less easy to show than 'open show'.

"Liberty horses, bare-back acts, these all audiences see. For me, I am shut away; it is very difficult. I feel my act not completely appreciated is."

Jenny told Menetti, "Mind, in one way he's right. It is difficult for the audience to see what's going on in cages."

Alfredo replied, "Darrling, a damn' good job. Maybe Trumelli get rid of zees man. I shell be ver' gled."

"Go on, luv. He's got to live same as the rest of us."

Unconscious that he was adapting a famous remark, Alfredo said, "So! I don't see no reason vhy 'e should lif', ziss man!"

She returned, "Freddo, for shame, that's not a Christian thought."

He chuckled, "Ees 'e Christian man? Me, I don't t'ink."

He winked delightedly at Genevra, who sat next to him at the table. She grinned back at him—how delightful he was, this handsome father of hers!—and said, "I think he's a bastard!"

"And I think," Jenny said smartly, "that it 'ul only need one more rude crack out of you, my girl, for me to give you the hiding you've been asking for!" Genevra, who had never been smacked in her life, remained unmoved, giving bits of meat to Haig and scraps of bread soaked in milk to the monkey. "I don't know why you're always so down on Holst. Mind, I don't like him, but I've something better to do than always be picking on him. I don't care for animal trainers; come to that I don't care for Germans, but as Trumelli says, he's got to offer acts the public wants. If they want lions and suchlike, they've got to have them. Genevra, don't give all your dinner to Haig, he's had his already."

That night Trumelli told Jenny, who repeated it to Alfredo, that several minor Royalties were 'in front'. He smiled his engaging, rather child-like smile, saying, "Darrling, I give just same show eff twenty kings and twenty qveens watch me. Alvays my best possible. Maybe after zey come an' say, 'Alfredo, pleaze teach me 'ow to do trapeze act.' No?"

He gave his act—as he always did, for his boasting was not empty—in the best possible way. Jenny never tired of watching his grace, his sureness and his swift, neat movements. It seemed to her that this act of his was akin to poetry; somewhere she had heard the phrase 'the poetry of motion', and surely Alfredo was the very epitome of its meaning.

They had been married thirteen years, and she could never recall a quarrel which had lasted more than a few moments and which had not ended with them both bursting into roars of laughter. He had not changed; his figure was still slim and beautiful. How often he had assured her that he owed so much to her, for she studied his diet with the greatest care, and firmly refused to allow him to eat dishes which induced the consumer to put on weight.

"Jennee, I wish more potatoes, pleaze," he asked.

To which she always replied, "I doubt wish 'ul have to be your master. Eat that luvely salad there, better for your figure, my lad."

Once when they had visited a theatre, some actor had spoken the words, "There are dragons in my path," and Alfredo had regarded this as a pearl of wit. Whenever Jenny refused to allow him to indulge in an extra glass of beer, or to eat sweet cakes, he would grin at Genevra and with his ridiculous wink say, "T'ere arre dragons een my pat'!"

Now as she handed him his props, he smiled and whispered, " 'Ave you 'eard zees prince laugh! I em sending a note to esk eeff 'e vill 'ave feesh an' cheeps wiz us after zee show, yes?"

His humour might not be of a very high order, it had a childish quality, but it was spontaneous, and he retained the ability to make Jenny laugh as she had always done.

The act was drawing to its close, the tricks were growing in daring and difficulty. The applause at the end of each came as if the audience experienced a sense of delighted relief that Menetti had accomplished what might well have been believed to be impossible. His smiles were constant, and Jenny thought, 'Bless him, he's enjoying himself to-night! He may be turned thirty, but he's just a great kid'.

She handed him the handkerchief for his last trapeze act saying:

"By gum, luv, you're good to-night!"

"Same es alvays, darrling Jennee."

He went up his long rope-ladder to the trapeze which hung almost at the full height of the great tent. His figure looked small, and Jenny thought 'kind of lonely standing up there looking down'. Then told herself that she was 'growing daft thinking such rubbish'.

The drums rolled, the trapeze swung, as Alfredo impelled it forward; he rose and stood poised, and Jenny could feel the tension in the audience increase. He was flying through the air, like a swallow in flight, he caught the second trapeze, and scarcely resting for a second prepared to make his return flight. The steady drum-roll continued; once more Menetti launched himself into the air.

Jenny, watching, heard herself scream, "It's not true! God, he's missed it!" She heard also voices shouting, screams from other women, saw Trumelli rush forward, and knew that something in gold-and-white leotards lay in a crumpled heap at her feet.

He was dead, his gay life finished on the tan of the big top. She remembered very little of what followed. A side tent, a doctor leaning over Alfredo—or what had been Alfredo—then rising and saying to Trumelli, "Instantaneous—nothing to be done. Why don't these fellows use nets, for God's sake?" That stung her into speech.

"My husband didn't use a net because he was a great artiste, and he didn't need any net. The sight of one made him nervous, he always said. That's why."

Genevra, white-faced and quiet, holding the monkey in her arms, while Haig lay at her feet, raising his head from time to time to stare at her in anxious affection.

"Won't I see him any more, Muther?"

Mrs. Zoppo answered for Jenny, "In Heaven, if you're a good girl, dear."

"But not now, not here?"

"No, ducky. You must try to be a comfort to you poor mother."

Genevra said listlessly, "Aye, I'll try."

Trumelli came and talked about insurance, and what should be done with the clothes used in the act. Jenny cried, "Give 'em away. I never want to see his luvely leotards again, nor his props neither."

"I'll find work for you, if you like to stay on, Jenny."

"Me—stay on! Without him! It's kind of you, Mr. Trumelli, but I shall go home to my muther in Manchester. Keep the caravan for yourself. Might use it as an office or something. By gum, it's been a luvely life. You've been very kind—always. My Freddo thought a lot of you."

She met his eyes and saw that they were filled with tears. He patted her hand, saying, "I thought a lotter him. Bin with me a long time. A grand feller."

They gave him a splendid funeral, with the band playing the Dead March in Saul, and the heartbreaking Funeral March of Chopin. Jenny had asked Philip Bailey, who was the conductor, if he couldn't play something from *Aida* or *Tosca*, but he seemed to think her suggestion slightly improper, and said that the English wouldn't approve, so she let the idea drop.

What did it matter, what did anything matter?

Josh and Lottie came from Manchester; they were gentle and very kind; they petted Genevra and Lottie tried to make dishes which would induce Jenny to eat. Jenny wanted nothing except to sit and think and remember. She went to the undertaker's parlour to see the wreaths, because it was too much trouble to refuse. Her mother read the cards, and appeared to get much satisfaction from the names which they bore.

"See, Jenny, the Italian Ambassador's sent one—what a size!"

Jenny replied in her strange dull new voice, "They always have them like that in Italy. They call 'em *tributi*."

"Here's one from Lord Studdington; it says, 'In sympathy for a great artiste'." Then suddenly, "Jenny, look at this; what a luvly wreath! The name's von Holst. German surely."

"Yes, it's kind of him to have sent that, because my Freddo never liked him. Oh, let's get away, Mum. I'll have cards sent thanking them all. The undertaker 'ul see to it all. I want to get it over and cum back with you and dad."

Only once did something of her old spirit assert itself. As they drove through London, where crowds had gathered, she said to Genevra, "He'd like this. He'd say, 'What an audience I've got!' eh?"

Genevra said sulkily, "He'd have liked the Monk and Haig ter cum; they oughter have cum an' all."

Lottie rebuked her. "Genevra, that's no road to talk. You don't tak' animals ter funerals, choose how."

"I seen a picksure once of a dog at a funeral. A king's funeral it was—so now."

After making that statement she relapsed into silence.

The rest of the day for Jenny was like watching a film which kept breaking, leaving gaps so that all continuity was lost. Two priests intoning, a little boy walking with a crucifix which she felt certain was too heavy for him. Standing by the open grave. Her mother crying bitterly. She'd been fond of Freddo, though she would insist upon calling him 'Fred', which didn't seem to suit him a bit. Trumelli, grey-faced and suddenly seeming so old. The clowns looking strange in their ordinary clothes. She wished they could have come in their white suits with the bright 'pom-poms'. A tall figure standing a little apart, his fair head shining in the watery sunshine. Holst! She thought that it was kind of him to come. Freddo disliked him, but she didn't believe that Freddo was capable of really disliking anyone very deeply.

All the grooms, the little Yorkshire head groom, O'Reilly, and Triplet and the rest whose names she had forgotten.

It was over; they turned away and walked back to the waiting cars; Jenny thought that it seemed heartless to leave Alfredo all alone. One of the priests was speaking to her; he had a nice warm Irish voice, and though she didn't attend very much to what he said, the sound was smooth and comforting.

"I s'ppose he's all right, Father?" Jenny said.

"Safer, better, happier than he has ever been, my child."

"I hope so, I'm sure." Then as an afterthought, "I'd like you to say Masses for him, very often. Dad," to Josh, "give the Father some money, will you? As much as you can spare, then I'll send some more, Father, when I get home. I shan't forget, I promise."

The priest smiled. "Neither will I, my child, rest assured of that. May God bless you, and Our Blessed Lady comfort you."

Back at the huge fair-ground everything was strangely quiet, for it was Sunday. More people shaking her hand, some bending down to kiss Genevra. They were to sleep that night at an hotel; Josh had arranged everything. "No use of drawing things out, only upset her more," he had said to Lottie.

"See as it's a nice hotel, Josh. I won't go to any third-rate places, an' we don't want any fuss about the munkey and that dog, neither. It 'ul only upset them both more'n what they are already."

Holst came and bowed over Jenny's hand; she said, "Thank you for the luvely flowers you sent. It was kind. Goodbye."

"I in 'Goodbye' do not believe," he said. "I leave Trumelli, I on my own shell work. Here I get no real opportunity. I hope, sincerely, we again meet one day."

Mechanically she answered, "I hope so, I'm sure."

A last interview with Trumelli, payments to be made, and as they sat together in the caravan he told her that he was going to retire.

"I'm getting old, Jenny. Tired of work. I'm planning to buy

54

a farm in Tuscany. The lads are good, they'll not find it hard to get new jobs. Only old Harry 'ul come along with me. Maybe Triplet an' a coupla others. Send me a letter sometimes, tell me how you're going on. The Italian agent—Bronelli, 78 Via Manzoni, Milano, will find me. Goodbye, it's bin a good time."

As they drove away, Jenny said, "That's the end of the act, eh?"

Josh cleared his throat, and answered, "The curtain goes up on another, think on, Jenny luv."

They were back in Manchester, living in the tall, rather over-furnished house at Stratton Street. The circus receded into the background, and when Lottie spoke of Alfredo it was as 'poor Fred'. Jenny never spoke of him at all. He was a kind of fragrant dream character. Sometimes she dreamed of him, dreams which were about the ordinary things which had made up their lives. She was cooking spaghetti for him—'just the way you like it, luv'—she was discussing a new trick which he proposed to introduce into the act, he was talking of Genevra and her attraction, their proposed tours. There was never anything astonishing or erotic about those dreams, but she woke in the morning conscious that she had been happy. Not wildly or deliriously happy, but possessing a quiet warm contentment. During the day which followed she would go about her work serene and smiling a little.

She worked in the house, for despite her protestations Lottie was finding the work just a little too much for her, and the two girls from Pudsey had married and been replaced by women who never, as Lottie said, 'really settled down'. Jenny was energetic, her cooking was good if not quite so excellent as her mother's, and with the help of one elderly woman with immense and startling false teeth, complete with bright pink false gums, they managed very well.

Genevra was sent to school. Jenny insisted upon a 'private school'. She might talk with a broad Yorkshire accent herself, might like to boast that Genevra was a 'reit Lancashire bairn', but she deplored the accent which the child had contracted. So Genevra was sent to a select and completely inefficient school, where the children were taught to 'mouth' their words, and where, except for the use of good open vowels which she heard at home, she would have spoken in exactly the same way.

She disliked the other children; she bragged and boasted that she had 'bin with the grandest circus in t'world' and that 'my dad was t' best acrobat. There's never bin anuther like him.' The other children gathered round, open-eyed and open-mouthed, to listen, but in their snobbish little souls they despised her for being 'someone who hes lived in a keravan, Mama'.

Genevra, though she loved an audience, was always glad to rush home. The 'visitors'—they were never called 'lodgers' at Mrs. Hostley's—liked her. They found her intelligent, and she never tired of asking them to tell her stories about the stage. Bransby Williams, no longer 'that young Mr. Williams', but still handsome and drawing huge audiences, would call as he heard her come in after school, "Is that my Genevra? Come and have a talk with your uncle!" For her he would do such imitations as he never even gave to the public. She watched and listened—and learned.

"You've come too late, my dear," he told her, "you've missed the greatest of us—Dan Leno and Marie Lloyd. The great single turns are going. Make the most of your time. Learn while you can. Now, watch . . . here's that nasty man Uriah Heep for you."

But Marie's sister Alice came, so did her other sisters—Rosie and Daisy Wood—and the child would stand wide-eyed, happy in being able to hear them talk. Florrie Ford, immense and essentially kind, said, "Now think of it, I knew your mother when she first started with John Tiller! To think that you're her daughter!" George Graves enchanted her, with his, "Well, well, well. Bless me soul! Jenny Mander's little girl, and as pretty as she was!"

Genevra said, "Mr. Graves, please tell me about *The Merry Widow*."

To which he replied, "The Widow! God bless me soul, what do you want to know about it, m' dear."

"Anything," she said, "just anything."

Josh took her to see Hetty King, and the next day they met on the stairs. It seemed impossible that this elegant, dignified lady could be the swaggering soldier she had seen last night on the stage. The lady said, "Good morning, dear. Who are you?"

Genevra said, "I'm Mrs. Menetti's little girl. Mrs. Hostley's my gram-ma, only she's not really called Mrs. Hostley."

"Then you're Jenny's little girl?"

"That's right, Jenny's my mum's name." Adding shyly, for though she could bluster and swagger with the best of them at school, Genevra was shy with these giants of the theatre, "M' gram-pa took me to see you last night. O-oh, you were luvely!"

There was a very gentle and beautiful young man who stayed

with them. His clothes, Genevra thought, were lovely. In a queer way he reminded her of her father, of whom she never spoke. He smiled at her, spoke to her in a voice which was full but never loud. She heard her grandmother say to her mother, "Nay, I must say I've never seen anything wrong. But it's a pity if all one hears is true. Mind, he's clever, and his act's clean."

Jenny said, "I' most cases all one hears isn't true."

Not only people from the music-hall came to Mrs. Hostley's, people from the theatre came also, wonderful people, whom Genevra was allowed to go and watch through the kindness of Mr. Huddington, the manager of the theatre, who gave Josh Mander tickets whenever he cared to ask for them.

Once a lady with a French name, and before she came, mum said, "We must have that piano tuned, for she's a pianist as well as an actress." The lady came and smiled at everyone, a smile which Genevra thought warmed the whole room. She was young, not very tall, and when she spoke it was something in the way dad had spoken—not quite English. She played the piano a great deal, not songs and waltzes but wonderful music which made Genevra stand outside the door, listening to each note and feeling that she was transported to fairyland, or at other times that she could have easily burst into tears.

It was worth going to school to mix with those silly and detestable girls to be able to come home and live in the same house with such people. Grandma had given her a book with blank pages all of different colours, bound in red leather, for Christmas. It was for these great people to write their names in. Some of them even did little pictures. Mr. Robey drew a picture of himself, with queer black eyebrows, and when Genevra said, "It's something like what you are, but you're a lot nicer," he roared with laughing.

She was thirteen, or would be thirteen in a few weeks, when mum said, "I'll take you to Belle Vue on Saturday, luv, if you're good."

Genevra, who would have preferred to go to the theatre where a certain Mr. Walls was appearing, said, "What's on at Belle Vue, Mum?"

"All sorts. A circus for one thing."

The child stared at her. "A circus! I'm going to no circus! I'd rather stay at home and talk to the Monk and Haig."

Jenny stared at her, "Then stop at home," she said, "I'll go by myself."

Impudently Genevra answered, "That 'ul suit me."

57

She was bitterly hurt. The thought that her mum, whom she loved and who had loved and known her dad, could go and watch a circus made her feel sick and cold with horror. The Liberty horses, the elephants—it might be some of Trumelli's elephants, ones she had known, for Trumelli had gone to his farm in Tuscany, with Harry Bagstock and Triplet and O'Reilly, and sometimes sent her brightly coloured postcards. There would be clowns like Zippo and Zoppo, lions with a trainer like that damned Holst, even—her mind halted—even an acrobat like dad. No, not like dad; as long as circuses existed there would never be another like Alfredo Menetti.

The next day as she went to school she saw a poster advertising the attractions at Belle Vue, and halted to read what it said. Hallet's Trained Elephants, Famous Thought-Reading Horse 'Thespes', Pure-Bred Liberty Horses trained by Signor Cavatelli, the Great Continental Clowns Zippo and Zoppo. Her heart missed a beat. How she would love to see Mrs. Zoppo again! After her abrupt refusal would it be possible to tell mum that she had changed her mind? "Sorry if I was rude, Mum. I just didn't know as Zippo and Zoppo were on the bill. May I come, please, and if there's any acrobats or lions, not watch them?"

She read down the bill, more names she did not know, then 'Von Holst and his trained forest-bred lions'.

Dad had once told her a story, someone had written music for it, all about a lady called Floria Tosca, and her sweetheart, a painter, Mario. It was terribly sad, and in the end the gentleman was shot. Dad had hummed some of the music, and there was a little bit that came nearer and nearer because it was meant to show that something terrible was going to happen. She could hear it now—'La, ta, ta tata tee'. All day it rang in her ears, and she imagined that it was coming nearer and nearer.

CHAPTER FIVE

GENEVRA said nothing; her grandmother said, "What's wrong, luv?" and she replied, in a voice which she knew was sulky, though she wasn't really sulky at all, but only disturbed and desperately unhappy, "Nothing, Grandma."

Josh asked, "Got a headache, ducky?"

She said, "Maybe a bit of a one."

Saturday came, and in the morning Genevra had answered a

ring at the bell and taken in a great bunch of red roses. The little envelope which was attached to them bore her mother's name. Instinctively she thought, 'Holst!' because she knew that, however Zippo and Zoppo might love her mother, they'd never send flowers like these, never for that matter send flowers at all.

Jenny took them, opened the envelope and said, "That's all right, luv."

Genevra longed to ask where the flowers had come from, but anxiety and sheer misery made her tongue-tied.

While they were having luncheon Jenny said, "Coming to the show?"

Genevra shook her head. "I'd rather stay with the Monk and Haig."

"Go on! You'd like it when you got there." Jenny's tone was encouraging, even faintly persuasive.

"I don't want to go!" Genevra blazed suddenly. "I've not forgot if you have. That Holst's there with his poor terrified cats!"

"Don't you speak to me like that," Jenny ordered. "If you don't want to come, stop away."

"That's what I'm going to do."

Lottie looked up from serving Josh with a second helping of steak-and-kidney pudding. "Genevra, ducky, don't speak rude to your muther."

Genevra lapsed into silence and gave her remaining bits of steak-and-kidney to Haig.

All the afternoon, when she had heard the front door shut behind her mother, she sat in her bedroom, with Haig and the Monk. There were moments when she sprang to her feet, determined to go to Belle Vue alone; others when she sat completely depressed and wretched, talking in a low voice to the dog and cuddling the monkey in her arms. The time seemed endless; she felt that she had been sitting there alone for years. When her grandmother called up the stairs, "Genevra—tea!" she pretended that she had not heard. Her acute depression had given way to a smouldering resentment. What did any of them care about her? Nothing! Her mother—whom she adored as she had adored Menetti—had 'gone off' to watch a man her father had detested. She would have loved to see Zippo and Zoppo, to have been clasped to Mrs. Zoppo's ample bosom, and to have been made much of, but instead—she was left to sit in her own room, with no one except Haig and the Monk.

Steadily declining into a state of acute self-pity, she began to cry. Haig stared up at her with loving, disturbed eyes; when her tears fell on the Monk, it shook its head in protest, and put up one of its tiny hands to pat her cheek.

The light was beginning to fade, there was a new cause for misery—even grandma had not continued her call to tea, and had not taken the trouble to come up and find out why she did not join them. She stroked Haig's smooth head, saying softly, "I'm what's called a Unwanted Child, Haig. My dad 'ud never have left me like this, never!"

The church clock was striking half past six when Jenny burst into the room. She was flushed, and rushed to Genevra.

"My angel, what's wrong? Grandma told me you'd not come down to tea. Tell your mum what's the matter. Don't you feel well? Let mum put you to bed, and bring you some nice milk and one of gran's little rock cakes. You've been crying! Darling, tell mummy what it is."

Genevra said, with quiet pride, "I've cried a lot—I never thought I'd stop crying. It was you watching a circus—and I wanted to see Zippo and Zoppo an' Mrs. Zoppo."

"And so you shall, luv. They're coming to dinner with us to-morrow. It's Sunday, an' as luck has it we've no one coming in while late."

"I'll not come if that Holst is coming!"

"He's not coming, luvey. Only them three."

Genevra flung herself into her mother's arms; with them round her she felt safe, secure in love which was solid as the world itself. She longed to blurt out all her ideas, jealousies and torments; instead she clung to Jenny, sobbing with relief. Her mother was home again; she hadn't asked Holst to come and see them, she had thought about Genevra, knowing how she would love to see the clowns again. She felt at once elated and disgraced.

"You and me, Mum," she sobbed gently. "That's all we want, you and me."

Soothingly Jenny whispered, "That's all, luvey, you and me."

Zippo, with Mr. and Mrs. Zoppo, came and Genevra was petted and made much of; she was clasped to Mrs. Zoppo's ample bosom, which smelt of 'Phul Nana', a scent which she affected, and Zippo told her silly stories, and Zoppo did tricks with handkerchiefs, and at the culmination of each trick cried, "Hello! Here we are again" in the traditional circus manner. The room grew very hot; Josh asked permission to remove his coat, and Lottie fanned herself gently with a copy of the *News of the World.* The air was heavy with the smell of good food, and again and again the guests were pressed to take more of the beautifully cold beer which Josh brought periodically from the cellar.

Jenny watched and listened, wondering what had happened to her. She had loved Alfredo; he had been dead for a year now, and she had never ceased to think of him with deep affection, and a consciousness of her loss. The first months had been agony, it had seemed that there was no reason for anything. She had worked mechanically, forcing herself to pretend to have an acute interest in the workings of the house and the comfort of its occupants. She had been charming to the clients, she had talked to them, laughed at their jokes, but always with a sense of resentment in her heart that they should be alive, pursuing their careers, while her Freddo was finished with everything that had made their life together so happy.

'Not,' she told herself, 'that I wish any harm to anyone. I don't want the O'Gorman boys to be where Freddo is, neither do I want any of them—George Robey, and Chergwin, and any of them. Only—I can't see *why* this should have happened to me and my Freddo. It's not as if we'd been wicked; maybe we didn't always go to Mass like we should have done, but it's difficult when you often move of a Sunday, and everyone's been working late on the "tear down". Now it seems as if life was hollow— empty—nothing's got any meaning any more.'

Then, a few days before she visited Belle Vue, she met Holst in the Oxford Road. He was walking with the swagger which she knew so well, his head held very high, towering above the people whom he passed with his long, easy stride. She had never really liked him, but now her heart seemed to miss a beat. He saw her and swung off his hat, smiling and saying:

"This a great pleasure is, Signora Menetti. I said once that I did not believe in saying 'Goodbye'. I knew that always we should meet again. Now I no longer am with Trumelli, he lives the life of a peasant in Italy. I work alone with my cats. Alles people wish to see Holst!" He laughed. "I am very glad. Now, will you a cup of bad English coffee with me take?"

Almost to her own surprise, Jenny enjoyed her coffee, though Holst grimaced at its wretched quality. He was studiously attentive, and it was interesting to hear circus talk again. She found herself watching his meticulously shaved face, his strong, firm hands—she missed the fact that they were cruel hands in addition.

When he said, "Perhaps you will kom to see the show, yes? On Saturday will be a good day? May I see you to-morrow and

C   61

bring the tickets with me?" she felt a sense of pleasant expectancy. They met the next morning when she was doing the shopping, and again Jenny sat and drank coffee with him. She looked forward to Saturday, and Genevra's refusal to accompany her came as a blow. She hated to leave the child at home, and when she returned to find her in tears she reproached herself for having been selfish and unkind. Holst, as an act independent from the rest of the circus, was remaining in Manchester for a month; his act was daring and to his audience it seemed that the ferocity of his lions was unquestionable. Jenny met him again and again and realized that—in some strange fashion—she was growing fond of him. He made no attempt to hide his admiration for her; he brought her flowers, chocolates and expensive fruit, presenting them to her with stiff little compliments. Once he said, with a touch of Germanic sentimentalism, which Jenny believed to be pathos, "I wish so much that your beautiful little girl liked me. I for children have a great love myself."

Jenny said, "Oh, well, you know what children are, Mr. Holst. They're full of fancies and likes and dislikes. Half the time they don't know what it's all about, anyway. But she's a highly strung little thing—and not so little, either—she's shooting up! I can't bear to upset her; when she gets upset it leaves her in a proper state for days."

He sighed, "Ah, well, so long as this child's beautiful mother does not me dislike, I can bear it. I could not bear to remember that you disliked me. I recall that at one time I felt that you did this, no?"

"I didn't know you so well then, Mr. Holst. A lot of water's gone under the bridge since those days."

A few days before he was due to leave Manchester, Holst asked her to marry him. She had known that it was coming, that she waited for his question with a sense of mingled excitement and apprehension. Even now she did not know if she loved him; certainly there was nothing in her feeling for him that had existed in her passion for Alfredo. Indeed she almost wondered if the main factor were not a longing to get back into circus life, to know again the happy care-free existence, where time seemed endlessly bright.

"You shall have everything that I can give you," Holst said. "To you I my whole life shall dedicate. Say that you will marry me, Jenny."

Her voice was lacking in any great warmth as she answered, "Yes, I believe I'd like to. Mind, I think mum and dad—to say nothing of our Genevra—will all be against it. Still, I've my own life to live, haven't I?"

He stretched out his hand across the little table where they had been drinking their usual coffee, and laid it on hers. He glanced round the rather dingy little place, then his eyes met Jenny's.

"You have changed this place by your giving of that promise to be my beloved wife. Never for one moment shall you this regret. You shall not be parted from your beautiful little girl. You will see that in a very short time she will have for me a profound and deep love. A love which will be returned from my heart."

He was leaving on the Monday for Newcastle. Four weeks later he had a vacant week, and then, he suggested, they should be married. Then their tour of England and Scotland would really begin. He was joining the old-established and very successful circus called 'Hugil's Monster Circus'; they were paying him well, and he was to have a small percentage of the profits.

Jenny went home to break the news to her family. She experienced no feeling of elation, her heart was beating very fast, and she was conscious of a sense of impending trouble. Once she even played with the idea of writing to Holst and telling him that it was all a ghastly mistake, that she could not possibly marry him, and did not wish to see him again. Then she remembered his magnificent figure, his smooth yellow hair, his fresh, fine skin, and imagined that she heard again his assurances of complete devotion, and his intention to devote the whole of his life to making her happy. She had never been a woman who wished to have trivial love-affairs, although there had been sufficient opportunities. In her intense love for Menetti there had been the love of a woman for a man, but also a protective motherly instinct which had absorbed her. Alfredo's figure, food which would contribute to the admirable condition of his fine body, had been her great and chief concern. Now, living in her mother's house, she did her best to be interested in the well-being of the artistes who visited there, but her efforts were objective. There was no actual personal feeling about them. She had been an artiste herself, and she realized that what would suit this person admirably might disgust another. She had flung herself into the work of the house, indeed she was proud of its reputation. If she were not cooking, then she was occupied with the rooms, the linen, the clean towels—all of which went to make up that atmosphere which made Mrs. Hostley's regarded as one of the finest 'rooming houses'—although that phrase had not yet reached England and professional rooms were still referred to as 'digs'.

While she had worked and given of her best, there had been always in her heart and mind the longing to serve people who were attached to her personally. She adored her child, but she—although never since Alfredo's death had she admitted it even to herself—wanted a man who worked for her and her child; a man who came in hungry and wanted the good food which she could prepare for him. At Stratton Street she was 'Lottie's daughter'; she wanted to be the head and front of a home of her own, even if that home were a caravan.

Genevra had gone to bed, and Josh returned from the music-hall. Their supper was a dish of tripe and onions, cooked only as people in Yorkshire and Lancashire understand. Lottie was, as Josh said, 'on top o' the world' because a Miss Gladys Cooper had booked rooms at Hostley's.

Lottie, leaning back in her chair, replete with the splendid dish of which they had partaken, said, "Mind you, I b'lieve as she's t'lovliest actress in t'world. London's pro'ply crackers about her. Then there's that clever little lad wi' t'lady as works wi' him. . . Wee Georgie Wood. Nay, seems to me as things get better every year. 'E's nobbut a bairn, but clever! Eh, I'm real satisfied."

Josh, fingering his moustache, which was streaked with grey, said, "I think that you may congratulate yourself, Muther—and wi' justice."

Jenny glanced round the pleasant, over-furnished room. Everything gleamed. Whatever would take a polish was polished. True the furniture was Victorian and Edwardian at their most hideous. Not that that fact mattered to Jenny; it was a homely, comfortable room, and dad and mum represented comfortable and homely people. People who knew their job, and did it to the very best of their ability. There were many things in the room which Jenny admired wholeheartedly. Her Freddo had been inclined to laugh at them, but she had stood her ground and defended them. There were two paintings. Freddo said they were copies; she didn't know or care. A stag standing at bay, and another stag, who might have been the twin brother of the first one, standing having 'one for the road' in a lake. There were two beautiful horses in bronze rearing their front legs, and two splendid young men hanging on to the reins trying to make them settle down. Josh was very proud of them; he called them 'Marley Horses'. Jenny had no idea who Marley was, or if, indeed, it was not the name of a particular breed or stable, but they were lovely creatures all the same, and every week mum rubbed them gently with a rag very slightly soaked in the best olive oil to make them shine.

There was a photograph of Jenny at the age of twelve, very stiff and self-conscious, another of Alfredo in his lovely leotards, standing in an attitude which seemed to indicate that he defied the whole world. Personal photographs given to mum—Ada Reeve—signed with a nice message—Marie Lloyd, Chergwin, George Formby and others. The room was the result of a lifetime spent on serving those 'servants of the public' in the best possible way. It had atmosphere; there was an air of intimacy and fulfilment about it. Jenny thought, 'It's a kind of sample of the whole house. Comfort, service which is given gladly and willingly. Now I'm going to chuck in my bombshell! Oh, I wish I didn't have to do it."

Her father said, "Jenny dear, you're very quiet to-night. Nothing wrong, I hope and trust?"

Lottie replied briskly—for she, too, had noticed her daughter's silence. "Nay, whatever could be wrong?"

Jenny said, "I don't know as there is anything wrong, Dad. It's only I've got some news for you. I'm going to be married again."

The effect of her announcement was electric; Josh exclaimed, "Well, I'm damned!" while Lottie started to her feet crying, "Our Jenny! Whatever are you telling us? Married! I didn't know that you were even courting."

Jenny laughed, rather shakily. "I scarcely knew myself, Mum."

"Well, let's hear all about it, my luv. The young man 'ud better come and see dad and me. You ought to have brought him home before this, Jenny."

"Somehow it wasn't possible, Mum," and she began to tell them the whole story of her meetings with Holst, his history as he had told it to her. Josh uttered one comment: "Seems a bit strange to me as a man with a title, who's had a college education, written books, should waste his time training lions."

Jenny found herself defending Holst, almost passionately. She extolled his bravery, praised the excellence of his act, his looks; she repeated his assurance that he was prepared to devote his life to her, and finally admitted that her reason for not bringing him to see them had been that Genevra had an unreasonable dislike for him.

"What does he feel about Genevra?" Lottie asked.

"He thinks she's lovely."

"Nay, any fool can see that she's lovely."

"He says that she'll learn to love him when she realizes how fond he is of her and me."

Josh asked, "Then you plan to take Genevra touring round with you?"

"Dad, I couldn't be parted from Genevra, not for the best man living!" Jenny cried passionately. "I'm worried to death that she'll be upset, but I've got my own life to live, haven't I, Mum?"

The next morning she told Genevra when she returned from school. To her surprise the child made no protest; she only stared at her mother, her blue eyes very cold, her lips compressed. Jenny realized that the child's face was utterly devoid of colour.

"You'll like being back with a circus, won't you, luvey?"

"I don't know, Mum."

"But you always used to love it," Jenny protested. "Why shouldn't you love it again?"

"Because it 'ul be all different. Before you lived with me and my dad, now you'll live with—Holst."

"Ducky, you'll not have to go on calling him 'Holst' that way; you'll try to be nice to him, won't you? He wants to be like a father to you. He says you're lovely and wants you to learn to be fond of him. You'll try, won't you?"

Genevra answered in a strange strangled voice, "I won't be rude to him, because that would mean I was rude to you. I don't want him to love me, because I shan't ever love him. I don't want him to be like a father to me, because that's something he can't ever be. I've had one father. I don't want a collection of them! I hope you'll be happy."

With that she turned and walked out of the room. In her bedroom she sat and talked in a low voice to Haig and the Monk. She did not cry, and if anyone could have heard what she said to the two animals they would have heard short, incisive sentences, statements which were completely unchildlike. Years later Genevra always remembered that day as the moment at which she ceased to be a child and suddenly 'grew up'.

Holst returned to Manchester and the wedding took place. Lottie wished to make a real 'do' of it, for she found Holst's careful and rather stilted manners attractive. She admired his looks, his fine figure, and listened entranced to his sentimental outbursts regarding Jenny and his longing to make her happy and to be worthy of her. When he greeted her with his stiff bow from the waist, and raising her hand to his lips brushed it lightly, she felt that he was a completely romantic figure. Josh, on the other hand, disliked him on sight. He was not a man to take violent likes and dislikes, but in Holst's case he took his stand immediately.

"Nobbut a fake, Muther. Paint and canvas made to luke like marble. I'm right grieved to see our Jenny getting married to such a man. I've no luv for Germans any road, and this one seems to me to be a partic'ly nasty specimen. However, Jenny's old enough to make her own choice, but I doubt—doubt sadly—it's not a good 'un."

It was Jenny who opposed her mother's wish for a 'right do', and insisted that the ceremony must be as quiet as possible. She and Holst would go for a five-days' honeymoon, return to collect Genevra and then begin their tour with Hugil's Circus at Dundee. Jenny was strangely quiet during the month before her marriage; she was very gentle with Genevra, but Lottie missed the sudden bursts of gaiety which had been characteristic of Jenny, even after Alfredo's death. She had said to Josh, "Nay, I know that life's a difficult business for that poor lass, but she'll always have the ability to 'bob up'. It may not last for long, she'll slip back into realizing—poor little soul—what she's lost, but there are—well —*minutes* if you know what I mean."

Now there were no 'minutes', no attempts at 'bobbing up'. Jenny seemed older, graver, less able to laugh at the jokes of Mr. Graves or Mr. Rob Wilton, less interested in her weekly visit to the music-hall, and less ready to come home able to recount the whole programme to Lottie with apt comments which had so often made Lottie cry, "Nay, our Jenny, give over! You make my sides ache! My word, you ought to have been a comedienne, not a dancer."

When Lottie told Genevra that she was to have a lovely new dress for her mother's wedding, the child stared at her in silence for a moment, then said, "Gran'ma, I don't want a new dress because I'm not going."

"Not going, luv! How's that? Oh, you ought to go. It 'ul be luvely."

Genevra said, "Not to me it won't be lovely, Gran'ma. I've told my muther that I'm not going. She just looked at me, and after a minute said, 'If you feel like that . . .', so I'm not going, because I *do* feel like that."

So Jenny Menetti was married to Friedrich Holst and only her mother and father were present; Holst explained that he was unable to bring a 'best man' because, having joined Hugil's so recently, he had made no intimate friends. He looked, even Josh had to admit, magnificent in a well-tailored suit, his linen immaculate, and his yellow hair gleaming like gold. The couple only returned to Stratton Street for a quick meal, before leaving to catch the train for Windermere. Genevra came down when Lottie called her, white-faced and quiet. She kissed her mother, and offered her hand to Holst, saying, "I hope that you'll both be very happy." He leaned forward to kiss her, but the child drew back, and Jenny saw that her nostrils were white.

"Please, Mr. Holst," she said, "I don't like being kissed except by my gram'pa and gran'ma and my muther."

He smiled. "But please remember to me how much pleasure it is to kiss pretty little girls who I so much love."

She shook her head and said, "Sorry—you'll have to find them somewhere else."

Five days later they returned to Manchester to collect Genevra. Jenny thought that the child looked strained, and Lottie insisted that she needed 'building up'. Holst, smiling and immaculate, declared that it was only excitement, and that the child was only longing to get back to the life of the circus.

"Am I not right, my dearest Jenny?"

She nodded. "Maybe you are, but I shall give her cod-liver oil and malt just the same."

When Jenny went upstairs to collect a few things which she had left behind, her mother followed her. Lottie sat down on the edge of the bed; she felt conscious suddenly of her age, wished that Jenny were not going away and leaving her to carry on the house. Vaguely she wondered if Josh were right when he said that Holst seemed to be a particularly nasty specimen. Josh was so often right in his judgments regarding people.

She said, "Jenny, luv . . ."

Without turning, and continuing to fold skirts and blouses, Jenny said:

"Yes, Mum?"

"You're happy, darling, aren't you?"

"Of course I am, Mum; why shouldn't I be?"

"I don't know, only if ever you felt you—well, weren't as happy as what you liked, remember dad and me's always here, and that this is your home, same as it's Genevra's. You'll mind that, won't you?"

"I'll think on, Mum." Jenny closed the suit-case and, turning, stood with her hands on the rail at the foot of the bed. She looked at her mother gravely and intently. "Of course every-thing's all right. It's—well, it's a bit *different*, but then my Freddo wasn't like anyone else. But Friedrich—funny their names should

68

be so alike, isn't it?—is terribly fond of me. There's nothing he'd not do for me." Suddenly she shrugged her shoulders, and added, "Of course everything's going to be all right! So'm I; so's Genevra once she gets used to the idea. You and dad don't have to worry, darling."

On the long journey to Dundee Genevra felt that she was travelling with people who were acting all the time. When Holst looked at Haig, and said, "How nice it is to have the little dog with us, eh?" she felt that he was making fun of Haig. When he asked if the Monk was good-tempered and clean, adding, "But how other is it for him possible to be with such a kind and clever mistress?" she felt a kind of chill down her spine. She kept looking at her mother, thinking how pretty she was, and wondering with a sense of panic if now she was married to Holst she would change towards Genevra. How terrible if mum should be different! How awful if she were to be 'shut out'! Dad and mum had always discussed everything in her presence, and even when she had barely understood what they were talking about, it had made her feel proud when dad said, "Ees zis not corr-ect, my Genevra?" or mum had said, "I'll bet that's what you think, too, isn't it, Genevra?" This circus which they were joining, would it be like Trumelli's? Would there be kindly people like Zippo and Zoppo and Mrs. Zoppo? Would there be animal acts? Those acts which she and dad and mum had always hated? Holst tamed lions—Genevra shivered—she knew how he trained them, too! She remembered that Triplet had said to her once, "Mind you, they calls it 'taming', but them trainers is just laying up trouble for theirselves. One day the lions gets sick and tired of it—then *woosh!* That's the finish of Mr. B——y Trainer!"

She knew that she wished that '*woosh*' might be coming to Holst, and coming soon! Curled up in her corner of the carriage, she dozed, the Monk in her arms and Haig crowding as close to her as he could get. The proximity of the two animals reassured her. *Everything wasn't* changed, there were still mum and Haig and the Monk; they all loved her, and even if Holst had been added to their number the odds remained four to one. At last she fell asleep, and did not wake until she heard Jenny's voice, felt the touch of Jenny's hand.

"Genevra, darling, we're there. Wake up, luvey."

She opened her eyes and looked into Jenny's lovely face. She was smiling, and Genevra's first waking thought was, 'It's all right, really she loves me better'n what she does him'.

Holst and Jenny had a very fine caravan, newly painted and

beautifully fitted. Holst said that it was his wedding present to 'my so beloved wife'. To Genevra's mind it seemed 'a poor kind of present, because it's his home same as it's hers. Like saying you give your wife a present when you pay the rent!' Genevra was to sleep in a caravan with Miss Lucy Hambro, who was a bareback rider of some distinction and was billed as 'La Belle Lucille', though she had no particular claim to the adjective, being a heavily built woman, with a rather flat white face. She possessed tremendous courage, and considerable skill. Her thighs and calves were immense and muscular. Standing on the back of a horse she looked impressive, and she was capable of doing extraordinary feats. Lucy Hambro was a Scotswoman, and when Hugil's toured Scotland the caption 'Yin o' ye'r ain' was inserted under her usual billing.

Her pleasant voice with its homely accent pleased Genevra immensely, and her kindness to the child was outstanding.

She said, "Now, ma dearie, you an' me's going tae get along fine! I've haired all about the animals. I'll not mind them a wee bittie. I've a great love for the wee beasts. Some time I'll tell ye stories o' my Scottie—my! Yon was a dog! His name was—what d'you think?—'Whisky'. That's a right name for a Scottish dog, eh?"

Genevra said, "Where is he now?"

"Nay, dearie, it was awfu' sad. Puir wee thing, it was last winter and he took pneumonia an' died. I nearly broke ma hairt! Eh, he was a real pal was my Whisky."

Yes, Genevra decided she liked Miss Hambro, who was as neat as a new pin about everything, and who kept her caravan shining and spotless. When she was not practising, she was always polishing, or scrubbing, or mending, pressing and washing her circus clothes. Genevra had breakfast with her, helped to wash up and tidy the caravan, and then—knowing that Holst would be working with the 'cats'—she tore over to Jenny's caravan.

Those were the best hours of the day, when Holst was out and she could rely upon having her mother to herself. Sometimes they would go out shopping, and Genevra thought that her mother became like she had been before dad died. She laughed at silly things; she said suddenly, "Let's go and have some chocolate and cakes and spoil our appetites for dinner, shall we?" They often walked round Woolworth's Stores, and spent a long time in the choosing of a new aluminium saucepan, or a few new glasses. Sometimes Jenny said, "Have you any money, luvey?"

70

"I've got four pence, Mum."

"Then you go and buy me a present, and I'll buy you one, eh?"

It was wonderful the things you could buy for three pence, and even more wonderful to see mum's delight at whatever Genevra chose for her. Those times when they went shopping together or sat in the caravan talking were the most precious moments of Genevra's life. Her intense dislike of Holst increased. She hated his arrogance, his criticism of mum's cooking—and dad had always declared that she was the best cook in the world! He was never actually rude in so many words, but the child came to look for the curve which his lips took when he sneered at anything; she knew that mum noticed it, too, and hated him for it.

His endearing phrases were nullified by what followed. "My beloved wife," he said once, when Jenny had prepared a particularly well-flavoured stew, "have you forgotten that I am not an Italian? This dish of garlic reeks!" or "My darling Jenny, while I applaud your child's love of animals, is it not possible for them to be fed when I my own dinner am not taking?"

Jenny never argued with him, and it was not until they had been married for three months that Genevra witnessed their first evident quarrel. Holst came in smiling, and taking off his coat sat down at the table. He looked good-tempered, and Genevra felt a sense of relief.

He said, "Well, Genevra, tell me how old are you?"

"Rising fourteen."

"I believe that you would like to work, to earn some money towards paying for your food and keeping, no?"

Jenny said, "Now don't be silly, Friedrich, what does the child want to work for? We don't need money for her keep! The idea!"

He turned slowly and stared at her with his cold blue eyes, which Genevra always thought were like pieces of hard stone, and asked:

"Who is the master here and the head of the family? Who earns the money, tell me that?"

Jenny flushed. "I've money of my own," she retorted. "I pay for my own child, thank you—and you know it! I'm not having her work. What work is there for her in this set-up?"

"I shall inform you," Holst answered, his voice cold and completely even. "Halfitz wishes an assistant in his act, to hand him his props, and set out his table. He will employ Genevra. That is the work she will do, my dearest Jenny."

"Halfitz," Jenny repeated. "Halfitz! That foul-mouthed old so-and-so! When he muffs a trick—and that's pretty often, for the old devil drinks far more than's good for him—it's a wonder the people on the ring-seats don't ask for their money back. I'm certain they hear his dirty talk! My child assistant to Halfitz, indeed!"

Very smoothly, his good-looking face completely unmoved, Holst asked, "Yet, my dear wife, I remember the time when you didn't mind being assistant to an Italian acrobat, or am I wrongly informed?"

Genevra saw her mother's face flush; she stepped nearer to Holst, and for a moment the child thought that she was going to strike him. Jenny's hands were clenched, and her voice sounded strangled and hoarse when she spoke.

"Damn you, how dare you mention my Alfredo and Halfitz in the same breath! My husband was an artiste, one of the finest acrobats of his day, as you very well know. Never you say a thing like that again, or you'll be rid of me and Genevra, for I'll go back to my mother. Listen to this, too—I'm carrying, and there'll be plenty for Genevra to do in a month or two! Let's have no more talk of this, I won't stand it!"

The change in Holst was astonishing; he rose and took Jenny in his arms. Genevra saw that his eyes were filled with sudden tears. He kissed her mother's cheeks, saying, "Ah, my wonderful wife. How happy you have made me! This what every man longs to hear is! I am the happiest of alles men. Little Genevra, come and kiss your clever, wonderful mother. How will you like a little sister or brother to have for a playmate?"

Jenny said, "That's all right, Friedrich, get on with your dinner while it's hot. C'm on, Genevra, ducky, and get your dinner. You'll not have this brother or sister for a long time yet. Are you pleased about it?"

Genevra nodded. "I am if you are, Mum, and please, I'll not work for Halfitz. I'd rather go home to gran'ma."

Jenny ruffled her hair, and laughed. " 'Course I'm pleased, and 'course you're not going to work for that old toad. Now eat your dinner."

Holst paused in cutting up his steak and looked at her, frowning.

"In this moment of my complete joy," he said, "you attempt your child to influence against me. Not very wise, eh, my dear wife."

"Get on! Influence no one! The way you talk!"

CHAPTER SIX

GENEVRA divided her life into definitely 'good times' and 'bad times'. The good times were when she woke early in the Spring, Summer, or early Autumn and left her bunk, moving very carefully so as not to disturb Miss Hambro. With the Monk carefully wrapped in his blanket, for he hated the cold, and with Haig following closely on her heels, she would open the door, and, descending the steps of the caravan, close it behind her. There, with the terrier crowding as closely to her as was humanly possible, and the Monk cuddled in her arms, she would sit on the steps and watch the countryside through which they passed.

She came to know the English country very well: the hills of Derbyshire, the glimpse of the lakes in Westmorland, the lovely dales of Yorkshire with their chattering little rivers. She saw the smoke hanging like a dark cloud over the Black Country towns, saw the long expanse of dull yellow sands at Redcar, and the old church and abbey perched on the cliffs at Whitby. Most of all she loved the journeys which took them over the moors, where the great rolling hills were dressed in their deep purple with splashes of golden gorse here and there. Even the sheep amazed and delighted her; she never forgot the first time she saw one—literally—run up a rough stone wall and disappear among the heather. She told Miss Hambro of the incident and that lady laughed.

"Dearie, you'll not find sheep like these we have i' the Nor-rth way down in Sussex! Ours are grand wiry little beasties, they can fend for themselves. My, they'd kill themselves i' a week if they were put on yon Downs. They *luke* for their food, *sairch* for it! Yon i' the South just eat steadily awe day long."

Those were the 'good times' when she watched the light growing stronger, the mists hovering over the fields to disappear as the warmth increased. She liked to pass through villages which were just waking from sleep, and often thought how pleasant it would be if she and mum could have a little cottage with a thatched roof and a little garden full of flowers. She often thought of that little cottage, and before she went to sleep at night dreamed waking dreams about it. Even on mornings when it rained she would wake and stand staring out of the caravan window, watching the whole countryside swept by sheets of rain, finding something very satisfactory in the steady downpour.

Breakfasts with Miss Hambro were 'good times', too. The smell of frying bacon, or well-buttered toast, the fragrance of the hot coffee—for La Belle Lucille had travelled the Continent, and learnt to love her morning coffee.

"Mind you," she said, "when it comes to a nice cup o' tea after my dinner or at four o'clock—there's no one readier nor me. Breakfast's different, then gie me coffee every time. Always providing that a pairson kens how it should be made."

She gave Genevra bacon with a slice of fried bread, and talked to her over the breakfast table, telling her stories of the circus. She had completely won Genevra's heart by saying, "In my many years o' circus experience I have never seen a handsomer man or a finer artiste than Alfredo Menetti. The things that man could do! I doot if a man was ever better loved or more admired. Aye, bairnie, you've something to be real proud of!"

Breakfast over, Genevra helped to clear away, to wash up and tidy the caravan, making—with Lucy Hambro's help and direction—'everything bright and ship-shape'. Then followed the announcement, "I must be away tae my work, lambie. Take care o' yourself. My kind regairds tae your mither."

Genevra would go back to the window and watch until she saw Holst's tall figure making its way to the cats' cages, then, catching up the Monk and calling to Haig, she would dash to her mother's caravan. It was exciting to watch the villages, the hills, moors, rivers, even the towns in the early morning; it was exciting when Miss Hambro said, "Noo, we've a change this morning. I got a nice finnan haddie for our breakfast. Say what you like, there's a rare flavour tae a haddie!" But there was no excitement to equal that of the moment when she opened the door and cried, "Mum! I'm here! Did you sleep well, Mum?"

Jenny always put down whatever she was doing, held out her arms and cried, "Here's my brightest and best! Let's have a nice cup of tea, eh?

Genevra felt, or sensed—for she had never attempted to put the feeling into words—that whatever estrangement had existed between them was over—completely over. They were closer than they had ever been; together they talked and chattered, laughed and made foolish jokes. At times Genevra wondered vaguely if her mother had 'come back to her' because she had 'moved away' from Holst. His name was never mentioned, and Genevra refused, in spite of Miss Hambro's pleadings, to enter the 'big top' and to watch the performances.

"I'd like fine for you tae see my act, Genevra," she said, adding a little wistfully, "Mind you, I know that Hugil's is no Trumelli's, it would be silly tae pretend it's—international. Only when you're not quite so young, nor maybe quite so good, as you once were—well, beggars can't be choosers."

Genevra always shook her head. "I'd love to see you, Miss Hambro, but I couldn't stand watching a show. Please understand. I know that you're the tops, because Charlie Bramer told me. He said, 'She's the best act in this show, damned if she ain't!' I bet you are, too!"

"Don't use that nasty talk, bairnie. If Charlie Bramer does, that's no call tae say you've got to. Mind on now, it's not pretty."

Genevra and Jenny rarely mentioned the coming child. Genevra flushed if ever the subject arose, and Jenny was self-conscious about it.

Once she said, "You'll be nice to the baby when it comes, won't you, ducky?"

"Of course, Mum; it 'ul be your baby, so I shall love it."

"Maybe you and me and the baby might go back to Manchester for a bit, eh?"

"That 'ud be luvely, Mum. I was thinking—wishing—you and me had a little cottage in a village. You know, with a garden, and a thatched roof, and maybe some hens at the back."

Jenny smiled. "Aye, luv, if wishes were horses beggars might ride."

The brightness was dimmed a little, their laughter became less frequent as Jenny prepared the dinner, and Genevra remembered that when the little 'wag o' the wa' clock struck twelve Holst would walk in. At half past eleven she took Haig and the Monk back to Lucy Hambro, and gave them their dinners. They always watched Genevra go with large wondering eyes, but they had come to like the bareback rider, and she assured Genevra that they 'settled down like twa wee lambs'. Dinner was always, to Genevra, a difficult meal. Holst returned tired and generally short-tempered. He ate enormously, but rarely allowed a meal to pass without some caustic criticism on the cooking or the selection of dishes. Genevra thought that the disagreements between Holst and her mother occurred more and more frequently. They were always about small things, but they seemed to grow and swell and assume enormous proportions. Holst liked to drink large quantities of beer at his meals, and one day it was found that only two bottles remained.

"*Lieber Gott!*" he exclaimed, "have you so much to do that

75

you cannot remember the beer to order? Here I am, the bread-winner, my lungs, my mouth, my nostrils filled with the stench of the cats, and I am told only two bottles of beer remain! It is intolerable!"

Jenny replied sharply, "I've said I'm sorry, what else do you want me to say? To burst into tears or what? Surely a couple o' pints are sufficient for a chap's dinner! I'd have thought so, any road."

He disregarded her outburst, and turning to Genevra said, "Take that jug, go down to the Rose and Crown and bring back a quart of beer. Be quick about it! Your mother will give you the money."

Genevra looked anxiously towards her mother; the change on Jenny's face almost frightened her; the lips were compressed into a hard, thin line; her breath came quickly; her eyes, blazing with anger, stared at Holst.

"You stay where you are, Genevra," she ordered without looking at the child, "you're going for no beer—anyway, they wouldn't serve you! Think on, Friedrich, my child's not running for beer for anyone. I don't give a damn who they are, or who they 'think they are'. If you want more beer—an' let me tell you you're drinking far too much in these days; one night you'll have too much, and one of your cats will know it, too, and that 'ul be the finish of Baron Count Grand-Duke von Holst!"

Genevra listened, scarcely understanding what her mother said. Holst, too, stared at his wife, his lips rolled back; he looked, Genevra thought, like one of his own snarling cats. He got up from his chair—he seemed to rise very slowly—until he stood towering above Jenny. Then lifting his beer-mug he flung the contents in her face.

"Take it all!" he shouted. "And also your food, which is fit only for swine! I elsewhere eat!"

He picked up his coat and walked out of the caravan. Genevra stood as if unable to move; when the door slammed Jenny lifted her apron and wiped her face, saying, "Well, what do you know about that? Come on, luv, help clear up this mess while I change my apron! My words, things have come to summat. Nay, don't look so flayed, duckie, he'll have forgot all about it in an hour. What he needs is to go down to the local, have half a dozen yobs tell him how clever he is, and he'll be as pleased as Punch. One thing I will lay—that he never asks you to go and fetch his beer for him again."

Her face had been quite calm, her voice even, but suddenly

she sat down and, covering her face with her hands, began to cry wildly. Genevra rushed to her, flinging her arms round Jenny's shaking shoulders.

"Mum, Mum, don't cry. You'll only please him if he thinks he can upset you. Who cares what he says or does? He's beastly, anyhow. My dad would have given him something to go on with! There, Mum, don't cry."

Jenny dried her eyes on her apron, then with a movement of irritation untied it and flung it into a corner, saying, "The damned thing reeks of beer! It's wet, anyway. Oh, Genevra, my luvey, what a mistake it's all been!" Then her usual spirit asserted itself, and she laughed. "What a carry on about a drop of beer, eh? Come on, my ducks, we'll have a cup of tea, there's nothing like a good strong cup when you're a bit het up."

It seemed that she had forgotten the incident, but Genevra could not put it out of her mind. She had watched Holst's face when he was talking to her mother, had seen the bestiality of his expression, and the thought came to her again and again, 'What if he ever hit her?'

On this occasion Jenny had been right, he came back for his tea of kippers, buttered toast, tea-cakes and bread and potted meat, his temper restored, anxious to recount the menu of the excellent meal which he had eaten at the Crown. Apparently, too, in the saloon-bar—he never entered anything but the saloon-bar, declaring that he refused to mix with yokels—several men had complimented him upon the act; he quoted their remarks at length and with zest.

"It is evident," he said, leaning back in his chair and picking his splendid teeth, "that my work the most admired of any is! These were not working men, believe me, but persons of distinction and education. What a pleasure it is for me to have pleasant conversation with men of my own standing and breeding! Hugil's must be careful, or they will lose their best act. I am a little tired of this circus, and my mind turns to greater things. Well, well, we shall see."

Genevra sat and watched him; her face was grave, and only when her mother spoke to her directly did she speak at all.

Holst looked at her, and said, "How this little one chatters! I feel that she must be very clever! Perhaps great thoughts pass through her brain, eh?"

Jenny said sharply, "Don't start picking on Genevra, I'll not have it!" Holst, well fed, and completely self-satisfied after his encounter in the Crown, for he throve on flattery and approbation, stretched out his long, elegant legs, and said, "Darling Jenny, why are you so—so prickly, tell me? I am only trying your child to praise, to encourage."

"It didn't sound like encouragement to me. Genevra, finish your tea, luv."

Things were growing strained between them, Genevra realized; more than that, gossip travelled like lightning in a circus, and it was whispered that Holst was paying too much attention to Hugil's eldest daughter. She was a brassy blonde, who sat in the cash desk at every performance, and smiled too seldom at women patrons, and too often at the males. Genevra, who still found the horses absorbing, heard hints, saw salacious grins and listened to suggestions from the grooms there. They liked her, they liked Jenny, whom they respected, even if she did 'keep 'erself tew 'erself'. She was always civil and pleasant, always had a 'Good morning' or 'Nice morning' for any of them as she passed. Holst they all detested, and their comments on him were salty in the extreme. Genevra's chief friend, Charlie, would stare after Holst's tall figure and mutter, "B——y swanker, thet's wot 'e is! 'Im an' 'is perishin' stinkin' cats. Not satisfied wi' them wot 'e 'as in cages neether, damn 'im. You keep clear of 'im, Genevra, my queen."

She sighed, "I do try to, but I must go and see my mum, mustn't I?"

"Certainly! Nothink wrong wi' your mum, barrin' her blarsted 'usband. Pity as she ain't got 'er 'ealth an' strent at the moment, as you might sai. No, we're sorry fer yer mum, kid; if she weren't like the way she is, we'd like ter see someone else a lot sorrier fer theirselves nor what we are fer your mum. Yeller-'aired cow!"

Genevra looked up sharply. "My mum hasn't got yellow hair!"

"Oberviously not," Charles replied, "but someone else 'as, an' would I be likerly ter refer ter yer mum as a cow? Come now, kid! Sneeze, yer brains is dusty!" Then to the mare he was grooming, "Oh, stand over, will yer? Thet's better. Ferget wot I said, kid. When I get me rag out my tongue runs awai with me, that's Gawd's solemn truth."

Holst had bought a motor-cycle and used to ride on ahead of the caravans when they moved from one place to another. Hugil's daughter drove a small Austin, painted yellow and upholstered in red rexine. They both left before the caravans got under way and were never seen again until the circus arrived. Then they made a great show of efficiency, directing everyone, talking in loud, self-assertive voices of what they had done, what they had achieved. Other performers glanced at one another meaningly, and Genevra, while scarcely understanding it all, thought, 'If there's something fishy, I only hope mum won't find out'.

Yet in her heart she was divided. If mum found out that Holst was 'carrying on'—and Genevra had only a vague idea what 'carrying on' meant—she might leave him. They might pack up and return to gran'ma and gram'pa in Manchester and be happy together again. On the other hand, if she went on without understanding that 'something was up', she was living in a life which contained no reality.

Genevra had picked up her knowledge of life in a haphazard fashion; the girls at school had whispered things, but she had said, "It's all lies. Not my dad or my mum never did that," because it all sounded so horrid and generally beastly. On the other hand she knew that women had babies, that they carried them—Jenny had said 'Tucked up all cosy, luv, near your heart, so's they won't feel cold or miserable'—for nine months. She knew that this had happened to mum, and felt that possibly that was why she loved her mother so much. She had heard foul language from the grooms, but it had left her completely untouched and incurious. True, when she used words which Miss Hambro disapproved of, and said, in her pretty clipped Scottish accent, "Genevra, my dearie, yon's a *nesty* word. I'd not use it if I were you," she tried to cease to use the objectionable expression; not because she herself knew why it was unacceptable, but because she trusted Miss Hambro.

They were moving southwards towards London. Not to play in a great place in London with all the nobility and aristocracy flocking to watch, but to a much smaller and less distinguished stand. Jenny, who was expecting her baby in a month or six weeks at most, travelled with Genevra by train, whilst Holst, clad in shining leather from head to foot, departed early on his bicycle. Miss Miranda Hugil also departed in her glaring motor-car.

The journey was long and tedious, Jenny sat silent most of the time, while Genevra held the Monk, and Haig watched them both with sentimental brown eyes.

Once or twice Genevra said, "You feeling all right, Mum?"

"I'm all right, luv. Bit tired, p'raps a bit worried, but I'm all right."

"I've some hot tea in the thermos, would you like some?"

"It might be nice."

She drank the tea, but she did not talk, and sat silent, her chin on her hand, staring out of the window.

Genevra watched her anxiously. "You'll feel all right, Mum, when you're all cosy and tucked up in bed in the caravan. We'll soon be there."

Jenny nodded. "Aye, we'll soon be there, luv. You're a kind little girl, Genevra."

"Nay, I just love you."

"Well, no one can say more'n that, my duckie."

The Monk was not well: he coughed a great deal, holding his chest with his two little hands as if it hurt him. Jenny suggested glycerine; he had taken it obediently. Certainly it stopped his coughing a little, but it did not actually cure it. He shivered often despite the thick shawl in which Genevra wrapped him, and yet his skin felt hot and dry. He cried if Genevra left him, and clung to her the moment she returned, his little hot hands clutching her as if she were his one hope. She adored the Monk; often, except for mum, he seemed her last link with her father. She had spoken to Charlie about him. Charlie had scratched his head and said, "Difficult, Genevra, ter keep 'em well. The climit's against 'em. Tew cold an' damp. You see, queen, they don't rightly belong 'ere. I of'en wonder if it's right ter cart 'em from their own 'omes. Not that you're not damned good ter the Monk —yer are. But there it is. Give 'im plenty ter eat, fats—thet's what 'e wants—fats. Cod-liver oil's a nice thing. Try thet."

Genevra had given him cod-liver oil; he had taken it obediently, and he certainly gained a little flesh, but the good effects seemed to wear off, and now on the dreary journey to London he cuddled against her, shivering and coughing.

They got to King's Cross, and Genevra insisted on taking a taxi to the circus-ground. The driver said, "It's a long way, miss! I'll 'ave ter 'ave part, at least, of me fare beck."

Genevra said, "Don't worry, you'll get it. Only get a move on."

He winked and replied, "All rite, young 'un. In you get."

They drove, it seemed to Genevra, through miles and miles of dreary streets, where people plodded along; she thought, 'None of them's laughing! An' what would they have to laugh at in a grey town like this? It's horrible.'

Jenny sat, still with her chin on her hand, and only spoke once to say, "Friedrich won't expect us. He'd never think we'd take a taxi."

"How else would we go, Mum?"

"By things called tubes and Underground. I didn't feel like it."

"Tubes—Underground! Oh, Mum, they sound horrible."

Jenny smiled suddenly and said, "So they are, my luv."

The taxi stopped, and Genevra, looking out, saw Charlie standing at the entrance to the circus-ground. He came forward and said, " 'Ello, Mrs. Holst, nice ter see you. Would you kere ter come and 'ave a nice cupper in our place? Y'know, it's 'umble but it's 'ome. We'd be proud."

Jenny took his proffered hand and got out of the taxi, giving her purse to Genevra and saying, "Pay him, luv. Give him a decent tip, he's been very nice."

Charlie took the purse saying, " 'Ere, give it me," paid the taxi and turned back to Jenny, offering his arm in a stilted and slightly ostentatious manner.

She asked, "Has my husband got here?"

Genevra saw Charlie's face, it was so guileless as to be guilty. She didn't know why she thought so, but the idea came to her. He said, "Now, I don't just know exackerly, but I 'ave a idea —no. I never seen 'im. Come'n and 'ave that cupper, an' I'll send over my stable-lad ter find out if he's in your caravan. You ken do with a cupper, I know. If yer can't, then you're the first lidy I've known as couldn't. Jest along 'ere, missus."

Suddenly Jenny twisted her hand from the arm which he offered, saying, "Nice of you, Charlie, but thanks just the same—no." Then turned and began to walk very quickly, not towards her own caravan but towards that which Miranda Hugil occupied.

Charlie cried, "Christ, don't let 'er go there or the fat will be in the flamin' fire! Genevra, stop 'er, d'yer 'ear, stop 'er! Fer Gawd's sake!"

Genevra ran, still clasping the Monk, and with Haig—thinking that it was his first run of the day, galloping at her heels. They reached the Hugil caravan, all painted in red and gold, and Genevra saw her mother rush up the steps and begin to batter on the door. Something drained the power from the child's limbs; she stood her mouth a little open, her face white as chalk. She had no idea what mum knew, all that she understood was that there was—something wrong. Charlie rushed forward, crying, "Now, missus, yon's not yer caravan. C'm on and 'ave that cupper char. Leave it be, missus; fer Gawd's sike leave it be."

Jenny disregarded his importunities and continued to batter on the door. Quite suddenly it opened and Holst's tall figure stood in the opening. There was light in the caravan and Genevra could see it streaming out, like a golden river. His figure looked dark against it, and Jenny looked very small and defenceless.

She heard his voice shouting, "Here, what do you do—tell me? Go back at once to your caravan. I am busy, occupied with business."

A woman's voice, shrill and metallic, cried, "Send 'er 'ome! Make 'er go 'ome. Are you a man or just a monkey?"

Charlie yelled, "Mrs. Holst, come 'ome and 'ave thet cupper."

For the first time Genevra heard her mother's voice. She was conscious that from other caravans heads were craning; she knew that there was something here which was of interest to everyone in the circus. Dimly she could see the figures of the grooms, the stable-boys; everybody was watching, listening.

Jenny cried, "Come out of that! Come home and behave yourself. I won't stand it. Come home and take it out of me, if you like—it won't be the first time—but you're not going to make me the laughing-stock of that moll you're chasing—and who you've caught, too!"

Genevra held her breath, saw Holst lean out and push her mother in the chest. Jenny was standing on the steps of the Hugil caravan, and Holst was a very strong man. She staggered, lost her balance and fell, rolling over twice as if she had lost all power to control her muscles. Holst stood watching for a moment, then stepped back into the caravan and closed the door.

Genevra rushed forward, crying, "Mum, oh my darling Mum!" but Jenny lay still, only groaning a little.

Charlie bent over her; his blasphemies were terrible, then he shouted, " 'Ere, bring La Belle Lucille! Some o' you lousers get cracking, do su'thing, fer Gawd's sake. 'Ere, 'elp, 'elp!"

The Monk shivered; mum lay groaning on the ground; she had cut her lip a little and a thin thread of blood ran down her chin, looking startling on her white face. Charlie was holding her hand and murmuring, "Yer're orl rite, missus. Buck up, yer scarin' the little 'un. C'm on, yer're orl rite." Jenny did not move, her eyes were closed, the only sound she made was that little, apologetic groan. Rushing towards them came Lucy Hambro; she flung herself down beside Jenny, making little noises of concern and indignation.

"Tut, tut! A nice thing! Ma certes! Puir darrling. Oh dear, oh dear!" Then, galvanized into practicality, "One of you run for a doctor. Quick. Take that blackguard's motor-bike. It's a matter o' minutes. Some of you, lift her, gently. That's the style—easy now. Her own caravan's the place. That's it. Come, Genevra, my bairnie. She'll be awe right. Oh, you'll see, you'll see."

Jenny was laid on her own bunk in the exquisitely clean

82

caravan of which she was so proud. Genevra sat on a hard chair and watched. The whole thing was a nightmare, and she remembered what had been her constant fear—'if ever he should hit her!' He had hit her, or at least pushed her, which amounted to the same thing. Miss Hambro and Mrs. Willis—wife of one of the clowns—were undressing mummy; they kept ejaculating softly, "Poor soul!" and "What a brute!" Mummy never moved nor spoke. Genevra thought, 'If only she'd speak to me, if only she'd say, "Hello, luv", I'd feel all right.'

All the time the Monk shivered and Haig whimpered softly.

She heard a car drive up; the door opened and Charlie's voice said, "It's the doctor." A tall man with a broad ugly face came in. He looked at Genevra and said, "Better send the child out of here. Get some hot water as quickly as you like. I've heard what happened—disgraceful. Look, little girl, if this is your mother— eh, oh, she is, well, better run away for a little. Can't you go somewhere and make her a cup of tea for her to drink when she's a little better? That's a girl!"

She rushed over to Miss Hambro's caravan, put on the kettle, set out two cups and saucers, for mum always liked her to have a cup, too, and then went out to sit on the steps of the caravan. She had sat there so often watching the lovely English countryside; now her eyes were fixed on the light which shone from the window of Holst's caravan. That caravan which he had 'given to my darling wife as a wedding present'. A sudden rush of light came from the caravan of Miranda Hugil, and Genevra saw Holst's tall figure descend the steps. In the shadow she could discern dim figures; she recognized them—Charlie, Atkins and Messer. Holst was making his way to his own caravan, when Atkins, moving forward, lurched against him. Genevra could hear Holst's voice raised in sudden anger.

"Where do you think you go! Never attempt me to jostle!"

And Atkins' reply: "W'at's wrrong, mister? If Ah slip it's not my fault."

"Not again let it occur!" Holst strode forward.

Messer, a wiry little Jew from the East End, bumped into Holst on the other side; he lisped, "Vot is wrrong mit me! Am I shicker? I am so sorry, Herr Holst. My 'eart is brroken!" but he sniggered, and Holst turned on him furiously.

"You swine. You damned Jew! You gutter-snipe, spawn of the Ghetto! Get out of my way, or I'll give you that thrashing which so well you deserve. I can see you both. . . . Atkins and Messer, sons of bitches both."

That was when Atkins hit him, crying, "Listen, Mister Holset, I'm a Methodist, my family are awl Methodists. Keep your mouth clean or I'll knaw how ter clean it!"

It was queer to be watching, listening to their brawl while mum was lying unconscious, and that strange doctor with the broad, ugly face and the kind voice was taking care of her. Their figures moved, dim in the half-light. Genevra could hear the muffled sound of blows, curses, grunts of pain; once she heard Charlie's voice crying, "Noa, don't kick 'im, it's tew dangerous. 'It 'im, thet's it—'*it* 'im."

She saw Holst disengage himself from his attackers, rise to his feet and set off at a run for his own caravan; saw Charlie spring forward and very neatly trip him, saying, "Didn't know as I was on the reserve fer Woolwich Arsenal, did yer, yer b——?"

Holst staggered to his feet. Charlie said, "Yer not goin' in there, not if we 'ave ter 'old yer." Holst stared at them, his face bloodstained and furious, then turned and ran back to the caravan of Miranda Hugil.

Messer shouted after him, "Rright, rrun beck to your fency lady! Mind, you 'ev blood on your hends! Gonof! To steal a voman's life!" and he spat rudely and noisily.

The door of the caravan shut, Holst was safe.

The three men walked towards Miss Hambro's caravan, their hands in their pockets. Genevra could hear them laughing softly.

Atkins said, "That was a right pasting if ever I saw one."

Messer said, "I hev neffer enjoyed myself mor'n what I did. My t'anks, Charlie, for making it possible."

Charlie merely nodded, and catching sight of Genevra said, "Hello, kid, 'ow's yer mum? Better, I 'ope."

"I don't know, Charlie. They told me to go out and make a cup o' tea. Mum loves a cup o' tea."

"Made it?"

"It's just ready, Charlie."

"Good kid. I'll go an' 'ave a decko or In'jun peep."

She watched him walk away, on tiptoe as if he might disturb mum. To Genevra it was like living in a nightmare. Everything was unreal. The impossible scene outside Hugil's caravan mum rolling on the ground, the caravan with its bright curtains and shining cleanliness in which mum and she had taken such a pride. How often had mum said, "Elbow grease, luv, that's the finest polish in the world. Lick into it, and sing something lively while you work. Not 'Home, Sweet Home', that makes you work slower, but something like 'Pack up your troubles' or 'All the nice girls love a sailor'." It was all photographed on her mind. The two women undressing mum—mum, who hated anyone to do anything for her—talking in low, quiet voices, while she sat on that hard chair cuddling the Monk to her—as she was cuddling him now. The doctor, telling her to go and make tea. The three men waiting for Holst, their fight and Holst's rush back to safety. Now Charlie was coming back, he looked queer, she thought, almost frightened.

He said, "Now, kid, come and speak ter yer mother. She wants you."

"Is she all right, Charlie?"

"You come along an' don't stand arguing, queen."

She took his hand and walked back over the uneven ground, still clutching the Monk to her breast. Charlie opened the door very quietly. Mrs. Willis was standing at the back of the caravan, wiping her eyes on her apron. Miss Hambro turned as Genevra entered, saying, "There's a grand bairn. Come and hae a word wi' her mither, but speak softly." The doctor leaned against the other bunk, saying nothing, only watching mum.

Jenny lay in her bunk, lying very flat, Genevra thought, with only a very small pillow under her head. She looked white and terribly tired. Genevra said, "Hello, Mum, it's me. How are you?"

It was a strange dead voice which answered her, a voice lacking all the colour and energy which belonged rightly to mum's voice.

"Hello, luv. I'm all right. Give me a kiss."

Genevra bent down and kissed her; strange to kiss mum when she didn't put her arms round you, and hug you close. She always smelt so nice, too, it was lovely to nestle your face in her breast and sniff long and luxuriously. Her face felt cold, and somehow a little stiff.

Genevra said, "Mum, you're cold. Let me get another blanket or a hot-water bottle, shall I?"

Jenny whispered, "No, ducks, I'm all right."

The doctor moved forward, and took her hand. Genevra knew that he was feeling for her pulse, like they did when you had what gran'ma called 'a nasty feverish cold'. He leaned down and said, very quietly, "Shall I send for your husband, Mrs. Holst?"

Jenny's blue eyes flickered, her mouth lifted at the corners a little. "Not on your life," she said, then raising her hand she pushed him away, though not roughly, saying, "Genevra, be a good girl . . . don't stay with—him. Goo' night, luv," and closed her eyes.

Mrs. Atkins put her arms round Genevra saying, "Come along with me, dear, the doctor wants to look after mummy. There's not enough room for us all," and they were outside the caravan, in the cold night air, with the Monk still holding his chest and shivering.

Later Miss Hambro came to talk to Genevra; she had red eyes and kept sniffing. Genevra knew what she had come to say, and said it first.

"My mum's dead, isn't she?"

Lucy Hambro sniffed louder than ever. "God has taken her tae Himself."

Genevra said, "I wonder why? I suppose He knew how she hated Holst. Damn his eyes! I shan't see mum again, eh?"

"You can come and look at her presently, my dearie."

Genevra shook her head, "No, that wouldn't be mum. She won't laugh, or drink cups of tea, or come to Woolworth's and buy silly presents. No, I'd rather not, thank you, Miss Hambro. Anyway, he might be there, and I'd kill him, like what Atkins and Messer and Charlie wanted to do. No, I'll stop here with Haig and the Monk."

She felt quite calm. Something had told her when she kissed mum's cold cheek what was going to happen. She thought that perhaps she had known when mum slipped off the steps of Miranda Hugil's caravan, and rolled over, then lay there groaning. It was the end of everything. Somewhere were gran'ma and gram'pa, but that was Manchester, and that was miles and miles away. She wasn't even very sure what gran'ma's name was, or what gram'pa was called except Josh. The house was called 'Mrs. Hostley's', but that wasn't really gran'ma's name. One thing was certain: she must get away, where to she had no idea, but away from Holst. Mum had said that: 'Don't stay with him.' If she stayed he might claim her, might tell people that he was her father, and try to keep her. She could see his furious, blood-streaked face, and shuddered.

Miss Hambro, good Christian soul, had returned to perform the last offices for Jenny. It was dark; Genevra sat very still, her mind working with a rapidity which was almost frightening. She put down the Monk in his basket, found her small private store of money which she had been saving to buy mum a really lovely birthday present. There was half a crown she had won from Charlie playing nap, two odd shillings, and some coppers. She tied them in a corner of her handkerchief. In the larder she filled a medicine bottle with milk for the Monk, took some biscuits, and a piece of corned beef for Haig. Carefully she packed them in the bag which she called her 'attachey case', lifted up the Monk, comfortably wrapped in his blanket, whispered softly to Haig, "C'm on, we're going," then, stepping very carefully in order to make no noise, slipped out and made her way out of the fairground to the high-road.

CHAPTER SEVEN

Genevra walked out on the broad high-road which led from Edgware, where the circus had its pitch. She had not the faintest idea where she was going, what she was going to do. All that she knew was that mum was dead, same as dad, that the laughing, happy life was over and that the world contained only herself, Haig and the Monk. True, in Manchester, gram'pa and gran'ma were living in a nice house, filled each week with kindly people who smiled and said, "Hello, Genevra!" when they met her on the stairs. But she didn't even know gran'ma's name, or the number of the house. She knew that Stratton Street was the third turning after you left the school which she had attended, that it had a shiny green door, and the windows were painted green, too. Gram'pa was something at a theatre, but which theatre Genevra could not remember, there were so many of them in Manchester. Maybe it would all come back to her when she didn't feel so—empty. Not physically empty, she wasn't hungry; she didn't think that she'd ever be hungry again; her emptiness was a mental thing. She didn't feel grief, she only felt dreadfully alone, and terribly worried about the Monk.

She went on walking and walking. She was not nervous or afraid, and once when a big policeman stopped her and said, "Bit late for a little girl like you to be out, isn't it?" Genevra answered with complete composure, "I've been to see my auntie, she's ill in bed. I'm all right, thank you. I've got my dog with me; he'd not let any harm come to me. Good night."

The big policeman said, "Fierce dog, is he?"

"Only if anyone gets cheeky, then he'd kill 'em."

He nodded. "Well, get along home, little girl. It's too late for kids to be wandering about. Good night."

She went on, steadily, without any idea of where she was going. The daylight had gone, the stars came out and twinkled down at her. Then the moon rose, round and shining and impersonally cold. Genevra had climbed a hill, a long hill which, with the weight of the Monk on her arm, made her pant a little.

By the light of the moon she saw the name Arkley on a signpost and vaguely wondered where on earth she was going, and how much longer she could keep walking.

Her feet ached, she felt almost exhausted, but she must find some place where she and Haig and the Monk could sleep. The Monk wasn't shivering or coughing so much, but she didn't like the sound of his breathing, it sounded as if he were panting. The shadows of the big trees, clear cut and somehow fierce in the moonlight, were disturbing; she thought that they were like tentacles—though the word was unknown to her—stretching out to stop her getting away, trying to drag her back to Holst. For the sake of hearing her own voice, she said to Haig, "Never mind what happens, Haig, we're not going back. We'll manage somehow. Give us time and we'll find gram'pa and gran'ma. Then we'll be all right. Just a bit further, luv."

She had visions of Holst on his motor-bicycle, tearing along the high-road to find her; there was no sound, but she grew nervous. At any moment she might hear him speeding up behind them. It was then that the shadowy form of a barn loomed up, just inside a gate. Genevra climbed the gate, Haig crept underneath the lowest bar. There was a door to the barn; she pushed it, pushed hard with a kind of desperate fear that Holst might appear suddenly on his bicycle. The door swung open and they went in. The place was almost a ruin, with a broken roof which allowed the moon to shine in and light up the darkness. In one corner were some sacks, and on them Genevra sat down.

Haig had drunk at various streams and puddles on the way; he sat near her, looking expectant, his bright pink tongue lolling, his eyes very bright and attentive. Genevra undid the shawl in which the Monk was wrapped. He lay very still, breathing quickly. His eyes looked piteous as if he questioned why this illness should happen to him. She gave him a little milk, and he took it obediently but without much interest. She tried to soak a piece of biscuit in the milk, and offered that to him, but he pushed it away with his cold little hands. Haig, on the other hand, ate his corned beef with relish, then lay down at her side, sighed profoundly, and slept.

After what seemed a long time, Genevra fell asleep, still and uncomfortable because she was holding the Monk and didn't want to disturb him.

How often had mum said, "Sleep's as good as medicine, nothing like it." If he slept he might wake up again in the morning quite well again.

She didn't want to think of mum, or of that last time when she had kissed her; she didn't want to think of anything. She was tired. She knew that if she allowed herself to think she would cry, then someone might hear, come into the barn and find her—and send her back.

The moon had gone, the place was incredibly dark. Genevra sat stiffly leaning against the dirty, rough wall. She must have slept, for the barn was almost light when she felt the Monk's hand on her face. She woke instantly and spoke to him gently. He must be better, he had always liked to stroke her face. His hand still felt dreadfully cold. She said brightly, "Are you better, Monk dear? Had a nice sleep? Now have a drop of milk and maybe a bit of biscuit. That's a dear."

She offered him some milk in a teaspoon, but he only lolled his head sideways, and his hand fell from her cheek as if it were too much effort to keep it there. He gave a long shuddering sigh, a sigh which brought Haig to his feet, to watch anxiously.

Genevra cried, "Monk, get better, darling—don't be ill. I'm here, so's Haig. Monk dear, oh, my Monk!"

The beautiful eyes closed, the hands fell at his sides; she knew that he was dead.

It was then for the first time that she experienced the real agony through which she had passed. Realization was forced upon her; except for Haig, and her grandparents—whose name she didn't even know—she was alone. There would be no more 'nice cups of tea', no more laughing and chattering, no more of mum's funny jokes, no more smiles for everyone. Mum's eyes were closed like the Monk's, and like the Monk's they'd never open again.

Genevra laid the Monk down very gently, wrapped his shawl round him, for even now she couldn't bear to think that he might be cold, then as Haig crept to her she lay on the dirty floor of the barn and cried as if her heart would break. The long, deep, hopeless sobbing of a lost child, a child without a home, without hope. How long she lay there she did not know, she only knew that the light had grown stronger, and that she felt utterly exhausted and weary. She ached—everything ached—her arms and legs; most of all she thought there was an ache in her heart which would last for always.

She sat up and Haig pushed his warm muzzle into her hand. He whimpered a little, softly, gently, as if he excused himself for making a noise at such a time. Genevra stared at him. "You're all I've got," she said. "You'll stick to me, won't you, Haig?"

She gave him the rest of the Monk's milk and some biscuit. She knew that her legs shook when she tried to stand, but equally she knew that she and Haig must get on. She must find some place where the Monk might be buried—buried decently. Soon they'd be burying mum decently, with Charlie and Atkins and Messer, and kind Miss Hambro, walking behind, or pr'aps riding in cars like they'd done when dad was buried. She set her teeth when she thought that Holst might ride behind mum, too, and maybe that yellow-haired woman, Miranda Hugil. Carefully she gathered up the Monk, knotting the corners of his shawl so that she could carry him more easily, and together she and Haig set out again on their journey, towards what goal Genevra had no idea. The first thing that mattered was to bury the Monk—'bury him decently'.

She walked more slowly this morning, her feet dragging a little. The Monk seemed heavier than he had ever done. One or two men on bicycles passed them and looked curiously at the slim child with the tousled hair, carrying a bundle, and accompanied by a small energetic fox terrier. They were on their way to work, and even if she attracted their attention for a moment they dismissed her from their minds and rode on. Once a motor-bicycle came roaring up behind them, and Genevra flung herself into a ditch at the side of the road, her heart beating furiously. The bicycle passed, she breathed again and crept out, more dishevelled than ever.

Houses began to appear, houses with bright, tidy gardens, well-hung curtains and brightly painted front doors. Genevra, looking at them, said to Haig, "One of these might do. There must be some nice folks living here. I'll pick the one that's got the biggest garden, then they won't mind the Monk being buried there."

'Killarney' was a corner house; if the other houses shone, 'Killarney' glistened. The paint was unbelievably glossy, the garden bright with flowers which seemed to be only recently awake. Genevra halted and stared. She was shaking, but she said to Haig, "This 'ul do. If they're nasty we must go somewhere else, that's all," and pushed open the bright green gate.

Tilda Lorimer, who had been Miss Mattie Colingly of the Odeon Theatre, was an early riser and proud of it. When Henry was at home and they sat up talking until all hours, then she didn't mind 'lying in' a little; but when Henry was away she liked to go to bed early, and if she did not actually rise with the lark, at least she rose before the milkman and the postman came.

She was pottering about in the kitchen, talking brightly to her elderly maid, Alice. Once upon a time Alice had been her dresser, and although Alice always said, "Yes, mum" and "No, mum," that did not prevent them being excellent friends. True Mrs. Lorimer retained a certain amount of dignity; she ate alone in the dining-room: really that was because it would have been difficult when Henry was at home to banish Alice. There were times when she would say to the maid, "I'll have a cup o' tea here with you, Alice," but she never made a regular thing of it.

She had been a successful artiste in musical comedy; her voice had been good if not outstanding, and her hair—it had been 'ash blonde' in those days—coupled with her pretty face and really fine figure, had, as the saying went then, 'drawn the Town to the Odeon'.

She had had many admirers, some whose intentions were strictly dishonourable, others who really believed themselves to be in love with her and who offered her marriage. To the surprise of everyone, when she was thirty, she had married Hilary Francis Lorimer, a 'solid man' who was said, somewhat vaguely, to be 'something in the City'.

Lorimer was a quiet fellow, not lacking in good looks, and obviously possessed of considerable wealth. He collected English water-colours, china—restricting his collection to the best period Dresden, Meissen, Chelsea and Battersea—and every book on dress throughout the ages that he could find.

Tilda liked him; his air of solidity was assuring. She doubted if she had ever loved him passionately, as she had once loved the Hon. John Mainsty. That had been different, like living in a dream with the pink limes on all the time. John would have married her, but he was a younger son, and knew that his aristocratic father and mother had already made their plans for him. He must marry money, and he knew it. The romance ended, the lovely dream was over, the pink limes put out, and Tilda married Lorimer.

They lived in a large, ugly house on the outskirts of Streatham, and Lorimer went to the City every day except Saturday and Sunday. Tilda's son was born two years after their marriage, and Lorimer gave her a very large diamond ring, a gold net bag, and a beautiful Chelsea group of a lady flirting with a gentleman in knee-breeches. This, after he had discoursed at length on its beauty and perfection, he took away and locked in one of his handsome cabinets.

He was delighted at the arrival of the child, a nice baby, who grew into an equally nice little boy. Tilda was happy with the boy, but she found the ideas of her husband somewhat restricting. She was a friendly creature and longed to keep in touch with her old friends at the Odeon. She soon realized that while Lorimer saw no reason why he, wearing the most correct and conventional evening dress, should not haunt the stalls of that theatre because he had fallen in love with Mattie Colingly, he had no liking—much less desire for friendship—with other lights of the musical-comedy stage.

When Tilda suggested that they might have a party in their very large and beautiful garden, inviting 'some of the boys and girls', he replied that he saw no necessity for such an entertainment. He inferred that the entertaining of his City friends and their wives was sufficient amusement. Indeed, Tilda found it so, and after those interminable and stiff dinners often recounted to Alice all that had been said, giving imitations of the guests which reduced Alice, as she said, 'to stitches'.

Gradually she forgot to keep in touch with her theatrical friends, and they forgot to invite her to their parties; she knew that she was bored to extinction. With the exception of the small Henry—who might be adorable but who was scarcely a companion—and Alice, Tilda was lonely. Hilary, returning from the City at his invariable hour, unless he was attending some City dinner, in which case he had his case taken to the Cecil and left there for him, changing there and remaining for the night, always greeted her in the same way.

"Ah, my dear!" as if, Tilda thought, he didn't expect to find her there!—adding, "And what news have you for me, eh?"

She always answered, "Same as usual, Hilary, the boy's growing more lovely every day. Nothing else."

They were sufficiently happy, in that their lives ran smoothly. Tilda was without 'nerves', and having married Hilary realized that she had a great deal to thank him for. He was unfailingly kind, she had everything—materially—for which she could wish, he was generous and denied her nothing. Her house was completely comfortable, if slightly oppressive; her servants—carefully chosen by Lorimer—well trained and respectful. Only at long intervals, generally when she saw his name mentioned in the newspapers, did she remember John Mainsty, and wonder what life might have been like if he had not been the younger son of a peer, and they could have married.

When Henry was eight years old, Lorimer was taken ill. He

showed great fortitude through a long and painful illness, and Tilda nursed him devotedly. He knew from the first that he was not going to recover and often talked to her concerning her position after his death.

"Hilary, my dear," she would protest, "don't let's talk of such mournful things. Anyway, it's not going to happen. You're going to get as right as rain, and we'll go to the south of France and have ever such a lovely time."

His tone, even when his voice began to weaken, was slightly reproving. "My dear Tilda"—for after she left the Odeon he never called her 'Mattie' again—"it is necessary to face facts. I have never allowed myself to evade any responsibility, and I do not intend to do so now. Henry is eight years old—in a few months time he will be nine. He will be in your complete charge. I impose no conditions. Should you wish to remarry—and I see no reason why you should not do so—far be it from me to penalize you."

He talked in this way for what seemed, to Tilda, to be hours. Even when he knew that he had little strength left, he gave her instructions as to what he wished done with his collection of china, his Birkett Fosters, and the rest of his possessions. He died as he had lived, quietly, without ostentation, and with dignity. The only time Hilary Lorimer had strayed from the narrow paths of convention was when he had married Miss Mattie Colingly of the Odeon Theatre.

Tilda was, as she told Alice, 'upset' by his death. She had not realized how she had depended upon him. The paying of gas and electric-light bills, rates and taxes were completely outside her ken. Hilary had even paid the firm who cleaned the windows. She felt lost and a little at sea.

Alice said, "O' course you're upset. It 'ud be on-natural if you were not to be. A *good* 'usband, I never knew a better, and I've seen a few in my time. Mostly other people's, admitted, but I've tried two out on my own—an' Gawd! what prize So-and-so's!"

Lorimer had left her everything; in his will he referred to her as 'my beloved wife, the finest helpmate a man ever had'. The lawyer, Mr. Carter, of Carter, Carter and Bowles, treated her with grave respect.

"You have been left a very considerable fortune, Mrs. Lorimer."

She replied, "Well, candidly, I never knew how much the poor fellow had. He was always generous, and naturally I gathered there was—well, enough. But I shall need it all. My Henry's going to have the best, and only the very best will be good enough. I want public schools, and universities and foreign travel—opportunities, that's what I want."

"All these things," Mr. Carter assured her pontifically, "will be possible and—more than possible."

She sold the house in Streatham, and sold it very well. With Alice she retired to live in a small but eminently well-run and even smart hotel in South Moulton Street. Henry was at his expensive preparatory school, he was entered for Harrow, and Tilda wanted to 'look round'.

It took her two years to find what she wanted.

"A house, Alice, that's not large and yet not poky. Modern improvements, plenty of power plugs, and plugs for extra lights. A couple of bathrooms, and a couple of separate lavs. Nice bit of garden, the kind of thing one man can keep in lovely condition. I must have flowers! Perhaps a little greenhouse for tomatoes— Master Henry loves them. We can't find a house like that in town, we'll have to go outside. Better for Master Henry, the air will do him good. London's no good for children."

Finally, as she and Alice drove in Tilda's smart car through Barnet, she clutched Alice's arm. "This will do. Look, those houses over there. Bennett, stop! Those are the very thing. Detached; nice piece of ground."

Then and there she got out of the car, found a foreman, and discussed the matter with him. He gave it as his opinion that she 'would not do better'. "It's a coming neighbourhood. Water's all right, Company's gas and 'lectric. Good service ter London. W'at was it you were reely wanting?"

"A house!" Tilda exclaimed. "What d'you think I want—a few hens and a cow or two?"

It appeared that a mysterious gentleman called 'Mr. Williamson' was 'somewhere round' and the foreman sent a small, thin man with a melancholy expression to find him. Mr. Williamson arrived, an anxious-faced young man, with sandy hair, and pale blue eyes. Tilda's energy and decision astonished him.

"A plot?" he said. "There are several plots. Did you wish to *build*, then, madam? Oh, to *build*. I can show you the plots with pleasure."

She chose her plot; the house must be detached. The new house must get all the sun possible. The young man with the pale eyes smiled wanly.

"That, unfortunately, madam, is a commodity we cannot guarantee."

"I know that. Where do you think I've come from? Honolulu?"

She plunged into the plans for her new house. She had her own ideas and, as she informed the architect, she was paying him to see how they might be put into effect. Bedrooms must have plenty of light and air, the bathrooms must be of the most modern type, the kitchen must have constant hot water, cooking stoves which were the best on the market, sinks which were deep and easily cleaned.

"Those details, Mrs. Lorimer, scarcely concern me as the architect."

"Then they *must* concern you! They're part of the house! If you don't know where to find such things, *ask*, my lad, *ask*."

There were times when he thought that he would throw up the job; not that she wasn't pleasant, but she was immovable when once she set her heart on anything. That matter of parquet flooring, of special airing cupboards, 'not only for the laundry, but for clothes if any of us comes in wet', all kinds of unusual things, even to the front-door steps being made of pinkish marble 'because it cleans quicker'. Finally the house was finished, the architect paid and, given a handsome present into the bargain. Workmen were regaled with a splendid supper of roast beef and beer. Tilda said, "It's now, Alice, that our work really begins. It's the furnishing I'm nervous of." She pinched her lower lip between her finger and thumb, a trick of hers when she was thinking deeply. "I wonder if I'd better wait till Henry has his holidays?"

"Master Henry! He's only twelve—what 'ud he know about furnishing?"

"Rising thirteen," Tilda corrected. "Master Henry's got taste, even if he is so young."

Henry on his return was consulted. He was a tall, slim boy, with fine dark hair, and a pale clear skin. The only thing he had insisted that he wanted of his father's had been the books on costume. He would pore over them for hours. It was obvious that his mother's wish that he should give his opinion regarding the furnishing of the new house gave him considerable satisfaction. Together they visited the depository where the furniture from 'Holmleigh' was stored. Henry inspected it critically.

"It's not a very good period, Mother," he said, almost as if he excused her and his father. "The wood is first-rate, it's the design that is so awful. Those chairs are nice—Chippendale—and the table's good. Those china cabinets are beautiful, but they're far

95

too large for an ordinary house." So Henry continued, selecting such pieces as he thought stood the test of the knowledge which he had gathered. He was a serious child, and confided to his mother that his house-master was "keen on all kinds of antiques, but mind," Henry warned, "they've got to be right."

Tilda, who so far as furniture was concerned did not know right from wrong, answered obediently, "Well, of course, Henry. We don't want anything that's not right, do we?"

Gradually 'Killarney' emerged, furnished, shining, and if not completely beautiful, at least filled with comfort and gleaming with exquisite cleanliness.

As Henry grew older and passed from his expensive prep school to Harrow, he showed his interest in furniture and furnishing had not abated. Again and again he came home during his holidays to announce that he had discovered this or that in some out-of-the-way antique shop.

"Now," he would cry in triumph, "we can get rid of that awful bookcase, and put in something really lovely!"

Tilda never questioned his taste, which she felt instinctively was good, and slowly 'Killarney' became not only a comfortable house, but one which was filled with really beautiful things. Henry's friends, whom he asked to his home during the holidays, might have come from 'the stately homes of England', but not one of them could stigmatize 'Killarney' as 'just a detached suburban villa'. They might regard his mother as 'rather obvious', but her genuine kindliness, her thought and plans for their enjoyment, completely won them over.

Henry at eighteen refused to go to Oxford, and when his mother said, "But what do you want to do?" he answered calmly, "I want to go into one of the really good shops in the West End, or Knightsbridge, so that I can learn about materials. I've got it all planned out, Mother. The thing that interests me is costume—of all ages. I'm going to get somewhere if I stick to that—believe me, I am."

Henry Lorimer at twenty-two was a self-possessed young man; he was tall and slim, his manner was excellent, and his appearance sufficiently handsome. He had worked—and worked hard—for three years at Messrs. Harris and George, in Knightsbridge. He had sucked up knowledge as a sponge takes up water, and at twenty-two was engaged by the great Levelle, as junior designer. He was indifferently paid, but he had a sufficient allowance from his mother to take a small but excellently appointed flat in St. John's Wood. He came home every week-end, unless he was paying a visit to one of his numerous friends. He was tremendously popular, for though many of the young men at Levelle's copied their employer in eccentricity of dress which bordered on the fantastic, Henry refused to alter his style of dressing. When some young designer appeared in a wine-coloured velvet jacket, with immense peg-top trousers, and asked Henry if he didn't think that it was 'divine', Henry replied that he thought the colour magnificent.

The exquisite replied, "Henry, you'd look marvellous in a coat like this of—midnight blue!"

To which Henry answered, "Midnight blue during working hours . . . daylight hours. . . . Oh, surely not!"

Clients were beginning to notice him, and Lady Monica Hallesley said to Levelle, "That young man has ideas, eh? I like this sketch for the dress he has done for me."

Levelle smiled, spread his hands and replied, "Yes, ideas! 'Oo put them t'ere? Me, Levelle! No, but he is a clever boy, one that weel go farr." He added rather bitterly, "Eef vimmen don't make a fool of heem. Remember Claude? Clever boy—now! Paff!"

Henry was apparently unaffected by the lovely ladies who came to Levelle's. He was anxious to execute the kind of drawings and designs they wanted, he was unfailingly polite, but they felt that he regarded them as vehicles for his art rather than as human beings. He loved his home, though the name 'Killarney' disturbed him a little.

"Mother dear, why 'Killarney'?" he asked, when he first saw the word embossed on a handsome beaten copper plate. "We're not Irish."

Tilda beamed at him. "You don't remember the song, Henry." Then in a voice which retained much of its old sweetness, she sang, "Heaven's reflex—Killarney," adding, "that's the reason, my dear. It is just that, 'Heaven's reflex' to me."

Henry smiled back at her, "Then it's the perfect name for the perfect house—with the perfect mistress."

On a chilly, blustery morning, when Tilda stood chatting in the kitchen with Alice, discussing what menus were most likely to appeal to 'Master Henry' when he came down for the week-end, she heard a knock on the front door. She said, "That's all right, Alice. I'll go; it's the post."

It wasn't the postman. She opened the door and saw a small girl standing there, with a black-and-white fox terrier at her side.

The child carried a little bag and a bundle which seemed heavy. Her face was completely devoid of colour, her fair hair tousled and dreadfully untidy. Her clothes were sufficiently good, but tumbled and stained. Her face held Tilda's attention. It was, despite its dirt and the stains of tears on the cheeks, a lovely face. It reminded her of that old picture Henry had brought home, of some lady in the Middle Ages. It was a perfect oval, with eyes set wide apart, a short, beautifully formed nose and a mouth which Tilda felt ought to be always smiling. Not laughing, particularly, but smiling gently and sweetly. The girl stared at her, and Tilda realized that there was something gravely wrong.

She said, "Well, little girl, what do you want, my dear?"

Genevra stared at the ample figure with its golden hair crowning a face which was still charming, even though it possessed several chins; there was a kindliness about this lady in the bright printed cotton dress which restored her confidence a little.

She said, "Missus, would you lend me a spade, and let me dig a grave in your garden somewhere?"

Tilda exclaimed, "A grave! You want a spade? Whatever's the matter, child? You're not wandering, are you?"

Genevra moistened her dry lips; she found it increasingly difficult to give explanations. "It's the Monk, missus. He died last night. He's got to be buried decently. You see—you see——." And with that she pitched forward on to her face and lay still.

Tilda stood aghast, then called, "Alice, Alice, come and help me with this little girl. Hurry, hurry, leave the bacon!"

When Genevra recovered consciousness she was in a room which seemed all white and pale pink. The window was open and the cool air touched her face. She felt strange and 'slack'; it was too much trouble to think how she could have come there. The door opened and someone said, "Now, my little dear, you're going to take a nice basin of bread and milk. I used to make it for my Henry, and he always says no one can make it as I can. Now let me lift you up, that's the style."

Propped on pillows, Genevra saw that it was the same lady she remembered seeing at the door, the lady with yellow hair. Not yellow like mum's, and certainly not yellow like Miranda Hugil's, but definitely yellow. She said, "Thank you—but where's Haig?—he's my terrier."

The lady sat down on a basket-chair near the bed; the basket-chair creaked a little as if in protest, for the lady was not slim. She laid her hands on her knees, and said, "Now eat that bread and milk, and I'll talk to you. Haig's as right as rain. He's had some bread and milk, and Alice has found him a bone. It's the bone from last night's joint as a matter of fact. Oh, he's all right." She leaned forward, and spoke more softly. Genevra decided that it was a nice, warm voice. "The poor little monkey, he's wrapped in a clean tray-cloth—he looked beautiful—so peaceful, just as if he were tired and taking a sleep—which I don't doubt he is, bless him. My gardener's found a lovely place for him, and we found a nice box. A big chocolate box my son gave me last Christmas. The gardener's going to put little stones round his grave and plant some really nice flowers. Now, don't cry, dearie, eat up your bread and milk, then Haig—it's a nice name, that—can come up and sit with you until you go to sleep again."

Genevra ate the bread and milk, felt terribly tired, and said, "Thank you very much, but I've got to be on my road. I think I can get up and start off."

Tilda Lorimer flung up her plump hands. "Start off! Oh, my dear, it's more than my life's worth—so to speak—to let you go until Henry comes. He'll be here this evening, then you'll feel better and can talk to him. No need to be scared of Henry, but he's got a headpiece on him, and whatever there is wrong, whatever has made you unhappy, you can tell him. You have a good rest, then a talk with Henry, and wherever you want to go we'll send you on by train. Henry might even drive you there in his car. He's a lovely driver."

Somehow the reiteration of the name 'Henry' reassured her; it was a nice, 'safe-sounding' name, Genevra thought, and she was so dreadfully tired. She lay down, her eyes already closing, murmuring, "May Haig come and sit with me, please?"

Tilda settled the bedclothes, went to the door and called, "Here, Haig, you're wanted." Through mists of sleep Genevra heard the patter of his feet on the stairs, heard him come into the room. The kind voice said, "Now lie down and don't disturb her. That's the style." Then the door closed and she was left alone except for the consciousness that Haig was close to her, and the reassurance of his heavy and contented breathing.

In the kitchen Tilda sat down heavily. Alice said, "Now we might have a cup o' tea, eh? My, that's a set-on, isn't it? Pore little thing, wanderin' about wi' a dead monkey and a little dog! It's a mystery, ain't it? I never see such a thing i' my life, never. Come to borrer a spade ter dig a grave for the pore little monkey! 'As she said anythink, mum?"

Tilda shook her head. "She's all in, Alice. When she wakes I'll give her a nice bath, and give her hair a shampoo. Mind, she's

99

as pretty as a picture, once we had her face sponged. I didn't even ask her what her name was; afraid of upsetting her. However by the time Master Henry gets here she'll be better able to talk. He's got a way with him, knows how to handle difficult situations." She sighed. "If she's half as good as she's pretty—oh, Alice, I wish we could keep her!"

Alice, busy with the tea-pot, replied, "Nay, it's early days to think of that, mum. Anyway, we must wait ter see what Master Henry has to say about everythink. There—that's a cup o' tea as will put heart into you with all the upsets this morning. I'll never forget the sight of that pore little monkey! I don't mind tellin' you that I shed tears."

"Oh, so did I!" Tilda exclaimed, as if in protest.

"That's so, mum, but you was always a easy crier, if I may say so. My tears comes hard, always has done. Just a slice of toast—yes, do, mum."

Upstairs Genevra slept soundlessly and dreamlessly, while Haig lay with his head on his paws wondering how they had come to be here in this house where none of the smells were in the least familiar.

CHAPTER EIGHT

GENEVRA had slept heavily, to wake and look round the pretty room, wondering at first where she was. Then everything had come rushing back—the dull ache because mum was dead and she would never see her again, worse than it had been when dad died. Somehow mum had seemed more nearly 'hers'. True she might have married Holst, but after the first estrangement between Genevra and her mother everything had come right again. There had been something innately personal in her association with her mother. Between them age had ceased to exist, and Genevra had never consciously felt that mum was any older than she was. She didn't want to cry any more, she had shed all her tears lying on the floor of that barn, with the dead Monk beside her, and Haig's cold nose pushing itself into the palm of her clenched hand. Only now, lying in this beautifully clean bed, with the cool air coming in through the open window, the recollection that she would never see mum again left her with a sense of dull sickness.

A woman she had not seen before entered with a tray covered

with a clean cloth, and Genevra saw that there was a little vase with two small roses in it as well as the various dishes.

The woman said, "Now, so you're awake! Here's a little dinner for you. Madam's own special beef-tea, and some crisp toast. You'll like that. It 'ul put strength into you. Sit up, my dear, and sup it up."

Genevra struggled into a sitting posture, saying, "Would you tell me where I am, please? I'm really quite well, you know."

"Tell you—why, yes. There's no secret about it, as I know of. You're at 'Killarney', that's the house of Mrs. Lorimer, the lady you saw. It's in Barnet. You've heard of Barnet Fair, eh?"

Genevra nodded. "Barnet Fair—yer hair. Charlie used to say, 'Luke at yer Barnet Fair!' when I was untidy."

"Oh, that's rhyming slang," the woman said. "Now drink up your beef-tea, while I take down your clothes and get them straightened out a bit. Then you shall have a nice warm bath and be ready for Master Henry."

"And Haig," the little girl said, "I've nothing left to give him. Might he have something, please?"

"His dinner's ready and waiting. Some nice boiled mutton, a couple o' bones, broken biscuit and so forth. Oh, don't bother your head about Mr. Haig. Treated like a king, that's what he is."

Genevra drank her beef-tea and ate her toast with relish. Vaguely she wondered if it showed lack of love for mum, to be able to eat at such a time. Then she remembered how mum had always said, "You'll feel a lot better, luv, when you've eaten something."

She got out of bed and set the tray down on a little table, then climbed back and lay with her hands clasped behind her head, thinking of the events of the last few days. How many days she could scarcely remember.

Mum with her in a railway carriage, and the Monk, and Haig; getting to London and driving and driving for miles and miles. Charlie waiting for them, mum going off to Hugil's caravan, and Charlie begging, "Come an' 'ave a nice cup o' char, missus." After that, noise, and dreadful pictures, shouts, a car driving up and a man with a kind but ugly, blunt face getting out. Making tea in Miss Hambro's caravan, because mum might want a cup. A fight, Holst with his face streaked with blood. Charlie, Messer and Atkins walking and talking together. Mum hadn't wanted that cup of tea after all. She was too tired. She had kissed Genevra and her cheeks and lips had been cold.

Genevra frowned. Mum had been going to have a baby! What

had happened to it? If it were still in the caravan, then someone must get it and she'd take it to gran'ma and gram'pa. This man 'Masterenery' who was coming—he might be able to tell her what to do about the baby. The woman with the fair hair and the thin one who had come in with beef-tea seemed to think that 'Masterenery' could do everything.

Slowly, lulled by the sounds which entered through the open window, the distant hum of motor-cars, the occasional furious buzzing of a bee, which having entered, wished immediately to get out again, the sound of far-off voices, Genevra slept. Once a cock crowed, and again—very dimly—she thought she heard Haig's voice barking joyously. Genevra sank into sleep again.

The light had lost some of its brilliance when she woke again, to find Mrs. Lorimer standing by her bed, smiling.

Genevra said, "Hello, missus."

Tilda said, "No, my dear, don't call me that, call me 'Auntie' —Auntie Tilda. Now, I want you to have a lovely warm bath, then I'm going to brush your hair and make it look lovely. Alice, dear soul, has washed the little collars and cuffs of your dress— she's pressed it, too. You'll look as nice as nip to meet Henry."

Genevra slid out of bed, almost tripping on the long night-gown which Tilda had put on her when she first went to bed. "Henry?" she asked. "Is he the same as 'Masterenery'?"

"The very selfsame. Now, put this shawl round you and run to the bathroom. Can you bath yourself or shall Auntie come with you?"

"No, I can manage nicely," Genevra assured her. "I always had a bath every day at my gran'ma's, and in the caravan I always sluiced down every night. Mum would have been angry if I'd not. So'd Miss Hambro, if it comés to that. No, thank you, I can manage."

A wonderful bathroom, all pink and white tiles, with shining taps, and the water, gently steaming, ready drawn. Water which smelt like flowers, and in which her body felt astonishingly smooth and soft. There was soap, too, of rose colour. She lifted it to her nose and sniffed. That smelt of roses, too. Like real flowers which mum sometimes bought to put in the caravan. Genevra lay down in the soft water, and sighed.

Speaking very softly, she said, "Mum, it's a shame you can't be here, too. They're kind and nice. They've given the Monk a decent funeral. Don't think as I'm not missing you. I'll miss you always as long as I live. I cried all my tears in that old barn. My heart's still crying. It 'ul always cry when I think about you."

Then because she felt that she might begin to cry again, she began to wash vigorously, and actually felt that the scent of the soap and the delight of feeling perfectly clean strengthened her. She dried, wrapped herself in the shawl and ran back to her room. Her clothes were lying ready, her dress was pressed, the collar and little cuffs starched and ironed.

Tilda began to brush her hair with a brush which was very hard, but the feel of the bristles on Genevra's scalp was pleasant. Tilda kept exclaiming, "My, you have got nice hair, dearie. It's so fine, and thick, and such a lovely colour."

Genevra said, "You should see my mum's, that's like real gold." Then she remembered that, of course, 'Auntie Tilda' couldn't see mum's lovely hair, and a strange lump rose in her throat and threatened to choke her. Tilda, continuing to brush smoothly and evenly, said, "I'm certain of it—certain."

Genevra was conscious of a great rush of gratitude because 'Aunt Tilda' had made no other comment.

When Henry Lorimer drove up to 'Killarney' in his very smart, if small, car, his mother rushed down the path to meet him. Henry halted for a moment before descending from the car, to look at the house, the garden and, most of all, his mother. He thought how pleasant the house looked, how gay the garden was with flowers and the pergola—which in his innermost heart he might stigmatize as being faintly suburban but which he had to admit looked very well with its climbing red and white roses, and lastly at his mother. She was fifty-six, he reflected, and she didn't look a day more than forty odd. She was, he knew, well and carefully corseted; hadn't he recommended to her Madam Masket, where Lady George Carteret got her stays? The effect was good; Madam Masket certainly 'knew her stuff'; so did Jules, who tinted her hair. He'd kept the 'brass' out of it wonderfully. Her clothes, too, were exactly right: after all, so they ought to be, he designed them himself. This dress which she was wearing was just what an attractive woman, not yet really 'middle-aged', ought to wear on a sunny afternoon in Spring. He was always saying to her, "It's the line that really matters. Very few materials are so hideous that they can spoil the *line*, if a designer knows his job."

He called, "Here I am! Nice to get home early, and to know that I've two whole days to play in!" Then stooping he kissed her and said, "How are you, sweet? I've not seen you for five whole days . . . an eternity, eh?"

She held him at arm's length, because she was never tired of admiring him. He did her credit—she never included the late Hilary Lorimer in her congratulations somehow—he was tall and well made, his features were clearly cut, even if the nose was just a little too long and inclined to be a little melancholy. Tilda dismissed that thought immediately, it seemed as if she were criticizing Henry.

'He's got nice eyes,' she thought, 'they're kind, and yet they're not soppy. Henry knows how many beans make five as well as the next one. Lovely hands, too, artist's hands, and good, narrow feet. I hate men with pudgy feet. His clothes are always nice, too —yet that suit—let me see—it must be three years old. He keeps them well; my dad was the same, even if he was a greengrocer. On Sundays when he was taking momma for a walk he might have been anybody. No, my Henry's a credit to me.'

She held his hand drawn through her arm as they walked into the house. "Well, I've got so much to tell you I don't know where to start!" she said.

Henry expressed surprise and concern. "They've foreclosed on the mortgage, cut off the gas, electric light and telephone, and you've lost a packet on the Lincoln! How often have I told you not to pick winners out with a pin?"

Tilda giggled happily as they entered the drawing-room. She always thought of it as 'the lounge', but Henry called it either the drawing-room or the sitting-room. Alice bustled in with the tea-tray; she smiled at Henry, saying, "Nice ter see you beck, Masterenery," and when he said, "Are you in this mystery business, Alice?" smirked a little, glanced at Tilda and said, "I've no doubt, sir, as the mistress will tell you all about it."

Tilda poured out tea. Henry did not take milk, and she dropped his thin slice of lemon into the cup with great care and concentration.

He leaned back, stretching out his legs and sighing with pleasure. "I've seen the most charming little writing-desk in King Street," he said; "a toy of a thing, walnut, painted very delicately with flowers. Italian, I fancy. It would look delightful over there instead of that perfectly monstrous set of tables. We must think if we can afford it."

"The tables are very useful," Tilda said mildly.

"But they're so ugly," he persisted. "However, tell me about this mortgage and the rest of it."

Again she giggled; it was a pleasant, melodious sound, a kind of friendly recognition that she found him amusing. "You know very well there's no mortgage on *this* house, nor ever will be on any house where I live. No, we've got a little girl here—such a pretty little thing, she came with a poor dead monkey and a fox terrier this morning."

Henry sat upright and stared at her. "My darling mother, what are you talking about—little girls and dead monkeys and fox terriers! Shall I telephone for Dr. Bowes?"

"No, my dear. Just listen and let me tell you about it. Only don't fluster me. It happened this way: I was in the kitchen talking to Alice when the bell rang. I thought it was the postman, and said to Alice that I'd go." So the story continued, with many embellishments and side-trackings, until at times Henry thought that he had lost the thread of it all for good. Tilda concluded by saying, "Now, Henry dear, what do you think of that, eh?"

"I think," he said, "that the sooner I telephone to the police and find out if they're scouring the country for this missing child, the better."

Tilda cried in admiration, "There now! I never thought of that! Trust you, Henry, to hit the nail on the head. But—" suddenly anxious—"you'll find out things a little before you let them take her away, won't you? I believe she's been unhappy. Children don't run away with monkeys and terrier dogs if they're happy at home. I've not asked her any questions; she was just done when she came here. Heaven only knows how far she's walked. From the look of her she'd slept out all night. So be careful, my dear. I'm not having any child snatched back to a home where it's unhappy, not if it's the law and whoever the law gets to help it!"

He nodded gravely. "Darling, with all your inconsequence you're wiser—yes, and kinder—than I am. I'll be very careful."

"You've not seen her, my dear."

"That can be easily remedied," he suggested. "Where have you hidden her?"

"She's with Alice and the terrier in the kitchen. His name's Haig. Her name's—I think it's lovely—Genevra."

"Genevra," Henry repeated, as if he wished to savour the name. "Well, let's see—Genevra."

Tilda went to bring in Genevra, holding her by the hand. Henry saw a child, tall and too thin, with soft fair hair, and wide-apart eyes. A skin which was very faintly touched with colour in the cheeks, and a mouth which was generous and looked as if it ought to smile readily. She moved easily, with what he recognized to be perfect balance.

He rose and held out his hand, saying, "How do you do? My name is Henry Lorimer."

She said, "I'm well, thank you. My name's Genevra Menetti."

"You're Italian?"

"My dad was an Italian—he was the great Alfredo Menetti. The best acrobat and slack-wire walker there ever was in the world. He was killed two years ago. He wouldn't use a net, he said it made him nervous. That was in London when Mr. Trumelli brought his circus here."

Henry snapped his fingers. "I remember! Of course! At Shepherd's Bush. I saw your father, and what an artiste!" He smiled. "And so good to look at."

Tilda said, "Now just look at that, that makes you two like old friends, doesn't it? That is nice."

"Of course," Henry agreed, "that is exactly what we are. Genevra—never let anyone abbreviate that lovely name, will you? Swear to me now that you will always insist on being called—by your proper name and not by some horrible abbreviation." He held up his forefinger, saying, "Now swear it on the head of Haig."

She nodded; this young man gave her confidence, made her feel that she was someone who 'mattered'. She said, "Yes, I will swear. How did you know about Haig?"

Henry said sagely, "Ah, that I can't tell you—at the moment, but if you will sit down I think we might talk more easily."

Suddenly panic-stricken, she clutched his wrist. "Listen, mister, I'm not going back to that Holst. I don't care if I walk miles and miles, I'll have Haig and he'll look after me. I've a gram'pa and a gran'ma in Manchester and they'll look after me. But I'll not go back to that blasted Holst, not was it ever so."

The little room was suddenly charged with hatred. Genevra's pale face had flushed, her slim body was tense with fear, her eyes clouded and filled with distress, and behind the distress . . . determination.

Henry pushed her, very gently, into a chair, saying, "My dear, delightful Genevra, I don't want you to go back to any blasted man, whoever he is. I'm all on your side. Now, do you think that you could tell me all about it? It doesn't matter if you cry . . . probably I shall cry, too, and my mother. Tears are good for everything. Now, could you bear to begin at the beginning?"

Genevra swallowed hard. This young man gave her courage, she liked his looks, his clothes—less ostentatious than those of Holst, but she felt that they were 'class'. His voice, too, was pleasant. Rather light, and friendly. She felt that he really wanted to know everything she could tell him. He had said, 'I'm all on your side'. Drawing a deep breath, she began her story.

She told him of 'dad', of his artistry, and his death. Of how mum had been attracted by this Holst—"always said as he was a German baron. I don't b'lieve it; no more did Charlie, nor Messer nor Atkins." She told of Holst's cats, his method of training them, of how, after he married mum, things had changed. Of mum's gaiety, of their good times together, their laughter, their silliness. She went on to say that mum had been going to have a baby, and that she longed to know what had happened to it now mum was dead.

"It's mum's baby," she said, "an' I'd look after it. I would, I'd work for it, only it can't be left with that b——y Holst. That's certain."

She heard Tilda draw her breath sharply at the word, but Henry was unmoved. He sat with his finger-tips pressed together, his face completely calm, merely nodding his head a little in assent. He said, very quietly, "Naturally, one understands that completely."

Then he began to talk, to explain that he must telephone to the police-station to find if enquiries were being made concerning Genevra. She took fright at that, and said, "No, no, don't do that. I can get on to Manchester. I'm not going to be dragged back— all I want to know is about that baby of my mum's. I'll not go back."

Almost casually, as if it did not really matter very much, Henry said, "My dear girl, no one wants you to go back. All I want to do is to make sure that this—unspeakable Holst can't make you go back. Can't you trust us?"

Genevra nodded, half sulkily. "Have it your own way, but I'll kill myself—and Haig—before I'll go back. Mind that, Masterenery."

Henry shrugged his shoulders, "That's all right," and went off to telephone. Genevra watched him go, thinking, 'After all, I was wrong. He doesn't care. For tuppence he'd send me back. Well, I'll not go. Nothink 'ul make me. I'll leave here to-night. It can't be so very far to Manchester, and once I'm in the Oxford Road I can find gran'ma's house. Maybe Auntie Tilda 'ul lend me five shillings. She's kind, not like that Masterenery, who only wants me to talk, and then—shop me.'

Henry returned; he was still very calm and cool. He sat down, lit a cigarette and said, "That's all right. The police are looking for a little girl——" He smiled at Genevra. "You're not so very little, are you? I told them that I *fancied* that I had seen such a 'little girl' go past this morning, and that I was prepared to scour the country-side in my car to find her. I shall let them know the result of my search. To-morrow morning I am going to Edgware, where it appears that Hugil's Circus is playing. I shall beard this monster Holst in his den, and return with some kind of an understanding." Again he smiled his engaging smile. "Be very sure that this gentleman will get very little small change out of me. Do you feel reassured, Genevra?"

Tilda said, "Now, Henry, don't get into any bother, will you?"

"My darling mother, what do you mean by 'bother'? If you mean shall I return to the maternal roof with two black eyes, most certainly—no! I shall have Charlie and Messer and Atkins behind me."

The fact that he mentioned her three friends by their names gave Genevra a queer kind of assurance. She didn't really like this elegant young man, who spoke what she had learned to call 'well put on'. She thought that he was affected, and something of a 'cissy'. His voice was so quiet, his movements so smooth and easy. She found his speech pedantic—though she did not know the word itself—and, she told herself, 'a bit old-maidish'. Still, he was going to see Holst, and she told herself that she must await the result of the interview.

'After all,' she thought, 'I've run away before, and I can run away again. I'm not frightened!'

But she was frightened, in her heart, and she knew it. She might swagger and make assertions, but there was still the definite fear of a child who realizes that it has no one to whom it matters supremely.

She said, "That's right—Charlie an' Atkins and Messer are good chaps. Messer's a Jew-boy."

"Really!" Henry said politely. "I have a great liking for Jews."

Genevra said, "Go on, have you?" Then, "What do you do, Masterenery?"

He said, "I design dresses for women to wear. It's rather fun. One day, when you're grown up, you must let me design some for you. I'm rather good, so they tell me."

"It's a queer job for a man, isn't it?"

Henry answered, rather pontifically, "That all depends upon your method of approach."

Not knowing in the least what he meant, Genevra said, "I s'ppose so."

Genevra slept soundly and dreamlessly, and was not awake when Henry drove off to Edgware in the morning. Tilda was worried, she imagined her son becoming involved in some brawl in which he might be battered and beaten. Henry had no such fears. Under his rather 'precious' manner there was a hard core of determination and mental strength. Life, in spite of the money which his mother lavished on him so generously, had not been easy for him. He had studied hard, had developed his eye for colour, and the temper of materials. He had ideas, and great ability. His progress had been almost phenomenal, and his employers were beginning to watch him with concentrated and even anxious care.

His clients liked him, not only for his skill but because he had the ability to make every one of them feel that their personal satisfaction was the one aim of his life. Designing came easily to him, and he was always ready to spend additional time in producing a new design if he thought that he might satisfy his customers.

He would watch one of them studying his drawing, not looking at the sketch itself, but with his eyes on the face of his client. If she seemed doubtful, Henry never hesitated. He took up the sketch, gave it a momentary glance, then said, "But you don't like it, madam, and therefore if you will give me another day I shall have something new to show you. I believe that I know exactly what you will like. Please trust me." His charming smile and his air of personal interest never failed to delight his clients. It was inevitable that many idle, completely unoccupied women, with more money than they could spend, and with time hanging heavy on their over-manicured hands, should imagine themselves in love with this good-looking young man, who had such perfect manners.

There had been difficult times, when Henry had wished that he had chosen any other profession than that of a dress designer. The Honourable Irene Fortlock, a slight anaemic blonde, had contracted the habit of sighing deeply whenever she saw him. Presents had followed, impossibly expensive things which Henry always returned, stating that it was in his 'contract' that he must not accept presents from his clients. Mrs. Gregory Foster, a well-nourished brunette, whose hair owed more to art for its colour than to nature, invited him to bring his designs to her luxury flat in Park Lane. Henry had gone, and looked back on the incident as one of the most terrifying in his life. The strange thing was that in spite of the fact that Henry was unprepared to accept their obvious advances, they still patronized Levelle's, and still demanded Henry's designs.

Some of these women had become his good friends; there was Mrs. Gossage, a morose, gaunt woman, the despair of every dressmaker in London, who came to him. She was like a clothes-horse; it appeared that her body was composed entirely of bones which stuck out at—what seemed to be—the most unlikely angles. Henry was sent for, and found her striding up and down the luxurious waiting-room like a caged tiger.

She swung round on him, demanding, "Who the hell are you?"

"The designer, madam."

"Can you design anything to suit me? Every damned dress-maker's tried to dress me. I never look anything but a guy. Too many bones and apparently all in the wrong place. Have a look."

Henry looked; he was interested. She had height, she carried herself well. Her craggy face was attractively ugly. He took out his notebook. He asked questions as to what type of dresses she wanted. She answered bluntly, even roughly. He smiled. "If you could give me two days, madam, I shall have something to show you which I hope will please you."

"I don't want to look like a poppy-show, remember!"

"Nothing was further from my mind, madam."

Two days later he produced designs which pleased her. He explained that he relied on line, and wished to cut down elabora-tions as far as was possible. Mrs. Gossage nodded. "I'm too tall, too lanky for frills and fussiness. Keep them plain. Now, let's talk about materials."

He made a success of Mrs. Gossage, and when she went to the first night of the new film—*Giants in the Causeway*—her photo-graph appeared in all the 'snob press' weeklies. George Gossage was delighted, and sent Henry a cheque for twenty-five pounds, which Henry duly returned, stating that it had been a pleasure and an honour to design clothes for Mrs. Gossage.

Gossage said, "Sent back my cheque! Is that damned cheek or —what-cher call it?—proper pride?"

"Proper pride," she said. "He's a nice fellow, if those damned fools of women don't spoil him."

There was also Lady Callcott, widow of a theatrical knight. For years she had fought against 'looking her age'; her clothes were fantastic and not a dressmaker in London dared to remon-strate with her for dressing in the style of a woman of thirty.

She, too, came eventually to Levelle's, and Henry was sent to attend to her. She looked like an over-dressed witch, her face painted and raddled until it almost ceased to look human. Her hands were like claws, the nails varnished with a pillar-box scarlet.

She said, "Are you the young man who dresses Clementina Gossage?"

Henry smiled, that disarming smile, although his heart sank at the prospect of designing clothes for Lady Callcott. "I have that honour, madam."

"I want to see what you can do for me. I don't want to look a hundred, remember!"

He thought, 'You can't be much short of that age, my poor sweet'.

He rallied his forces. He was frightened, for he knew that she would prove a valuable client if she were satisfied. He came forward, and drew up a chair, saying, "Would you allow me to sit down?"

"Why not?"

He spoke conversationally. "I like to study my clients——"

She rapped out, "Ugh, you call them 'clients', not 'customers', eh?"

"I do, madam. I think it's a nicer word. I am going to be very frank. I know that I am risking your displeasure, but I can't help that. You're a very lovely woman, madam."

"*Was*," she corrected, "I'm a hag now, and I know it."

"Your dressmaker does you less than justice."

"He's Claude Mallet—dressed half of the Royal Family!"

Henry smiled. "Yes, the other half look so much more elegant, don't they?"

She chuckled, "I suppose that *you* dress the—other half?"

"Only a quarter of them, madam, but I have hopes—madam," he edged imperceptibly nearer. "I looked you up in the Theatrical *Year Book* when I heard that you were coming—oh, may I order tea for you? China or Indian? Yes, we make very good tea here!" He rang, ordered tea and returned to his chair. "You first played at the Adelphi in *Little Miss Curly Locks*—your first appearance in London. You had played in the provinces before then. *Age*, that is the accumulation of years, doesn't matter, but looks do, and the memories of people matter also. Let me dress you! Not with all those frills and feathers and dyed furs, but as you ought to dress—with loveliness and dignity. There, you have a perfect right to walk out, and ask Levelle's to give me the sack!"

Lady Callcott stared at him. "I shall do nothing of the kind. I want that tea you promised me, young man."

The tea was brought, she drank it very strong and half filled the cup with sugar. She sipped it, nodded, and said, "If your clothes are as good as your tea—they do very well. Now, let me know what ideas you have for me. No need to pull your punches, my rheumatism's not so bad to-day; if it had been I should have bitten your head off!"

Henry brought out his sketch-book, he showed her what he had in mind. She listened, nodded, and said, "Maybe you're right—yes, I believe that you are. I shall look like a ruin, but still——"

He said, "Madam, have you seen the Fountains Abbey? It's the most lovely thing you ever saw."

"Eh, a ruin?".

"I said that it was very lovely, madam."

"Have it your own way. Only if I don't like your clothes I shall go back to Mallet."

Two weeks later Lady Callcott emerged wearing one of the dresses which Henry had designed for her. Her hair was undyed. Henry had recommended a man he knew who had, as she said, 'dealt with it'. She looked her age, and yet miraculously seemed years younger.

She said to Henry, "They'll say that I've given up the fight, y'know."

"On the contrary, madam," he replied, "they'll say that you have won it!"

Again and again Henry dealt with clients who were known by the trade to be difficult. He never became subservient; he was always himself, charming, and essentially kind. He gave every woman a sense that she was the most important and interesting of all his clients. Levelle was delighted; Henry's salary was increased; he was even given a share in the business.

Levelle, an undersized Frenchman, whose knowledge of fabrics was untold, but whose knowledge of actual design was negligible, said, "I 'ave 'eard that you liff wit' Lady 'Elen Crr-rosse, eh?"

Henry raised his eyebrows and answered, "Really? How amusing!"

"Ees eet not tr-rue t'en?"

"I have no knowledge of it, sir. Why not ask Lady Helen?"

Levelle laughed. "You are just oyster! Forr myself, I 'ave lived wit' many vimmen. Why not? Don't 'arm no one! W'at do you say in Eenglish—mak' 'ay vhile the sun is shinin'."

Henry said gravely, "An excellent proverb, sir."

He had never felt attracted to any of the women who came to Levelle's. Possibly, he told himself, he saw too much of them and they held no mystery for him. He was a perfectly normal young man. When he was sent to Paris for the firm he had no scruples about enjoying himself, but he always returned to 'Killarney' conscious of a slight sense of relief. Commercial love-making was pretty hollow, and it was pleasant to return to Tilda's well-run house, and immerse himself in matters which held interest for him.

He was not an unfriendly young man, though he did not make friends easily. He had a certain retiring spirit, and his own work absorbed him. He was totally unable to understand the type of young man he met in connection with his work. To him they seemed affected and to affect characteristics which never rang quite true. He had no particular dislike for the men who were obviously attracted by their own sex, provided that they seemed 'real' about it all. But the posturing, mincing young men who, he felt certain, merely adopted that attitude as a pose, sickened him. More, they made him acutely uncomfortable.

On the morning when he set out for Edgware he experienced a slight feeling of excitement. The beauty of the girl Genevra had impressed him greatly. He kept thinking how lovely she would be in five or six years' time, when she had outgrown that slight 'legginess'. How delightful to dress her, to make her strikingly individual! Once or twice Henry smiled, thinking what a strange business it all was. Strange and tragic, even though there might be comedy interludes. This German lion-tamer! What were lion-tamers like in private life? he wondered. Men called 'Charlie, Messer and Atkins'—Genevra had said vaguely that they were 'with the horses'. His mind ran on wondering what life in a circus might be like. Genevra might speak with a broad Yorkshire accent, but her manners were good, and the tone of her voice, Henry remembered, delightful. She had poise, too, and during the time she had talked to him had never broken down, though once or twice her voice had faltered a little. He admired her control as much as he admired her potential good looks and her lithe slim body. With a growing feeling of excitement he reached Edgware, and demanded to know the location of Hugil's Monster Circus. As he drove towards the field where it was situated he smiled again, thinking, 'A new rôle for me—a squire of dames! Now for the German!'

CHAPTER NINE

As he got out of his car, Henry sniffed the air with appreciation. The smell took him back to those exciting moments of his childhood, when he had visited a circus, and smelt the scent of the beaten turf, the astringent odour of the stables, the slightly 'meaty' atmosphere which hung about the cages of the wild beasts. The old excitement caught and held him. Here he was, Henry Lorimer of Levelle's arriving to interview the man who trained—lions. Again he smiled. What a story to recount to the more friendly of his clients! How Mrs. Gossage would throw back her head and, showing a full set of most admirable false teeth, roar with laughter!

He stood staring at the circle of caravans, wondering what they were like inside, if it were really possible to live in them week in, week out in reasonable comfort. A smallish man with slightly bandy legs came towards him. Henry said, "Excuse me, I wish to see a certain Mr. Holst. Can you tell me where to find him?"

The little man ejected a straw which he was chewing, and asked, "What d'yer wanter see 'im for? Anythink ter do wi' young Genevra? I mite tell yer 'er pore mum's been buried this mornin'."

Henry returned smoothly, "Then in that case, if the funeral is over, I imagine that I can see Mr.—er—Holst."

Charlie pulled down the corners of his mouth. "I'll tell yer w'at, 'e's a barstard, narsty low-down animal! But thet's his caravan over there—that red-an'-gold 'un. Mind yer—watch 'im, 'e's a narsty customer."

"I believe that I have a personal message for you," Henry ventured; "are you Charlie, or Atkins or Messer? Oh, Charlie! Well, Genevra sends her love to you all. She has a great affection and respect for you all."

The little man grinned suddenly. "Thet's a grand little girl, thet one is. None o' us never took ter a kid like w'at we did to Genevra. Mind yer, 'er mum was a nice lidy, affable an' kind as could be. Pore soul."

Henry hesitated, then said, "And, Charlie, what about the baby? Genevra's worried in case Holst should keep it."

"The biby?" Charlie looked blankly at Henry for a moment, then said, "Oh, the biby. Well, thet pore lidy 'ad a miss. The biby never drew breath as you mite say. There isn't no biby. Tell Genevra as it parsed away immediate after its birth. Lucky fer it, too, pore little so-an'-so."

They parted, Charlie giving his last piece of information: If Henry had any bother with Holst, "Open the door, gie a whistle, an' me and Atkins and Messer 'ul be along. No need ter thank uz, it 'ud be a pleasure ter give 'im a damned pastin'. If so be as you don't require our assistance, then we'll be proud an' 'appy ter see you in the Crown about openin' time."

Henry made his way across the trodden-down turf, and mounting the steps of the red-and-gold caravan, knocked on the door. A voice bade him enter, and he found himself in a neatly and well-furnished room, where a tall man sat at a table, his face supported on his hands. A good-looking fellow, with shining yellow hair, and a fresh complexion.

Henry said, "Are you Mr. Holst?"

The man replied, "Baron von Holst, at your service."

Henry commented politely, "Really! How do you do, Herr Baron?"

"Why here have you come, please?"

"To discuss with you the matter of your step-daughter, Genevra Menetti."

The man rose, his fresh colour deepened, his hands were clenched. Henry thought that he had never seen eyes which were so completely cold and yet burning with anger.

"Of this child I have no wish to know. A wicked child, completely bad. Let her go where she wishes. Her poor mother is dead; she this morning early was buried. This child steals a valuable dog, and also a monkey of great intelligence. If I happened a revengeful man to be—I am not—I should send the police to find these two so-clever animals."

Henry with considerable elaboration lit a cigarette before he spoke. Holst watched him intently, his hands resting on the table, his body leaning forward. Henry blew out the match, said, "Is there an ashtray anywhere?", then placed his match with careful exactitude in the saucer which Holst pushed forward.

"The police can't do much about the monkey," he said, "it died yesterday. I didn't think that the dog was particularly intelligent. A nice pleasant little dog—nothing more. I believe that Genevra has a grandfather and grandmother living in Manchester. She had better go to them when her visit to my mother ends, don't you think so? Then—do you mind if I sit down? It is so tiring to stand, isn't it?—there is the question of money.

I knew Menetti's act very well—did I say that I was connected with the theatrical business? I don't think that I did. Menetti left a considerable amount of money, all to his widow. Has she—might I ask—left a will?"

Holst—his eyes seemed to protrude a little, and to be increasingly bloodshot—said, "Alles is left to me. I the will have."

"Then," Henry's tone was like honey, "you will have no objection to my seeing it, I am sure."

Holst's control appeared to give way; he shouted, "Tell me what has all this to do with you? Who are you, meddlesome fellow? Is it not sufficient that my wife this morning is buried, that I have two performances to-day, but you must come here to worry me? Answer me!"

Henry smiled, examined the end of his cigarette with care, then said, "My good Herr Baron, sit down. You make me feel exhausted when you raise your voice so! Menetti was a friend of mine, and asked me to be the executor of his will. I know what he left and to whom he left it. Either you show me your late wife's will or—and I should be so unwilling to do so—I must perforce, institute proceedings. I should dislike so much to be forced to take such a step. The little girl had always the address of my mother stitched into the lining of her dress. This is how she found us. My mother has always been devoted to her, and will leave no stone unturned to see that justice is done to the poor little thing. Now—" and his manner became more brisk— "that will, if you please, Herr Baron."

Holst's good-looking face looked suddenly sulky. "It with my lawyers is."

"The name of your lawyers?"

"I forget at this moment."

"A-ah! I have friends waiting for me outside, Herr Baron. I wonder if they could refresh your memory. Their names—or the names by which you know them—are Charlie, Atkins and Messer. Shall I call them?"

The effect upon Holst was electrical. The flush faded from his cheeks, he leaned heavily against the table, his fingers opening and closing.

Henry, delighted, said crisply, "Well, I am waiting!"

Holst licked his lips. "There is no will. I this caravan gave to my wife when we married. I claim that, it is for my living necessary. I shall give you her books of the bank in London. She took money from there. Now—please go! Here are the books! How like alles English you are—thinking of only money. Possessing no culture, no fineness. No understanding of gentlemen."

Smiling, Henry took the bank papers and cheque-book and placed them carefully in his pocket.

"You've done very well out of it," he said, "you've got the caravan. You're a comic race, aren't you? Baron von Holst—neither 'von' nor 'Baron' unless I am greatly mistaken. Behave yourself, don't imagine that this child—Genevra—is not well protected. My mother and I—as well as her grandfather and grandmother—also my mother's father and mother—the Earl and Countess of Westingham—are deeply interested in her welfare. One day she will be an exceedingly wealthy woman, this child, Genevra. May I wish you a very good day? I hope that one of your wretched lions eats you!"

As he left the caravan he was unable to repress a chuckle. He had never known that he possessed such imaginative powers. 'The Earl and Countess of Westingham'—it sounded like characters from a third-rate melodrama! Tilda's father had kept a greengrocer's shop in Pimlico, and her mother had been a mantle-maker in the City. He had only seen Menetti as a performer! But—he chuckled again—it had worked!

A voice behind him said, " 'Ow d'yer git on, guv'nor?"

It was Charlie. Henry grinned. "First rate, chum. Is it opening-time? Go and collect the others and let's go and celebrate."

In the bar of the Crown they duly celebrated. Henry recounted his interview with Holst, the three making varied comments and interruptions at intervals. "Luke at thet!" and "Did yew ever 'ear the like of it?" Charles gave it as his opinion that "It's what's called in bukes—the long h'arm o' conhincidence. Thet's wot it is, blimey!"

Atkins said, "To think as you knew 'er father! That's a thing, that is."

Henry wagged his head. "It all goes to show what a small world it is."

"You sed it, Guv'nor, you sed it. Small world."

They parted on the best of terms, promising to 'look each other up' whenever it was possible. Henry, pressed to go and take a look at the horses, went with them, and while his knowledge of horseflesh was strictly limited, he was so satisfied with his obviously active imagination that he passed several observations in which the words 'hocks', 'pasterns', 'well ribbed up' figured with great effect.

"Oberviously a judge o' 'orse-flesh," Charles stated.

Atkins returned, "Knew it immedjetly. Can't miss it."

Henry drove back to Barnet in a contented state of mind. To-morrow—no, to-morrow was Sunday—but on Monday he would interview the manager of the bank in which Jenny's money had been deposited, and get a true picture of the state of Genevra's position. Then it would be necessary to find the grandfather and grandmother in Manchester. They had a right to the child and, in all probability, Holst had not acquainted them with the fact that their daughter was dead. It wouldn't be easy to break the news, but he'd do it. He might even take Genevra to Manchester with him. Somehow the thought gave him great satisfaction.

Tilda met him. "You're all right, Henry darling?"

"Right as rain, Mother. It was like taking candy from a child."

"She," with a backward jerk of her head towards the house, "has been worrited all the time you've been away. Watching the clock, and asking how many miles it is to Edgware. Poor little soul. Eh, I wish we could keep her here. She's the best little thing, though sometimes the language she uses is shocking."

Henry said easily and confidently, "She'll get over that, it's mixing with grooms and so forth. I think I'd better take her with me to Manchester to-morrow to find her grandparents."

Tilda's face showed immediately dismay, "Oh, Henry, then we shall lose her!"

"Darling, she must go to her own family; we can't go about snaffling other people's children, however nice they are. Well," noticing her expression of disappointment, "I'll see what can be done by sending a telegram. She knows what her grandmother's *called*, but says that's not her real name. It's all very puzzling."

It gave Henry a sense of pleasure when Genevra greeted him, even lifting her face to be duly given a kiss. She did not immediately ask after his interview with Holst, but wished to have news of Charlie, Atkins and Messer.

Henry replied that he had 'found them charming fellows', adding that he hoped to meet them again.

"An' Miss Hambro?"

"I'm afraid I didn't see that lady. I saw—Herr Baron von Holst."

Genevra replied, " 'Baron' my foot! Messer says he's no more a baron nor what *he* is! Nasty bit of work. I hope one of his cats eats him!"

"I should like to associate myself with such a wish," Henry said.

Genevra giggled. "You do talk funny, Masterenery, don't you? Like what books do, eh? But," quickly, "it's nice. I think you're lovely, like a prince—like Mr. Novello's like a prince."

The name of the actor recalled the fact that several times Genevra had mentioned actors and music-hall stars; had spoken of them in an easy, familiar fashion, as if she actually knew them.

"How do you come to know so much about actors?" he asked.

"Me? Why, my gran'ma lets rooms to them. They're the best rooms in Manchester; you ask anyone. Ask Mr. Robey, or Mr. G. H. Elliott, or Wee Georgie Wood—they'll all tell you that Mrs. Hostley's is the best rooms in Manchester. My gran'-ma's mum was Mrs. Hostley, and it's always kept that name. See?"

"Nothing could be more clear."

Henry consulted his engagement-book, found that he could afford at least three days to devote to Genevra and her affairs; only one or two clients—whose needs were not pressing—must be asked to make other appointments. Tilda beamed when he told her, not only because it was the greatest joy of her life to have Henry at home, but also because she had become sincerely fond of the child who had arrived under such strange circumstances. During the day while Henry was at Edgware, Tilda Lorimer had watched Genevra closely. She had admired her self-control, a self-control which she realized was not the result of lack of feeling for her dead mother. Genevra had spoken of Jenny several times. Once she said—when her voice shook a little—"I want to talk about my mum, because it eases things here," and she laid her hand on her chest. "It's when I don't talk about her that I get a kinder pain, then it rises and gets into my throat and makes me cry. D'you see what I mean, Auntie Tilda?"

So Henry, in spite of his apparent inability to be practical about anything except dress-designing, interviewed poor Jenny's bank manager, and found that Genevra would benefit to the extent of two thousand pounds. It appeared that Jenny had deposited a will with the bank; more, that she had been astonishingly thrifty and had saved a good deal of the money which Holst had given her for housekeeping. Henry grinned contentedly when he heard that, thinking, 'The brute. I'm glad the little Yorkshire woman managed to extract some pennies out of him. I bet it was hard work!' He returned to Barnet satisfied that the child would not want for anything. When he told her she seemed completely unimpressed.

"It's quite a lot of money, Genevra."

"I'd rather have my dad and mum than all the money in the world. Oh, Masterenery," she hesitated, "what about mum's baby? I wanted to ask last night, but—somehow I didn't. You know how it is, don't you?"

Very gently he told her that the baby had died with its mother. She said, "Was it a boy or a girl?" and, slightly dismayed, he said that he believed that it had been a boy.

Genevra sat on a low chair, with Haig at her side watching her with intent and adoring eyes. She was leaning forward, her chin on her hand. It was not, Henry thought, the attitude of a child, but of a person of mature years. There was a stillness and quietness about her which he found soothing and arresting. Even her voice—with all its imperfections of accent, her various lapses into bad language—did not disturb him.

He thought, as he watched her, 'You're going to be all right, my dear. Another four years and you'll be a beauty. If they'll send you to a decent school, get that accent right, and eliminate your more "purple" expressions, you'll go a long way. I wonder which road you'll take? I wish that I could talk to you—as your mother might have done. You mustn't be allowed to make a mess of your life—to marry some worthy tradesman, or even one of your adored theatrical "princes", unless they can keep you properly. Keep you properly—bring you to Levelle's so that I can dress you!'

Genevra did not move, and he stretched out his hand and touched hers with his finger-tips. "I'm so sorry, Genevra."

She raised her eyes and met his. "Thank you, but I don't know as I'm all that sorry. I'm sorry for the baby, having to die when it hadn't, as you might say, had a start, but, after all, it was only half mum's. Atkins used to say 'It's true'—I can't really imitate the way he talks—'that you've got to have two to make a quarrel, same as you've got to have two to make a baby.' Well, s'ppose *his* half had been the strongest, an' the poor baby had grown up like that bastard—that would only have meant more bother for everyone. Even the baby—with something of mum's loveliness in him—wouldn't have liked it, because mum's part and that stinker's would have been—kind of—at war inside it all the time. No, I expect it's better as it is. Still, thank you very much for everything you've done. One day, maybe, I'll be able to pay you back. Oh, not in money, you've got plenty of that, but some other way."

The following day Henry did not need to take Genevra to Manchester, for a tremendously long telegram came, in reply to his, from Josh Mander, announcing that they were both coming to Barnet. Henry showed it to Tilda, with the comment that the reputed extravagance of the theatrical and music-hall professions must have tinged the spirit of Josh Mander. "Did you ever read such a telegram in your life?" he asked. "No words missing—it's written like a letter."

Tilda said, "Very proper, too, Henry. How'd you write if you'd heard that your only daughter was dead, and you not there to take a last look at her? Henry, I don't want you to grow *critical* about people; live and let live, dear. You can't measure everything and everybody by a foot-rule you've made yourself, to your own fancy. It may suit you, but other people use—other foot-rules."

"I accept the rebuke; thank you, Mother."

Josh and Lottie arrived at 'Killarney'. All the morning Genevra had watched luncheon being prepared by the admirable Alice. Henry had brought Genevra a new frock when he went to London, a frock which gave her great satisfaction. It was very simple, in a soft dark blue material, with beautifully fine white cuffs and collar. He made her turn round and round when she first came down to the drawing-room wearing it, his face very serious. He seemed to be someone quite different, she thought, when he was looking at the dress.

"Turn round—now sit down! Yes, it's all right, and you look charming in it, quite charming. Always insist upon being dressed *plainly*, Genevra. Don't let people imagine that you want decorations, frills and so on. You're sufficient decoration in yourself."

To her own surprise she felt her face flush, "Oh, do you think so? Do you think as I'll be nice-looking when I'm grown up? My mum was lovely, an' my dad—oh, he was handsome. I've got photos of them in my *attachey*-case. That was all I bothered to bring, barring food for the poor Monk and my Haig."

As she sat in the kitchen, delighted to be given small things to do—beating eggs, whipping cream—for both Alice and Tilda liked and fully appreciated good food, though Alice told Genevra that "Masterenery never seems to know what 'e's eating. The Missus an' me gets prop'ly disheartened sometimes. There's a lovely dish I make—got it out of a book written by a French gentleman. Veal with a cream sauce. D'you think as Masterenery ever notices it? Times w'en I've given him something that, as you might say, took no cooking at all, he'll say, 'Alice, that was astonishingly good'. He's more concerned with flowers on the table, lace mats an' the like, is Masterenery."

Henry had told Genevra that her grandparents were coming, and—because he believed that the child had common sense—explained to her that he and Tilda would like to speak to them alone first. Genevra had nodded, and said that she understood.

"It 'ul be better," she agreed, "then you can tell them about mum, an' the baby and poor Monk. I'll only cry if I'm there an' that 'ul upset gran'ma and gram'pa. I'll just wait while you send for me, Masterenery."

Josh Mander descended from the car heavily. He was wearing a very dark grey suit, which Henry thought looked as if it had been made out of felt. His heavy face, with the large moustache, now heavily streaked with grey, seemed to have been drained of most of its colour, his whole skin appeared to be too big for him, as the skins of old dogs often look. His wife was dressed in mourning; the materials were admirable; everything was admirable, Henry decided, except the cut of the clothes.

'She's a handsome woman', he thought, 'but what a crime to "bunch" her up like that, making her stick out where she ought to stick in! Some of these provincial dressmakers have a lot to answer for!'

Lottie advanced, and held out a tightly-suède-gloved hand to Tilda, saying in a carefully controlled voice, "I shall never be able to thank you enoof."

Josh, removing his hard bowler hat, also offered his hand, and said, "Me and my wife's more than grateful to you. It's been a blow—say what you like—a blow."

In silence they entered the pretty room, with its bright chintz, its really excellent furniture, took stock of the elegant young man who accompanied them. In spite of all her grief—and it was real and profound—Lottie felt a sense of satisfaction that if her granddaughter had run away and managed to pick up people who had been good to her, she had chosen people who were obviously—something.

Tilda Lorimer saw them both seated, then said, "Henry dear, the sherry and biscuits." Somehow the fact that Mrs. Mander 'let to pros' made her feel easier in her mind. After all, they were connected with the same profession, they probably knew the same people. She wondered if she could not detect the smell of the greasepaint! Lottie was calm, and Josh seemed to be carved out of wood; it did not appear to be likely that either of them would indulge easily in emotion.

Tilda said, "It's all very sad, and my son, Henry, who went to visit this man—Holster——"

Henry, engaged in pouring out sherry, said, "Holst, Mother dear, Holst."

"Very well, then—Holst—will tell you all about it. The first thing that happened was this dear child arriving at my front door with a little dog and a dead monkey." With endless elaborations she told the story; even the funeral of the poor Monk was dealt with in detail and with deep emotion. She had not lost her histrionic ability and, although perfectly sincere, enjoyed the recital.

Mrs. Mander listened, nodding her head from time to time, and at intervals ejaculated, "Luke at that!" or "Nay, that's a reit do, isn't it?" Josh said nothing, but stolidly sipped his sherry at intervals, only once nodding towards Tilda and murmuring, "Another kind love, I'm sure."

Carefully and with restraint, Henry told of his interview with Holst, and with the bank manager. Tilda, as he spoke, felt that this was actually the funeral service of poor Jenny Menetti. Here were her mother and father, the father apparently unmoved, but Henry—sensitive to such things—realized that the stolid man was suffering. His wife from time to time dabbed her eyes fiercely with a small handkerchief, muttering, "Oh dear, oh dear, and to think that I actually liked the brute—nay, it's a strange world."

He was asked questions, he promised to take them in the morning—"for, of course, you will stay here for the night"—to visit the grave of their daughter, adding quickly, "At the risk of seeming impertinent, might I beg that you will not take Genevra? She is highly strung, she has been through a great deal during the past few days. Far better—if I may suggest—that she thinks of her mother as she knew her when she was alive. . . ."

Josh said heavily, "Why, I don't know. It's not altogether nachurel for a child—speshully a girl—not to visit her mother's tomb."

Lottie answered very quickly and briskly, "Josh, this gentleman's quite right. There's no call for Genevra to go to some nasty graveyard. Let her think of our Jenny same as what I always shall: bright, laughing, looking reit bonnie. Mr. Lorimer, I'm on your side. Leave the child at home!"

After that things seemed easier; both Josh and Lottie accepted a second glass of Henry's admirable sherry; Tilda began to ask questions regarding the various theatricals who had stayed in Stratton Street, and was delighted to find that she knew the names of so many, even having a personal acquaintance with a few of Mrs. Mander's 'regulars'.

Tilda, smiling and delighted, said, "Now what about seeing that dear child. I promise you, Mrs. Mander, except for my Henry's scruples, I'd have loved to have kept her. That's a lovely child——"

Henry interposed, "Mr. Mander, you will forgive me, sir. That child must go to a first-class school. She has everything! In another few years she will be a raging beauty. She's clever, she's kind, and she has poise. I beg you give her every chance. She's worth it."

Lottie Mander looked at him intently, "D'you reelly b'lieve that? I've always known as the child was clever, and pretty——"

Henry interpolated almost fiercely, "Pretty! She's going to be lovely! And," with due weight, "good."

Mrs. Mander continued, "Thank God we've done well. There's nothing—within reason—we can't give to her—and with God's help— we *shall give* her. Josh will go into this matter of the money her poor father left—oh, Mrs. Lorimer, what a dear feller he was! My Jenny was the light of his eyes—eh, Josh?"

Josh repeated, "The light of his eyes—no more an' no less."

Genevra was sent for, she came into the room, her eyes bright, her hands outstretched. Henry thought, 'See how Beatrice lightly like a lapwing comes', then wondered if he'd got the quotation right and tried it in several other ways, and each one seemed wrong. Meanwhile Genevra was embraced by her grandparents, Mrs. Mander dabbing her eyes fiercely again and again, while Josh ejaculated at intervals, "How's that grand dog of yours, Genevra? What's his name—Haig? I'll like to see him again," or "Well, that's a lovely dress you're wearing. I doubt if I've ever seen you look nicer."

Genevra regarded them both with affectionate gravity. She smiled at them impartially, gave them information regarding Haig and told them that 'Masterenery' had bought the dress for her. Josh beamed and enquired of Henry in a hoarse whisper, "You don't think black more—well, proper?" To which Henry replied rather irritably, "For Heaven's sake, no!" Josh subsided, muttering, "All right, I just asked. No harm in asking."

Luncheon was elaborate and rich; after it both Mr. and Mrs. Mander retired to rest. Lottie said, "Nay, I doubt if I ever ate such food i' my life. I've been to the Midland scores of times— yes, i' the French restaurant, where the food's good, mark you, but never like this. I shall never be able to thank you for your goodness to this poor child, never—not was it ever so."

Henry was conscious that he was tired. The last two days had exhausted him and he had never possessed much reserve of energy. He always said that he 'used it up as he went along'. He lay back in one of the big chairs in the drawing-room and closed his eyes. When he opened them, feeling refreshed and restored, he found Genevra sitting near him. Her eyes were watching him.

He said, "Hello, Genevra."

She answered, "Hello, Masterenery. I'm going away to-morrer. What do you want me to do?"

For a moment he resented her question. What did it matter to him what this pretty child—this nice child—did with her life? It was unlikely that her path would ever cross his again; he wasn't sure that he wished it to. She was a disturbing influence, and Henry had grown to dislike being disturbed. He blinked his eyes, and replied, lazily, "Well, be a good girl, Genevra."

He watched her eyes widen, brighten, and then turn suddenly cold. She demanded, "That's all you care! I thought that you were a prince! I thought you'd be wise an' tell me things. My life's in front of me. M' gran'ma's lovely, so's my gram'pa, but they don't *know* things like what you do. I don't want to just take over Mrs. Hostley's, I want to do something for myself. Same as what my dad did, an' my mum while she broke her ankle—and all you can say is 'Be a good girl'. What's being good, any road?"

Henry sat up suddenly; he was unaccustomed to small fire-brands like this child. He blinked his eyes, and stammered, "But —Genevra—I've only known you for—what?—three days. . . ."

She stormed at him in her thin childish voice, "Three days . . . three days, or three years? I b'lieve you can know someone i' three hours better'n you can know other folks i' three years. I know you, Masterenery. I've lost my way without my mum. What is it what sailors use to show them the road on the sea— I know, because Atkins told me, an' he'd been a sailor—a chart! Can't you give me a chart? I want to find my way about. Can't you do somethink?"

Henry stared at her, then licked his lips, which were suddenly dry, and said, "This isn't me, Genevra. This is probably the wisest man who ever lived. He understood the heart, he under-stood—I think—everything. He wrote plays, and generally this part is played by rather silly old men. It's a great part, just the same. This man—but they're the words of the man who wrote the play, of course—said: 'To thine own self be true, and it must follow—as the night the day—thou can'st not then be false to any man.' Does that mean anything to you? Be yourself, Genevra. See that people don't change you, don't make you mean or furtive or—or unworthy. There, darling, is that any help?"

She nodded, so that her fair hair swung backwards and forwards. Her eyes were grave, her lips curved into a little smile.

"That's grand," she said, "my mum would have liked that, Masterenery. I will be true to—what was it?—my own self. D'you know what I want to be? An actress! I will, too. My gran'ma was an actress, my mum was a dancer, my dad was an acrobat—the best ever. I want to be in the theatre, an' I'll be in it or die. One day, Masterenery, I'll say words like that—from the stage—I will! D'you b'lieve me?"

He sat staring at her, half hypnotized, then he, too, nodded, and said, "Yes, I think that I'd believe anything you said, Genevra. God, darling, I wish that I were younger—or you were older. No, not that. I wouldn't rob you of a day of your youth. Only—only——"

Instantly she became almost maternal, she leaned forward and touched his hand very gently. "Nay, don't fash yourself, my dear. I said that you were a prince, an' you are. I've got a long road to go—maybe I'll meet a lot of strange folk along the road. I have already, if it comes to that. But—but——"

He said, "Journeys end in lovers meeting, is that what you're trying to say?" then sprang to his feet and cried, "Genevra, this is all wrong, for me to talk to a child—as you are—in this way. Listen," he caught her hands and held them, "forget what I've said. I've been half asleep, been overcome by too good a luncheon —whatever you like. I'm going up to town, yes—now. I'll get my mother to make my excuses. Now, listen to me. Learn and learn! Get a good accent. It's charming now but it—won't do. Stop swearing. Never mind how good Charlie and Atkins and Messer are, their speech won't fit into ordinary conversation. Good chaps, but they don't talk in the way you must. You won't *stride* ahead, striding only tires you. Forge ahead, Genevra. See your goal and make for it. Get there. If I don't meet you again——"

She said, "Auntie Tilda's asked me to come and stay here for my holidays. . . ."

Brusquely he answered, "I might be away. I generally go abroad."

Then he added quickly, "If I don't see you again, until you're a star—or broken by the stage—but you won't be, you can't be

126

—then we'll smile. Goodbye, darling—oh, you're going to be so lovely. Goodbye."

She smiled at him calmly, "My dad used to say *arivederci*, and I think that's nicer. I shall—this is another word of my dad's— go *diritto. Arivederci*, Masterenery."

He stared down at her, half-ashamed, bemused, and uncertain of himself. He recalled the women who came as his clients, and compared them unfavourably with this child. He felt some reassurance in the word 'child', and said aloud, "Oh, you *nice* child." She tilted her face upwards towards his, and Henry bent and kissed her, saying as he did so, "What was it your father said? *Arivederci*."

He walked quickly out of the room, and Genevra heard him running upstairs. She sat down and fondled the soft, smooth head of Haig. She did not move, and some moments later she heard the sound of the car coming out of the garage and driving away.

BOOK TWO

CHAPTER TEN

SHE did not see Henry again, and when Tilda announced at supper—a cold meal at which Alice served one of her 'speshul' salads, which Lottie pronounced as being 'something quite out of the ordinary'—that Henry had remembered an appointment for an early hour the following morning, and had regretfully returned to London, Genevra thought, 'That's just another bit of heartache—not the same as losing mum, or even the Monk, but there were so many things I wanted him to tell me. He *could* have; the others would if they could but they just can't'.

They left the next morning for Manchester. Tilda wept openly at parting with Genevra, excusing herself by saying again and again, "It's silly, but I'd not have believed that I'd have got so fond of any child in a few days. Remember, ducky, that if your grandpa and grandma will let you, you can always come here for a nice holiday. Henry would be as pleased as Alice or me."

Genevra replied gravely, "Thank you, Auntie Tilda. It's very kind of you." As they drove through England on their way to Manchester she was very quiet, only answering when asked some question. Lottie thought, 'Poor little soul, it's upset her—all this —mor'n she'll admit. Say what you like, it's all been a shock.'

Josh watched his grand-daughter, his heavy face serious and intent. He wondered what she would do with her life. Josh was a great believer in people knowing 'what they wanted to do with their lives'. She was startlingly pretty, he decided, prettier than poor Jenny had been at that age. To be very attractive, to Josh, meant 'temptations and lions in the path'. Genevra would be a responsibility. One which he and Lottie would accept gladly, but a responsibility all the same.

When they stopped for luncheon at an old inn he watched Genevra noting everything, listened to her when the waiter said, "Can't take a dog in the dining-room; against the rules of the hotel." Genevra stared at him, not in surprise but with a kind of cool contempt.

Lottie expostulated, "Now, I'm sure he'll do no harm, he's the best little dog in the world. Just make an exception"—she smiled, and most people melted before Lottie's wide, warm smile—"and I'll make it all right—for everybody."

"Sorry, madam."

Genevra spoke calmly, her childish voice sounding thin but not shrill. "Where will he have his dinner—my dog?" she demanded.

"Why, in the kitchen, or the garden—I don't rightly know."

Genevra turned to Lottie. "May I have my dinner—and Haig's —served in the garden, please?" Then turning back to the waiter, "And I s'ppose you charge for the dog's dinner?"

"Generally eighteen pence——"

"Then," very briskly, "see that it's not scraps, or a lot of kag-mag off of other people's plates—or I'll send it back. C'on, Haig."

Lottie would have expostulated, but Josh said, "Nay, let her go, she'll be all right, will that one." He chuckled. "I'll bet Haig gets a reit dinner! Lottie, we've got to put on our thinkin'-caps regardin' young Genevra. She's got something in her as is— *onusual*, distinctly onusual. There must be no lapping her talents oop i' napkins and suchlike."

Lottie, drinking some thin soup in which small pieces of carrot and tinned beans cut into tiny dice floated, said, "This is what they call Julienne in half the hotels i' England. I know what I call it! I mind Mr. Graves—or was it Mr. Wilkie Bard?—saying to me that England had the best food an' the worst cooks i' the world. You were talking about Genevra; well, she'll have Hostley's one day. That's a good enough living for anyone; it's done uz very well, Josh."

He leaned forward and patted her plump, well-kept hand.

"She may not want to take over Hostley's, my luv. There's a French sayin'—though as you know I'm no French scholar, but I learned it when we had a French act on the bill. Nice feller he was, and spoke a bit of English. It's this—*outrer pays outrer moors*. That means—other countries, other ways of doin' things. Well, what suited uz might not suit our Genevra. We got to keep an open mind, my dear—that's it, an open mind."

Genevra met them in the entrance-hall. She announced that Haig had done very well 'on the whole', but added that she considered it a small portion for one and sixpence.

Again Josh chuckled. "Nay, luv, you're set on letting 'em all know as you coom from Yorkshire, even if you do live i' Lancashire. Value for money, eh?"

"Why not, Gram'pa?"

The following evening Josh, who had been 'setting stages' most of his life and still had a passion for 'setting' them for every possible occasion, said, "Now, Lottie my dear, you sit there; Genevra luv, come an' sit near me. First just get me a nice bottle of Worthington. That's the idea. Now we're all cosy an' set, I'd like to have a little—conference. It's about you, Genevra luvey. What," he spoke with weight, "do—you wish—to do with your —life?"

Genevra smiled at him; there was something so comfortably kind about her grandfather. And with all his kindness, a certain childish love of 'making an act' out of anything. She thought, 'If he could he'd have liked the fire lit, and a red lime thrown on us to make it all look like what he thinks should be "home, sweet home".' She said, "Do with my life, Gram'pa—well," her smile widened, "I'd like to enjoy it!"

He responded warmly. "A good answer—a damned good answer, my pet. But—" and he returned to his slightly weighty manner—" 'ow do you propose to set about enjoying it? That's the point, isn't it?"

"First of all I'd like you and gran'ma to send me to a school where I can learn to talk prop'ly——"

"Talk prop'ly!" Lottie exclaimed. "But you do talk luvely. I mind when you were here with your poor mum, that luvely lady—Miss Ellaline Terriss said to me, 'What a dear little voice your grand-daughter has!'"

Genevra nodded. "It's not my voice, it's the things I say with it—that's what's wrong. I want to learn to say po'try, and then when I've learnt enough—" she drew a long, deep breath—"I want to do what you did, Gran'ma. I want to go on the stage!"

"Now," Josh cried, "we're gettin' to the milk i' the coconut!"

Lottie said, "What—musical comedy or music-hall?"

"Neither. I want to act like Julia Neilson, an' Doris Keane, an' Marie Lohr. I want to make people cry—and laugh and *feel* the things I want them to feel. Oh, Gran'ma, Gram'pa—I've set my heart on it! Let me have a try any road."

Her big handsome grandmother nodded. "Well, it's history repeating itself. I said just the same to my dear mum and dad. After all, Josh, you might have taken up something different to stage managing, mightn't you? Maybe it's in her blood, as the saying goes. My mum and dad gave me every opportunity. I don't see why Genevra shouldn't have a chance—only mind, luv, we're having no duds in the fam'ly. Your mum—God bless her —was a luvely artiste; so was your poor dad—one of the best, a tip-topper. I wasn't so bad, was I, Josh?"

"Oh, wunderful—absolutely wunderful. Only remember, Genevra, it's a job beset with temptations, pitfalls, and there are —lions in the path."

So a highly respectable school for young ladies was found to which Genevra went every day, and where—however much she might hate it all—she worked without ceasing to learn to 'speak properly'. She was given 'elocution lessons' by a thin, rather dried-up little woman, who was inclined to mince her words, and who tried to teach Genevra to say 'barth' instead of 'bath', and 'grass' introducing several r's into the word. Genevra, acutely uncomfortable, grew scarlet about the ears, and protested, "Nay, I'll never get my tongue round saying 'May I hev a glarse of water before Aye go to my barth.' It sounds daft to me!"

"But," the small woman persisted, "thet is the correct way tew speak."

"Of course, if you say so, Miss Williamson, I'll do my best."

Genevra learned to say a poem which made her feel acutely miserable, which she spoke with great effect, being allowed to linger over the sentimental passages, and make sudden and inexplicable changes of tempo. "This is tew indicate the galloping of the horse, yew see," Miss Williamson assured her. Genevra learnt the poem, and although its actual meaning was always a little obscure, she felt sorry for 'poor Loraine Loree' and most sorry of all for the baby, who was the only person who cared when Loraine Loree was killed. She learnt about the 'Revenge' and loved to bawl the line, "Are you man or are you devil?" at the top of her voice. As a great step forward she was allowed to speak—or rather whine—Prince Arthur's speech to Hubert, when Miss Williamson cried, "Splendid! Now try to make your voice shake a little at the words—'*must* you put out mine eyes?' It gives an enhanced sense of what is known as pathos."

Accordingly Genevra learnt to bleat like a sheep caught in a thicket, and felt it to be very effective. She enjoyed learning, she found that she could absorb poetry as a sponge absorbs water. If she read anything through twice she found that she had a very fair idea of the words, then she began to work on the details—choosing with particular care the bits which were highly sentimental or dramatic.

At home she used to recite to Lottie, while Josh smoked placidly, and made no comment. Lottie was always ready to say delightedly, "Luvely, dear. Made me cry, it did really. That pore little Prince and that horrible man! I'm glad that we don't live in those times!"

At last, tired of her grandfather's silence, Genevra asked, "Gram'pa, is it good? Tell me—truly. Don't try to kid me."

Josh removed his pipe from his lips, and sat silent for a moment. Then he spoke—slowly, as if he weighed each word.

"I think that you're talking nicer, Genevra. An' you don't swear any more. I fancy—mind you, I may be wrong—that you don't speak quite natural, but that's not for me to say. As for the po'try, you say it very nicely, but—it's *ham*, my ducky. No, don't be disappointed. Bawling and shouting, making your voice tremble, may catch—some of 'em. Now listen—once I heard Sir Henry Irving in a play called *Becket*. A priest who was murdered in Canterbury cathedral. I ferget for why exactly, some row with the king.

"Now this Sir Henry had a bit to speak about a moor-hen—that's a kinder bird that lives in wild places—he found frozen on her nest. So far as mem'ry serves me, he said that she was dead but that her eggs were warm. That doesn't sound much for anyone to tell an audience, but he didn't make his voice shake, he didn't shout, it was the quietness of it all that *hit* you! And—" he leaned forward and drubbed with his forefinger on Genevra's knee—"and it fairly broke your heart. Now, I b'lieve as we're on the wrong track. You're learning po'try, but are you learning it the right road? I don't b'lieve that you are. Next week there's a gentleman called Sir Frank Benson coming with his company, playing Shakespeare. I wish you to go every single night, an' to three matinées. Then, when the Saturday show's over, cum an' talk to me and gran'ma. I'll lay as you'll have something to say. 'Oo," he demanded, "cares a damn about this lady wi' a baby at her knee? 'Oo'd call a horse 'Vindictive'—enough to put every punter on the course off of it! Bleating about having his eyes put out. Oh, I know it's Shakespeare, but it's all said the wrong road.

"No, Genevra, I've heard 'em all one time and anuther. I've heard Sir Henry, I've heard his son—H.B.—I've listened to Madam Sarah Bernhardt an' Mrs. Patrick Campbell—both talking French, but you knew every word they said. I've listened to Seemer 'Icks—playing comedy, admitted, but it was *acting*. No, you've 'got it', that I b'lieve, but we've got to find someone who'll train you. Otherwise, in anuther couple of years you'll be a great success at smoking concerts, p'lice benefits, and the like. That won't do. First, you've got to go to a *class* school, where, if they have a mistress to teach this elocution, she's someone who knows what she's talking about. What d'you say?"

Lottie said, "Go on, Josh, I think you're hard on the pore little soul. I'm sure that piece about the baby always makes me cry!"

Genevra, her hands clenched, cried passionately, "Gram'pa, you're right! It's all too easy. I want other things, too—I want to learn French, I want to know what literachure is. I'd like to learn to fence, and half a dozen other things!"

So Genevra was allowed to continue at the school for young ladies, and to learn a great deal more poetry, which she delivered very badly, and as gram'pa said again and again, 'It's just *ham*, an' you say it in a hammy way'. Genevra went to the Shakespeare plays for a whole week, and came home feeling that she had lived in another world. When Lottie said, conversationally, "Where'd you like to go for your holiday, Genevra?" the answer came promptly:

"Stratford, please, Gran'ma."

Josh gave her a complete set of Shakespeare's works, and she devoured them avidly. Lovely words, exquisite phrases, wonderful imagery ran through her brain. In her own room she sat down to learn some of the passages which gave her such delight. She read them, trying to remember the phrasing and intonations of the actors and actresses she had heard; only when she left the book and tried to speak the lines did despair overtake her.

It wasn't the same; nothing she could do made it sound the same. They had given the words life, had even brought added beauty to words already beautiful. When she spoke them they sounded cheap, over-coloured, false.

Meanwhile Josh was at work. He wrote for information, he asked questions of people he knew who had daughters—daughters who were receiving the best educations money could buy them. One great music-hall artiste said, "My girls—two of them—go to Deepdene. It's expensive, but I believe that it's worth it. They have a woman who comes down every week—Doggerty. She's famous. If you can afford it, Mander, let your grand-daughter have special lessons with her. Don't have her *taught* to speak nicely, she'll *absorb* it all. The child's no fool."

So Lottie flung herself into an orgy of buying clothes, new trunks, and everything necessary. When Genevra protested, she replied, "I'm not having you go among a lot of swell girls and pulling a pore mouth. You'll go looking as good as the best, and —I hope—a bit better than most."

Curiously enough, Genevra liked her new school. She had a quick ear, and rapidly began to speak the same type of English is the other girls. She never found it easy to use anything except the broad 'a' of the West Riding, but otherwise her pronunciation was natural and correct. To her the highlight of the week was the visit of the lady who came from London.

She was elderly, not particularly nice-looking, but she was dynamic. To Genevra, when she read a passage of Shakespeare, of Keats, Shelley, or even Wordsworth—whom Genevra never liked and never learned to like—she seemed to be a new person. She was gay yet astute as Portia, she was swaggering but full of charm as Viola, as Queen Eleanor she was a heartbroken, apprehensive woman. When she spoke Ophelia's lines her years dropped away, she was a strange, puzzled creature, loving love and yet fearing it. Genevra's own private lessons were a delight tempered with a sense of her own ignorance and inability.

She worked—how she worked! She asked to be excused games in order that she might give the time to her study of the various lines which her teacher set her. She felt that she could never attain to greater heights than when the plain, elderly lady, listening intently, said, "Very well done, Genevra, we shall make something of you! I am very much pleased with you."

For nearly three years she was at Deepdene, and at eighteen returned to Manchester. She had grown tall, was still very thin, with fine wrists and ankles, and a complexion which could scarcely have been more perfect. Her voice had deepened a little, but not so much that Haig—growing old and inclined to be lazy, and to dislike being taken out for walks on wet days—did not recognize it immediately and rush forward to show that his love and devotion had not decreased since she was home last.

She discussed the matter of her future with Josh and Lottie. Josh grinned, twirling his moustache, now quite grey, all the mahogany having been removed by time. "Now what about giving uz a taste of—what was it?—about that lady with a baby? The one that rode a horse?"

Genevra laughed. "Gram'pa, that's mean! I'll recite to you some other time. Now I want to talk about—*me*."

He returned, "Show me the woman as didn't, and I'll show you a miracle."

She said, "I've learned to walk, to speak, to use my voice, to study lines quickly. Lots of other things, too. Now I want to have a chance to put them into practice. There are companies called repertory companies. It's hard work and the pay isn't much, but you're learning all the time—if you want to. I don't want to stay there too long. Then I want to go to a theatre in London, called —the Old Vic. I don't care what I play—I'll carry on tea-trays, or announce carriage, or hand hats and coats."

Lottie exclaimed, "London! My luv, you can't live in London by yourself!"

"Lots of girls do, Gran'ma. They don't seem to come to any great harm."

"Well, I don't know, I'm sure. It 'ul need a lot of thinking about."

"The great thing," Josh announced, assuming his weighty voice, "is that Genevra has a plan. Always work to a plan. Know where you want to go—and go there!"

It seemed astonishing to Lottie that Genevra, whom she had regarded as being only a child, should evince such energy and strength of purpose. Josh wagged his head and announced, "Our Genevra's all right. She's got a head-piece, that's what she's got."

She wrote to various repertory companies, and was finally asked if she would go to Cothampton for an interview. Lottie wished to go with her, but Josh objected. "Let her go by herself, it will learn her to stand on her own feet."

Accordingly, Genevra presented herself at the old Theatre Royal at Cothampton, and was told to wait in the auditorium. There she watched, for a considerable time, a young man with untidy yellow hair and equally untidy clothes taking a rehearsal. From time to time he waved his arms and cried in tones which were almost piteous, "Dar-ling, no! You're angry with him, you're not asking him to have a chocolate!" or "My ang-el, you're in love with this fellow—don't keep it a dead secret, that's not the author's idea at all!" At last he flung his hands high above his head, and said:

"All right—which is exactly what it isn't, but—break for an

hour." Everyone scurried away, and he turned and stared into the auditorium where Genevra sat. Then, ejaculating, "Ah, there you are!" he came through the pass door and over to her.

"You're Miss Menetti? Are you English?"

"My father was Italian, my mother was English."

He nodded, a lock of yellow hair fell over his forehead, he pushed it back irritably. Genevra said, "Why don't you have it cut if it worries you?"

"I've not *time* to get my hair cut! What did you think of the rehearsal?"

She asked, "What's the play? It's not *Yellow Sands*, is it?"

"It is!" He appeared to be delighted that she had recognized it. "Yes, it's good old *Yellow Sands!*"

"It may be good," she agreed, "it's certainly old. I don't think that they're getting the accent quite right, do you?"

"Not quite right." Then suddenly, "Can you speak dialects, Miss Menetti?"

"I studied them. Scottish—not too bad, more Glasgow than Edinburgh, I'm afraid. Cockney—I learnt that from Charlie, a groom in a circus. Yorkshire and Lancashire, and broken French and Italian."

He stared at her, then said suddenly, "Would you like to play in *Romance*? The Doris Keane part?"

"You've not engaged me yet!" she laughed. "Anyway, it's old, that play! Don't you do new plays? Or Shakespeare?"

He waved his hand towards the entrance of the theatre. "Let's go and have some luncheon. It won't be very good, first because there isn't anywhere very good in this town, and secondly—I've not got a lot of money."

"I'll toss you who pays for the luncheon," she said. "Yes, whether you engage me or not."

He stared at her. What a strange girl she was. Not in the least nervous, and this, he knew, would be her first engagement. Of course he was going to engage her. He liked her voice, her slight air of assurance, which yet was not conceit. Her looks, too—were rather staggering. That hair, which his stage experience had taught him was 'the real thing and not out of a bottle'. Her bright blue eyes, with dark lashes. He could think of a dozen parts she could play—always supposing she could act at all."

Gravely they spun a penny, and Genevra said calmly, "I pay. Come along and let's talk business. First of all—you are Filmer Turner? I thought that you must be. Now, where do we have this luncheon?"

"I think at the Crown. That's the best place. Not only because you're paying for it, but because it's good for me to be seen there —with my new leading lady. I can't afford to pay much, you know. Not even to anyone who is going to play leads."

"I don't think," she objected, as they entered the gloomy entrance-hall of the Crown, where the smell of yares of roast beef and cabbage seemed to permeate everything, "that I've any right to play leads. Only if you were stuck and I was the only possible person to play. I can promise to 'dress well on and off' because I have a very generous grandmother. I can study quickly; I enjoy work. But I've no experience. I've studied with Miss Doggerty; she thought that I was quite reasonably good. She advised me to go into rep to learn."

Turner nodded gloomily. "The only profession where you are paid to learn your job. Strange, isn't it? When could you join us—three weeks' time? I'll find some new plays by that time. I'd like to try Pirandello's *Six Characters*. Do you know it?"

Genevra shook her head. "No, but I shall in three weeks' time."

"Salary?"

She laughed. Turner decided that she had a good laugh— neither a giggle nor a roar. "I've honestly not the slightest idea."

"We can't afford more than six."

"I'll take it. Where do I live? I don't know anything about this town."

"I'll find out and write to you. You might share with Miss Mercia Carrington—she's awfully nice—good company, too."

"I can't share a bedroom with anyone. You see," confidentially, "I've got a dog called Haig, and he must come with me. He sleeps in my room, and, anyway, I must have a room to myself."

"Could he play in *Peg o' my Heart*?"

"He *could*, but he won't. I don't approve of animals on the stage. I've lived in a circus, you see."

He didn't see, but he felt that this girl was a find. If only she had as many easy and natural inflections in her voice on the stage as she had in ordinary conversation, she'd be wonderful. When she said that the dog 'could' but 'won't', Turner had detected a certain curious grim tone in her voice. Her whole expression had changed, her lips narrowed, her eyes looked suddenly cold.

They ate indifferent beef, cabbage which appeared to have been swimming in green water and dried itself insufficiently, and potatoes which were a dreary and unpleasing shade of grey. Turner drank beer, Genevra drank nothing, not even the coffee which she ordered and left untasted.

Turner went back to his rehearsal, Genevra caught the afternoon train back to Manchester. She felt excited, rather uplifted. For the first time in her life she was conscious that she would earn money by her own efforts; that she would have definite work to do, and that it depended upon her how well she did it. She was—beginning her career! Six pounds wasn't a great deal on which to live, but probably other people didn't earn much more. If they could manage, so could she.

That night they talked; held their usual conference in Lottie's comfortable, overcrowded sitting-room. Lottie beamed at her grand-daughter; Josh nodded his head, murmuring, "A very nice start; what you might call a *auspishus* start. Only, my girl, don't you go casting yourself, nor letting them cast you, for 'Lady Isobel' or 'Josephine', nor any of those old plays. They're not suitable. You've got somethin' to sell—give yourself a chance to sell it! Just get me a bottle of beer and we'll drink to your good luck!"

Before she left Manchester to begin work, Genevra went to stay with Tilda Lorimer. She had visited her several times, always hoping that Henry might be there. She disliked realizing how much she hoped that he might be at 'Killarney'. He was always away—once he had been in America, once in Paris, once staying in the south of France with Mr. and Mrs. Gossage. Genevra had shrugged her shoulders and tried to believe that she didn't really care if Henry were there or not. After all, she'd only known him for a few days—she shivered when she remembered some of the events of those days—he had looked upon her as a little girl for whom he had bought a beautiful dress—because he was sorry for her. Well, now she was eighteen, she was going to be a real actress, to learn long parts, and make a success. She might find Henry different, but not so different as Henry would, without doubt, find her.

Nothing had changed at 'Killarney', except that here and there Henry had introduced some fine piece of furniture which Tilda, in her turn, introduced with immense pride to all her visitors. Not because she knew anything about the work of Mr. Hepplewhite, Mr. Sheraton or Mr. Chippendale, but because she could wave her hand towards the various pieces saying, "My son found that! Great knowledge of good furniture. He dislikes modern stuff, yes, no matter how expensive. What he really cares about is

—design and the graining of the wood, or the polish—whichever it may be."

She was delighted to see Genevra. Held her at arm's length, exclaiming, "Well, my girl gets prettier every time I see her. And you're going on the stage! Rep, eh? This evening I'll go through my stage jewellery—I've lots and lots of it. There's my old make-up box, too—that might bring you luck. I didn't do so badly, y'know, ducky."

Genevra was enchanted. "Oh, Auntie Tilda—how wonderful! Anything—for we have to find everything, and with a new play next week, you can just imagine! I've lots of clothes, grandmother is so generous, but even so—I shan't have sufficient."

Tilda said solemnly, "You shall have a wardrobe like what the old Odeon used to have! When I make a promise I keep it. Now come and have a word with Alice."

Alice discussed the dinner at great length, she voiced her old complaint that 'Masterenery' never bothered what he ate. "Now ter night, I've reely spread meself, as you might say, Miss Genevra. Clear consomme—and when I say 'clear' it's 'clear' what I'm talkin' about. Whitebait with thin brown bread an' butter. A lovely little loin of lamb, green peas—from our own garding, an' new pertaters. Then a souflay! What d'you say to that?"

"There is only one word—magnificent!"

"Will Masterenery say that? Not likerly. He'll sip the soup, he'll eat half a dozen whitebait, p'raps a tiny loin chop, and mess a few peas about on his plate. The souflay—and you know what my souflays are like!—he'll have a piece as big as a bee's knee and say, 'Alice, a delightful dinner, thank you very much'. I often wonder what his wife 'ul do with him!"

Genevra said, with more urgency than she intended, "He's not going to be married, Alice?"

"Married, miss, not Masterenery! No, I said that in a manner o' speaking. He's taken up with his work. He's a partner now, y'know, in Levelle's. Doin' ever so well."

Genevra said mechanically, "Oh, I'm so glad."

She was in her bedroom when Tilda called, "Genevra, ducky, here's Henry."

Genevra stood for a moment staring into the mirror, asking herself if she was really attractive, or if Henry would think her hideous. No, he couldn't think that, for without conceit she knew that she wasn't hideous. Would he hate her accent, think that her movements were clumsy? Not unless Miss Doggerty had

lied, for she had said that Genevra moved smoothly and beautifully—and she was not accustomed to paying compliments. She
touched her hair, set her collar and cuffs at exactly the right angle,
and descended the stairs. It was nearly four years since she had
seen him—Masterenery. He stood waiting for her, his face turned
towards the stairs. He looked taller than she seemed to remember;
and thinner. Anyone less prejudiced might have said—older.

He was wearing a suit of dark brown, and yet it looked light
somehow. There was a faint white line running through the
cloth; perhaps that was what made it look lighter. She saw everything—his tie was a dark brown, it also had white lines running
through it. It was sombre but looked—what was the word?—
rich. As she came down the stairs she called, "Hello, Masterenery!
I began to think that I should never see you again."

He held out his hands—such nice hands, Genevra thought—
with long fingers and big, well-kept nails. He smiled and said, "Is
it really my little Genevra? It seems impossible. It's nice to see
you."

She took his hands, leaned her face forward and he implanted
a kiss on either cheek, saying, as he held her away from him,
"And so you're a potential actress, eh?"

"I start in two weeks at Cothampton. I don't know what
they'll want me to play . . . I'll play anything. I don't suppose
that I shall be very good—not at first—but I will be—eventually."

Henry said gravely, "I am quite certain that you will be."

He was the same, Genevra thought, and yet different. Just as
kind, with the same ability to make you feel that you were the
one person in the world with whom he wanted to talk or to
whom he wanted to listen. She watched his head, during Alice's
perfect dinner, bending slightly towards her, as if to sit upright
might make it possible to miss a single word. He asked very few
questions, but listened to all her answers to Tilda's with grave
attention. When dinner was over and they had drunk their coffee,
he said, "Have you been into the garden? Would you like to go?"

She remembered the Monk; his grave was there, in this
garden. She knew that her cheeks flushed, because—although she
had thought of him so often—she had forgotten him in the
excitement of meeting Tilda and Alice and Masterenery. Everything came rushing back—the Monk's little cold hands against
her cheek, his fits of shivering, his eyes filled with appeal as if he
asked why this deadly sickness should happen to him. She recalled
that last morning when she had offered him milk, how he had
tried to drink it, but at last turned away his head as if he begged

139

her not to worry him. Then . . . that last little shiver, and he had lain dead in her arms.

She stared at Henry, her eyes swimming with tears, and said, "I'd like to go into the garden, please."

He walked beside her, silent and, she felt, understanding. They reached a little plot of ground, surrounded by closely clipped privet bushes. There was a little stone, inscribed, 'In memory of the Monk'. Genevra caught Henry's hand, "That's you——" she said. "You did that, didn't you?"

"Any friend of yours, Genevra, is a friend of mine," he answered.

She held his hand tightly, and swinging round said, "Look, Masterenery, I talk better than I used to, I've learned a whole lot of things, but I'm still the same Genevra you once knew."

He looked at her, his face still and intent, then said, "Are you, darling? You were always terribly attractive, now you're devastating. Shall we try—try—to leave it at that?"

Genevra looked back at the Monk's grave, then back to Henry's grave face. She said, "Why should we try? We're here. We're young. Life belongs to us, Henry."

"Are you sure that it does?"

"For me—at least."

She saw a flicker of a smile on his lips. "Ah, but you are Genevra."

Genevra turned back and stared at the neat little grave that marked the resting-place of a small unimportant monkey, and with the sight of it came back so much: mum laughing; going shopping with mum; the day Holst had tried to get mum to allow her to assist some nasty old man who did conjuring tricks; mum lying on the bed with a doctor with a kind, blunt face watching her; Miss Hambro and Mrs. Atkins crying; mum kissing her, and . . . that was the last time Genevra had seen her. Her eyes were swimming with tears; she still held Henry's hand, and without turning to him said, "Do you mind leaving me alone—just for a little?"

Henry said, "My dear, I do understand," and slid his hand out of hers and was gone.

Later Tilda took her up to her storeroom and brought out wonderful artificial jewels, discoursing on each piece. "I wore this when I played *The Lady from Montmartre*, and this when I acted in *The Circus Girl*. That was on tour, but it was a big success all the same. Look, these were what I had for the last act of *Little Miss Nobody*. Lovely, aren't they?"

So it went on, until Genevra was surrounded with artificial jewels and the place looked like the setting for the 'Jewel Song' from *Faust*.

Tilda said, "There, we'll do the dresses to-morrow, ducky. Let's get down and have a word with Henry before we go to bed, shall we?"

Henry was seated in his own particular easy-chair, reading *The Times*. He looked up as they entered, rose and said, "Now, Mother dear, what about a nightcap? I suppose that our Genevra doesn't indulge in such things—eh?"

Tilda said indignantly, "I'd think not? Genevra, ask Alice to make you a nice cupper tea, ducks—or cocoa if you'd like it better."

With Genevra out of the room, Tilda said, "Lovely girl, eh, Henry?"

He looked up from his paper. "Genevra? Oh, charming, dear, quite charming."

She hesitated. "Henry—you've never thought that—well, that perhaps you and Genevra——"

He interrupted her almost violently. "Mother dear, what utter rubbish! I've not even seen the child for four years. What do I know about her? My dear, don't get ideas like that into your head, and for God's sake don't put them into hers. She's charming to look at, but what do I know about her? What does she know about me? Half London imagines that I'm Mrs. Gossage's lover —it's not true, but there it is, the story is in circulation. If it's not Mrs. Gossage it's Lady George Grilton! Oh, you've no idea the reputation your son has got!"

"I don't believe a word of it. . . ."

Henry replied smoothly, "Neither do I, but it amuses people to—shall we say—speculate? Leave Genevra alone, dearest. She's going to do things and go places."

Tilda sighed. "Very well, Henry—I just thought . . ."

He looked up and smiled. "Mother dear, if only people wouldn't *think*."

Tilda, after yawning widely, picked up her glass and said that she would finish it in bed 'over a book'; Genevra poured herself another cup of tea, kissed Tilda and said that she was coming in a minute.

Henry sat staring at a Chippendale cabinet which he had recently bought.

Genevra said, "You're very quiet, Henry. . . ."

"I'm very tired. Women in search of clothes can be very tiring, my dear."

She frowned. "I don't think that I enjoy being called—'my dear'."

"Don't you? I think it's very nice—a kind, comfortable kind of thing to call anyone."

Meditatively she said, "I've not seen you for nearly four years. Then you quoted Shakespeare to me. Polonius, do you remember?"

Henry smiled. "And now—when you're going on the stage—I should like you to read Hamlet's advice to the Players, and remember every word."

"I've read it; learned it by heart."

"Splendid. I hope that you profit by it, Genevra."

She shrugged. "Oh . . . profit . . . !"

"I imagine that it was written so that actors—yes, and actresses—might profit by it."

"I suppose so. Henry, you're not like you were four years ago. You were kind, and told me things. Tried to help me. Now you think I'm just a silly little thing who wants to 'go on the stage'. Henry, I'm going to make a success—you'll see."

Henry Lorimer looked round the room as if he had never seen it before, he noted everything as if he saw it for the first time. His eyes came back to Genevra Menetti. She sat with her hands lying loosely in her lap, she looked neither bored nor eager. He thought that she only—waited. For what? She was lovely, and he was conscious of her beauty. At that moment he might have told her that he loved her—and meant it. Henry was a person of integrity, an integrity upon which he prided himself. He was possessed of a knowledge of the world. Genevra might be only eighteen but she had seen quite an amount of the seamy side. To begin life as an actress might not mean luxury, but at least it meant the happiness of attainment, the gathering of knowledge. Genevra must have her chance.

He said, rising, "My dear, I am sure that you'll make a success. I don't for one moment think you a silly little thing I regard you as one of the pluckiest people I know. Genevra, I'm sorry, but I'm all in. Good night."

CHAPTER ELEVEN

She was disappointed. Henry had left her alone, saying once more, as his parting, that he was 'all in'. She thought, as she sipped her tea, that if he wanted her to remain and talk to him she would have forgotten that she was tired, and even if her eyes had been closing with the wish to sleep, she would have pinched herself in order to keep awake.

She had only wanted to talk to him to find out what his opinion was of her intention to go on the stage. She had no idea of wishing to be made love to. At eighteen she had never been conscious of an attraction to any man. True, there had been boys —brothers of girls she had known at school, and whose homes she had visited—who had wanted to hold her hand, and had said huskily, "I say, Genevra, you're so lovely. Let me kiss you, darling. May I?"

She had been slightly amused, because kissing seemed to her such a very small and unimportant thing. They had kissed her, usually clumsily, and breathing hard, they had whispered, "Darling—darling—darling," until she was bored and wriggled out of their embraces. They had written her long letters, sent her boxes of chocolates, handkerchiefs and the like. She had answered their letters, and felt a little disconcerted at the fantastic expressions which they used. Gradually their letters had ceased, and she had felt a sense rather of relief than deprivation.

Only once when she was staying with a school friend—Ursula Morgan—had she been afraid of a man. He was considerably older than the usual type of young man she met. He was, in fact, a friend of Ursula's father. He was tall, very thin, with a narrow, rather twisted mouth. They told her that he was 'in the diplomatic', and what that meant she neither knew nor cared. During dinner Genevra had caught him watching her, watching from half-closed eyelids which were wrinkled and reminded her of a lizard she had once seen in the zoo at Hamburg. Later, he refused to play bridge and came and talked to her. His voice was low but very distinct; he spoke slowly as if it were almost too much trouble to speak at all.

"Where did you get that attractive name? Genevra . . ." He let the sound of it trail away into nothingness.

"My father and mother gave it to me. They spent their honeymoon in Geneva."

"And you're as lovely as your name."

She shrugged her shoulders. "I'm not bad."

He said abruptly, "Come into the garden. It's hot in here."

They walked out on to the close-clipped, smooth lawn, and he took her hand, saying, " 'On such a night as this, when the soft wind did gently kiss the tall tree tops——' "

Genevra interrupted him. "You're getting it wrong. It's 'the sweet wind' and it's 'did gently kiss the trees'. It's from *The Merchant*."

She felt his hand slide away, knew that he stiffened with annoyance. Then he said, as if fighting down his annoyance, "Very well, my little student, have it your own way. Genevra, be kind to me."

She stared at him. "I am—I've come out walking with you!"

He came closer and put his arms round her, holding her to him, leaning down so that he could kiss her, find her lips. He whispered, "You're so lovely. You'll always turn men's heads. Genevra . . ." he said the name as if it actually tasted sweet, "Genevra, be kind to me."

Suddenly she was afraid. She felt that the dice were loaded against her. This thin-faced man, with his elegant clothes, his smooth, easy movements, his low voice, knew—all the things which she had only heard whispered about.

She twisted out of his arms, and stood facing him, her head flung back, her eyes very bright. "Don't talk such rubbish! I believe that I know what you mean—and the answer's—no, and no, and no again. Impertinence! Who the devil do you think I am? I'm Genevra Menetti and I'll thank you to remember it!"

He stared at her, his lips closed into a thin line. "I suppose that you have no idea who I am?"

"Not the slightest. Someone told me, but I've forgotten."

"I'm the British Ambassador in Colcuri. My name is——"

Genevra answered, her voice faintly shrill, "I don't want to hear it. It's of no interest to me. To me—you're—you're just a dirty old man."

He turned away and walked off; she—still furious—spun round on her heels and went back to the house.

Now, sitting alone in Aunt Tilda's pretty room, Genevra poured out a third cup of tea and thought about Henry. She hadn't wanted him to kiss her, to hold her close and ask her to be 'kind' to him. She had wanted to talk about her own affairs, to ask his advice—and he had sighed and told her that he was 'all in.'

She leaned back in her chair; the house was completely still; outside cars passed at long intervals. She thought that she might have been alone on a desert island. She thought of Aunt Tilda, sound asleep, her mouth a little open; of Alice, her hair in curlers, her face smothered in cold cream; of Henry—she imagined that he lay very straight and still, his slim figure scarcely making a perceptible mound under the covers.

She smiled, and then said very softly, " 'Stood Dido with a willow in her hand Upon the wild sea banks, and waft her love To come again to Carthage.' " Then, smiling more contentedly, she repeated, " 'To come again to Carthage'—well, this room would do for Carthage!"

She sat stiffly upright, someone was coming down the stairs. She held her breath and waited. Very carefully the door opened, and Henry came in. She said, "Hello, Henry, couldn't you sleep?"

He said, "It's time you were in bed, Genevra. Still drinking tea! You'll never sleep."

He was wearing a silk dressing-gown and she could catch a glimpse of his pyjamas, very bright and exotic. His hair was smooth. She thought, 'Even if he's been in bed, he's combed it when he got up again.' She said, "It's so nice sitting here—quiet and peaceful. Would you like me to make you a cup of tea, Masterenery? This is cold . . ." She lifted the lid and peered into the pot. "Anyway, I've drunk it all."

He had come farther into the room and taken his usual chair. "I don't think that I want any tea. I'm afraid that I was churlish, but I was tired. It's a long day in the West End, with silly women quibbling about this and that, whispering scandal, and longing to hear more. I think that I've been asleep. Anyway, I feel better."

"I'll get you a drink—shall I?"

"That would be very pleasant."

She brought him the drink which she prepared for him, and sat down watching him sip it with appreciation.

"Henry," she said abruptly, "what do you think of my going on the stage?"

He stared at her and sighed. "I hope it will give you all you wish for."

"I don't ask what you *hope*. I ask what you think."

"It's a hard life, Genevra. Where one person makes a success there are fifty who never get anywhere."

"I might be the—one person."

He smiled. "Fifty to one against!"

"I'm not afraid of long odds. Outsiders do come in sometimes, y'know."

"I suppose that I don't want you to be hurt—or disappointed —or disillusioned, Genevra."

"But why should I be any of those things? I don't say that I am —but I might be—the exception."

He frowned. "I don't like the risk for you. Genevra, I've known you for a long time——"

"Not so very long. Once when I was a small girl for two or three days. Since then you've always been away when I came. You don't know much about me, Henry."

His voice was irritable when he answered. "In actual point of time, I may not have seen much of you. But I've been in touch, through my mother. I don't like the idea of your going off on your own. This place—Cothampton. It's some one-eyed place in the Midlands, isn't it? They'll underpay you and overwork you."

"I shall be learning my job, remember—and being paid for it."

"Living in beastly rooms, mixing with cheap people, having a lot of second-rate young men with blue chins wanting to make love to you——"

She flared up at that. "How do you know that they're second rate? How do you know that I shall live in—beastly rooms? No man in the world is going to make love to me—unless *I* want him to! You're being very stupid."

He set down his glass and stared at her. She thought that he looked sulky, as if she had beaten him in their argument and he was not too pleased about it.

At last he said, "I suppose that you'd not consider giving up the whole thing and—marrying me, eh?"

She laughed. "Noble little Henry! You'd marry me to save me from the young men with blue chins, the beastly rooms and the second-rate people. No, my dear, it's sweet of you. Candidly, I expect that Aunt Tilda put it into your head. I'm a common little girl—not so little either now—I'm as tall as you are!— my great-grandfather was a pork butcher, my grandfather a stage manager in a music-hall, my own father an acrobat and juggler. But"—she was allowing her temper to get the better of her, rising and standing looking down at Henry—"I'm going to try to do things and get places. I thought that you'd understand, want me to make good. Instead you sit there glooming, and— as a kind of second prize to make up for not even trying to make a career for myself—you ask me to marry you. And you don't even say that you love me! All right—let's see what happens!"

He too rose and stood facing her. "But, Genevra, you know that I've always loved you. When you were a little girl—when I first saw you . . ."

"Yes, amusing. A scared child, who wanted to bury a dead Monk! A kind of performing animal myself! A child who swore, and talked badly, and was lost and miserable. It must have made a lovely story to tell your aristocratic clients. Consider giving up the whole thing to marry you—love not included in the arrangement! Thank you, Henry—now *I'm* all in, and *I'm* going to bed. Good night."

"Genevra—wait, let me explain. I can explain if you'll give me the chance——"

"You had your chance! Good night!"

She went to her room, leaving Henry sitting slumped in his chair, his hands hanging between his knees, wondering if he really had wanted to marry her and how much her refusal had actually wounded him. He had felt her attraction, known that it would be easy to fall violently in love with her; but Henry Lorimer distrusted violence in any form. More still he distrusted himself. He had lived his life at Levelle's for so long, he returned to his own home to be made much of, pampered and considered. He knew that he was—technically, at least—what is known as a good son.

He was generous to his mother, he made her a sufficient allowance to keep the house in a high state of comfort and even luxury. He was devoted to her, recognizing her admirable qualities and enjoying her shrewd comments on life in general. But a mother was one thing—a wife another. Now, if he were tired, if he wished to go to a party, a theatre, the ballet or the opera, he had only to telephone to Barnet and announce that he was staying at his flat in town. Was it likely that a wife would accept that? Henry doubted it. He had no wish to live in London. He enjoyed his quiet evenings, the cool room or the well-kept garden.

He drank what was left of his whisky-and-soda, set down the glass, and turning to the beautiful Queen Anne mirror which he had bought a short time ago, he stared at his reflection.

He nodded. 'She was right. I was wrong. I'm a selfish, self-centred swine. What on earth should make Genevra want to marry me? Do I really want to marry Genevra? I pride myself on my tact—with clients—but I can't exercise a little when I ask a girl—and such a girl—to marry me!'

Genevra rushed up the stairs to her room, her cheeks flaming, her eyes suddenly dark with anger. So that was how men asked you to marry them!

Henry 'supposed' that she'd not 'give up the whole thing' and marry him! What right had Henry to suppose anything of the kind? She was furious, she felt disillusioned, disappointed. For years—ever since she first came to 'Killarney'—she had thought of Henry as something removed from other people. She had admired him as a child, she had thought of him very often while she grew from a child to a young woman, and always—half unconsciously—when she read a play or book which she liked or admired, she had cast Henry for the rôle of hero.

True, she hadn't seen him since she was barely thirteen—and five years to Genevra Menetti at eighteen seemed almost a lifetime—but she had kept him alive in her memory. The supreme test of all masculine behaviour to Genevra had always been, 'Is this what Henry would do?' or 'Is that what Henry would approve?'

She hadn't been 'in love' with him. How could you be 'in love' with someone you knew when you were thirteen and had not seen for five years? It was that mentally she had come to rely on him, to measure other people by the standards which she believed to be his. Now, when she had imagined that he would talk to her, advise her, promise to give her his moral support should she ever need it, he had first excused himself—on the ground that he was 'all in'—and then, having come downstairs again, had dared to express a doubt that she would marry him and give up her cherished ambitions.

'If he'd said did I think that I could love him sufficiently', she thought—'if he'd said that he loved me—it might have been different. But just that cold-blooded sentence!" She bathed her eyes, which were red more with tears shed in fury than for any other reason, and as she stood before her looking-glass, managed to shrug her shoulders in a fashion which was sufficiently convincing to herself at least. 'Oh, well, I've learned a lesson. I suppose it's worth something to have learned anything. I shan't forget.'

As she lay in her cool bed, stretching luxuriously, she mentally rewrote the scene, deciding what Henry might have said—so differently.

He might have said, "Genevra darling—I loved you the very first moment I saw you. I went away just for that reason. I stayed away whenever you came to visit my mother. Now—you're back again, and here am I. Genevra, try to forget that I'm much older than you are. I'm twenty-seven, you're only eighteen. Nine years, my dear. When you're thirty—just at your very best and most lovely, I shall be nearly forty."

Forty to Genevra at eighteen seemed like something which was rapidly approaching old age.

That was how he ought to have spoken to her! That was how a man in one of Noel Coward's plays might have spoken—only much better! She could imagine an orchestra playing 'I'll See You Again' or 'Some Day I'll Find You' very softly while Henry spoke. Well, he hadn't said anything like that. He had been slightly patronizing, and 'supposed' that she wouldn't do this or that. Genevra clenched her hands; she breathed through her nostrils as she had seen actresses do in moments of tense drama.

'I'll show him! I'll make him realize what I can do—what I will do!' In the middle of imagining a wonderful scene in which she—after a great and successful first night—received the deafening applause of the audience; with the setting changing to her dressing-room, 'crowded with flowers and seething with people', Henry would enter. Immaculate, slim, perfectly groomed, shaken out of his slightly superior attitude, remembering only the mistake he had made. Leaving the side of the Earl of Some-thing-or-Other, she would hold out her hand, saying, "Ah, Henry—how nice of you!" He would stare at her, and say very quietly, "I didn't believe that you could do it. You've done it. My congratulations."

"That's kind of you, Henry." Cool, admirably polite, faintly cold.

"Genevra, do you remember that I once asked you to marry me?"

She laughed, a rather brittle—she liked that word—sound. "Why, yes, I believe that I do. How amusing!"

"I'm serious now. Genevra, will you marry me because I love you?"

"Henry dear," the brittle tone had gone, her voice was at least two tones lower, "you're too late—I've just promised to marry Wilfred—the Earl of Something-or-Other."

Henry, speaking very low and rapidly, here began a long and very lovely speech, during the composition of which Genevra —fell asleep.

At breakfast the next morning, when Aunt Tilda talked, as she always did, very brightly, and the delicious smell of good Wiltshire bacon and fried eggs filled the air, Genevra ate with an appetite. Henry came down late, looking, she thought, as if he had not slept too well. He looked at the bacon and eggs, lifting the cover and staring at them as if he owed them a personal grudge, replacing the cover and sitting down to take dry toast.

Aunt Tilda said, "Henry dear, no eggs and bacon?"

"No, thank you, Mother dear. Genevra, good morning."

She replied very brightly, "Good morning, Henry. I hope that you slept well."

He answered, "No harm in hoping. Did you?"

"I always sleep well here. There's nothing to disturb you, is there? It's all so quiet."

"That's good. I find the traffic noisy. I'm off to town this morning. Would you care to come up—if you've any shopping to do? I could meet you for luncheon wherever you wished."

She saw Aunt Tilda's face pleased and at the same time a little anxious. She smiled at him. "I should love to come. Only give me time to change and make myself a credit to you. Where shall we go? I once went to the Ivy. I'd love to go again. Could we?"

He buttered his toast without raising his eyes. "I think that it can be arranged. I'll telephone while you're—making yourself even more beautiful."

Genevra turned, beaming to Aunt Tilda. "Listen to that! Henry, if you didn't seem exactly like my elder brother, I might begin to imagine that you admired me. Only men never do really admire their sisters, do they? At least not until they take their cue from other men! Aunt Tilda, may I be excused?—that's what I used to say when I was a little girl."

She went out, still smiling, and Tilda, pouring herself another cup of tea, said, "She's a pretty thing, isn't she? And such a dear child. I still think that you might go further and far worse, Henry love."

Henry replied grimly, "I imagine that Genevra thinks she can go further and fare better, Mother. Last night I made a botch of our talk. I said all the wrong things and none of the right ones. She thought that I was being patronizing—and it was entirely my own fault I admit—and she was annoyed."

Tilda gasped, setting down her tea-cup with such force that the tea splashed into the saucer. "Henry—do you love her?"

"If I knew, I'd tell you," he said. "At the moment I don't know."

"Oh, my dear! I do hope that it's not going to make you unhappy. But you ought to know your own mind, y'know. Well, I can only hope that it turns out all right. Be nice to her to-day, ducky, and see what happens." He did not speak, and she said anxiously, "I believe that you do love her, Henry—now be honest."

He threw down his napkin and rose. "Listen, Mother. I tell you that I don't know. I mean it. I've been spoilt. Made too much of. Yes, partly by you and Alice, partly by circumstances. I expect things to fall into my lap. When they don't, I'm puzzled and disappointed. Probably it's much better this way. So we'll go out and Genevra will be charming to her elder brother. There," he bent down and kissed her cheek, "don't worry."

Genevra was charming, she looked delightful. Henry wondered where she got her clothes. They were not 'exclusive' they didn't bear the hallmark of individual designing; but she wore them beautifully. Everything about her was fresh and crisp, her gloves without wrinkles—except where wrinkles were necessary. Her shoes excellent, her stockings were fine and fitted her really lovely legs.

As he held open the door of the car, he said, "May I be permitted to say how very nice you look?"

She laughed. "Praise from Sir Hubert Stanley—thank you, sir."

As they drove towards London, Henry, with his eyes on the road ahead, said, "I want to apologize for last night. I was stupid and insensitive."

Her smile was brilliant. "My dear, you were tired, you told me that you were 'all in'. You ought not to have come down again. And I suspect that last whisky-and-soda was just a little too strong. Let's forget all about it."

"You have—forgotten? And—one word—I most certainly was not influenced by the whisky-and-soda!"

"I had forgotten," she admitted, "and now we're both going to forget."

"Very well."

He left her in Bond Street, and drove on to Levelle's. During the morning his clients found him less amusing than usual. Mrs. Gossage asked if he had a headache, Lady Mary Forsyth told him that he wanted a holiday. She added, "We're going to Cannes. Why not come along? You'd enjoy it." Lettice Manvers frowned when he displayed less than his usual interest in her long-winded and involved story of her latest love-affairs. He listened—only half attending—to the impression which Griogri Lapinski had made upon her. What the devil did he care about Lapinski! A sleek-haired little creature who wore excessively waisted coats, danced magnificently, and whose mental development had stopped short at the age of fifteen.

She said, "Henry, you're not attending. Usually you're such a poppet when I come and pour out my heart to you. This morning you're—yes, you're positively grumpy."

"Forgive me. I've such a lot to think of. We've never been so busy."

"What are you thinking of? Not dress designing, I'm certain."

He nodded as he re-draped a fold. "A kind of designing."

"You're trying to be cryptic, Henry."

"Never with you, my dear. You'd see through me in an instant."

She went away, lunched with her best friend, Charlotte Bennings, and said, "My dear, such a thrill. That divine Henry at Levelle's is in love with me. I began to tell him about Lapinski, and he shut up like a clam. Like a clam, my dear. Looked sulky, disgruntled, and said that he had a lot 'on his mind'. Of course, I've *suspected* it for months, but literally months. It's rather a thrill, isn't it?"

Charlotte Bennings, who was always anxious to speak in the highest terms of her best friends, announced at a small intimate dinner that evening that Henry Lorimer was head over ears in love with Lettice Manvers and was liable to do something desperate if she didn't give him some—she was careful to add 'some additional'—encouragement.

Henry lunched with Genevra at the Ivy. Signor Abel smiled and bowed, behaved delightfully; and Genevra was charmed. Henry pointed out the various celebrities to her, and she looked at them, her eyes very wide.

She sighed. "I'll be one of them—one day. Do you believe that, Henry?"

"Very few things would make me happier than to see your name in lights in the West End."

She chattered, told him about the company she was joining at Cothampton. He listened, only half attending, busy with his own thoughts.

'She's lovely, vital, she has charm, and she has determination too. I want desperately—with one side of me—to marry her. The other side, and I believe that it's the wiser side, tells me to be thankful she did lose her temper last night. I'm as ambitious as she is. I'm only twenty-seven. I've a long way to go yet. Levelle's getting old. I'm the person with the new ideas, the push, the energy. He's still good, still a great artist; but he's old, old, old. I'm a partner now; in a few more years I can pay what he wants for his share of the business—and make it run on my lines, according to my ideas.

'Married to Genevra—or even for that matter really in love with her—would be to lay myself open to limitations. I have my art, even though it may not be the art of the theatre.'

That thought came almost defiantly.

He stared at her across the table; she was staring—her eyes

wide—at Dame Marie Tempest, who was seated at her usual table receiving like a queen her various acquaintances who came, quite literally, to pay tribute.

Henry's mind halted. 'Then there's her side of the matter. I doubt if she would ever be sufficiently fond of me. She's sufficient unto herself. She has always fought her own battles and she always will. Heaven forbid that in those battles I should be— the enemy.

'Lovely Genevra, things are better left as they are. We've both got imagination; you might even come to imagine yourself in love with me, and nothing would be easier than for me to imagine myself in love with you. Surely it's time we went? People are going, and even if Genevra is content to sit and stare —most discreetly, I admit—at Ivor Novello, it's time we went.'

He glanced at his wrist-watch. "Genevra, do you know the time?"

She turned and smiled at him. "I've no idea. It's been wonderful. I've seen people—close to. It's made me determined more than ever that, one day, I'll come to the Ivy, and young, untried actresses will stare at me and sigh and think, 'One day I'll be what you are to-day'. Oh, Henry! Thank you for bringing me. It's given me—inspiration."

He signed to the waiter to bring his bill, and said, a trifle drily, "I'm glad that you have enjoyed yourself."

She sighed, "Oh, I have."

"It gives me inspiration—that was what you said?—to come here. I look at these famous actresses and think how much better my models are, and how ravishing I could make them look if they'd come to me. They will come, one day."

For the remaining three days of her stay their relations were easy, friendly and noncommittal. On the last evening Henry took Genevra and Tilda to town. They dined well, and went to a theatre. Tilda looked magnificent, Genevra lovely.

Henry was conscious half-way through the first act that he was watching the stage less and Genevra more. She sat leaning a little forward as if unwilling to miss the slightest movement, to lose the smallest inflection. He glanced at his mother; after all, she had been an actress, she loved the stage and everything appertaining to it. Did all stage people feel the same passionate interest in the plays they saw? Tilda was leaning back comfortably in her stall. She was interested. Henry saw her smile gently at some of the lines, but he found nothing in her still good-looking face to compare with the intensity which he found in

Genevra's. The realization made him feel vaguely disturbed. If her expression was an indication of her interest in the work which she had chosen, there was very little chance that she would be turned from her goal. Not, he added hurriedly as if to reassure himself, that he wished to turn her from it. If the girl was intent upon becoming an actress, it was a good thing that she felt as she obviously did.

She talked very little during the intervals. When Tilda asked if she was enjoying the play, she only gave her a smile which held all the assurances in the world.

Back in 'Killarney' they drank tea and Tilda kicked off her very smart shoes, saying, "Henry, duck, run and fetch me my soft slippers. These are all right when I want to cut a dash, but —'oh, my poor feet!' as someone or other used to sing when I was young." Then, as she slipped on the shoes which Henry brought, "Ah, that's better! Well, it was quite a nice evening. Thank you, Henry."

Genevra said, "It was a wonderful evening. Thank you, Henry."

"You liked the play?" he asked.

She frowned. "The play—I don't think that it was a very good play, but the acting was beautiful. They—those people—make it all *look* so easy. You feel that you could do it just as well, but in your heart you know that you could do nothing of the kind."

"The art which conceals art," he suggested.

She nodded. "That's it. That's what is going to be so terribly difficult to learn. But I *shall* learn it!"

Henry thought, 'She said that as if she flung a challenge at me!'

The next morning she left for Cothampton. She tried to read as the train wound its way out of London, but she was far too excited. She sat staring out of the window, scarcely seeing the passing landscape. Had her mother felt like this when she first left Manchester with the famous Tiller Troupe? Had gran'ma experienced this sense of entering a new world when she joined the first company in which she played? Did Aunt Tilda remember how she felt when she walked down to the Odeon for the first time?

She thought of all the parts she would like to play—Juliet, Ophelia, Desdemona, Portia, Trilby—how she would love to play Trilby! It might be an old-fashioned play, she didn't believe that the construction was very good really, but—oh, Trilby! The Duchess of Towers in Peter Ibbetson. *The Importance of Being Earnest*—privately she thought the girls' parts both rather silly, she'd like to play Lady Bracknell or the governess. Yes, even though you had to look a sight, it would be tremendous fun to play *By Candle Light*—but it took someone like that French actress to play that part, to play it properly. If only she could learn to act like she did, or the American—what was her name? —Lynn Fontaine! They made it all seem so easy, so effortless. If only she could have seen those great people of whom gram'pa said, "Aye, giants, my dear, giants. They were bigger nor life size, if you know what I mean. I don't b'lieve—except in one or two cases—they come like that now."

Ellen Terry, Irving, Duse, Tree, Lewis Waller, Hawtrey, Mrs. Patrick Campbell . . . She tried to imagine what it must have been like to go to a first night at the Lyceum, to Her Majesty's—as it was then—to the Haymarket, to the St. James's. 'The glory that was Greece, the grandeur that was Rome.'

The train was slowing down; she asked a man in the opposite corner, "Is this Cothampton, please?"

He nodded. "Aye, that's it. See how dark the sky lukes. That's a sure sign as Cothampton's doing well. Wheer there's muck— there's money." He rose and began to lift her bags down, placing them on the seat near her. She knew that he was staring at her and felt her face flush a little. He was a big burly man, with a scarlet face and small twinkling blue eyes.

"You don't live i' Cothampton, do you?"

"I shall be living here. I'm"—she knew that her flush deepened—"I am joining the repertory company here."

"Go on! So yer a' actress! Luke at that! It 'ul be Filmer Turner's company. Mind you, there's weeks as they're very good —but some other weeks neither me nor my missus can make top nor tail on it all. Here we are." He rose and thrust his head out of the window. "If I'm not mistaken, there's Turner 'isself come to meet you." He bawled, "Here you are, Mr. Turner—I've brought summat for you!"

The big man handed out her bags. Turner—a lock of hair still falling over his forehead—hurried forward.

"Hello, Councillor Thwaites, how are you? Good morning, Miss Menetti—come ready to face a lot of hard work? Anything in the van?"

Genevra laughed. "Two trunks and a huge skip—it's got 'Mattie Colingly' painted on it."

Thwaites shouted, "Mattie Colingly! Nay, that beats all. How did you come bi that? I mind Mattie; used to be the shining light at the old Odeon. Come on, Mr. Turner—I'll gie you a hand."

Later, her luggage extracted from the van, Thwaites held out a hand like a ham.

"Glad ter have met you, Miss Menetti. Aye, I got your name quick! Hope to bring my missus to see you very often. Maybe some Sunday you'd come an' take a bite of dinner wi' us." He threw back his head and bawled a great gusty laugh. "I've always heard as actors are always 'ungry! My missus is a champion cook. Just drop us a note ter say as you're coming. Glad ter see you an' all, Mr. Turner. Well, s'long."

In the rattling taxi Turner told her that he had booked rooms for her with Mrs. Rattery, and that she would share a sitting-room with Ruth Power, a girl a little older than herself who had recently joined the company.

Genevra's first question was, "Can I keep my dog there? He's with my grandmother now, but I want to go and bring him as soon as I see if everything is all right."

Filmer said, "I mentioned the dog to old Mother Rattery, and she said that she didn't mind, provided that you didn't expect her to cook lights for him."

Genevra replied with some indignation, "Haig doesn't eat lights—they're not good for dogs!"

The house looked clean; it was unimposing with a bright green front door approached by two steps which were hearth-stoned and immaculate. Turner opened the door and shouted, "Mrs. Rattery—here's your lodger!"

From a distant kitchen came the sound of a husky voice. "All right, no call ter 'oller. No one's deaf i' this house, not as I know of."

Mrs. Rattery emerged, allowing a smell of Irish stew to penetrate into the passage. She was very stout, with scanty grey hair scraped back from her forehead. She wore a very large, very white apron on which she wiped her hands as she came towards them.

"Is this the young lady? Glad to meet you, I'm sure. My God, what a amount o' luggage! Come ter stay, 'ave you?" She laughed wheezily. "Luke's like it. Oh, some's for the theatre, is it? That's better. Noo, wheer's t'little dog? I 'ope as he is a little dog, not one o' them like gert calves!"

"I'm going home to bring him," Genevra said, "as soon as I can. He's a very well-trained, obedient little dog. His name's Haig."

Again that wheezy laugh. "Noo, that's what I call a name! If 'e lives up to it, 'e'll be all right. Dadda an' me like animals. Noo, are you 'aving yer dinner 'ere? I've Irish stew, and when I say Irish stew I mean Irish stew, not kag-mag, same as what some makes."

Filmer Turner said rather nervously, "I was going to ask Miss Menetti to have luncheon with me, we've a lot to talk over."

Mrs. Rattery nodded. "Very well, she can 'ave the Irish stew for 'er supper. Let 'er 'ave a look at her room. You go into the sitting-room and wait for five minutes. Would you like a bottle of beer? I'll get it. You'd like one an' all, Miss What's-it?"

The sitting-room was spotlessly clean and not uncomfortable. A table in the centre was covered with a dark-red serge cloth, there was a sideboard bearing a very large cruet, a tantalus containing three empty decanters, and a china figure of a woman in a state of nudity. There were two rather doubtfully 'easy' chairs upholstered in dark-green plush, an upright piano, its top covered with photographs of former occupants of the room. They were signed with assurances of affection to 'dear Ma' or 'to dear Mrs. Rattery, one of the best'. The mantelpiece had evidently been cleared to make room for Miss Power's personal photographs. There was a naval officer, an elderly gentleman who looked as if he might be a solicitor or a doctor, a stout elderly lady, presumably Miss Power's mother, and various china models of animals—a dog wearing a top hat, a cat with one paw extended towards a ball, and several ducks arranged in a line.

Turner said, "They're the best rooms in Cothampton. You'll find Ma Rattery all right. He's a plumber, so the bath's in order! Ruth's quite a dear; her father's a doctor in Birmingham. Ah," as the door opened to admit Mrs. Rattery, "the beer!"

She poured it out for him, saying, "That 'ul be eightpence."

He gave her the money, and said to Genevra, "Now would you like to see your bedroom while I get rid of this?"

She followed Mrs. Rattery upstairs, was duly shown the bathroom and the 'lav', Mrs. Rattery explaining that while there was "one in t'yard, Dadda being a plumber thought we might as well 'ave a 'indoor' as well. Nice, isn't it? Noo, this is your bedroom, 'ope you'll like it. I could have a fresh let every week, but I like my permanents better. I get ter know their ways an' they get to know mine. Suits everyone all round."

Genevra said, "It's a very nice room, the bed looks very comfortable. Would you tell me what—what your charges are? I should like to stay here, but I don't want to—well, I don't know what you charge! I might not be able to afford it, you see."

Mrs. Rattery sat down on a bedroom chair, her vast bulk seemed to overflow its seat. She planted her broad red hands on her knees and breathed deeply.

"Joost starting, aren't you? Well, mind you, I could get dooble, an' 'ave been *offered* dooble, but what I say is right's right, an' wrong's no man's right. I'll ask you same as what I ask Miss Power. Three pounds—bedroom, sharing sitting-room, plain breakfast, good dinner, nice cupper tea an' a bit o' 'ome-made cake at four, an' supper. The dog's food you must buy yerself. I don't mind two baths a week, but if you've got fancy ideas an' want one a day, like what Miss Power does, then that five days as you pay for—at sixpence a day. Laundry—that's your business. If you're away fer a week, week-end, whatever you like, I take nothing off, *and* I shan't try to let your room to anyone else whiles your away. There, you 'ave it!"

Genevra said, "I think that's very fair, Mrs. Rattery. I'm sure that I shall like living here. And you will find Haig a darling."

Mrs. Rattery heaved herself from the frail-looking chair, blew out her cheeks and replied that no one hoped more than what she did that Genevra would find No. 37 Wilmington Street—as "literally thousands of pros 'ave done—a 'ome from 'ome."

"I'm sure I shall."

Again they lunched at the gloomy hotel, Filmer saying rather shyly, "This time we won't toss for it. I'm in funds. We had a good week last week. We took a chance with *Milestones* and they simply ate it. I say, have you read those plays of Pirandello's? Oh! Good. What do you think about *Six Characters*?"

"I think," Genevra said, pushing away her plate, which contained some light-coloured liquid stated on the menu to be '*crème suprême*', "that you'll enjoy it tremendously, and that the audiences—if there are any after Monday night—will think that you've gone crazy."

He pushed back his lock of hair and stared at her with his light-blue eyes.

"But you? Wouldn't you like to play it? That girl's part?"

"Of course, I should love it. But is that the point? Don't you want to fill your house?"

"I want to produce artistic plays as well." His tone was slightly defiant. "I believe that you can do both! I'd like to do *The Cherry Orchard*—yes, and *Three Sisters*. Anyway, the week after next we're doing *Caesar and Cleopatra*." He stared at her as if he challenged her to question his right to produce Shaw at Cothampton. Genevra was dissecting a particularly tough piece of mutton; she

158

did not raise her eyes, but said gently, "And what do I play? The old nurse?"

He stammered a little. "Well, no—I thought Madge—Miss MacClintock—would play that, and—of course—Charlotte Mason—Cleopatra. They're both very good. Brewster Hallam —Caesar, and, of course, Charles Bradstock—Britannicus. Mason, I think—unless I play it myself—Anthony."

Very demurely she said, "I have an idea there is a slave's part which I could play."

Turner appeared less apprehensive. "Oh yes—yes, there is. Then I've got a copy of Sardu's *Tosca.* I believe in it! I'm working on it now. It's got some old-fashioned phrases in it that need— or I think that they need—alteration. I believe it will go like hot cakes."

"There is a peasant woman in the church scene," Genevra said reflectively. "I've only seen the opera, but I believe that I could play that. She doesn't speak—she only prays. What are you doing this week?"

"This week—oh, *Love on the Dole.*"

"And next week?"

"That's why I wanted you to come to-day. We're doing *Hedda!*" There was a note of triumph in his voice.

"And Miss Macauley—sorry, I've got the name wrong——"

"MacClintock."

"Yes, of course—will play Hedda?"

"Of course, no one else in the company could touch it. But I want you to play the young woman—she has a lovely scene in the first act—you remember?"

Genevra smiled sweetly. "Oh, perfectly, a kind of agreeable stooge to Hedda. Can I have the part at once? If we could go round to the theatre perhaps you could let me have it."

CHAPTER TWELVE

GENEVRA thought that she had never worked so hard in her life. There were Saturday nights when she reached 37 Wilmington Street too tired to eat the supper which Mrs. Rattery had provided for her. Other times when the conversation of Ruth Power drove her almost to madness. Genevra wrote to her grandmother:

She is a nice girl, and I have come to the conclusion that I loathe and detest all 'nice girls'. She is more concerned with what new films will be-

chowing next week than what kind of houses we are getting. She tells me about the men who have 'fallen with a loud crash' for her, which one is a 'darling boy' and which 'a dreadful fellow—simply frightening'. And I want to study!

Still, in spite of Miss Power, she was learning many things Never to go to someone else's dressing-room with the words, "I say, could you lend me a little number five?" or, "Have you the odd spot of powder, it's early-closing day and I—well, I just forgot." She learned that leading ladies and leading men must be treated with respect, whether you liked or despised their work. She was a very quick study, and could have gone down to a first rehearsal practically word perfect, but she learned that to do this was to gain the reputation of 'swanking' and 'showing off'.

She was given small parts, and accepted them gratefully and worked at them, trying to extract from them the last ounce of meaning and 'character'. Turner watched her, refraining from acting on impulse and risking giving her a really big part too soon. He knew that to do so would rouse indignation in the somewhat massive breast of Madge MacClintock. Madge might not be a really good actress, but she was reasonably sound, and her assurance was such that no part ever dismayed her.

Charles Bradstock once said, "Ask her to play Lady Godiva and she'd do it—even if she had to wear a badly dressed wig and go to the turkish baths every day for a fortnight. That's our Madge!"

The company were all very nice to Genevra. She was unassuming. She was never late for rehearsal but always arrived early. Haig was content to sit by her chair and guard her bag while she was working. They all admitted that she was startlingly pretty, that she worked well, and that she did not 'give herself airs'.

Ruth Power said, in her highly cultivated drawl, "We-ell, she's sharing rooms with me, I know all about her. Just tell me, please, what has she got to—give herself airs about?"

Brewster Hallam, who played the heavy parts, and admitted that he played them 'ham, m' dear, but I like to think that it's reasonably good ham', said, "I don't suppose that this little girl has anything to give herself airs about. She is 'as God made her, —she's got 'something', and I like to think that God gave that 'something' to her."

Brewster's stock phrase was 'I like to think . . .'

Really, Genevra thought, they were nice, kindly people. True, at the end of the first week George Mason, who played young and—when they offered—heroic parts, said to her, "Miss Menetti, if you feel that I can be of the slightest use to you, do come round to my rooms and we'll put in an hour's work together."

She said, "That is kind of you! I am only playing such small parts that I have plenty of time to study others—I'd be so grateful for your help."

He smiled; his smile was one of his chief assets. "I'm delighted."

She had gone, and it appeared that he wished to study plays far less than he wished to study her. There had been an argument and he had told her that she was a 'prudish schoolgirl' and a good deal more in the same strain. Genevra listened, gravely attentive, and said, "Thank you for all your help. Good-bye."

Filmer Turner watched her, found himself watching her at every performance. No matter how small a part she played, she brought something to it. She was young, inexperienced, and yet in some strange way she had 'finish'. It seemed natural to her to know how to 'walk a stage', her 'attack' was admirable, she neither over- nor under-played such parts as she was given. He knew that he was thinking far too much about her. He was a sincere and earnest young man, with ideals and ambitions concerning the stage. His father was a rich manufacturer and Filmer was his only son. On the strength of several fairly good performances with the O.U.D.S., and a course at the R.A.D.A., Filmer had contrived to convince his father that he was 'the new type of producer'. His father decided that to finance a repertory company was less expensive than financing chorus girls—a thing which he had done at great expense to his family in his own youth. Filmer certainly worked hard, and the deficit at the end of his first season was considerably less than Turner senior had dared to hope.

True, he had only visited Cothampton twice, because he liked plays which were either lively or 'musical'. He found his son's productions too heavy, they required too much mental exercise to understand them, even if they were really worth understanding! However, the boy appeared to be happy. Turner, Limited, were making money hand over fist making bicycles and—under strict secrecy—rather inferior munitions for the Government. Later Filmer would settle down, forget all about his tuppenny-ha'penny company and his wretched actors and actresses and understand that a clear turnover of £15,000 a year was better than producing plays which half the audience didn't understand and the other half slept through.

There had been that incredible play by some Russian, *The Cherry Orchard*, in which some stoutish woman had meandered on about some trees. Fred Turner had not been able to make head or tail of it. Filmer hadn't given himself much of a part. He had wandered on and asked people to 'come to the Volga', but somehow he had *meant* something. What exactly Fred didn't know. There had been a lovely girl in the show, playing a part which was just damn' silly about her dog eating nuts. As a matter of fact, he had a dog at 'Risingly Hall' who ate nuts and liked them.

Later, when Filmer had supper with his father at the Crown, Fred said, "You ought to give that pretty girl a better chance. She's wasted. All that about her dog eating nuts! Damn it, Tip eats nuts—there's nothing in it. But she's lovely! Give her better parts and you'll pull in all the lads of Cothampton."

Filmer, who looked grey in the face with utter weariness, said very patiently, "I know, but she's not ready. I'm nursing her."

Fred roared. "So long as you're nursing her as pretty girls ought to be nursed—on your knee—you're not wasting your time!"

His son stared at him, then drank his wine. He swallowed hard, then said, "I'm going to let her play . . ."—he drew a deep breath—"Hedda."

"Never heard of the play! What is it? Comedy?"

"That," his son said gently, "depends on how you look at it."

His father sighed. "Oh, it's another of those 'thinking' plays, eh?" He poured out another glass of wine. "Mind, you hadn't much to do, but somehow you—well, you got away with it. You ought to play heroes. It's you who pays the bills, or"—with another gusty laugh—"I do, and so why not have some of the—what's the word?—koodoss?"

Filmer went back to his rooms and sat until early morning reading *Hedda Babler*. In the morning he sent for Madge MacClintock to come to his office. She entered, tall, massive and assured. She was still a handsome woman, possessing a fine full voice with good tones. Filmer said, "Sit down, Madge dear. I loved your performance last night."

"Thank you, darling. It's a devil to learn, and candidly I don't think that the audience liked it much. Look here, Filmer, I know it's old-fashioned, but I believe they'd eat it. What about *The Royal Divorce*?"

Pushing back his heavy lock of hair, he stared at her, then saw deliverance.

"You play Josephine, of course."

She nodded. "I seem to be the only person *to* play it."

"Exactly. I believe that it's an idea. And the Emperor?"

"Darling, why not Brewster? He's smallish, and he's good—when he likes. It's a hammy play, but I'm prepared to bet that they'll love it."

Again Filmer said, "Madge, it's an idea. Now, this is another thing"—he was careful to say 'another'—"that I want to discuss with you. I want to do *Hedda*."

She said piously, "Oh, my God!"

He picked up a rusty pen which lay on his desk and tried to make a pattern on the blotting paper, which was so old that had long ceased to be pink and had reached a stage of funereal black. Anyway, the points of the nib were crossed.

"I felt that you'd not want to play Hedda. And after all, Madge darling, a week's rest won't hurt you. Heaven knows that you carry the burden and heat of the day, don't you? I've an idea. Let's try little Menetti! What do you think?"

With a hint of coldness in her rich voice, Miss MacClintock said, "She can only fail. Of course, she's too young . . ."

"Hedda was, I think, twenty-six."

"Mrs. Campbell played it when she was sixty!"

He smiled, and laid down the rusty pen. "What about a glass of beer? I've got some here." He rose and wiped two dirty glasses on a still more dirty towel, then opened two bottles of 'Crowther's Special' and poured them into the glasses. He raised his own and said, "Here's love." To which Miss MacClintock replied:

"All you wish, etcetera."

Filmer reseated himself. "Then you approve? I felt that you would. It's an experiment, and might be interesting. Thanks awfully for your help, Madge dear. And you'll have a really good week's rest and come back to—pull them in!"

That night after the performance, he said to Genevra, "May I walk home with you? Or would you come—I wish that you would—and have supper with me at the Crown?" He smiled suddenly, and she thought how pleasant it was to see him, momentarily at least, looking unworried and unharassed. "I had my guv'nor here last night, and—he was generous. Do come, please."

"Can Haig come?"

"Haig comes, or we break the whole place into small pieces!"

The head waiter beamed at her; of course the little dog could come. Might be that there was a nice bone 'lurking somewhere and suitable for a nice little feller'. He was an obedient dog, and lay contentedly under Genevra's chair munching his bone in complete contentment.

Filmer leaned his elbows on the table. "My guv'nor thought you were wasted in that part last night."

She smiled. "I agree with him—don't you?"

He drew a deep breath. "Genevra, you're only just starting. I *know* you're good, but you've got to prove it to other people. I'm going to take a big chance. Next week we play *Nothing But the Truth*, and the week after that—*Hedda*. You play—Hedda."

The effect on her was electrical. She sat bolt upright and stared at him, her lips parted a little. Filmer felt that her suppressed excitement lit up the whole gloomy dining-room, that everything gained additional brightness. Her eyes met his, glowing with happiness.

"Filmer . . ." she breathed. "Me—to play Hedda! You're not making fun of me? Swear you're not!"

To his dismay he saw that her eyes had suddenly filled with tears. He stretched out his hand and touched the tips of her fingers.

"Darling, of course I'm not. You don't know how hard it's been, Genevra, not to snatch all the best parts for you, only I realized that it couldn't be done. It wouldn't have been fair to you, it wouldn't have been fair to the other members of the company. Darling Genevra, say that you're pleased and happy. Tell me that you'll love playing it. Tell me—oh, Genevra, my dearest, couldn't you say that you love me a little?"

The soft expectancy, the excitement, died; her voice had sharpened when she answered him. "You're not giving me the part because—because you think you're in love with me?"

Filmer smiled. He had never yet been conscious of the difference in their ages. Now he knew that she was years his junior. There was something anxious and yet childishly defiant in her attitude. An older woman, one who was ambitious, would not have cared why he offered her the part, it would have satisfied her that it was given to her.

He spoke very softly, and his voice could be very charming. "My dear, I offer you the part because I believe in you. I want to know if you could ever be fond of me, because I'm a man and I love you. I ought not to have asked you all those questions at the same time—forgive me. Now, will you play Hedda?" Her smile, the light which returned to her eyes, gave him the answer. "And do you love me a little, darling Genevra?"

She laughed. "I ought not to try to answer both questions at the same time—so we've both made a mistake. Listen, Filmer, at the moment I'm so filled to overflowing with gratitude that I *could* say anything—and mean it too. I won't. I do like you so much. You've been so kind and sweet to me. Love—I don't know. Give me time to think it over, will you?"

Eagerly he said, "Of course, of course. But think of it, darling. We could work together; make this rep the best in all England, have people coming to see our work—as they might go to Stratford."

She thought, 'Yes, to listen to the *Royal Divorce* and *Nothing But the Truth!* I don't want to stay in Cothampton. I want to—see my name in lights in the West End!' Aloud she said, "Filmer, just give me time. If I'm to play this part, I daren't let my thoughts turn to anything else. It's"—she drew a deep breath—"it's my first real part. Oh, Filmer, what if I made a hash of it! I'd leave the stage for good—" she laughed—"for the good of the stage!"

"You won't, you can't, you mustn't."

"No, I won't, I can't, I mustn't," she repeated, as if she were taking a vow. "Filmer, let's go. Your news has tired me. I feel empty and not quite certain if this is really—me. I want to go home and read the play—I have a copy there. In the morning——"

"You'll give me your answer?"

"I'll try to."

She sat up until the early hours of the morning, reading the play, trying to visualize it all, attempting to hear the necessary inflections. At last, worn out and yet still conscious of great excitement, she went up to bed. Even then she could not sleep. The play—the play—the play! Her first chance! Then later the thought of Filmer. She knew that she didn't love him, that she never would love him. Equally she knew that she liked him very much indeed. There were moments when, young though she was, she knew that he was inclined to skate over the most difficult passages, and even to give way to actors who protested, "Filmer, old boy," or, "But, Filmer darling, that's how I feel it." He was weak, Genevra felt; he ought to have his own clear-cut ideas, his mind filled with exact, definitely printed pictures. There was often no question of even saying, "I know, Brewster, but just try it my way," or, "Madge dear, let's see how it works out according to my ideas." Not because he believed their methods to be better than his, but because he enjoyed working at the 'highlights' and was content to assert himself only when the work in hand interested him.

Could she love him? She might, but she most certainly didn't want to be tied to him for the rest of her life. Filmer would be happy to go on with his rep company until such time as his father cut off supplies. He was ambitious for the Turner Repertory, but not for Filmer Turner as an actor.

She remembered his anxious, kind, thin face with its heavy lock of hair, saw again his long-fingered nervous hands, just touching her own. He had asked her if she could love him. She remembered another man—so unlike Filmer Turner—who had asked her to marry him, and never mentioned love at all. Henry —so smooth, so beautifully groomed, so fastidious. She had tried not to think too much of Henry, and indeed since she came to Cothampton her work had occupied her to the exclusion of most things except the necessity of smiling at the butcher in order to persuade him to add an extra bone to Haig's daily piece of skirt or liver. Henry had not written to her, but then she'd never had a letter from him in her life. Aunt Tilda wrote every week, letters which told her that Henry was busy, that Alice had been suffering from neuralgia, and that Tilda herself had had rheumatism in her left foot. The garden was looking nice, Henry wanted her to go to Paris with him, but it seemed a long journey for such a short time. Henry would send his love if he knew she was writing. Genevra shrugged her shoulders under the sheets.

"I'm afraid, my dear Henry," she said softly, "you've missed the boat so far as I'm concerned."

Never, in later years, did Genevra work so hard at any part as she did at that of Hedda. She was fully conscious that she was far too young, too inexperienced, to play it; but she determined that it should repay her for all the work that she put into her study of the character. Filmer was patient; Genevra knew that he had his own ideas as to how the part should be played, but he was— apparently—content to watch her evolve something entirely her own. Indeed, she wished so often that he would be more decisive, that he would order her to do this and that. He never did. He listened, watched, and only when they were alone—except for some obviously bad move, or indistinct line—did he talk to her about the character which she was trying to make come to life.

Once again, during a wait at rehearsal, he said, "Genevra, do you think that you could love me?"

She answered, "My dear, at present I'm in love with Hedda. I can't think of anyone else. Give me time to get this over."

At the dress rehearsal she was lamentably bad. She muffed her entrances, she allowed her voice to get out of control, lines which should have been whispered she gave in a shrill tone which robbed them of all actual emotion. When it was over, she said to Filmer, "I couldn't very well have been worse, could I?"

He blinked his eyes. "A bad dress rehearsal is said to mean a good first performance, y'know."

"Not unless the—the stuff is there all the time! That's what frightens me. Is it there?"

"I believe so, Genevra darling."

She leaned forward and impulsively kissed his cheek. "Bless you!"

Mrs. Rattery said, "I'm coming, never mind what. Noo, you'll have a couple er beaten-oop eggs before the show. Lay down i't' afternoon. Get yersen prop'ly rested. I've 'eard as it's a difficult part ter play."

Genevra breathed piously, "My hat! Difficult!"

Later, Genevra sat in her dressing-room numbed and with a sense of dullness creeping over her faculties. What did she know of Hedda, what did she care? She couldn't make her 'come alive', what was the good of trying? Old Brewster came tapping at her door. She turned furiously and almost shouted, "Come in! What *is* it?"

He entered, and stood smiling at her. "My dear, I'm an old actor. I'm a ham actor, but I know! Listen, let Hedda play herself. You've worked, studied, analysed—now leave it to her. Good luck, m' dear, and all the best."

He was gone; she went on mechanically with her make-up, thinking hard. He was right. She'd let Hedda play herself.

Filmer came in, white-faced under his make-up. "Darling, you'll be wonderful. God bless."

She nodded. "Thank you—sweet of you."

The call-boy's knock and cry of, "Half an hour, please"; later, "Fifteen minutes, please," and at last, when she was dressed and waiting, "Overture and beginners, please." Genevra shivered.

She thought, 'My gran'ma has done it, my mother did it—they all faced first nights and audiences far more critical than this one. Aunt Tilda's done it—well, so can I!'

She walked down to the stage. Her face felt stiff, and it was difficult to smile and reply, "Thank you so much!" to people who whispered, "All the best, Miss Menetti." Madge MacClintock was there, she smiled almost too sweetly. "My dear, you brave child. All the best of luck!"

Genevra waited; she thought, 'Even now if I liked I could run away. No one could force me to come back! I can still go if I want to.' Then she answered herself, 'You damned little coward, at least you know your lines. Go on and say them!'

Her cue!

She went on, wearing a dress which Aunt Tilda had worn in *Ladies, Ladies!* at the Odeon. The audience saw a very young, very lovely girl, with tightly braided hair of corn colour. She moved smoothly and with a sense of swift assurance. Her voice was full and deeper than they expected from so young an actress. They were not a particularly educated audience, neither were they critical in the sense that a highly trained journalist is critical. They scarcely understood the play. To many of them it seemed to be a 'lot of talk about nowt'; but whenever that young girl with the foreign name was on the stage, she roused their interest.

A man in the stalls with a woman who was too well dressed to be an ordinary patron of the theatre at Cothampton, whispered, "What do you think, Mother?"

Behind her hand she whispered back, "Henry—she's got it!"

He sighed. "I felt that too."

Filmer Turner, watching intently, thought, 'It's there. She's making one fault after another, but she's sincere. She's speaking naturally. Moving beautifully. They can *hear* her. Oh, she's got it all. She only needs production. Heaven knows if I can teach her anything. God, she's lovely—lovely—lovely!'

When the shot came at the end of the play, that shot which told the audience that Hedda was dead, Filmer heard the long, shivering sigh which ran through the audience. It was as though they had said, "We shan't see her again! Eh, I'd have liked her to come on once more."

The applause was adequate; only when Genevra came on did they let themselves go. They shouted, they applauded. Still shaking, she took her calls, smiling her delightful, youthful smile. Filmer waited, the applause continued. He stepped forward.

"To-night you have seen the first really big character which Miss Menetti has played. She is glad, and I, as her manager, am glad, that she has pleased you. The rest of the cast are, to you, old and well-known friends. We know how good they are, and what we can demand from them. They have assurance—and rightly; Genevra Menetti needs that assurance which only you can give her. Thank you."

Back in her dressing-room, Genevra slumped in her chair, her hands hanging at her sides, her eyes closed, her mouth a little open as if she craved for air. Brewster came, his voice loud and resonant in her ears. "Well done, little girl! Oh, well done!"

Madge MacClintock held her hand to a warm bosom and said, "Darling, you were really very good—very good indeed. It's *such* a part! We're all delighted."

Genevra murmured, "I'm so glad. Thank you."

Filmer, still white-faced and without his make-up, kissed her hand and said very softly, "I'm not going to say that it was faultless, it couldn't be. But, darling, it was so—alive, so real. Bless you, and thank you."

She smiled at him. "Dear Filmer!"

"I wish that I were a better producer, darling—more worthy of your talent."

Almost sleepily she said, "Don't worry, you've done very well up to now, bless you."

He was standing watching her when another knock came on the door. The dresser opened it, and looking back over her shoulder, said, "A Mister an' Missus Lorimer ter see yer. Can they cum in?"

She sprang to her feet. There was Aunt Tilda, wearing restrained but magnificent clothes, her hair beautifully done, her face wreathed in smiles. "Genevra darling—oh, an' to think that you wore that dress of mine that I wore in the second act of *Ladies, Ladies!* Oh, I was so pleased! It brought you luck, dear. You were marvellous. Mind, it's a tiresome part—I didn't know honestly what half of it was about—but you spoke up beautifully, looked lovely. Bless you, darling! And look who's here!"

Henry came forward, his hands outstretched. "Genevra dear, my most hearty congratulations. You looked divine—you spoke beautifully—you acted . . ."

Breathlessly she said, "Yes, I acted . . . ?"

"With conviction. You carried me away by that if nothing else. I believed in your Hedda."

"Henry—and you've come all the way from London."

Henry smiled. "Before long people will come from half over the world. A drive from Barnet to Cothampton will be nothing."

She had forgotten Filmer; she stood before Henry, her eyes

very bright, her hands clasped. "But there were parts where I was so bad!"

He nodded, smiling. "Incredibly bad, but sincere. Keep that swiftness of movement. One day I'll dress you—though I admit that my mother's clothes suited you admirably. Bless you, we must rush. I've got to drive back to London to-night. I'm off to America this week—not for very long. By the time I come back you'll be playing all kinds of immense and wonderful parts." He leaned forward and said softly, "Don't you think that you ought to introduce your friend to my mother, darling?"

Tilda had made the introduction herself, and was babbling away very happily to Filmer. She turned to Henry and said, "This clever boy has done the production. Well, I must say that it did you credit. That sofa in the first act wants to be larger; Genevra and that girl sit like hens on a perch. You want to give them room."

Filmer, with that charming smile which came so seldom, said, "Mrs. Lorimer, one day shall I be able to persuade you to come and play for me? Think what fun we should have!"

She hit him gently, in the manner of the Edwardian actress. "My dear, whoever heard of such a thing! Who remembers me?"

"More people than you suppose. For one—a well-known councillor here in Cothampton!"

She laughed. "Now, we don't want any scandal before my son! You know the old saying—more folk know Tomfool than Tomfool knows. Now, Henry ducks."

She embraced Genevra, and Henry kissed her gently on the cheek, saying softly, "You were quite right—don't give it up—for anyone."

Genevra stood watching them until the door closed. Henry had come all the way from London to see her. Henry had worn his lovely clothes which made him look more slim and elegant than ever. Most of all Henry had said, "Don't give it up—for anyone."

She turned to find Filmer still watching her; this time she smiled and said, "If you'll go out, I can change!"

He started. "I'd forgotten. My father and mother are here— will you have supper with us and one or two other people at the Crown? My father has everything arranged." He laughed "I can promise that there won't be Julienne soup."

He looked appealing. Genevra longed to get home to talk to Haig about the evening, and then to creep into bed and play

Hedda all over again. Instead she said, "Filmer, I'd love to. Give me ten minutes and I'll be ready."

As she removed her make-up and dressed she kept thinking, 'If only Henry had said, "Don't give it up—for anyone—not even for me," how different it would have seemed!' Still, he had come; he had taken trouble; he had said that she had been 'incredibly bad' in parts, but—and that had taken away all the sting—she had been sincere.

While her dresser, Lizzie Marchmont, puffed and blew as she fastened hooks, Genevra said, "One day will you come and dress me in London?"

"I'd not wunder at that, m' dear. You're carrying yer future all before you as the man said when—— Oh, I never meant to say that! Theer, you're ready. 'Ave a good time. Good night, miss."

Filmer was wearing a dinner-jacket, and together they entered the gloomy portals of the Crown and asked for Mr. Turner's private room. Genevra was nervous, she had a vague feeling that she was being paraded as a possible wife for Filmer; when she saw his father and mother she felt certain of it. A large man with a starched shirt which bulged a little came forward and said, "Glad to have the pleasure, Miss Menetti. Let me interdouce you to my wife." Mrs. Turner was small and spare, with sharp eyes and a tight-lipped mouth.

"Very nice performance, I must say, Miss Menetti."

Filmer said eagerly, "Her first big part, Mother. Marvellous, eh?"

"With all respect to everyone—I thought the play just silly. Trivial, if you know what I mean. But I must say that you looked lovely, and what pleased my husband so was—you spoke up!"

"Filmer, your son, insists upon us—speaking up, Mrs. Turner."

Madge MacClintock was there, Brewster Hallam, Charles Franklin and little Charlotte Mason; also two other men whose names she never heard, both of whom assured her that they intended to come to the theatre again and again. They both looked chinless and Genevra disliked the way their eyes travelled up and down her figure as they spoke. The supper was as bad as most other meals she had eaten at the Crown, the only difference being that this was pretentious. She was unutterably weary; in a kind of haze she heard Hallam's voice booming, listened to Madge's carefully enunciated vowels, and the rather shrill if quite pleasant laughter of Charlotte Mason came to her from a vast distance. She was conscious that Filmer watched her eagerly, that he tried to make her talk to his father; and she felt again that she was a filly being cantered up and down to show its paces. Turner paid her heavy compliments, and she did her best to appear bright and to be reasonably amusing; all the time her thoughts were following Henry's car on its way to London. He was going to America. What might he find there? If only he could have stayed and they might have sat talking at 'Ma' Rattery's, instead of wasting time eating indifferent food, and listening to Hallam's recollections, Madge's accounts of her various triumphs, and old Turner's inane compliments!

Filmer whispered, "I believe that you're tired——"

"Tired! I'm only half alive. Can I go home without seeming to be rude?"

"I'll take you."

He spoke to his mother, and a moment later Genevra was saying good night, thanking people—whom she saw through a mist of intense weariness—for a wonderful evening, then she was out in the cool night air, with Filmer holding her arm.

CHAPTER THIRTEEN

DURING the weeks that followed Genevra played many parts—parts sufficiently large and difficult to have staggered an experienced actress. She knew, in her heart, that very often she never got 'below the surface', that the best she could hope to do in the limited time given to production was to give a kind of broad impression of the part. Only here and there was it possible to polish and develop with that care which she longed to give to the characters which she played. Always she told herself that 'one day' she would have enough time; that 'one day' she would be able to think and develop, polish and elaborate.

Filmer continued to be devoted; he never worried her, and when at last, in reply to his question as to whether she could love him sufficiently to marry him, she replied, "Filmer dear, I do like you so much. Only I don't want to marry anyone. I want to—get on. Can't we go on being the good friends that we are? To be engaged would only spoil things. In all probability it would spoil our work together."

He held her hands tightly, and for the first time she noticed that his were inclined to be clammy. As she withdrew them she longed to wipe her palms on her handkerchief.

He said, "If only you realized what it means to me, Genevra!"

She laughed. "But I do—I'm a very conceited young woman."

"I'd do everything to make you happy—everything."

"Listen, Filmer dear. You can't make other people happy. We've all got to make our own happiness. Just as we've all got to make our own way in the world. Go on producing me, and oh, darling, do be more strict. Don't let things go because they're 'nearly right'. Make us go back, and back and back. You've got plenty of ideas, you must see the play as a complete whole. Make us see it! Curse at us, break our hearts, shout, rave, do anything, but don't let us go on making mistakes! It's not only the 'highlights' in the play that matter, that need polishing and making slick, it's the whole play. Filmer, do have more—more—what's the word?"

"Self-assertiveness," he suggested, "if there is such a word."

"If there is no such word, at all events that's what I mean."

"I'll try, Genevra darling. Will you try to—well, to be fond of me?"

"I am fond of you, but you know as well as I do, just being 'fond' isn't enough. I do like you so much."

Turner laughed. He hoped that it 'rang hollow', and said, "That is, I suppose, the most damning thing any woman could say to a man."

Genevra shook her head. "Not nearly. At least I've not offered to be a sister to you. My dear, you've no rehearsal this afternoon, do go and read that new play. It might be a winner."

He replied moodily, "They never are winners."

It was one evening in December, when she had been at Cothampton for nearly eight months, that she came home to find Mrs. Rattery waiting to speak to her.

"I'm not altogether 'appy about 'Aig, miss."

"Haig! He's not ill? He was all right this morning. I didn't take him to rehearsal because he didn't seem to want to come—it was cold and wet. He hates the wet streets. Tell me—what is it?"

"He's hangy. Won't lie down; just stands theer. His breathin's a bit on the quick side. Wouldn't luke at 'is food—nice bit o' liver, as you know. Takes as much ter drink as yer can give 'im. 'Ow would you like Rattery ter run fer the vet? I've 'eard as 'e's very good, 'as a way with dogs, they tell me. Just a young chap, 'e is.'

Genevra was cold with fear. Haig was ill; she was forced to be out all day at rehearsal! She rushed into the kitchen; there he stood, his legs rather wide, breathing with terrible rapidity. She went on her knees at his side, and he turned his head, his eyes meeting hers, questioning and yet patient.

She said, "Darling, what is it? You can't be ill, Haig. You've never been ill. Oh, what can I do? If only you could speak to me!"

She lifted him and carried him into her sitting-room. Ruth Power was away for the week. Genevra often thought that she was away more often than she was in Cothampton. Mrs. Rattery followed her; she put the little dog down on the hearthrug.

"I shall want a fire kept on all night," Genevra said, "I don't care what it costs. He must be kept warm. It's a chill, I believe."

Mrs. Rattery answered with some asperity, " 'Oo said as theer'd not be a fire kep' on all night? Not me, was it? 'Aig 'ul not go short of anything in this 'ouse, allow me ter tell you. O' course there'll be a fire kep' on. You can sit with 'im while— what shall we say?—three, then eether Rattery or me'll come and take over. Noo, what-t-ever you do, don't start ter cry, miss, you'll ondly upset 'im. Faint'earted, that's what you are, y'know. Show as much spunk as what 'e's doin'—bless 'is 'eart."

Rattery returned with the veterinary surgeon, a young man called George Powell. He was tall and broad, with wide-set eyes, and a skin that was burnt by exposure to the wind, sun and rain. His clothes smelt of tobacco and fresh air. As he entered the little sitting-room Genevra felt a wave of assurance sweep over her.

He said, "Where's my patient? What's his name? Haig— that's a good name, isn't it, my boy?" Genevra watched his fingers as he ran them over the dog's firm little body, saw him take out a stethoscope and hold it over Haig's ribs, saw him listen intently, then, nodding his head—he had very close-cropped, thick hair—he rose to his feet.

She said, "Well?"

"It's pneumonia. Put him into a gamgee jacket. Can you make one?"

"Give me the idea," she said. "I'll make it."

Speaking very rapidly, he told her. "You have some cotton wool?"

"Luckily, lots of it. I use it in the theatre. He won't die, will he?"

The young man smoothed his rather heavy chin with his fingers. "Pneumonia depends on the nursing. More than medicine. It's not easy to nurse. You have to have great patience and perseverance."

Mrs. Rattery said, "We've got 'em both 'ere, don't worry."

174

He was seated at the table scribbling on a pad which bore his name and address. He stood up and handed it to Genevra. "One of you knock up old Bilstow in the High Street. Tell him it's urgent. If he's difficult, tell him that I go to Hammond's in future—that will put the fear of God into him. I suppose you know how to give medicine to a dog, eh? Into the side of his mouth. Get him some Brand's Essence, he won't take much, but t's good for his heart. I'll be round in the morning—early." Then he turned back to Haig; his voice changed, he knelt beside him. "You'll be all right, my brave lad. Pneumonia can't down a chap like you. You'll beat it every time. Keep up your heart, I'll look after you." He rose. "Good night. Keep him warm. I'll be here early."

That night was the longest Genevra had ever spent. She sat watching the little dog panting for breath, at intervals she offered him some of the essence which Powell had ordered. He took it obediently but without any real interest. She gave him his medicine and tried to believe that she saw an improvement in his breathing. She talked to him softly, gently, repeating what Powell had said. "You'll be all right, darling. A thing like pneumonia can't down you!"

He looked at her, his eyes questioning, as if he asked why this should have happened to him. She was relieved by Mrs. Rattery, who grumbled that the fire was being allowed to die down, who muttered at intervals, "Savin' coal at the risk of 'is precious life! I never did, s'elp me God!"

Genevra went down to rehearsal thankful that she was playing a small part; she knew that she looked heavy-eyed and rehearsed badly.

Hallam said, "Tired, m'dear? You want a holiday. Ought to have one."

She said, "I've been sitting up with my dog. He's ill—pneumonia."

"Tut, tut, nasty thing! Still, I've kept dogs all m' life, nursed a round dozen through pneumonia, never lost one. Warmth, that's the thing."

They were kind, every one of them; even Mason came and said, "So sorry, Genevra, to hear your dog's ill. Beastly for you—and for him, eh?"

She rushed back at midday. Haig was still standing, his legs spread a little wider, his sides heaving. George Powell had been and was coming again. He had said that the dog was 'holding his own'.

That night he was worse; even Genevra's inexperienced eyes could see that. He turned his head away when she offered him the meat extract, as if it were too much trouble to swallow it. She begged him, "Haig, my darling, try to take it, to please me. To please me—you've always done what I asked—always. Look, my sweet, it's so nice." He only moved his head away and sighed.

Another long night. Powell called in about twelve. He stood looking down at the dog, frowning and serious. "Wonder if he'd take oxygen. Might try. I'll bring a container in the morning. I'll come early. About seven. That too early for you?"

"No, I shall be here."

He looked at her. "Gosh, you look tired! Try not to worry. This is likely to be the turning-point—y'know, no use blinking—one way or the other. We're doing everything. I'm going to give him an injection. Keep his heart going. He's got the pluck of the devil. A gallant fight."

Another long night; early morning with Mrs. Rattery entering to grumble again that the fire looked 'half dead'. Strong cups of tea. Powell's arrival with oxygen, and watching Haig breathing the gas into his overstrained lungs.

"See how it's done?" Powell asked. "Give it again—every hour. Not too much, don't want him worried. To-day will see the turn—one way or the other. Good fellow—this chap. Got great heart. I'll be back later."

Before she left for rehearsal, Genevra knelt beside him "Haig, you know that I want to stay with you; but you're a 'pro' dog, you know that we've got to do our jobs. You do understand, don't you? Keep going, my sweet, keep up your heart. You're going to come through."

At midday she saw that Mrs. Rattery's eyes were red. Genevra asked, "He isn't worse, is he? What did Mr. Powell say?"

"What-cher mean—is he worse? He's all right. Powell says 'e's a dog in a thousand. C'on and get yer dinner. No use sayin' as yer can't eat, you gotter eat. I don't want you ill on my 'ands, it's bad enoof wi' our pore 'Aig. There, 'ave a try."

Rattery walked about the house in his stockinged feet; his voice was hoarse when he spoke. "Funny thing, 'e'll take that gas stoof from me better'n what 'e will from the missus. Likes me, I honestly b'lieve."

Mrs. Rattery said, "Powell 'ul be back about four."

The rehearsal dragged. For the first time Genevra felt that Filmer was a 'niggling' producer. He seemed obsessed with trifles, silly things that didn't matter. She clenched her hands.

176

'If only he'd get on!' Four o'clock, and Filmer, pushing back the lock of hair which fell over his eyes, said, "That's all for to-day. For heaven's sake leave your parts at home in the morning. Genevra, I've never known you fluff so badly, and it's only a small part, confound it!"

She stared at him, half dazed, then said, "I'm sorry, Filmer."

Mrs. Rattery met her at the door, she spoke in a whisper. "Don't make a row, walk quietly. 'E's laying down. Powell says it's the turn."

Genevra staggered suddenly; the stout woman caught her arm. "Noo, easy does it, easy does it. No call to take on."

She said, "The turn? Do you mean Haig's dying?"

" 'Dyin'?" Mrs. Rattery hissed. "I tell you 'e's laying down! Sleepin'. Breathin' easier. Managed ter take a bit o' scraped steak, like wot I used ter give our Clifford w'en 'e almost died wi' scarlet fever. Not a lot, but 'e'll take a bit more later. Powell 'ul be back about six."

At six Genevra was waiting for him. Haig was still sleeping, the sleep of complete exhaustion. The broad young man came in walking very carefully. He looked down at the sleeping dog and grinned.

"I told you that he had a great heart. Mind, he's not really out of the wood. Needs feeding up, lots of care, no rushing out in the cold. Tear off a bit of his gamgee jacket every day so that he won't catch cold. That Mrs. Rattery's a wonder. She and you have saved him." He breathed deeply. "I thought that he was going to slip us this morning! But he fought like a trooper."

Genevra tried to speak evenly and failed completely. "Then— then—you believe that he'll get well?" and suddenly burst into tears.

She was desperately tired, her overstrung nerves relaxed too suddenly, she felt that she—like Haig—had come through a long and terrible illness. She stood, her hands covering her face, sobbing wildly. She felt Powell's arms go round her, holding her closely to him. His voice was very gentle when he spoke.

"No, you mustn't cry, darling. You've been so good. Of course he'll get well. We'll see to that. I shall send him a tonic in the morning. To-night you can get some rest. Old Ma's got a camp-bed she'll bring in here for you. There, my sweet, don't cry." He bent his head and kissed the back of her neck, very gently and tenderly, murmuring, "Now, that's better, you'll feel all right now. Look up, sweet, tell me that you're pleased with

177

me for making your dog better—with your help, admittedly. You've been wonderful, you and old Ma. There . . ."

She raised her head, conscious of what he was saying.

"Pleased with you! I'm so grateful—there isn't anything I'd not do to show my gratitude—nothing. Oh, it's all so marvellous! To think that he's better!"

Powell pulled out a cigarette-case, saying, "It won't hurt him, they're mild. You? Do you good." He lit her cigarette and his, then said, "I know what I wish you could do—to show your gratitude. I wish that I could take you to the theatre to see an actress called Menetti. If you saw her, you'd realize what takes me there every week—and not only once a week either. I've been watching you for weeks. Falling deeper and still more deeply in ove with you.

"Oh, don't think that I've been attentive to Haig because he was your dog. I'd be the same with any dog. Only it was rather wonderful to be in the same room with you, to see you without make-up, hear you speak your own words and not some author's."

She said, "Mr. Powell—I don't quite know what to say . . ."

"Don't say 'This is so sudden', " he answered, and laughed, showing his beautifully white teeth.

Genevra looked at him curiously. He was a good-looking young man; he looked clean, well groomed. His eyes were kindly and his mouth smiled easily in spite of its determination. She saw his expression change; the little dog had stirred, and she knew that for the moment Powell had forgotten her. He dropped on his knees. His voice when he spoke was almost incredibly gentle. "You're better, my fine lad, eh? Look, here's your mistress. You've given her a bad fright, so be nice to her." Then to Genevra, "Tell Ma Rattery to give you some of that scraped steak, will you, and a saucer of water?"

Haig took a little scraped steak, rather languidly lapped a small quantity of water, weakly wagged his tail when Genevra spoke to him and then sank into sleep again. Powell rose, saying, "Now we can go on—from where we left off. You're not engaged, are you?" She shook her head. "That's good, it would all have been so much more difficult. Do you like me at all?"

"But Mr. Powell, I've only known you for three days."

"I know, but you get to know people awfully well in a short time when you're fighting for a life. It's like meeting people on a sea voyage. It's not a matter of time, it's all that you pack into the hours."

"Yes, possibly, but even so——"

"For a brilliant actress you're quite astonishingly tongue-tied!"

"You've admitted that you have only heard me speaking lines which someone else wrote," she reminded him.

"I know, but—Genevra, lovely, darling Genevra, come here." He held out his hand, and to her own surprise she took it and he drew her to him. She felt his arms go round her again, felt his kisses on her cheek, then at last he kissed her mouth, warmly, with love but without passion.

"Kiss me, Genevra!"

"No—not yet."

"Yes, now!" For the first time she heard his voice harden a little. "Yes, now. Then you must go to the theatre. Darling, please . . ." She pressed her lips to his, and heard him draw his breath sharply. Almost abruptly he let her go, saying, "I'll be back about eleven—to see that my patient is going on all right. *Au revoir*! my sweetest."

He was gone, closing the door very softly, moving without noise. She stood as if half dazed. What had happened? This young man had told her that he loved her. He was coming back after the theatre. He had kissed her, begged her to kiss him. Was he serious? Did he—could he—mean anything to her?

That evening she played badly and she knew it. The part was not either large or important, but she resented the fact that George Powell had the power to make her thoughts constantly turn to him. She tried to give a good performance but again and again the thought of Powell intruded. She was mechanical and she knew it. He had saved Haig. She had left the little dog sleeping—exhausted, gathering strength while he slept. How different it was now when he woke, when she offered him food; he took it quietly, gratefully, and returned immediately to sleep. Before she had felt herself a brute, trying to persuade him to take what she offered him. He had been so patient and obedient, but she had felt that he was asking, "Why do you bother me? I don't want it. Please leave me alone." Now his eyes might still be heavy, but they were bright; his skin felt loose and relaxed, his breathing was normal. All that he needed now was care and attention.

With all her relief, a relief which left her feeling almost weak, she knew that she was excited at the prospect of seeing George Powell again.

At the end of the performance Filmer came round to her dressing-room. He was scowling, and in some inexplicable fashion she realized that she was facing the anger of a weak man. He talked to her in a way which she felt was 'womanish'.

He said, "Your performance to-night was beneath contempt. Do you know that?"

"I'm sorry. I did my best. I've not slept much for the last two nights; my dog——"

He broke in. "I'm not concerned with your dog! You're an actress, not a dog-breeder. Because it's a small part you're asked to play this week you're disgruntled. You think that you ought to play leading rôles every week. Well, I'm directing this theatre! I expect people to play to the very best of their ability."

She said, "I know, Filmer. I'm terribly sorry. I shall be all right to-morrow night."

His voice was shrill as he answered, "To-morrow night! You'll be all right! For the last three nights your performance has been —been positively lamentable! But," he mimicked her tone, "you'll be all right to-morrow! If your precious dog is better, you'll be able to do your best. A pretty state of affairs."

His usually pale face was scarlet, his eyes cold and furious. This was not the man she knew, who had always been so kind, so gentle. This was someone who was venting his spite on her. She was taken aback. She didn't love him, but she had valued his friendship. Now—all friendliness was gone.

She flared, "I've worked, and worked hard, ever since I came here. I've played small, insignificant parts—I've played big ones when you felt you wished to cast me for them. If you want to find faults, why not go and talk to some of your other artistes? They can do with it, believe me. Other people are more often out of the theatre than in it! I've only had one week free, and for that I had to thank you again and again. You behaved as if you'd given me the earth! Why not speak to Miss Power? She's a small-part actress, and she is more at her home than she is in Cothampton!"

Filmer, his nostrils white, snapped, "Leave Miss Power out of it!"

Genevra thought, 'This will develop into a brawl unless I put an end to it'. She said, "I'm allowed to give a fortnight's notice. Please take it now."

She saw his face fall; knew that he was disturbed. "But—I want you to play *Fedora* in three weeks' time! I mean—well, you can't——"

"I leave in a fortnight from now. I think that's all there is to be said. Good night."

"No, no!" He came towards her, his hands outstretched. "Genevra, you can't behave like this. I've been so fond of you. I always hoped that one day——"

"But you hadn't sufficient understanding to make allowances, eh?"

"Genevra, you know that I'm terribly fond of you. I wanted you to come home to my father's place for a week-end. My father and mother know what I feel about you."

She had turned and begun to take off her make-up. Without turning round again she said, "Felt. Past tense, Filmer. Take Miss Power to your home."

Again he began to protest; she remained aloof, merely interpolating a phrase here and there. His sentences were to her silly and meaningless. She saw him clearly for perhaps the first time. A weak man, possessing insufficient knowledge for the work which he had undertaken. She felt assured that her attraction for him had died. Ruth Power, with a solid background, with no critical faculty, and with a readiness to hail him as a great producer, was what he really had hoped to find in her. As Filmer warmed to his opportunity, he elaborated. There had, he told her, been many times when she had argued with him, when she had shown very plainly—'and before the whole company'—that she disagreed with his ruling. He had offered her devotion, she had merely used him as a means to obtain good parts and further her own ambitions.

Genevra, still without turning, said, "Call my dresser, will you?"

"That's another thing!" He almost screamed. "A dresser. Other ladies in the company can do without a dresser—except Miss MacClintock, but you—you have to have your own dresser!"

That made her turn to face him. "Damn it, I pay her—you don't! Mind your own business and—get out!"

She was shaking as she walked back to her rooms. She had made her decision, she would leave in a fortnight. To hell with his production of *Fedora!* She would go back to Manchester, to gran'ma and gram'pa. Both she and Haig would be none the worse for the rest and the good food which Genevra knew would be waiting for them there. Or she could go to Aunt Tilda's. . . . She shrugged her shoulders. Henry had not written to her. He had taken the trouble to come to see her play Hedda, probably because Aunt Tilda had persuaded him to bring her.

She thought, 'What's Henry Lorimer to me—and, obviously, what am I to Henry Lorimer?'

Haig was asleep. Mrs. Rattery reported that he had taken several spoonfuls of beef essence, some milk into which had been poured several drops of brandy. "Good fer the 'eart, brandy is." He looked completely peaceful, even his breathing was almost normal.

She said, "I've given in my notice. I leave in a fortnight."

Mrs. Rattery said, "You never say! What-t-ever's 'appened? Noo, I'm real sorry about that. It's that Turner, I'll be bound. What you ever sore in 'im I'll never know. Pasty-faced thing! 'E's a pore actor, an' Rattery thinks very little of 'is productions. Well, I am grieved. 'Ow long? Eh, ondly a fortnight! Nay, that's a reit do, that is. Well, I allus say as it's 'ere ter-day an' gone ter-morrer. Why, we must get the little lad reit afore you leave." She stared hard at Genevra, then said, as if with some super-human effort, "I'll be sorry ter see you go. Both me and Rattery think a lot of you. I'll say good night. I've made up the camp-bed there. You'll be able ter sleep. God bless!"

Genevra remembered. "Mrs. Rattery, Mr. Powell is coming in to see Haig. I'll let him out. Don't wait up."

Mrs. Rattery nodded. "Yon's a man, yon is. Not some 'alf-baked lad wi' 'is 'air falling all over 'is face. Aye, you let 'im out. Goo' night."

Genevra made up the fire, gave Haig his tonic and some milk, after which the dog went peacefully to sleep again. She smoothed his coat and looked down at him, her heart filled with thankful-ness to—George Powell. Haig slept soundly, his breathing even and steady; it was obvious that he was better, only needing sleep and good food.

She started as she heard a tap on the window. She listened; it came again. She slipped out and opened the front door. Powell stood there smiling.

"I didn't want to disturb the whole house," he said. "How is he?"

"Sleeping—quietly, breathing easily."

He nodded. "He's over the worst. Can I come in?"

"Of course." Genevra knew that her heart was beating heavily. Powell followed her in, and moving softly, in a way which seemed astonishing to Genevra, for he was heavily built and his shoulders were very broad, he looked down at Haig.

"I shan't disturb him. Sleep's as good as medicine to him." He turned and looked at her, his smile widening. "Well, darling, are you glad to see me?"

Rather primly she pointed to the table. "Will you have some

supper? Mrs. Rattery's brawn is very good, she makes it at home here."

"Rather. Nothing I'd like better. Look, let me carve." When they were seated, and he had carved the brawn in beautifully thin slices and laid them with great care on the plates, he said, "I say, what fun! One day when you're a great actress, I'll come to London and we'll have supper at the Savoy together, shall we? Because," his voice was serious, "you are going to be a great actress. I've seen you in everything you've played here. You make the others look like tuppence."

He talked and she watched him. He was an exciting person to watch, though she could not have said why. His hands were very quick in their movements; they were sufficiently sensitive, with very fine reddish hair on the backs. His clothes were not particularly new, but they were well cut and well kept. His linen, she noticed, was immaculate.

He ate with appetite, but carefully cutting each piece with attention as if he wished it to be uniform with the others which he had eaten. Once or twice he turned to her and smiled. She saw how bright his eyes were, how they seemed to shine as if someone had placed a light behind them.

They ended the meal and Genevra said, almost shyly, "I generally make a cup of tea. Would you like to have one?"

He nodded emphatically. "Love it! Only let me do it. I know all about making tea. You sit still."

He brought her a cup, strong and fragrant, then sat down near her to drink his own. He stirred his tea with grave concentration, then looked up and met her eyes very steadily.

"This is serious, Genevra. For me, at least. What are you going to do about it?"

She said, "I don't quite understand. Are you—are you asking me to marry you?"

"I'd love to, if only I could! I was married two years ago, just a month before I qualified. She didn't like being married to a man who might be called out at any hour of the night or day. She didn't really like animals a great deal. She lives with her people in Shrewsbury. I expect one day she'll want a divorce. She's young and very pretty. She'll marry again. Meanwhile— I've fallen in love with you, Genevra. I've been in love with you for months. Seems dreadful that it nearly cost poor Haig his life to make it possible for us to meet, eh?"

She stared at him. She was terribly tired, her scene with Filmer had shaken her; she had never imagined that a man could scream and grow vituperative as he had done. It had disgusted her. She had always known that he was weak, but to have had to face his spite and his venom had shocked her. Here was this young man, obviously well balanced, kindly, and to whom she owed a great debt—he had saved Haig. That alone warmed her heart to him. He simply stated that he was in love with her.

She said, "I'm sorry that your marriage wasn't a success. It must be very lonely living here alone—with just your work to occupy you."

Powell laughed, softly, but with real enjoyment. "Darling, what a queer little thing you are! Yet you can play Hedda. There, you've finished your tea. No, of course you mustn't have another cup—you'll never sleep. Genevra, come away with me for a week-end. My dear, remember 'love's stuff that won't endure'. Let's catch at lovely things. I swear that I love you. If it were possible, I'd ask you to marry me. It's not. Then—oh, why let it all go?"

He rose and came to where she sat, and stooping put his arms round her, lifting her to her feet. He held her closely, whispering, "Darling, don't be afraid. I shan't hurt you. You mustn't shiver like that. Genevra, come away with me—on Saturday. I'll arrange everything—say that you will."

She said, "I'm leaving in a fortnight's time——"

"You mean that? Master Filmer Turner, I suppose? He's believed that he was in love with you. Damned wet! He's in love—or imagines himself to be—with every woman in the company. I live here, I know. Nasty little tick! So you're going." He kissed her cheek, very softly and tenderly. "Poor little Genevra —and you have so enjoyed playing good parts, and you've played them so well. And, dear, what about me? I've only two weeks left, to love you, to be happy with you! Darling, let's snatch at happiness! There is so little time. You'll go and heaven knows when I shall see you again. The world's waiting for you. I shall be stuck here. Kiss me—yes, please kiss me."

She liked the sensation of his arms being round her, liked his firm solidity, his deep quiet voice. She raised her head and kissed him. His arms tightened round her, he was whispering childish, silly but beautiful things. His mouth was hard against hers. She knew that her own will was being subjugated to his—or had she any will at all? She didn't know. He meant warmth, security— of a temporary kind, at least—she felt his breath coming quickly.

She said, half laughing, "You mustn't breathe like my poor Haig did!"

He stooped a little, lifted her in his arms, easily, securely. She was conscious of a moment of wild panic, then knew that she wanted his love—wanted it wildly, completely. He carried her to the camp-bed which Mrs. Rattery had made and laid her down very gently. She felt his body lying beside her, heard him whispering that she was the loveliest thing in the world—and drifted away into a state which was neither sleeping nor waking, only sensible that he was erasing all the venom that Filmer had stung her with, wiping out all the old unhappy things. Time had stopped, and when it began to move again she lay in his arms listening to his voice.

CHAPTER FOURTEEN

THEY sat in the old-fashioned sitting-room of an inn to which he had taken her when she met him outside the station at Birmingham after the performance on Saturday. He had taken Haig with him earlier in the day. He had told Mrs. Rattery, "Going into the country. I've got him a new coat. Very smart, isn't it? Miss Menetti's visiting her people, and fresh air's better for him than Manchester, eh?"

"Noo, I don't know. I've always liked Manchester. Theer's some 'go' in the place. Not like this dead-an'-alive 'ole! Mind as 'e doesn't catch cold. I'll never forgive you if 'e does."

Powell laughed. "Ma, remember that he's going with his own private and personal medical adviser!"

She nodded. "I know all aboot that—just the same, think on what I said."

Genevra had not known how tired she was until she climbed into the car and cuddled Haig to her. Powell swung the car out towards the country, the shabby streets were left behind; half asleep, Genevra saw fields, detached cottages, and in the distance the faint outline of hills.

She sighed. "How nice the air is!"

Powell glanced at her. "Close your eyes and just breathe it, then."

The inn was small, with a long sloping roof. They entered into a stone-flagged passage, where an oil-lamp swung, flinging great dancing shadows on the white walls. It felt and even smelt warm.

The little sitting-room was hideous and comfortable. The fire leapt and danced; a very large lamp, elaborate and ugly, hung from the centre of the ceiling, but the light which it gave was kind and mellow. A round table stood in the middle of the room, it bore a woollen mat of red and green upon which stood an aspidistra, its leaves shining as if to prove that care was lavished upon it. A wide horse-hair-covered sofa was placed along one side of the room, and over it hung old hunting-prints—rather spotted—in wide maple-wood frames.

Genevra and Powell sat facing each other in old-fashioned chairs which proved to be considerably more comfortable than they looked.

He smiled across at her. "Nice ugly room, eh?"

"Both," she answered. "You've been here before?"

She saw his eyes dance suddenly. He nodded. "Yes—they know me here."

"Alone?" She wished that she hadn't said that, and yet she had felt impelled to. His smile widened.

"No, my sweet, not alone."

Genevra raised her eyebrows. "Oh—I see."

He laughed. "That's just what you don't do, my dear. You're trying to make me confess that I came here with some lady of the chorus from the Birmingham pantomime—or some other such silliness. I came here fishing with a man called Tom Heathcroft. If you ask Baines—the landlord—he'll be only too delighted to show you his visitors' book."

She flushed and leaned down to pat Haig. "I'm sorry. I suppose I had a kind of spasm of jealousy. It was stupid—and impertinent. Please forgive me."

"I could forgive you a good deal more than that."

She raised her head and sent him back his smile. He watched her, content and reassured. How lovely she was, and how her every movement held him. Suddenly she asked, "George, do you think this is all—terribly wrong of us?"

He stood up, filled his pipe slowly and with intense care before he answered. Genevra found that his silences did not irritate her. There was something purposeful about them. He wasn't just—making time, trying to evolve some comforting piece of sophistry. He was really thinking of what she had asked.

Finally he said, "Honestly, I don't, Genevra. I can't see that we're hurting anyone. I love you—completely—I believe that you're fond of me. We're neither of us the kind of person who is only out for—sensation. We really enjoy being together, talking. I haven't deceived you. You've not deceived me. That little twerp—Turner—never meant anything to you. You thought that he had more knowledge than he had. You wanted to profit by it. Well, he just couldn't deliver the goods. What you've done in Cothampton you've done through your own hard work, ability, and—inborn acting power. No, I don't think that we're a pair of wicked, licentious people. I believe that we're two people who love warmth, kindness and companionship. Don't worry, darling."

"I won't." She added, "Ruth Power comes back on Monday."

He nodded. "I know. And in about ten days—you'll be gone. Where to, I wonder?"

"Manchester first, then—well, it depends what offers. I'd like to do some more rep work."

"You might find something not too far away," he said, "then I could always come over and give an eye to Haig, eh?"

"That had occurred to me, George."

Genevra, as she lay in bed that night, stretching out under the cool coarse linen sheet which smelt faintly of lavender, knew that she had been 'tightly strung' for years. The events of her childhood, the death of her father and mother, the change of environment, her determination to prepare for the stage, her entrance into the Turner Company and the parts which she had studied with such intensity and concentration had all served to make her strained and always working 'on her nerves'.

Under everything, and over everything, she knew too that she loved Henry. Why she should love him she did not know. He had been kind when she was a little girl, he had always been kind—but always inexplicable. Whenever she had thought that she was growing to understand him, to imagine for a moment that he wished to understand her, he had seemed to build a high wall between them. He might have appeared to be interested, even absorbed, in her and her projects, then suddenly he had changed—as it were—moved away from her. His visit to Cothampton had moved her deeply; she had realized that she hoped—for so much. He had gone, and since then she had only heard of him through Aunt Tilda.

She looked back on the six months which she had spent at Cothampton, and knew now how lonely she had been. True, Filmer Turner had assured her from time to time that he loved her; but what she suspected was, in reality, that he loved a good audience, someone to whom he could expound his rather pedantic formulas for making a success of a play.

Genevra knew that she was a far stronger character than Filmer could ever be. After having seen and talked to his successful father she knew too that old Turner held his son's work in no great esteem. He hoped to keep him busy and occupied until such a time as Filmer would tire of the stage and be prepared to 'settle down' and—make money.

'They're afraid,' she thought, 'that he'll marry some girl just because she's attractive—and then drift. They'd have welcomed me, because I make no bones about the stage being my chief—probably my only real—interest. They imagined that I'd either spur him on to do something good, or bully him to death so that he'd be glad to escape into the comparative peace of his father's works'.

Then, after six months of intensive hard work, when she had always been conscious that she was tired—not only through hard work but through a sense of frustration because she knew that Filmer Turner could never give her the direction and production which she longed for—Haig's illness had come to take from her the small remaining amount of energy which she still possessed. When she had felt that the last of the sand in her own particular hour-glass was running out, leaving her weak and exhausted, Filmer had indulged in his scene with her.

She had returned home to find Haig better, and a few moments later George had come in. He was all the things which Filmer had not been, never could be. He was calm, efficient, essentially kind. He neither 'fussed' nor 'blustered'. His big solid figure had filled the small stage of Mrs. Rattery's sitting-room. He had given orders—without giving offence. He had announced what he was going to do—and he had done it. He seemed filled with confidence; there had been no hesitation in his methods with regard to the dog. Then he had told her that he loved her. There had been no more hesitation in his lovemaking than there had been in his treatment of Haig. She knew that she had been weak, possibly she should have refused to listen to him; but she remembered that she had been exhausted, remembered that fact not in extenuation but as a reason for her readiness it allow him to make love to her.

She admitted, too, that she was hungry for love. She had felt starved, disappointed. She had indulged in dreams of Henry, she had thought for a time that Filmer Turner might give her what she longed for. Both had failed her—or she believed so—and when George came with his strong, very steady and almost unemotional kindness she had welcomed it.

She was happy with him. She knew that marriage was impossible, she even doubted if she really wanted to marry him.

Kindness, companionship, love and warmth, these things she knew that she longed for.

That night she slept dreamlessly, and woke to find the wintery sun shining, Haig demanding that he should be allowed to go out immediately, and for the first time in months she bathed and dressed conscious that she smelt with appreciation the scent of frying bacon which ascended the narrow stairs.

George was waiting for her. She looked at him attentively.

"You look magnificently 'tweedy'," she said.

He laughed. "I'm going to make both you and Haig come walking with me."

"Don't say it in that threatening tone! I like walking."

"And it won't be ' 'ammer, 'ammer, 'ammer on the 'ard 'igh road', you know. That's not my idea of a walk. Fields and narrow tracks, places where you can really *see* things."

It suddenly struck Genevra that she had rarely, if ever, taken a walk such as he described. When she was a child her walks had been taken with Jenny through the streets when she went shopping. Her father had always been working at his act, and came back to the caravan too tired to wish to take more exercise. Gram'pa and gran'ma never walked a yard if they could take a tram or a taxi, and Aunt Tilda believed that to stroll gently round the garden was all that anyone required to keep them in perfect health.

Now, when breakfast was finished, George gravely inspected her shoes.

"Not ideal, but we must make the best of them."

Indignantly she cried, "They're beautiful shoes!"

"I was thinking of their practical qualities. Assessing them as things in which to—walk."

Haig in his fine new coat rushed ahead of them, behaving as if he had never known a day's illness in his life. Genevra breathed deeply. The air was like wine, she thought.

"Doesn't it smell good!" she exclaimed.

He laughed. "As good as greasepaint and powder?"

"Ah, that's different—that's a significant smell, it means that you're in the theatre, going to work, going to try to create something. This is just open and free and clean."

She was interested in everything; she liked to hear him telling her about the wild things of the countryside, and laughed like a child when they came suddenly upon a hillside where rabbits were playing.

He said, "Now clap your hands and watch!"

In a second there was nothing to be seen after the brief flash of white bobbed tails disappearing into the burrows. He turned their path so that they walked beside the slow-moving river, and made her look into the water to catch sight of some perch which were lying there, lazily and as if they slept. He told her about his fishing holidays, of his ambition to go salmon-fishing, to go to Norway and fish there.

"Shall we go to Norway one day, Genevra?"

"If you'll leave me at home when you go fishing. I don't like seeing things killed. Or"—quickly—"if I wasn't playing."

"Work really does come first, eh?"

"Darling, it must or it's better to leave it and do something else."

He took her to a farmhouse. It belonged, he said, to Baines' brother Jim. She sniffed the smells of the farmyard, begged to be shown everything. Jim Baines was delighted; he beamed on her, and said, "Nay, you'll see nothin' as bonnie as w'at you are yerself, not i' my farm nor no other." She surprised him when she came to the horses; her comments on their heads, ribs, fetlocks and general condition amazed him.

" 'Ow cum as you know soa mooch about 'osses, missie?"

"I was brought up in a circus, a circus where they had the finest horses you could hope to see. I spent most of my waking hours with the grooms. Oh, how I used to swear! They did it as a matter of course, but when my mother brought me home, my poor gran'ma was terribly shocked."

George said, "You should hear how I swear when I'm operating!"

Baines laughed. "Nay, most chaps swears; they mean nout bi it."

As they walked home, Powell said, "I never knew you'd had anything to do with a circus. Tell me about it—then show business is in your blood?"

She slipped her arm through his, and without any straining after effect told him all she remembered; of her handsome, adorable father, her pretty mother, even about Holst. He listened silently, making no comment until she ended her story, saying, "And so—here I am!"

They had reached a stile, and as she stood looking into his eyes he caught her to him, saying, "Dear little Genevra, you've had some bad times. I wish that I could make up to you for them all! Damn it, if I were free, would you marry me?"

She answered gravely, "If I felt about you then as I do now —yes."

They left early on the Monday morning, for Powell had his surgery to open. At Birmingham he left her, taking Haig back to Cothampton. That night she began playing her last part with Filmer Turner's Repertory Company. A fairly large part, one which required a great deal of hard work and gave small returns. Genevra had told Powell that it was 'a stupid part in a silly play'. During her waits the various members of the company came up to her, always with the same question on their lips. "Genevra, is it really true?" or, "Darling, you're not really leaving!" Some of them, she felt, were actually sorry to lose her, others—and she smiled—were thankful to be rid of her. She noticed that Filmer was particularly attentive to Ruth Power, who came in to 'watch the show' and was not playing, only rehearsing for the next week's production. The next morning, at rehearsal, Genevra said to Filmer, "My fortnight's notice ends next Thursday. There isn't much point in my rehearsing this week, is there?"

He replied coolly, even insolently, "None at all. I was going to suggest that you didn't bother. Miss Power, I believe, will be admirable in the part."

Genevra said, "I hope so. Thank you."

She wrote to her grandmother, packed her skips and boxes, and on the following Saturday left Cothampton for the Gallant Huzzar, where George was to join her in the evening.

Mrs. Rattery had let her go unwillingly. "Nay, I could do wi' a lot more like you, luvey. I fair 'ate ter see you go. Aye, an' Rattery does an' all. As fer losin' Haig—well, I don't know what ter say. It's like what losing a child is!"

"Perhaps one day I'll come back, Ma. Come back a real leading lady."

"Ye're lady enoof noo—as fer 'leadin'', 'alf Cot'ampton's ondly cum ter Turner's flea-pit ter see you!"

"Would you turn out one of your permanents for me?"

"I'd turn t'damned world oot fer you!"

She carried away many memories which were happy, remembered small actions, kindly phrases, which warmed her heart. One day, she determined, as she sat in the little local train which rattled along towards Bilsbeck, where Fossick would be waiting with 'the trap', she would come back to Cothampton. Come back, not as one of Filmer Turner's company—if it existed so long— but as an actress with a name which was known not only in England but in America as well.

She cuddled Haig to her more closely. "It's all coming, my dear, it's all coming."

Baines, his face shining from the use of much soap and water, wearing a suit of startling tweeds which were too small for his stout figure, called, as the train drew to a standstill, " 'Ello, miss! 'Ello, 'Aig!" in a voice which sounded like distant thunder. When Genevra left the station, at which she was the only arrival except some empty egg-boxes and a crate containing chickens, Baines announced, somewhat unnecessarily, "I've fetched t'trap, miss. Can yer joomp oop?"

Genevra enjoyed her week-end. Her enjoyment was not merely physical; she liked being with George; she was not certain that she was not in love with him. She liked his solidity, his sound sense, his essential kindness and his obvious longing to do everything she wished. She knew that marriage with him was impossible, and even that a continued association could only end in disaster. She would be working—he was more or less tied to Cothampton. She knew him sufficiently well to realize that he would never—for any reason—neglect his practice. That being so, it was inevitable that their meetings would grow less and less frequent, and that slowly the love which he felt for her, and the affection which she felt for him, would fade. Other interests, other people, would enter her life and his, and this present state of things would become something which was actually outside their lives, only to be dragged into them from time to time.

For that last Sunday, they loved and laughed, found life filled with colour and brightness. Genevra knew that she was relieved to have finished with Filmer Turner. She had learnt all she could from him, and now she longed for work under some producer who would have knowledge vastly superior to her own.

On the Sunday evening they sat together in the ugly little sitting-room. George smoked in silence, his eyes always turned towards Genevra. She stared into the fire, trying to make pictures, dream dreams and see visions.

Finally he said abruptly, "And to-morrow you go to Manchester."

"Yes. You have the address?"

He laughed. "I wonder if my letters—I write such poor letters —will mean anything to you? Well, if you don't answer them, remember that so long as I live I shall be indebted to you. It's been so lovely to be with you, to know you—yes, to love you. You're a rare person."

She felt that her eyes suddenly stung with tears. At that moment she loved George Powell very dearly. He was so understanding. There had been times when he could—and had

—asserted himself, but they were few and far between. His behaviour after their first week-end together, when she had returned to Cothampton, had been completely discreet. Twice they had supper together at the hotel, and several times he had met her, as if by accident, and walked home with her. Now his tone was faintly regretful, but there was no hint of overstressed sentiment, and no trace of whining. He was not attempting to make any demands on her. He only told her that he was, for always, in her debt.

She stretched out her hand, and he took it.

"George dear," she said, "I don't know. That's honest, at all events. I'm beginning, and the beginning is almost invariably hard work. I just—don't know. That sounds terribly hard, dreadfully offhand, but it's true. Now, here, in this funny little room, I love you very dearly. How can I promise that, separated, this love can last for the rest of my life? There'll always be a sort of tenderness for you; when I think of you I shall know that a kind of warmth steals through me—but love! It's such a strange thing, my dear. Do you find me very hateful?"

"No," he said. "No. I think that I understand. Darling, you're barely nineteen! How much, despite all your travels and experiences that you told me last Sunday, have you really known about what people call life?"

That night she slept in his arms, and cried a little because their time together was over, and something told her that although she might see him again, things would never be the same.

"I don't want to let you go," she whispered, and George bent over her, kissing away her tears and assuring her that at any time, anywhere, she had only to send for him and he'd leave everything and come to her.

She said, "I believe that you mean it too."

He kissed her again, saying, "You know very well that I do."

The next morning he left very early for Cothampton; their parting was subdued but without any apparent emotion; later, Genevra and Haig were driven by Baines to the station, and that afternoon she was seated in the familiar room in Stratton Street, feeling that she had never been away.

They were glad to see her, anxious to hear what she had done and what she intended to do. Gran'ma said, "My luv, by the look of you a rest's what you want. Never mind rushing about for a new shop right away. What do you say if you and me went off for a bit of a holiday?" She sighed. "Nothing I'd like better than to see Paris again! Would you like to go to Paris, luv?"

Josh said, "Thet's right, snatch her away just as she's coom home ter see her old gram'pa!" But he smiled as he said it, and Genevra knew that he was what he himself always referred to as 'funning'.

Ten days later they went to Paris, and Lottie gave it as her opinion that it had 'changed sadly, not the same life as there used to be'. They stayed for a week, during which time Genevra's feet never ceased aching, for her grandmother was indefatigable. She loved staring in shop windows, found museums and picture galleries highly stimulating, and was ready for a music-hall at night. She adored the good food, and made copious notes in order to attempt the same dishes for some of her clients when she returned to Manchester.

At the end of the week they returned to London, and went to Barnet to stay with Tilda Lorimer. Henry had given his mother a car of her own, and the gardener had been given driving lessons. Genevra refused to drive with them every day, pleading that she must go up to town and see about work. Henry had not appeared, and Tilda explained that he was busier than ever. "There never was anyone like my Henry for work!"

So Genevra went to London, and did the round of such agents' offices as she knew—which were not many—until finally she reached the last on her list, in Shaftesbury Avenue. She was shown into the most untidy office she had ever seen, where a woman sat behind a desk littered with papers. Genevra wondered how she ever found anything!

She smiled and said in a voice which Genevra felt was not only pleasant but sounded as if she were really interested, "Now, what do you want? You're lucky, I was just going out to luncheon. Tell me about yourself."

Genevra told her as much as she could remember which might be germane to the business in hand. The woman nodded. "Not bad—in six months. Like rep work, or is it too hard for you?"

"Too hard! I want hard work—I don't mind, I mean, how hard it is, if I can find that I'm getting on."

"Um, let's see now. How old are you? Nearly nineteen. Specialize or just take what's given to you? That's right! Oh, I obviously don't mean that you should play old ladies!" She laughed, and Genevra felt warm and reassured. "I believe I could fix you at Bristol—Harvey Cartwright's rep—or I might even get you in at Leicester. I wonder which would be better. I've got all your particulars, yes. Living in London? Only this week, then back to—where?—Manchester. I shall be in Manchester next week. I'm going up to see Frank Millet's new show. Have you a telephone number?" Genevra produced it and gave her the card. "Good, I'll telephone you. So if you hear that Miriam Warner wants you, you'll know who it is. Good-bye, and the best of luck. You know about commission and all the rest of it, do you? Good heavens, look at the time! I'm late."

She seized her bag, and was through the door, still calling "Best of luck," before Genevra realized that she was gone.

Far too shy to ring for the lift, Genevra made her way down countless stairs into the street; she thought that she would like luncheon, and surely the Ivy was somewhere near here? Vaguely she remembered. Would they refuse her a table? Dare she mention Henry's name? She pushed open the door and went in. Immediately she wished that she had gone somewhere else. How terrible if they looked her up and down and then said that it was impossible to find her a seat as she wasn't a regular customer!

A grey-haired man in commissionaire's uniform said, "Are you waiting for someone, miss?"

She said, "No, I want a table, just for me, please. I have been here before, with Mr. Henry Lorimer."

He said, "I'll see," and came back to say that they thought they could find a place for her. She went into the crowded restaurant, and to her delight it appeared that there was a table, and she was ushered to it by Signor Abel himself.

He said, "But Mistaire Lorimer is 'ere now! I shall tell 'im that you 'ave come!" He beamed at her; so good an Italian as Abel, he could not but smile at anyone so attractive.

Genevra, hoping that she looked as if she lunched or dined at the Ivy several times a week, studied the menu and gave her order. She leaned back and watched the people. There were one or two whose faces were familiar. That was surely Bobbie Andrews, and with him—she knew so well—Lilian Braithwaite, tall, elegant and—she had heard—always amusing. Dame Marie Tempest—instinctively Genevra felt that she always sat at the same table and that everyone paid court to her. A lovely woman, with fair hair and a comprehensive smile, which never slipped into being merely mechanical; she heard someone at the next table whisper, "There's Dorothy Ward!" How exciting it all was! If only one day she could come here and know that people said, "There's Genevra Menetti!"

Then she heard Henry's voice. "My dear, what are you doing here?"

He looked, she thought, magnificent. No one wore clothes as Henry did, and his smooth-looking grey-blue suit, with its restrained tie, suited him admirably. She looked up and smiled.

"I'm lunching at the Ivy," she said calmly.

"But why didn't you telephone to me? I'm lunching with a friend I'd like you to meet. Will you come and lunch with us?"

"I'd rather have luncheon alone, Henry, thank you. I'd love to come over later—perhaps to have coffee with you. Yes?"

"Delightful. We're over there. You're staying with my mother?" He paused for a second, then said, "I'm running down there to-night. Could I take you back? I shall be leaving Levelle's at five sharp. Could you be there or shall I call for you somewhere?"

"I shall be there."

"Then," and he prepared to bow himself away, "you'll come over for coffee? Lovely."

She ate her food slowly, thinking, thinking, thinking. How good it was to see Henry again; how Henry made other men seem rough and even a little uncouth. George Powell—she had scarcely thought of him since she left Cothampton. Yet George was a nice person, kind and considerate. Filmer—he had almost faded from her memory. That young actor who had wanted to 'help' her—what was his name? She remembered—Mason! The sight of Henry had served to dim her memories of them all.

She finished her meal, paid her bill, saying, "I'm taking coffee at Mr. Lorimer's table."

The waiter said, "Ah, Mistaire Lorimare—I shall show you, madame."

Henry was at a table with an elderly but very smartly dressed woman. Genevra thought that she must be considerably over forty. She was quite remarkably plain, and yet there was something attractive about her. Her eyes were good, she had beautiful teeth, but her skin was sallow and looked dull and thick.

Henry sprang to his feet. "Ah, Genevra—Mrs. Gossage, this is my very old friend, Genevra Menetti."

The woman said, "She doesn't look as though she could be anyone's—very old friend! What a charming name!"

Genevra said, "I think that it's rather nice. My father was an Italian."

"You know Italy?" Genevra shook her head. "My dear, you must go there. After all, it's your own country and, Henry, was it Disraeli who said that the person who did not know Italy always suffered from an inferiority complex? I think so. You're an actress, Henry tells me, and you can't afford to have inferiority complexes!"

Henry said, "I saw her play Hedda; I did indeed."

Mrs. Gossage said, "Ridiculous! And yet, how old was Hedda? Only twenty-five or twenty-six. This child—must be—what? Twenty?"

"Nineteen," Genevra said.

She shrugged. "Yes, but Hedda was never written for girls of even twenty-five. What else have you played?"

"I played the step-daughter in *Six Characters* and Frida in *Henry the Fourth*." She chuckled, a sound which Clementina Gossage found delightful. "I never allowed the producer any peace until he put on both those plays. Oh, what terrible flops they were too!" She realized that she was talking a good deal, flushed and said, "Oh, and lots of other parts. Now I'm looking for someone else to employ me."

Clementina said, "That sounds ominous. Why did you leave the other company?"

"For one reason. I realized that the producer—this sounds conceited—couldn't teach me anything."

Mrs. Gossage turned to Henry. Genevra felt that she might not have been at the table judging from the way Mrs. Gossage spoke.

"Henry, you've seen her. Is she good? Has she possibilities?"

He nodded gravely. "I thought so. My mother was entranced, astonished."

"What do you think about sending her to Melton Carter? He has those two theatres—one at Follingly—that's a town filled with respectable, retired people who, when they're not playing bridge or golf, like the theatre—and the other at Lelton, which is simply a manufacturing town—full of mills and factories and people who go to the theatre to be interested or amused, not as a social duty. Bags of money, and he's clever. If he hadn't had that accident he'd have been playing here in London. I never saw a career open more brilliantly. Poor devil! He produced *Carthage 702*, and then—to prove that he could do serious stuff—*Skeleton Leaves*. Plenty of money. His father was old Jonas Carter of the patent window frames, the 'Letgo' Car, and half a dozen other things. Let's send her to Melton, shall we?"

Genevra said, quietly and with considerable diffidence, "I have an agent."

Henry said, "You have? Who?"

"Miss Miriam Warner."

Mrs. Gossage said, "Oh, Miriam! I know her. Very well, I'll give you a note to take round to her. She's just near here; Gloucester Mansions, I think."

"I've just come from there."

Henry laughed. "Genevra knows all the ropes."

"All the same, you go to Carter if you can. It's rather an extraordinary company. Two theatres, and you play a week at each one. Henry, get the bill and I'll drive this nice child to my place and give her the note for Miriam, then she can meet you at five."

They drove to Mrs. Gossage's flat, which was in Arlington Street, in a car which to Genevra appeared to be rather longer than the Ivy itself. Henry put them into the lift, a thing which looked like a monster bird-cage, all gilt and pieces of glass, and waved them good-bye, saying, "Five, then, Genevra."

The flat staggered her a little, it was so silent. Your feet made no noise because the carpets were so thick; the bells made no noise, the servants who answered them made no noise. Even their voices sounded muffled and subdued.

The room into which Mrs. Gossage led her was white. Genevra realized that it was not quite white, and supposed it to be the tint she had heard referred to as 'off white'. Mrs. Gossage said, "This is the room Henry designed; it's excellent, I think."

Genevra thought, 'Designed! What design is there about it? One picture, and that's ugly. A grand piano, a thick white carpet —and a long time it will stay while in London!—and four great sofas covered with dirty-looking white ribbed silk. If that's what Henry calls designing—welll' She said, "I've never seen a room like it, never."

Mrs. Gossage smiled, and when she smiled the expression redeemed the plainness of her face. Genevra, watching her, thought, 'She's plain, she's positively ugly, but—oh, she's groomed to the last hair! Her clothes are perfect, I suppose Henry designs them. She's certain of herself, as those actresses I saw at the Ivy to-day are sure of themselves. That's what I've got to have. Poise, certainty, balance'.

Now she said, "You'll have tea, won't you? I can write that note to Miriam while they bring it." She rang. A silent-footed servant came, was given the order, and closing the door silently, vanished.

The note was written on thick grey paper which felt like cardboard.

Genevra said, "Forgive me, you've not sealed the envelope."

Again that smile which made you forget the plainness of the face.

"I don't seal letters when my friends deliver them for me, my dear."

Tea arrived, pale liquid which tasted astonishingly good, which gave off a scent which was delicious. Mrs. Gossage said, "Cream or lemon?"

Genevra thought, 'I'll show her!' and said firmly, "Lemon," which made the tea taste, she thought, extraordinary and not particularly pleasant.

"I'll telephone to Miriam," Mrs. Gossage said, and Genevra listened to a conversation which seemed to be completely composed of, "I wish you would—that would be kind," and, "Yes, Genevra Menetti—charming name! . . . Coming now with my note . . . Oh, you thought so—well, you ought to know, my dear . . . Very well—yes, if you can. Manchester—of course, young Millet's show—might be interesting. Good-bye, and I shall be grateful. I don't think that Melton will regret it. Yes, writing to-night. Good-bye."

Again a servant was summoned. "A taxi for Miss Menetti, please."

She was on her way to Shaftesbury Avenue, Mrs. Gossage's note in her hand.

Miss Warner, seated again behind her untidy desk, said, "So you know Clementina Gossage, eh? I've known her for years. She's a grand woman. She suggests"—she read the note as she spoke—"that you go to Melton Carter. I admit that I hadn't thought of it. Oh, he's very good. Interesting man. Tragic business—that accident. He's sure to be in Manchester—I'll telephone to you. Oh, if Clementina recommends anyone—it's a certainty. Nice of you to have come back to me. I appreciate that —very much. Good-bye, see you in Manchester."

Genevra made her way back to Levelle's; there at the kerb stood Henry's car, and a moment later Henry himself ran down the steps and called:

"Hello, Genevra, how nice this is!"

He drove northwards, over Oxford Street, along Gloucester Place and past Lord's before he spoke. Genevra sat quietly, watching his keen, rather lean face.

At last when Swiss Cottage was left behind, he said, "And how did you like Mrs. Gossage?"

"As much as and a good deal more than I like most people I meet. She was marvellous to me. Gave me a note to Miss Warner, telephoned to her and—well, she couldn't have been kinder. She told me that you designed her room."

"I did. What do you think of it?"

"Not much, Henry dear. Stick to dress-designing."

"It has been admired—considerably admired."

"Why?"

He laughed suddenly and unexpectedly. "Honestly, I don't know."

"Her clothes are lovely."

He gave her a quick smile. "Ah, then you approve of that side of my work, eh? I must stick to that, then. Oh, Genevra, it is nice to see you!"

CHAPTER FIFTEEN

GENEVRA looked back on the evening that followed as something which had been completely satisfactory. Alice, as always when Henry came home, prepared a meal which was a masterpiece. Aunt Tilda beamed at everyone; Lottie and she told stories of their young days on the stage which were amusing, if towards the end of the evening they tended to become a little ribald.

Henry and Genevra sat talking long after Tilda and Lottie had gone to their beds, each bearing a glass of whisky and hot water in which a slice of lemon floated.

Henry sighed with contentment, lit a cigarette with an air of satisfaction and said, "Now, tell me all about yourself—what you have done and what you're going to do. I've not seen you since that night when you played Hedda."

For one wild moment she wondered what Henry would say if she told him about George Powell. Would the news affect him, make him angry? She watched him intently, and felt that in all probability he would only shrug his shoulders, and possibly tell her that she had been foolish and that George had behaved like a cad. She asked, instead, if he knew anything about Melton Carter and his repertory company.

Melton Carter had been, Henry said, a very promising young actor. He was marked down by the critics for success; he had good looks, a good voice, a great deal of money which he had inherited from his father Sir Jonas Carter, and his maternal grandmother, the Hon. Julia Blakestone. He had played Shakespeare with distinction, his comedy in modern plays was regarded as excellent, he took a theatre and decided not only to act but produce.

His first production, *Carthage 702*, had been acclaimed as a complete success. It had run for nine months. Then Carter sent out two touring companies and produced *Skeleton Leaves*, with which he repeated the success of the first venture. He played the lead, a strange neurotic character needing careful and skilful treatment. The play was booming; 'house full' boards were out for every performance; people declared that the play would run for months. It was in its second month when Carter, making his exit, stumbled and pitched head first down a flight of stairs which led to the cellars of the theatre. In spite of orders given that the door must on no account be left open, someone had forgotten! The result was that for weeks Melton Carter lay in hospital while the doctors waited for him to die. He possessed a fine constitution and slowly began to recover. He found himself held firmly in splints and mechanical devices which felt like plate armour. He gathered strength, asked questions, and listened, his face unmoved, while the great surgeon Sir Franklin Bates gave his verdict.

Carter would live, provided that he lived reasonably and exercised a certain amount of care. It was inevitable that he would suffer a considerable amount of pain, and he would always walk with great difficulty.

"That puts paid to the stage?" Carter asked.

"I am afraid so."

"Then I must be content with producing. Oh, well, it might be worse."

He had taken two theatres—as Clementina Gossage had told Genevra—and had recently finished a very successful season.

"Does Mrs. Gossage know him?" Genevra asked.

"Oh, very well. He's a great friend of hers," Henry said.

"Are you a great friend of hers?"

"I think so, and of her husband's. They've both been remarkably kind to me. She's evidently prepared to be interested in you, Genevra."

Genevra sighed. "I wish that I could afford to dress as she does! I will—one day. I'll have a flat in Arlington Street—and", she laughed, "it won't be furnished in that dreary 'off white'!"

For the remainder of their stay Henry came to Barnet every evening. There were times when Genevra thought that he was really falling in love with her. He dropped what she stigmatized as 'his superior manner' and talked naturally and easily. When she spoke of her work he appeared to be interested; he brought her flowers, expensive sweets from London, and on her last evening showed real regret that her visit was over.

"It's been nice to have you here. You don't come nearly often enough, you know. You ought to make a point of sharing your favours between Barnet and Manchester!"

She said, "You're so often away!"

That was a mistake, and she knew it the moment she had spoken.

Henry answered, with less than his former warmth, "But my mother loves to have you here; you can't come sufficiently often for her."

He said, "Good night," explaining that he had to be away very early in the morning. Levelle's were having a dress show which for beauty, luxury and costliness would outdo anything which London had seen.

Genevra said, "If I'm still out of work, shall I come and be a model for you? I can walk quite nicely."

He smiled. "I'm afraid that there is very little chance of your being out of work. Good luck, my dear, and great success." He leaned forward and kissed her cheek, kindly and with affection.

"Good night, dear Genevra."

Back in Manchester, Miss Warner telephoned. She was to go down to the Midland and ask for Melton Carter's suite. He was interested not only in what Miss Warner had told him, but with what Clementina Gossage had written.

Genevra rushed down to the Midland, entered its somewhat gloomy portals and was escorted to the lift and finally to Mr. Carter's suite. The door was opened by a tall serious-looking man with a melancholy expression and immaculate and very conventional clothes.

"Yes, Mr. Carter is expecting you, Miss Menetti." He lowered his voice. "You know, perhaps, that Mr. Carter is an invalid; this is not one of his good days. He is in considerable pain."

She was taken into the room where he lay on a sofa. Genevra saw a tall, exceedingly thin young man with a haggard, clean-shaven face. His eyes were very bright and sunk deeply in his head. She supposed that he was handsome, though the evident marks of pain engraved on his face robbed him of much of his possible good looks.

He held out his hand. "Ah, Miss Menetti—Genevra Menetti. How do you do? I'm afraid that I can't get up to greet you—or I *could*, but I dislike giving myself additional discomfort. Sit down, won't you?" He watched her as she seated herself, and said, "Thank God you've learned how to sit down. Half the people I interview either twist themselves like snakes or slump untidily like a sack of potatoes. You've been with Filmer Turner, eh? I heard about you from Lorimer. Turner's an ass, isn't he? Pretentious ass! Did you find that you learnt anything?"

Genevra smiled; Carter, watching, thought what a pleasant smile it was, how pleasant she was to look at altogether. She said, "I learnt to work hard. But—well, Mr. Turner wasn't sufficiently strong. I mean, he never seemed to me to know *all* the play, he only concentrated on the high spots."

He nodded. "And you played . . . ?"

"Anything, everything. Good parts—I mean big parts—and small ones."

Carter said, "I'm glad you didn't say 'bad parts', because my answer to that is, 'There are no bad parts, only bad actors and actresses'. And Clementina Gossage thinks that you might like to come to me. One week at Follingly, where they come to the theatre when they're tired of playing bridge, and Lelton, where they come because they love the theatre and really know quite a lot about good acting. Each play gets two weeks, which gives us two clear weeks for rehearsing the new one. Oh, it's not enough, but it's better than a bare week. Is that the real colour of your hair?"

His question came so abruptly that Genevra flushed. "Of course, and my skin is its real colour and my eyelashes are not stuck on!"

She saw him raise his eyebrows, as if her bluntness surprised him, but he made no casual reply. His next question was, "What did Turner pay you?"

She told him.

He nodded. "I'll give you nine. I advise you to have rooms in Follingly and to stay at a small hotel—Mr. Wright will give you the address—in Lelton. It's turning out all right, Hubert, that hotel, isn't it?"

"I've had no complaints, except from—as I told you—from Miss Strong and Mr. Fillerton."

Carter replied, "Those two damned people would complain of the Kingdom of Heaven, if ever they got there." Then he held out his hand to Genevra. "That's settled, then, eh? Will you be at the stage door of the King's Theatre at Follingly on Monday at ten? I warn you I am bad-tempered, self-opinionated, excessively rude and a slave-driver. Does the prospect frighten you?"

She took his hand and held it for a second. "Not in the very least. Those are all qualities which I possess, very largely, myself. Good-bye."

The tall thin man took her to the door of the suite. He gave her a wintry smile. "I think you amused him. My name is Wright —Hubert Wright. I'm the manager. I'll send you the contract. We have your address? Yes, Miss Warner gave it to me, I remember." He lowered his voice and almost whispered, "It's a great privilege to work with him. He's brilliant as a producer. What a loss to the stage as an actor! Well, Miss Menetti, I shall see you at Follingly. Oh, what about clothes?"

"I think that you'll find they are—at least—adequate. I have quite a lot of Edwardian clothes too—they're very good. Good-bye."

Two days later she received her contract, and a note from Hubert Wright stating that if she arrived, as he trusted that she would, on the Sunday she would find that Mrs. Thackle, of 15, Albion Street, had rooms, recently occupied by Miss Strong, which she could take if they seemed suitable.

Haig was left with her grandmother, and Genevra left on the Sunday morning for Follingly. It proved to be a very neat, well kept town, with a slightly self-conscious air. The streets were wide, the shuttered shops well kept so far as paint and varnish went. People—Genevra supposed on their way back from church —looked well dressed, highly respectable, and, like the town in which they lived, rather self-conscious.

Albion Street was small, the houses had tiny gardens filled with golden privet and laurel bushes. Number 15 appeared to be no better and no worse than its neighbours. Mrs. Thackle, a small, thin, dried-up woman with her hair scraped back from a high and bony forehead, opened the door, saying, "Might you be Miss—the lady with the foreign name?"

"I'm Genevra Menetti."

"Come in, will you? I do hope as you'll not be like that Miss Strong. A holy terror she was. Wore me to litt'rully skin an' bone. Her tempers! I've got a nice bit of beef cooking for our dinners if you'd care to have a cut off of it. My Yorkshires are pretty good—mind, I find 'em chancy. Sometimes they'll almost push the top off the oven; next time—they're flat as what pancakes are. There's no telling. How do you like your room, miss?"

It might have been the twin of Mrs. Rattery's; not quite so clean, and lacking the same amount of polish on the furniture.

Genevra asked the price; Mrs. Thackle said that she'd prefer to leave that to Genevra.

Genevra said briskly, "Oh, that won't do at all. I can't sell and buy!"

"Shall we say—three pounds?"

"Every other week I shall be away at Lelton," Genevra reminded her.

"For the weeks as you're away, shall we say—two pounds?"

"My rooms mustn't be let to anyone else, remember. . . ."

Mrs. Thackle expressed a kind of hurt surprise. "Miss, as if I ever would!" with such emphasis that Genevra felt certain that was exactly what she had hoped to do. "No, when you're away that gives me the chance that I'm always waiting for. There never was a woman like what I am for cleaning. Morning, noon and night I'm at it. My gentleman lodger—he works nights, you'll scarcely never see him—calls me the non-stop express. Very nice young man he is, been with me three years now. He works at the gasworks, nice steady job it is too. He has the little bedroom at the back. Yours is at the front. Lovely sunny room. Last Bank Holiday Mr. Howsditch—that's his name—distempered it something lovely for me. I told him no perfessional could have done it better nor what he did. He'll be glad to take your luggage up for you, I'm sure."

Mr. Howsditch proved to be a short, immensely broad young man with red hair and a face heavily powdered with freckles. He emerged from the kitchen in answer to Mrs. Thackle's call of "Gerald!" blushing deeply and expressing his willingness to carry Genevra's luggage upstairs by saying, "This it? 'Ere we go, then! Quick's the word an' sharp's the action."

He put the baggage in the positions which Genevra indicated, then stood breathing heavily.

She said, "Thank you very much."

He answered, "Nothink ter thank me for. 'S' pleasure. I did this room. Tasty, isn't it? Well, s'long."

The room was small, it looked clean, though the bed sagged ominously in the middle. The smell of roast beef ascended the stairs. Genevra thought of her grandmother's rooms, with their running water, large towels and good solid furniture, and sighed. The towels provided for her use by Mrs. Thackle were thin and cottony; it struck her that they were not unlike Mrs. Thackle herself—small and inadequate.

She went down and ate her dinner. The meat was good, though the Yorkshire pudding had obviously been made on one of

Mrs. Thackle's 'off days'. It was heavy and leathery. The potatoes were hard and waxy, the greens swam in a shallow bath of green water. An immense and badly cleaned cruet held a battery of bottles, all empty except one, which contained some dark sinister-looking fluid. In addition to the meat there was a shivering pink blancmange and some withered-looking prunes.

Mrs. Thackle entered after twenty minutes, saying, "Would you like a nice cup o' tea, and shall I clear? Do you like the cloth taken off or lef' on? Some likes it one way, some another."

"Taken off, please. Can you tell me how far Cothampton is from here?"

"Now, I never was one for j'ography. I'll ask Mr. Howsditch."

Again in answer to her call of "Gerald!" he came, and Genevra put her question to him.

"Cot'ampton?" he repeated. " 'Seasy. Thirty-five miles from 'ere, an' a bare thirty from Lelton. Good road all the way. I've done it plenty o' times on the ole motor-bike. 'Snothing!"

That afternoon Genevra wrote letters—to her grandmother asking that a selection of towels might be sent to her, asking for news of Haig and giving as pleasant a picture of her rooms as she could do with any truth. She wrote to Aunt Tilda almost the same letter except that she did not ask for towels, and substituted queries regarding Henry and Alice for those about Haig. Lastly she wrote to George Powell; next week she would be at Lelton, she supposed, but would let him know.

She felt no great desire to see George. True, he would be someone to talk to; he would flatter her vanity by assuring her that Turner's rep wasn't the same without her, and say how much he had missed her. She knew quite certainly that she did not love him; whatever she had felt had become nothing more than a tolerant affection. He had written to her several times, brief affectionate letters telling her nothing in particular and barely covering two pages. Still, she knew that to spend Sunday in some small hotel in a mill town would reduce her to a state of acute depression—George might ward that off at least.

She went to bed early, found her bed less uncomfortable than she had expected, and in the morning experienced the pleasant surprise of discovering that the bathroom was not only clean but that the water was really hot. She dressed carefully, had her breakfast—which consisted of a fried egg, slightly speckled through having been cooked in a pan which was not completely clean, two bits of bacon, and tea which was a rich dark mahogany in colour.

As she was leaving the house Mr. Howsditch entered it. He was wearing a boiler suit, and grinned a greeting.

"'Morning, miss. I've finished—you're starting, eh? Wot a life! S' long."

The theatre was solid and old-fashioned, but it was well kept, and at the stage-door entrance everything was beautifully clean. The doorkeeper gave her a 'good morning', saying, "An' your name, miss? Might you be Miss Menetti by any chance? Right ahead for the stage. You're a bit on the early side, but Mr. Tancroft an' Miss Trent are there. Stage manager and A.S.M., miss."

Charles Tancroft hurried forward to meet her. He was small and energetic, with lightish hair which seemed to bristle on his head. The girl was thin, young and looked eager. She said, "I'm Freda Trent. You're staying at Mrs. Thackle's, aren't you?" She laughed, a high, uncertain sound. "She'll talk you to death! Oh—here are the rest of the company."

She rushed away, and Genevra heard her greeting them with a warmth which was slightly overdone. She watched them all carefully; her impression was that they were a more experienced selection than she had met at Turner's. So much the better, she would have to work to keep up with them. A tall, rather stout woman came towards her holding out her hand.

"I'm Nellie Gosforth, Miss Menetti. I'm at Number Fourteen, next door to you." Her voice was rich, heavy and well modulated. "If I can be of any help, in anything, you've only to come in. Don't forget."

There was a stir at the side of the stage, and Melton Carter appeared leaning on the arm of Hubert Wright, with the stage-doorkeeper on his other side. Genevra watched his entrance with horror, though she contrived to keep her face expressionless.

Carter was very tall, incredibly thin; his face was pallid and his eyes lacked all expression except that of intense pain. She saw how heavily he leaned on Wright's arm, saw too that he dragged his right leg as if it were completely useless, while the foot twisted inwards helplessly. She saw that there was a Madeira chair with an extension down stage, and into this they lowered him carefully.

His face was damp and his breath came rapidly. She thought, 'How does he do it? He's got sufficient money apparently just to remain an invalid, and he must subject himself to this every morning!' No one actually watched him; several of the company turned their backs and appeared to be absorbed in conversation, others read their mail. At last Wright said, "Mr. Carter is ready, ladies and gentlemen."

Everyone turned as if spun round by some invisible force.

Carter, breathing more easily, said, "Hello, everybody. Nice to see you. The only new member of the company is Genevra Menetti—you can talk to her at the end of the rehearsal. I hope that we're going to have a very successful season. I have four new plays—I believe in three of them, the fourth I think is rubbish. It will probably be bought by someone in town, produced there and run for two years.

"The one which I propose to do now is called *Laughing Jove*. The hero is not Jove and he certainly doesn't laugh. Fortnight's rehearsal and then the old scheme—a week here, a week in Lelton. Small cast, so the people not concerned can be polishing up the next play—a revival. I'm proposing to do *His House in Order*." He laughed suddenly. "Yes, Jane dear, you're for it! Still, James will play opposite to you—with the requisite dignity and 'love locked out' by circumstances over which he has no control. Charles Tancroft has the parts ready. Now, Hubert, whom do I need?"

Hubert consulted the list which he held, and read out slowly, "'Miss Gosforth, Mr. Caxton, Mr. Stuart and Miss Menetti.' Miss Trent will play the maid's part, Mr. Firth the butler—it's quite a nice part, Harold."

Carter suddenly barked, "Give them the parts. Let's read the thing."

Hubert said, "I have them; the rest of you—I shall take rehearsal in the circle bar to-morrow at eleven. Good morning."

Everyone pulled up hard uncomfortable chairs, and prepared to look both interested and intelligent. Carter, the full script on his knee, beckoned to Tancroft, saying, "Don't mark anything this morning. Just get a rough idea of time, and we'll cut to-morrow.

"Nellie dear—Mrs. Hewson; Tommy—her husband; Martin —the young man; Miss Menetti—Mrs. Hewson's adopted daughter; Freda—the maid; Harold—the butler. Well, I don't think that he's really a butler, he's more a house-man. It's not a sufficiently big house to have a butler; besides, at Lelton they regard butlers as comic characters. Now, Nellie—keep it fairly light for the first act."

Genevra realized that they were good, they read—on sight— smoothly and easily. Carter listened intently, rarely stopping anyone except to make some reasonable suggestion. She was nervous, she was afraid that her voice would shake; but she retained sufficient control to read easily and naturally.

At half past twelve Hubert glanced at his watch, and Carter looked up at him and smiled.

"Time up? All right."

Wright said, "Break, ladies and gentlemen; back at half past two."

Carter whispered to him, and he called, "Miss Menetti—just a moment, if you please."

Nellie Gosforth came over to the long chair and said in her rich, full voice, "How are you, Melton dear? You're looking better."

He grinned, a grin which struck Genevra as being particularly young and boyish. It seemed to take some of the lines from his face. He stretched out his hand and took hers.

"Of course I'm better. I've been listening to your voice most of the morning. Go and have some luncheon, bless you."

She laughed. "Fried liver and bacon with 'mashed'!"

"Go and eat it!"

Genevra stood waiting; he waved to Nellie Gosforth and turned back to her.

"Listen," he said. "It's not the lead. This is in confidence. It's a more difficult part—actually—than Nellie's. She's a good actress, by the way. I want—the first act—complete confidence. You've lived with these people all your life, you trust them, believe in them. Then in the second act I want to see that confidence almost tottering, certainly badly shaken. Only at the very end, ten minutes before the curtain of the last act, do I want to see it re-established. Not the *same* unquestioning confidence, but something that comes from your own knowledge of yourself. Do you know what I'm driving at?"

"I shall when I've read the play through. It's difficult to tell from just a part, isn't it?"

He looked over his shoulder and said to Wright, "I've always said that they all ought to have full scripts, haven't I? Give Miss Menetti one now."

Quietly Wright grumbled, "Most of them would reduce them to ribbons in two days." He handed the script to Genevra saying, almost pleadingly, "Do try to keep it reasonably tidy, won't you?"

As she left the stage she heard the sound of Carter being helped out of his chair and then the dragging of his useless foot and leg across the stage.

In the afternoon Charles Tancroft had marked roughly the

entrances and exits, using two chairs set together for a sofa, and so on.

Her own part intrigued Genevra. She had sat reading the play all through her luncheon. Mrs. Thackle had provided her with cold beef, some brilliantly yellow pickles and mashed potatoes which contained small hard lumps like pills.

She said, "You see, it's washing day—there are times when I have mince. My mother used to call mince 'the washing-day dinner', but the joint was a bit bigger'n usual and I thought we could finish up that. After to-day p'raps you'd like to order for yourself, many prefer to do that. I'm no French cook, but anythink in reason comes easy to me. I had thought of a nice bit o' fish for supper, but Monday's a bad day for fish—the boats haven't come in or suthink. I never reelly know what. It's not a good day for meat neether, not reelly. Nor yet for tripe. How'd you like eggs and a nice bit of ham—cut thickish, eh?"

Genevra said weakly and mechanically, "Yes, very nice, thank you."

The afternoon rehearsal was more exacting than the morning one. Carter grew impatient, complained that no one listened, or that if they listened they did not understand. By the time it was all over Genevra felt exhausted. That night she wrote to George that she would meet him on Sunday for luncheon at the Golden Hind at Lelton. She went to bed feeling dispirited and lonely.

Slowly she felt that the play was taking shape, and slowly too she saw what Melton Carter had in his mind, how he was preparing to work out his pattern and design. His work delighted her; even when he grew caustic and sarcastic she knew that he never wavered. Once when Martin Stuart offered a carefully worded objection to Carter's reading of a line, the reply was, "Let me hear how you'd do it, Martin," then with a sudden and unexpected chuckle, "then we'll go on doing it my way, eh?"

Once he called, "Miss Menetti, for God's sake don't allow yourself to be refined. Shun refinement as you'd—I hope—shun the devil."

Again he stopped her. "Sorry, my dear, you're saying 'mooch' —the word is much! No"—irritably—"not 'match'—*much*. Can't you hear, or do you come from Wigan?"

She said calmly, "No, Manchester," and he flung back his head and laughed.

"Just the same you can't be allowed to say—mooch. Try again."

On Sunday morning she woke and knew that one week was

behind her. In another seven days she would be actually playing the part of 'Mollie Hallet'. The idea excited her. Next week Carter would begin, as he had said, to 'fill in, put in light and shade—and in all probability drive everyone, including myself, crazy'.

For the first time she was revelling in the consciousness that she was working under a producer who knew his work. The thought gave her confidence and a sense of security. He took practically no notice of any of the company except Nellie Gosforth and old Thomas Caxton. Sometimes Genevra wished that she could talk to him, really talk, ask questions and listen intently to the answers. If only he were able to stand, walk about, and actually *show* how he wanted this or that played! True, Hubert Wright, in moments when Carter's irritation grew, would walk forward and say in his slightly deprecatory fashion, "I think this is what Mr. Carter wants. Like this . . ." and Carter would shout:

"That's right, Hubert! You should have been an actor!"

About ten o'clock on the Sunday morning Mrs. Thackle came to ask if Mr. Howsditch might have a word with Genevra. He came into her sitting-room, where the mangled remains of a kipper lay on her plate, smiling brightly. " 'Mornin'. 'Ad a two-eyed steak, I see. Very nice too. I was wunnering if you'd kere for a run on the ole bike. Pillion, y'know. Ondly too 'appy if you kere for a breather. What-cher say, eh?"

She thanked him. "I have to go to Lelton, thank you very much."

"I'll run yer-r-over. Delighted."

"I think that I'd rather go by bus or train. I'm not very good at riding on a pillion." She reflected that she had never ridden on one in her life.

"Jest as you like. Bus at ten-forty-two. Lelton—eleven-ten. I'll show you w'ere the bus station is. Ondly five minutes' walk. I'll be on the spot, ready and waitin'."

She had a moment's panic at the thought that Mr. Howsditch might be going to accompany her to Lelton, but when she went out he was standing by his motor-bicycle and informed her, "Take you to your bus stop, then it's me for the wide-open spaces. Oh, 'oo will o'er the downs with me? No offers? Then I'll go bi me little lonesome."

As the bus bumped along she thought about her meeting with George. It was ugly country, comparatively flat and with hideous eruptions of mills, coal pits and slag tips. She did not feel in the least elated, rather a kind of numbness filled her. It would be pleasant to see him—at least she supposed that it would be—

but she knew that she would far rather have stayed in Albion Street, working at 'Mollie Hallet.' What would there be to say to George? They would eat an indifferent luncheon and possibly go for a run in his car; he would kiss her, and—drive her back to Follingly.

Before there had been a certain amount of glamour about their meetings, an expectancy; now that had died and nothing was left. Yet she had liked him, almost loved him, and not very long ago either.

She found the Golden Hind in a side street; it looked old, and she was thankful that it had not proved to be some dreadfully modernized place. Genevra made enquiries about the rooms allotted to Mr. Carter's company, and to her surprise they greeted her warmly.

The landlady, a tall, golden-haired woman, beamed at her. "Say what you like—give me pros every time. I was a principal boy myself. Oh yes—I'll show you some photographs one day. Prince Charming, too big even then for Aladdin—Dick Whittington, Robin Hood—oh, lots more. Then I married Percy—he was Percy Pellet, the comedian—and we settled down here at the Golden Hind. I'll give you 'Bessie Bonehill'—or I wonder if you'd like 'Kate Carney' better. All my rooms called after pros! Nice idea, eh? Novel, and—to pros—homelike."

Genevra told her that she was expecting a friend, and that they would want luncheon for two. Mrs. Pellet exclaimed, "Would that be the good-looking fellow waiting in the smoke-room? Yes, he's there, behaving like a caged lion, only he looks happier!"

George stood completely still when Genevra entered, then as his face flushed slowly, he came forward, saying, "Genevra, I'd forgotten how lovely you were! How good to see you! Tell me all about everything."

He kissed her affectionately, attended to her wants, lit her cigarette for her, and for a few moments she felt that she was back in Cothampton or at the Gallant Huzzar. He asked affectionately after Haig and his health, gave it as his opinion that she would be wiser to leave him with her grandparents, for, "Say what you like, Genevra darling, stages are draughty places, and you don't find landladies like Ma Rattery in every street."

They ate a surprisingly good luncheon, and George suggested a drive. She accepted willingly, for she was beginning to feel that she had nothing left to say to him. The silences were growing longer, then both of them began to say something—completely trivial—at the same time. Both said, together, "No—what were you going to say? Please go on."

The other replied, "No, nothing important; what were you saying?"

They had driven into the country for about six miles when George said, "Genevra, I've something rather difficult to say—do you mind if we stop and—I say it?"

"No, George—nothing bad, I hope?"

He said, "It's difficult. You see, I am terribly fond of you. I always shall be. My wife wants a divorce. She wants to divorce me for desertion. Apparently it can be done. Fairly easily. I'm tired of Cothampton. Not sufficient scope. At Lessington there's a vet, rather elderly. Wonderful practice. County people, bloodstock, racing stables. I'm pretty good with horses. I'd like to go in with him as partner. That's what he wants. Later, when he retires, I should take over the whole thing. Genevra, if I get this divorce through, will you marry me? I do love you. I'd work hard for you. It's a nice house, Georgian. Lessington's a pleasant kind of place."

She said nothing; he stretched out his hand and took hers.

"Genevra, will you?"

She said, at last, "George, I'm an actress—first, last and all the time."

"There's a good amateur company there," he told her hopefully. "I made enquiries. They did *Mrs. Dane's Defence* this Spring."

"Darling, that wouldn't be the same."

"It does mean so much to you?"

"More now than it ever did!"

"Perhaps—some day . . ."

She turned and faced him. "George, you're not to wait for me. You're young, you ought to have a nice wife, some lovely children, a home, dogs and things. I shan't leave the stage—it sounds silly for me to say this when I'm just starting in my second engagement. But I shan't always be in the provinces! I know it; it's not conceit, I swear it's not. Thank you, dear, dear George—but you must find some nice girl who isn't . . ." she laughed, "stage-struck."

He met her eyes steadily, gravely, regretfully. "There'll never be anyone like you, Genevra. Never."

"One day you'll write to me and tell me that you've found her," she said.

"I doubt it. I don't feel like it."

"Not *now*! not at this minute—but in a year, two years' time. My dear, will you drive me back to Follingly? I've got to work."

"Work on Sundays? What slave-drivers these people are!"

She leaned forward and kissed him lightly. "My dear, we *love* it!"

When he left her, he asked almost pathetically if he would see her again.

"Why not? Only I'm going to be terribly busy. But I'd love to see you."

"To meet," he hesitated, "just as we've—met to-day? Not—not . . ."

"Not as it was when I was at Cothampton. George, I don't regret anything. Why should I? Why should you? But that was —then; this is—now."

BOOK THREE

CHAPTER SIXTEEN

GENEVRA remained with Melton Carter's company for over two years. She played a variety of parts, and with each of them came a growing consciousness that she was becoming a mistress of her art. She had profited by Carter's production. Again and again he had shouted, "For heaven's sake read Hamlet's advice to the Players. Menetti, don't batter yourself to pieces. Leave something for the next act!" There had been times when she had replied briefly and abruptly and his reaction had always been to answer quietly, reasonably, so that she felt a certain sense of shame at having lost her temper.

She never knew if he was pleased with her work or not. At the end of a first performance he called everyone on to the stage. Wright handed him his notes and he went through them slowly and carefully, though his face might be grey with fatigue and lined with pain. His commendation was sparing; at the best it amounted to, "That scene was played beautifully, Miss Heriot. In the scene that rollowed you lost all that you had gained." Or, "My dear James, you sounded like a ram caught in a thicket when you were supposed to be making love to Miss Menetti. In the act which followed you got back to normal and were very good —very good indeed."

He never grew intimate with his company, once or twice

Nellie Gosforth or Tom Caxton were asked to dine with him, but that only at rare intervals. For the rest of the company, the only sight they had of him was in the theatre, with Hubert Wright in close attendance.

Nellie Gosforth said to Genevra one evening when they had supper together at 15 Albion Street—Mrs. Thackle having surpassed herself by providing a roast chicken, well cooked, and bread sauce which was not more like a bread poultice than such a sauce usually is—"Melton's interested in you, my dear."

Genevra laid down her knife and fork and said eagerly, "Do you mean that he thinks I shall make an actress—one day?"

The elder woman smiled. "I'm not allowed to say anything. But—as the old women say when they read your cards—there's brightness round you."

"Tell me!" Genevra begged. "Just give me a hint."

Nellie shook her head. "It's more than my life is worth. Possess your soul in patience, and please give me some more of this excellent chicken."

Genevra had seen George several times; each time he had been his usual kind self, and each time conversation had grown more and more difficult. Then one Sunday she went over to Lelton and lunched with him at the Golden Hind. He was alternately silent and boisterous, and at last Genevra said, "George, you've some news for me? Out with it!"

He flushed deeply, crumbled his bread and finally said, "What you said the first time we met here has come true. The man whose partner I'm going to be—we sign the contract next week —well, his daughter—her name's Helen, she's about twenty-five, very sweet girl, and——"

Genevra said, "And you've fallen in love with her, George?"

He still continued to make pellets with his bread, and mumbled, "I suppose that I have. Genevra, do you think me an awful cad?"

"My dear, why should I? It's what I've longed for you to do. You're far too nice, too clever, to be wasted; it's your ordinary duty to make some woman happy. I'm delighted. Tell me all about her."

He drew a deep breath and slowly began. As he continued, his account of the beauties of Helen Cannon's nature gathered way. Genevra listened, thinking, 'That settles everything. Now I shall be able to work every Sunday without feeling it my duty to come over to Lelton. Dear George; how infernally dull she sounds!'

He ended his recital with, "Mind, Genevra, she isn't lovely, as

215

you are, but there is—just—something about her—well, I couldn't explain, but it gives you a sense of happiness and content. I believe that you and she would be great friends," he repeated—"really great friends."

She said, "I am certain of it—certain," thinking, 'I should be bored to death! But I'm equally certain that he will be terribly happy. Bless him, what a nice person he is!'

She had been free for one or two weeks, and had returned to Manchester to find Haig slowly putting on the dignified weight of an elderly dog. She longed to have him with her, but with Melton Carter all productions were intensive, and she knew that Haig might grow restive. He had a touch of rheumatism, and when it asserted itself he liked to stand up, wander round and lie down again, giving vent to great sighs of relief. She could imagine Carter demanding, "What's that dog doing here? I like dogs as well as the next man, but rehearsals are not the place for them!" Genevra knew her own quick temper, and could imagine the rejoinder which she would make. No, Haig was better left in Manchester.

Twice she went down for a couple of days to stay with Aunt Tilda. She only saw Henry once, when he seemed distrait and absorbed. He made an effort to appear interested in her work, asked the right kind of questions and uttered the right kind of comments.

He said, "Carter told Clementina Gossage that he had great hopes of you. He said that you 'had it all'. Candidly, because he's had some success I can't see that gives him the right to be patronizing!"

She replied warmly, "I don't call that patronizing. If you knew how hard he works! It can't be easy. I believe that he's always in pain."

He smiled at her, that aloof smile which she hated. "If he didn't like producing plays he is under no obligation to do so."

"You don't understand, Henry, maybe it's just something he can't help doing, now that he can't act!"

"Oh, my dear," he said, "that kind of assertion won't stand analysing."

Genevra shrugged her shoulders, dismissing the matter. "How is Mrs. Gossage?" she asked.

"Quite well, but poor George is dying. Nothing to be done. He's let all the surgeons in London and on the Continent have a look at him. She's completely devoted to him. Poor devil!"

"Young?"

216

"About her own age, I imagine—fortyish—little over, I think." Henry sat watching her; she was turned twenty, and he wondered if ever again she would be so beautiful. Her voice had deepened and become more rich. She dressed well, for her grandparents were generous. Her hair looked so bright and alive. Henry felt that he wanted to touch it with his fingers—very lightly and caressingly. Her eyes were extraordinarily blue, not the milky blue which he disliked so much, but a clear, almost gentian colour. Her complexion, for she used 'make-up' carefully and with restraint, was perfect.

He thought how much he would like to marry her—then his thoughts halted and seemed to shy away from the idea. He was more or less established, his salary was very large, his ambitions boundless. The same thing applied to Genevra. She had the stage in her blood, she was determined to make a success. Henry had not the slightest doubt that she would attain all that she was working for. How could she help it? She had looks, she moved beautifully, and—although he had seen her only once on the stage, and that when she was at the very beginning of her career—he knew that she had that strange quality which makes an actress.

Clementina Gossage had told him that Carter thought very highly of her, adding, "Now you're not to tell her that, Henry. These young girls, particularly lovely young girls, must learn everything the hard way, the slow way."

'She'd never marry me', he decided, 'the stage means too much to her. She is young, she has ambitions, longings. She must satisfy them. I believe—honestly—that I love her; I think that I loved her the first time I saw her. Poor little scrap, with her dead monkey buried in the garden and her dog. I think that is why I still look back on my interview with that awful animal-trainer with such satisfaction. I felt that I was fighting for her. But she's in love with the stage, and until she has satisfied her ambitions, or seen them broken, she'll have no time for any man. She might take a lover'—instinctively Henry knew that he loathed the idea that such a thing could happen—'but he'd always come second to the part she was studying at the time. Oh, lord, what a mess it all is! I could make her happy. I'm certain of it.'

She raised her head and looked at him. "You're very silent."

"I was thinking——"

"About . . . ?"

"You, as a matter of fact. Do you remember that once I asked you to marry me?"

217

She nodded. "Very well—and the word 'love' didn't come into it; do you remember that too?"

"If—now—the word 'love' *did* come into it," he asked, "what then?"

Genevra shook her head. "The answer would be the same, I'm afraid. You see, I've tasted just a few of the sweets of success —if even in a very small way. I've learned that I can exercise a certain power over an audience, make them feel what I wish them to feel. I want more—much more."

Henry did not answer, and they sat silent, both occupied with their own thoughts. Genevra wondering if in reality she didn't wish to be Henry's wife more than anything else in the world and yet conscious of the tugging of her heart-strings when she even contemplated giving up the work that she loved and which she felt she was beginning to understand a little.

Henry, watching her, entranced by her beauty, recalling the tones of her voice, the ease of her movements. To live with Genevra would be a continual joy—a joy to his eyes, his ears, a satisfaction to all those emotions which stirred him. Yet his own work fascinated him, and its fascination had grown with the years. He, too, wanted to be famous. To earn a huge salary with Levelle was not enough; so long as he did that he was—no matter how good he might be—only adding laurels to the crown which Levelle wore so elegantly, and towards which he contributed less and less every year.

At last Henry said, "I wonder if we're not both chasing illusions; running after something that doesn't really matter very much, that will be forgotten in a very short time? We might both be wiser to pin our faith, our hopes, to what we know to be realities, don't you think?"

She said, "I don't know. I'm not certain that I know which is illusion and which reality—or if I did if I should know which was the better and more sound. Probably we're both chasing through a thick wood—a vast forest even—and we shan't *know* until we find ourselves out of the forest and standing in the open country again. Added to that we're individualists. You have your ambitions, I have mine. We may love each other—there again I don't know for certain how much that love is worth; but neither of us is prepared to give up our own personal ambitions. We might like to have our cake and eat it—or is it eat our cake and have it?—but at the moment we're obsessed with the beauty of our own cake. I'm too uncertain of my possible ability. I haven't really had to try my strength fully. You haven't yet reached the goal which you've set for yourself. Once that has happened"—she shrugged her shoulders—"who knows?"

Henry rose and mixed himself another whisky-and-soda. "In the meantime, one of us, both of us, may fall in love with two other people, and what then?"

"Oh, my dear, we've got to take our chance of that! Either of us might suddenly find the real thing. If it offers, then we shall have to decide. This conversation here in Aunt Tilda's drawing-room isn't a declaration from you to me, or me to you. It's a kind of reviewing the position at the present moment."

He came back to his chair. "You're cold-blooded, aren't you, Genevra?"

She retorted cheerfully, "Not in the least, but I'm single-minded."

In a tone which was half tolerant, half amused, he asked, "What exactly do you hope to get out of this career of yours?"

Genevra knew that a year ago she would have been stung into some quick retort; now she was wiser. She smiled at him, a charming, wide smile.

"Exactly what you hope to get out of that career of yours," she said.

"Fame, adulation, money—those things? Your name in lights, invitations to wonderful parties, perhaps offers from America, Hollywood, eh?"

She shook her head. "I don't know. I have never actually formulated what I really hope for. I hope that whatever I am asked to do—on the stage I shall have equipped myself sufficiently well to be able to do it properly. That's as far as I have dared to look."

"Look here," he demanded, "I believe sincerely that I'm in love with you. All right, go on with this acting for—shall we say—another four years. If by that time you've made the success which you believe you can make, then you will have no doubt made your own decision. If not, if you're still working in a stock company in the provinces, will you marry me?"

"You're prepared to keep yourself free for four years? Remember, Henry, you're young, good-looking, successful. You're constantly meeting women who would give their ears to marry you, if only because you could design them dresses which would make them the envy of other women! Four years—it's a long time."

"I'd wait four years with the hope of you at the end of them."

She rested her chin on her hand. "I wonder if *I* am," she said thoughtfully. "So much might happen in four years. I might be anywhere. Henry, I can't say that I'd wait. I'm not sufficiently sure of myself. When I'm with you I'm happy—generally, when you don't infuriate me! I think of you quite a lot when I'm away. I compare other men with you, generally to their disadvantage. But to promise to wait, no, my dear, I can't do that."

He shrugged his shoulders. "Very well. I'll offer an amendment —if you are not starring in Hollywood, if you are not playing lead in New York, or making a world tour, I'll come and ask you to marry me. If by that time you've married a member of the aristocracy, of course, I shall understand, and wonder when I see pictures of your wedding-dress in the *Sketch* and the *Tatler* why you didn't come to me to design it."

"Aren't you being rather stupid, Henry? I think it's time that we both went to bed. Good night."

She left for Manchester the following day. Henry drove her to London, but made no reference whatever to their conversation. He was kind and attentive, but she felt that he had rebuilt the wall of reserve behind which he took shelter.

She returned to Follingly, to receive assurances from Mrs. Thackle that the house had been cleaned from top to bottom. "Not a speck anywhere. My word, I've worked morning till evening. Mr. Howsditch said to me, 'What-t-ever are you wearin' yourself out for? It's not as if the place wasn't like what a new pin is already!' I said, 'Never mind new pins', I said. 'Shining, spotless cleanliness is what I'm aiming at!'"

To Genevra's surprise there was a note waiting for her from Carter, asking if she would come to dinner, and stating that he would send his car for her at seven. She had never been inside his house, which Nellie Gosforth assured her was very beautiful, and felt vaguely excited. What was it Nellie had said about a surprise, a surprise which she averred was a dead secret. Had Carter found a new play? Was he going to cast her for a really big and important part?

She dressed with additional care, and was ready and waiting when the car came for her. The house stood in considerable grounds, well outside the city boundaries. As far as Genevra could judge in the dim light of early evening, it was Georgian, and very dignified and beautiful.

Hubert Wright came into the hall to meet her. "How nice that you could come, and at such short notice. Melton is delighted. He is in the library; he likes it better than the big drawing-room."

Genevra stared frankly round her. "How lovely this is!"

"Of its type," Wright said, "it is considered very good."

The library was brightly lit; Genevra felt a thrill of pleasure at the rows of books, with the light gleaming softly on their fine bindings. The room was high with a decorated ceiling and a huge and very tall fireplace. Carter was lying in a long chair. He smiled and held out his hand as she entered, saying, "It's very kind of you to take pity on two dull people, Miss Menetti."

"It's very kind of you to ask me to your lovely house."

She saw his eyes brighten. His voice was almost eager when he answered, "It is a nice place, isn't it? One day you must come over and see it all. There's some pleasant panelling in the drawing-room; my aunt, who—bless her—left me the place, had no taste and stripped it of its nice old paint. I had it repainted; they didn't make a bad job of it either. I don't usually admit that it has been repainted! Hubert, let's all have cocktails to celebrate Miss Menetti's return!"

She saw Hubert's eyebrows rise a little as if in protest. Carter said impatiently, "Oh, for heaven's sake, man, one won't hurt me. Let me be human for once!"

As Hubert mixed the cocktails, which later Genevra had to admit he did very well, Carter said, "That's the worst of having a friend who believes in what doctors tell him and has a conscience. If old Rumpty Tuffty, or whatever his name is, told Hubert I wasn't to have any air at all, he'd have every window in the house hermetically sealed—and join me in a miserable death."

His tone was light, but under it Genevra found something of genuine affection and liked him all the better for it. He sipped his cocktail with obvious enjoyment, then—his eyes still shining very brightly—said, "You're longing to know why I particularly wanted you to dine here to-night, aren't you?"

Genevra felt suddenly that, in spite of all his knowledge, his ability and his insistence on discipline in his company, he was like a small child, holding out clenched hands and chanting, "Nickerty, nickerty nick nack—which hand will you tak'?"

She said, "Miss Gosforth said that there might be a surprise waiting for me."

Carter almost shouted, "If Nellie's told you, I'll never forgive her!"

"But she didn't tell me anything. I asked her to, pestered her with questions; she was adamant!"

His face cleared, the heavy scowl vanished. "Ah, she's a good scout, our Nellie. Now listen—you've been with me for two years, haven't you? You have worked like a black. Oh, I've watched, I know. You do, too, Hubert, don't you? Well, at last I've got—a play. What I call—a play. It's—it's something that *ought* to be produced. I'm going to take a theatre in town. I'm going to put it on as well as anything can be put on. I'm not engaging new actors and actresses. I'm taking certain members of my own company. I'll show the West End that I can make actors and actresses!"

Genevra drew a deep breath. "Are you going to make me?"

He waved his empty glass towards Hubert, saying, "As you are strong, be merciful—give me another cocktail. She's as excited as I am!"

Hubert replied, as he took the glass—taking it, as it were, under silent protest—"Don't get too excited; you've only just begun to talk about this project to Miss Menetti."

He turned back to her. "Am I going to take you! Good God, I'm going to give you the chance of your life! It's a part that needs—everything. I believe that you can give it what it wants. There, that's as good a compliment as you will ever have paid you. The author's unknown and, for myself, though I've taken an option on his next two plays, I doubt if I shall take up either. His fourth—if he stays the course—possibly. You shall have the full script to take home with you to-night. Three acts—one set—except for one small box set we can set inside the full stage one. It's got—as I read it—everything. Comedy, tragedy, and sanity all the time. I shall take Tancroft, because I believe in him as a stage manager; Freda—good girl, that—will carry on here while he's away. Hubert will manage—and dart up and down to give an eye to things here. When he's away dear old Tommy Caxton will manage.

"Jane Heriot—I might have taken Marcia Bland, but she irritates me—Hubert, don't make 'tut-tutting' noises; Miss Menetti knows that this is all tiled in. Felix Manvers—he's come on a great deal, that chap—Jimmy Cowper, Harold Firth and Nellie—oh, and yourself. Six—there are two or three small parts, but I'm getting Miriam to fix them for me. I can rely on Miriam. Hubert is working to get a theatre; it must be a good one or I won't consider it."

Hubert said mildly, "There are two which, you might say, are in the bag so far as we are concerned—both excellent."

Carter continued, "We'll have Lorimer do the dresses, and you must all have everything you want. Hubert, again don't make those clicking noises! Of course none of them will get everything they want! That's only the way one talks to actresses to rouse their enthusiasm! Now, Miss Menetti—what do you think about it?"

She knew that she was shaking, that her head—and it was not the result of one of Hubert's cocktails—felt swimming. Town, a good part, a wonderful production. These things were coming to her—Genevra Menetti.

"You think that I'm sufficiently good?"

Carter answered in his old abrupt manner, "If I didn't I shouldn't have considered you, should I?"

"May I talk to you when I've read the play?"

"Of course, but remember I believe in it. It's a play that will make people talk. Make them—I hope—want to come again. Oh, how good to be back in a London theatre again; good to see people coming in, to read the criticisms—good or bad, doesn't matter so long as they're interested. To go down to the theatre every night and know——"

"Dinner is served, sir."

Carter's face changed. "Damn!" he said firmly. Then with a sudden and unexpected burst of fury, "Damn, now I've got to move, and remember that I'm like a blasted log. I'd almost forgotten, almost imagined myself playing the part that Jimmy Cowper will play! It's insupportable—it's——"

Genevra interrupted him gently. "Do you mind if I go and powder my nose and wash my hands? That cocktail has made them feel sticky."

He turned his coldly furious face towards her, and said, "That's very nicely done. You'll go and powder your face, which doesn't need powder, and wash your hands, which aren't sticky, to spare my feeling of having you watch me being hauled into the dining-room. Miss Menetti, I am indebted to you for this charming display of tact. Withers—show Miss Menetti a bedroom where she can wash her hands, and then show her where the dining-room is. Send Brownlow to help Mr. Wright to help me."

"Certainly, sir."

In the bedroom into which she was shown she found everything that she could possibly—or impossibly—have wanted. Withers hovered at the door for a moment, then giving a small artificial cough, said, "Excuse me, miss, don't take any notice. It's only natural after all. There are times when his affliction gets him low, as it were. I will return in five minutes, if that is convenient to you. Thank you, miss."

Scents, powders, every kind of toilet requisite Genevra had ever heard of, a bathroom gleaming with bright tiles, a sunken bath, the faint sweet scent of expensive bath salts, towels of every size and kind. The bed covered with an eiderdown of such quality as she had never seen before in her life.

She had always known a certain degree of comfort, but for the first time she saw luxury. As she washed her hands, which, contrary to Carter's assertion, were sticky after holding the cocktail glass, she stared at her face in the mirror. She frowned, thinking of the little scene in the library.

'He's got everything except what he really wants. He'd give it all up, live in rooms such as I have at Mrs. Thackle's, if only he could play the parts he longs to play. It must be heartbreaking. Imagine casting a play, in which you believe, and having to find other people for the part—the parts, for he could play anything —that you long to play yourself. Poor devil! Poor unlucky devil!'

Withers knocked on the door and gravely escorted her down, only halting for a moment to say in a low voice, "I apologize, miss, for passing any comment, but I felt that you might understand. Miss Gosforth always makes allowances; I'm sure that you will too."

Genevra smiled. "But, Withers, of course! How could I fail to?"

"Thank you, miss."

Carter was seated at the head of the table. He seemed to have recovered his equanimity and smiled at Genevra when she entered. The food was excellent, and she thought, 'Fancy, two men to wait on three people, and in all probability five or six others have worked to get this meal ready!'

Carter ate very little, but his spirits were rising and he kept asking Genevra and Hubert questions.

"Lots of billing, Hubert, eh? No use spoiling the ship for a ha'p'orth of tar. When do you think we can make a start? There will have to be some new people engaged for Follingly and Lelton, of course, to replace those we take to town." He turned and smiled his engaging smile at Genevra. "Mind, Miss Menetti, I'm not suggesting that *actually* any of the people I am taking to town *are* replaceable. We must do what we can. Get on to Miriam to morrow, Hubert. Genevra—I beg your pardon, do you mind being called 'Genevra'? It's such a lovely name. You don't mind? Good! Then, Genevra, do you remember the first play you ever did here—*Laughing Jove*? It's a part something like Mollie Hallet, only better, stronger, more highly charged. Lovely clothes you must have. Will Henry do his best, do you think, for a provincial company?"

She said, "Henry couldn't do anything but his best. That's how Henry is."

He nodded. "That's nice, Hubert, isn't it?"

Hubert said, "I believe that it's true about Lorimer; he's an artist."

"Umph, umph! Listen, Genevra, you can talk—in the first act—the least hint of—what is it?—Lancashire or Yorkshire?"

"Lancashire, and there's a great difference, you know."

He laughed. "I don't know. They all say 'bi gum', don't they?"

She shook her head. "They may. I've never heard them except on the music-hall stage."

He was excited. She felt that for weeks he had nursed this project, had planned and schemed. She knew that already his whole plan for the production was clear. She had ceased to be Genevra Menetti and had become the character in this new play which so delighted him. Again and again she saw him watching her, intently and yet impersonally. She knew that he was already 'producing' her, giving her the inflections which he felt were right, telling her to move here and to make that gesture there.

She hid her excitement, but all through the rather long and elaborate dinner she found it difficult to think of what she ate, her mind was constantly turning to the play, that play which she would lie awake reading until the small hours. Then she remembered her last talk with Henry, recalled his questions as to what she wanted, his rather sarcastic comments concerning lights, dresses and pictures in the *Tatler*. Four years, she had said, and now if only the play were a success, if only she could do justice to the part in which Carter believed so firmly, her dreams might come true; not in four years, perhaps in four months. As she ate a tiny and delicious little cutlet she wondered if Henry would ask her to marry him; that thought gave her additional cause for excitement.

She loved Henry, not wildly, not romantically, not emotionally, but in a fashion which had become almost a habit. Her love was tinged with admiration; admiration for what he had attained, for his poise, his ability. Suppose—suppose that Henry fell in love with one of his clients?—'society ladies' was how Genevra thought of them. She wondered what she would feel, and the word came to her mind instantly—furious! Carter was speaking to her, she had missed the first part of his sentence but caught the latter part.

". . . you won't leave us, make an aristocratic marriage, and make it necessary for Hubert and me to find a new actress?"

Genevra, forcing her mind back from her relationship with Henry Lorimer, managed to smile, "You must see to that in my contract. You must 'tie me up'."

Hubert said gloomily, "Marriage nullifies all contracts, I've always heard. Not many of our actresses have left us to marry, have they, Melton?"

"Only the ones we were jolly glad to get rid of. Their departure was well worth a case of silver fish-knives and forks."

Dinner ended and, with Withers standing at his elbow, Carter said to Genevra, "If we have coffee in the library would you like to wash your hands again?", but this time he smiled as he said it, and she felt that his irritation had vanished for the time.

"Why not have coffee here?" she asked. "It's a 'pro' habit to sit over a dinner-table for hours, you must know that!"

He turned to Withers. "You hear that; we're actors and actresses here, and we shall sit here and fill all the ash-trays with burnt-out stubs, talk scandal, and tell each other how good we were as Napoleon, or Josephine, as Sydney Carter or Minette. Coffee here, please."

"Very good, sir."

When she was leaving Hubert came with her to the car. As he helped her in he said, "You've done him good. He's so plucky, but now and then he realizes his—his handicap, and gives vent to these fits of irritability. Now he'll be filled with excitement to know what you think of the play."

"What do you think of it?"

He pursed his lips. "Frankly, I think that it should be good —very good box-office. Good night, Miss Menetti."

That night she lay awake reading the play *Playing Cards*. She was held by it, the play was well—and in parts even beautifully —written. There were strong situations which, to Genevra, never seemed forced but which came naturally and with complete reasonableness. The characters were well drawn, clear and definite, there was adequate development, and it was evident that the author had some considerable knowledge of stage technique. It was half past two when she closed the script and turned out the light. Even then she could not sleep, for the play and its development, particularly the character of the young woman— Susan—intruded and drove sleep away.

Carter was right, Genevra felt, to believe in the play. Was he right in believing in her? To play, even to play to the very best of your ability, before Follingly and Lelton audiences was not the same as playing to an audience made up of sophisticated playgoers. Then there were the critics—those famous names of which she had heard, and whose comments she had read so eagerly in the Press. Imagine if James Agate, Ivor Brown, Hannen Swaffer, or Darlington rose in their wrath and demanded to know why Melton Carter should have inflicted this half-trained, inexperienced, rough provincial actress on a West End audience! Better, far better, to beg Carter to let her stay in Follingly, and to choose someone else to go to London and play 'Susan'.

The daylight was filtering into the room when at last, exhausted, uncertain and utterly miserable, Genevra fell asleep.

The next morning—or rather the same morning, for Genevra had only slept for a few hours—she went down to the theatre. She felt that she had been away for years, that the people she knew so well were coming back into her life after years of separation. She eyed Nellie Gosforth, and the others whom Carter had named as prospective candidates for his London venture, doubtfully. He had not asked her to keep the matter a secret and yet she did not feel that she had any definite right to mention it to them.

As the Town Hall clock was booming ten o'clock he arrived and made his slow and painful progress across the stage. Genevra had never grown accustomed to it, never ceased to feel an overwhelming sense of pity and compassion. They lowered him into his long chair, he held his usual low-voiced conversation with Charles Tancroft and Hubert, then came his greeting, "Good morning, ladies and gentlemen! Now, if you'll all come a little nearer, I have something rather startling to tell you."

Speaking slowly and choosing his words with obvious care, he outlined his idea for a London production. Genevra listened and marvelled at the way he practically made those who were not chosen for the production feel that he was leaving them behind because, "After all, Follingly and Lelton are my first ventures. They've been praised and admired, and I must have that standard which we—you—have achieved maintained. It is only natural that I long to try my wings—" he laughed—"such as they are—in London again. What the result may be none of us knows. If it is a success the possibilities are almost limitless."

He gave them additional information. "Hubert, this wise old thing who looks after us all, insists that we have two plays. I don't think that he has a great deal of faith in the one which I have chosen."

Hubert, in his clipped and precise voice, said, "My dear Melton, not at all, but you must have a second string. You ought to know that!"

Carter laughed. "Well, I've got it! I'm going to revive *Skeleton Leaves*—that play which was such a success financially and such a terrific disaster for me! Felix, if you play my old part, take care that all doors leading to cellars are shut! Now—are we ready?" He gave them the rough outline of the play, which they were to rehearse for the following fortnight, as was his custom. His last injunction was, "Remember, it is a comedy: keep it light. Tommie—none of those chest notes; and Nellie, dear—don't play 'Augusta' like 'Lady Bracknell'."

Outwardly the work of the company went on as usual, but to Genevra it seemed that there was an undercurrent of excitement. Wright was continually going to London. Several times Carter went with him, and rehearsals were left in the hands of the elderly, white-haired Thomas Caxton. Then one morning when 1936 had slipped away and 1937 was nearly two months old, Carter announced at rehearsal that he had found a theatre.

"Trust Hubert to hold his horses until he could get everything his own way!" He was smiling and looking suddenly younger and happier, Genevra thought. "Wily old devil that he is, he waited and finally pounced. It's the Queensway! Lovely stage, acoustics couldn't be better. Mellett was the architect, remember. That speaks for itself, eh, Tommie?"

Caxton nodded. "Undoubtedly. A first-class theatre, couldn't be better."

"We take over March 29. Notice how Hubert steered clear of signing for April 1! I want to open at the end of the month. Three weeks' rehearsals here and two in town. There! Now let's get on." At the end of rehearsals he called Genevra over to him, and said, "Well, are you pleased?"

She said, "Very excited, and desperately frightened. You're certain that you haven't changed your mind, that you wouldn't rather have someone with—with a name?"

He opened his eyes very wide. "Where could I find anyone with a nicer name than Genevra Menetti?"

"Don't make fun of me! I'm serious."

"I should hope so. It's a serious business. Will you come and have dinner to-morrow? I'll send the car. Yes, please do."

"I should like to. May I bring the script?"

"Why, yes, if you like, but I warn you, I'm not going to have an informal rehearsal all through dinner!"

That evening when he sat with Hubert drinking coffee after dinner, Carter said, "Hubert, a devil of a thing's happened. It ought not to be a devil of a thing—wouldn't be under ordinary circumstances—but I believe that I've fallen in love with little Menetti."

"My dear Melton . . ." There was dismay in Hubert's voice.

The other man nodded. "I liked her from the very beginning. She's lovely to look at. Gosh, how lovely she is! She's a great worker; one day she's going to be a very, very fine actress. And she's kind. She's sensitive. D'you remember that night when she came to dinner, and asked if she might wash her hands——"

Hubert nodded. "I remember perfectly."

"I've noticed that when I come on the stage at rehearsal she is always immersed in her letters, her part, a newspaper." He sighed. "Well, if I can't get her out of my system, what am I going to do?"

Hubert looked at him gravely. He noticed, as he had done so often, the finely cut features, the wide, eager eyes, the whole expression of high intelligence. He watched the long-fingered, thin hands moving restlessly; saw the broad shoulders, and how well the head was set upon them. He thought of those dreadful moments when Melton had to be lifted in and out of the car, helped across the stage; of the days when he suffered, when his temper grew irritable, and his tongue bitter.

"Do you think that she is fond of you, Melton?" he asked.

"Good heavens above, no! To her I'm a play-producing machine. Oh, she likes me quite well, and because she's a decent woman she's damned sorry for me. Even suppose—and it's an insane idea—she did like me, like me quite a good deal—how can I ask any woman to marry me? Imagine any woman tied to a thing like me! She'd want a normal marriage, want children. God, the very idea, even in my wildest dreams, of me marrying is revolting. She's not some cold-blooded fish, Genevra Menetti. With an Italian father, not likely! No, Hubert, the only thing to do is to try to get it out of my wretched system. Thank God London's looming ahead, and if she looks as lovely as I know she will, half the men in town will be chasing out of the theatre to hang round the stage door."

"That won't help you much," Hubert said gloomily.

"I've got to help myself," Carter returned. "Well, she's coming to dinner to-morrow. See that we have something pleasant to eat. God only knows what she lives on in those rooms in Albion Street."

That night when he lay in bed, carefully helped there by Withers, Melton Carter knew that his determination to overcome his disability, to submerge his bitterness at the sudden termination of his career as an actor, had been shattered. Whether he could rebuild it, retire still further into the solitude which, except for his work in the theatre, he had deemed necessary, he did not know. He was still young, only thirty-two; when last the great London specialist had seen him he had assured him that there was not the slightest reason why he should not live for years.

He had immersed himself in his work, had realized with satisfaction that already people were beginning to talk with respect and admiration of the productions at Follingly. More than once well-known critics had come to see the first night of a production, and their opinions had been reported in the London Press. Follingly and Lelton were successes, and he had made them so. He knew that by his unremitting attention, his ability to convey his wishes clearly and logically to his company, his insistence on everyone giving of their very best, that he had created a repertory company which was unique. Admittedly he was not handicapped, as so many of such companies were, by want of money. He could afford excellent scenery, excellent clothes, and salaries which enabled his actors and actresses to live in reasonable comfort.

He had almost come to believe that his work satisfied him. He had never been particularly concerned with women. When he began his work as an actor he had been too engrossed to wish to devote his time to anything except his actual work. There had been small incidents, amusing, trivial, transitory, but they had passed and left no mark upon him. When he had first made his success in London, women had run after him, flattered him, and for a time he had 'taken his fun where he found it'. Queer to think that he could only remember their names with an effort. Then, after his accident, he had lain helpless and useless for months, and when his strength came filtering back it had been Hubert Wright who said, "I wonder that you don't start a repertory company. Something that should be the best of its kind. You've plenty of money. You're a first-rate producer."

He had answered angrily, "Don't be a damned fool! How can I act—like this?"

Hubert had answered mildly, "I didn't say act. I said produce."

The idea had taken hold, his imagination was fired. After all, it meant that he would not be completely cut off from the theatre which he loved. Success had come, his ambitions had grown, he had made plans eagerly. Then he had engaged Genevra Menetti. He had liked her, admired her looks, believed that she had talent. Slowly he had found that the thought of her came to obtrude more and more, that when he read plays he read eagerly, longing to find a part for her which would give him more opportunity of talking with her, rehearsing her, advising her. While she had been away he knew that he had missed her, missed her more with every day that came. When he saw her on the stage, engrossed—or apparently engrossed—in reading a letter, in spite of the pain which his dragging leg always caused him he had caught his breath with sheer pleasure because she was there looking lovelier than ever, and because he would hear her voice and be able to watch her.

Previously he had given himself mental warnings, 'Melton, you're dangerously near falling in love with little Menetti!' Now, lying awake, longing for sleep and oblivion which did not come, he realized that what he had feared had become an accomplished fact. Genevra Menetti had complete possession of his heart.

CHAPTER SEVENTEEN

WHEN Genevra arrived the following evening it was obvious that Melton Carter was in one of his irritable moods. He picked up a telegram, and flicked it with his finger in disgust.

"Stupid! Lorimer can't come up this week because George Gossage has died, and I presume that Henry has to stay to console the widow."

Genevra said, "Well, they're great friends of his; they've been very kind to him. I think it's sweet of Henry."

"Would you expect me to postpone a production if your husband died, and you wanted me to sit and hold your hand?"

She replied very calmly, "That would depend upon how close our friendship was; how well you had known my husband; on a dozen things."

"Don't talk rubbish," he snapped. "The world can't stand still because George Gossage dies!"

"The world isn't being expected to stand still. Henry will be here next week. He works astonishingly quickly, he won't keep you waiting."

She watched his lips twist into a sneer. "You're very loyal to Lorimer!"

"I've every reason to be. Henry and his mother have been very good to me. One day, when you're in the mood to listen to stories, I'll tell you how and why they were so good."

His ill-humour left him. Genevra thought that there was something almost childish in his attitude; whatever he wanted must be available when he wanted it. Any delay, any disarrangement of his plans, made him work himself into a fury. Now he smiled and suddenly held out his hand, and said:

"I'm sorry. I was behaving badly. I suppose that I was disappointed. I hoped Henry would come down this week-end, talk about designs, and get down to making sketches. I'm sorry for Clementina; she's a grand person, and she was devoted to old George. Tell me this story, please."

Genevra laughed, and sat down near his long chair. "You've been spoilt," she said: "given everything you wanted. It's bad for you."

"I have! Damn it, I wanted to be an actor——"

"You wanted to be a creative artist . . . well, you are! It's all coming to you. You'll be inundated with offers to produce. Your career has only been diverted from one channel into another, possibly a wider and better one."

He asked, "My dear, why don't you recite to me those lines which begin, 'Do the thing that's nearest, though it's dull awhiles' or 'So we all must shine, you in your small corner'? They'd come in admirably in that little sermon you've just given me."

"Because——" she refused to allow his irritability to affect her—"I don't know either of the quotations."

"Your education must have been neglected!"

"It was; not only neglected but, until I came to live in Manchester, non-existent. Where is Hubert?"

"He's gone to town; he'll be back in time for dinner. Will you ring for Withers to bring cocktails? Now, tell me that story; I'm really in the mood for a story."

Withers gravely brought them both cocktails, and Melton said, "Be careful that the glass isn't sticky, Withers. You remember last time. Miss Menetti dislikes getting her fingers dirty."

"I have paid particular attention to the glasses, sir."

As the door closed Carter settled himself more comfortably in his long chair, and said, "Now—the story!"

She told him very simply of her mother's death, of her escape from Holst and the circus, of her arrival at Tilda Lorimer's, and as she spoke Melton listened with an almost painful interest. She looked so lovely sitting there with the light catching her bright hair, sitting—he noticed with satisfaction—still, not twisting and turning. Her voice was low, but very full and held a promise of power in its lower tones. The story was full of essential pathos, but she never stressed anything; even the death of the Monk was told quietly and evenly. The story was ending, her voice had taken on a slightly quicker tempo.

"So now you understand why I am so grateful to Henry and Aunt Tilda, don't you?"

"And don't you think that any average decent people would have done the same?" Carter asked.

Genevra shook her head. "Not in the way they did everything. Imagine Henry, who loathes disputes and arguments, going to see that dreadful man Holst!"

"I notice that in the end everything comes back to Henry," he said. "You're not engaged to Henry, are you?"

"Of course not."

"In love with him? Is he in love with you? You needn't answer if you don't want to."

She sipped her cocktail reflectively. "I don't know. I think that perhaps we are just a little in love with one another. Henry asked me to marry him. I refused. I think that one-half of me loves him very much, that part of Henry loves me—not, perhaps, half—rather more than a quarter. We're both ambitious. Neither thinks the other's work as important as—well, as our own. We both want to justify our belief in ourselves. Henry, of course, has, to a great extent; I'm just beginning. I expect that it all sounds very muddled and stupid."

He held out his glass. "Will you give me another cocktail and will you have another?" She brought it back to him; he stared up at her, and said, "You said that I have been given everything I wanted. Well, at least I can help you; give you the opportunity to justify yourself. That's something. Are you going to be grateful to me?"

"I am grateful already; you've taught me so much."

He lit a cigarette, very carefully, as if the fate of nations depended upon its being lit with the most perfect exactitude. He blew out the match, stared at the end, which glowed for a second, and then turned black. Only then did he look again at Genevra. "Tell me something, quite honestly. No overdone gentleness. You're an honest person, I believe. Do you think that any woman would marry me?"

"I think that many women would marry you for many reasons," she said.

"What are the reasons?"

"You're rich—very rich. You're successful; you're going to be even more successful soon. You would be in a position to gratify a woman's personal ambitions if she were an actress, a dress designer, a scenery designer——"

"You haven't mentioned that any of them might conceivably love me."

Genevra leaned forward and impulsively laid her hand on his arm. Her eyes were very gentle and kind, he read compassion in them, loved her for it, and resented the reason for its existence.

"Melton," she said, "this is a futile conversation. All supposition. How can I really know? I'm not experienced. Many people could—and do—love you. Love to one individual means one set of emotions, to another—something completely different. Talk of something else, my dear. We shall only get into deep water, and—" she laughed softly—"I'm not a very good swimmer."

He caught her hand in his, lifted it to his lips and kissed it. He held it firmly, but not tightly, she knew that she could have drawn it away had she wished. His fingers were very long and fine, his hand was smooth and yet had no trace of undue softness. She thought of it as the hand of a man who was, by nature, energetic.

He said, "It hasn't by any chance occurred to you that I might be in love with you, Genevra?"

Then she did draw her hand away, and glanced at him as if his words had startled her. "That's not—not why you've cast me for this part?"

He smiled. "My dear, however much I loved you—and remember I have not even said that I do—not all the King's horses and all the King's men would make me give you a big and important part unless I knew—knew, mark you—that you could play it. Oh, I'm sufficiently commercially minded for that, believe me. But if I told you that I was in love with you what would you say?"

She looked at him, her thick white lids a little lowered. "I should hope that it wasn't really love, only an attraction."

"Why? Henry?"

"No, my dear—work. Listen, I can hear Hubert's voice in the hall. We must talk of something else——"

"I don't want to! I want to talk about you and me in relation to you."

She rose and put down her cocktail glass, then turned and smiled at him. "Your relation to me is that of a very famous brilliant producer who is expending a great deal of time and effort in teaching a quite unknown Lancashire actress not to say 'mooch'!" The door opened and Hubert came in; Genevra said, "Hubert, poor frozen creature. Do you want a cocktail?"

Melton said, "Make some fresh, Hubert. There's nothing left in the shaker but iced water tinged with vermouth. The last one Genevra gave me was dreadful!" He chuckled. "Ah'd mooch rather 'ave one that 'ad a bite ter-r-it! How's that, Genevra?"

"Awful! How fortunate that you don't have to play dialect parts!"

The tension had eased and for the remainder of the evening Melton was ready to become immersed in the play. The three of them discussed the character of 'Susan', argued how it should be played, and which lines had worth and which might be sacrificed for the good of the play.

Only when she got back to Albion Street did Genevra think again of what Melton had said, to speculate as to how much or how little he had meant; to hope that if there had been any seriousness in his words it would not affect her relations with him during the rehearsals of *Playing Cards*.

She knew that she liked him so much; there were so many things in his character which appealed to her. She admired his courage, his knowledge and his imagination, but she had never felt an attraction for him as she had felt for Henry, or even—for a short time—for George. She consoled herself with the hope that he had only been indulging in an attempt to flirt with her. Poor Melton, there must be times when his infirmity irked him unbearably!

Rehearsals continued; work was harder than ever, for not only were the proposed London company playing every night, but they were often getting ready for the next week's play. True, Carter was keeping to revivals; plays in which the artistes already knew their lines and only needed them brushing up. March was drawing to an end, and Carter had decided that his company were to take a long week-end vacation.

Everything was well in train, and he was determined not to allow them to grow stale. Henry Lorimer had been to Follingly, he had sat in the stalls and made sketches, he had talked at length to Jane Heriot, Nellie Gosforth and Genevra about their clothes, the colours best calculated to harmonize with the décor, returned to London and sent back his finished sketches.

Genevra had dined with him one evening at the Golden Hind at Lelton. She had thought that he looked tired and that sometimes his voice sounded listless.

"I was sorry to hear about Mr. Gossage," Genevra said.

Henry nodded. "Bad business, although he knew that he couldn't get better. She's lost without him; he had always attended to everything, her financial affairs and so on. Poor Clementina."

He crumbled his bread, and asked suddenly, "How old are you now?"

"Twenty-two."

"You ought to be a success in London. Have you decided where you're going to live? I ask because Clementina is going away on a cruise, I think—and told me that she'd be only too happy to offer her flat to you while she was away." He smiled. "You once told me that you wanted a flat in Arlington Street, didn't you?"

She cried, "How kind, but of course I couldn't accept it! I couldn't possibly live up to that flat!"

"Would you like mine? It's convenient, quite comfortable, in Bury Street. My old man and woman are very capable."

"Are you going to be away as well!" Genevra asked, and Henry heard the sudden sharpening of her tone with a certain amusement, even satisfaction.

"I'm always away a good deal, and I expect that I always shall be. There is always the house at Barnet, and now I have a better car the journey backwards and forwards is nothing. I warn you that my mother will be mortally hurt if you don't escape there at the week-ends!"

"May I think over about your flat? Of course it would be wonderful, but I'm sure you'd hate it—I mean hate not being able to occupy it yourself."

"How often am I there? I shouldn't hate it, unless I knew that you gave wild parties where no one uses an ash-tray, but everyone lays down lighted cigarettes on a grand piano or a Chippendale cabinet. Think it over. By the way, what is Carter paying you for town?"

"Ten—as I get here—and a percentage."

Henry rapped out, "What percentage?"

"Two."

He pulled out his slim gold pencil and on the back of an envelope made some rapid calculations, then scribbled over the figures to obliterate them and returned his pencil to his pocket.

"Not too bad, though not wildly generous if the play is the success he believes that it will be. You ought to be able to save money, Genevra."

"I've been saving money for quite a long time, Henry."

When he left her he told her that he was returning to town in the morning, adding, "I'll see you at the dress rehearsal. I hope that you'll like the clothes."

Genevra spent her long week-end in Manchester. She watched her grandparents closely, and with some sense of anxiety. For the first time in her life she realized that they were growing old. Lottie—she calculated—must be sixty-six or sixty-seven; Josh a year or two older. They were well preserved, active, and Lottie boasted that she could 'do a day's work better than these bits of girls who neither clean nor let it alone!'

"I believe that I shall try to get foreigners. Mrs. Holmes, at Number Twenty-five, has two, wonderful workers, clean as they can be. She got them from Austria." She made the statement as she might have said 'from Lewis's' or 'from the International Stores'.

"You never think of retiring, Gran'ma?"

"Now, Genevra dear, what on earth should I do if I retired?" She gave a pleasant chuckle. "Come to that, what would the profession do without Hostley's? Mind, things are changing; lots of the old faces aren't coming on tour any more. You miss them. It's all right folks laughing at pros who say, 'Ah, those were the days!' But it's true—those *were* the days. Looking back—and when you get to my age you spend a lot of time looking back—it seems that people were gayer, they laughed more, and more easily. They gave more and didn't demand so much. But retire—not yet, m' dear, so long as I keep my health and strength—not yet."

The world, even to Genevra at twenty-two, was changing. Haig moved slowly. When she asked him to come for a walk he came because he was too much of a gentleman to refuse, but she often felt that he wanted most to lie still, and only at intervals get up, stretch his stiff limbs, and go to sleep again, sighing luxuriously.

She sat and watched him, remembering that he was nearly fourteen years old; had he ever been quite the same since his illness at Cothampton? How good George had been then! She wondered if George had married his partner's daughter, and if they were happy. For quite a long time she had exchanged letters, always promising to come to Lelton 'one day when I am not too busy learning a new part', but slowly the letters had become farther and farther apart, and now they had ceased altogether.

"Now, Haig, dear," she said, as they sat alone in Lottie's pleasant, inartistic and overcrowded sitting-room, "I'm going to London. I can't take you because I shall be working terribly hard, and I don't want to leave you with people you don't know—

however kind they may be. You stay here with gram'pa and gran'ma, where you've everything you want—except me."

He looked up at her; his brown eyes seemed to her to be suffused, their whites were growing rather yellow and a little bloodshot. She knelt down and held his head in her hands, whispering, "Haig, I wish you could come with me. That would mean I should have someone to talk to. I'm in such a muddle, darling. Only, you'd hate it. I'll come back. If ever you were ill I'd send on an understudy, whether they liked it or not, and come to you."

When she left, Josh said, "The best, dearie, all the best. Gran'ma and me'll be up for your first night. Staying with Tilda at Barnet. Mind, never move on the stage onless there's a good reason for doing so. Don't hurry your exits and entrances—they may have to be quick, but never hurried! Think on, speak up, and let the chaps at the back of the gallery hear what you're saying. The author's wrote it, and so, presumably, he wanted it to be heard. That's a good girl, and there's a fiver for you."

She had accepted Henry's offer of his flat, and drove there on an evening when the rain was slanting down on the pavement, and everyone scurried along under umbrellas looking pinched and miserable.

Henry's flat was warm and comfortable; the stout, elderly woman and her long, angular husband were anxious to do everything possible for her. The man, wearing neat clothes which almost amounted to a uniform, said, "Mr. Lorimer's express orders, miss. Anythink that you want is to be pervided immediately. Mr. Lorimer is out of town at the moment, but he gave instructions that flowers were to be placed in your room."

Genevra's heart warmed suddenly. Henry had remembered. Henry had given instructions regarding her! To Henry perhaps she meant something after all.

Flowers. . . . Her careful Lancashire soul made her imagine what they must have cost, and as she looked at them with intense pleasure she made a little clicking noise with her tongue.

"T'click, t'click! What they must have cost him!"

Rehearsals began. The stage seemed far too large, and everything a little strange after the theatres to which—after two years —she had become accustomed. Carter made his entrance, and, as always, Genevra was intent upon her letters or reading an advertisement for some special kind of 'make-up' with simulated interest.

"Good morning, ladies and gentlemen."

There he was, lying in his long chair, Wright standing beside him, with Charles Tancroft on his other side. He looked well, Genevra thought, and excited.

"Run through," he ordered. "Charles, get some chairs to mark the entrances, and stick something on the stage for the chairs and tables. That's the idea. Everyone knows their lines. Ready! Act One. Let it go." During her waits Genevra saw various people drift into the stalls; she thought that she recognized Miriam Warner; once she imagined that Henry came in and slid out again, moving soundlessly. Other people she did not know, who seemed to have a right to come in and slip away again without comment from anyone.

At a quarter to one Carter said, "I believe that it's shaping. Back, everyone—no books, remember—at half past two." He laughed. "It takes longer to get luncheon in London than it does in Follingly!"

Hubert repeated, "Back at half past two, please—everyone."

Tancroft called, "Half past two—Act One. Those not concerned please come to me and get instructions regarding wigs, if necessary, and clothes. Thank you."

Carter called, "Miss Menetti, please."

She went over to his chair. He said, "Found somewhere pleasant to stay?"

"Henry's lent me his flat in Bury Street."

She saw Carter scowl suddenly. "Oh, really! Very convenient."

"It's charming, and Henry is going to be out of town a great deal, or staying with his mother at Barnet. It seemed an ideal arrangement."

"Quite." His voice was still very crisp. "Now, I want you to go down as soon as possible to see the clothes Lorimer's making for you. Nellie will go down this afternoon. She's only got a very short scene in Act One, and someone can read for her. I'd like you to go to-morrow, without fail. Better telephone Lorimer to find if he'll be there. I can't have you fobbed off with some understrapper."

"I shall see to it."

During the weeks that followed Genevra lost count of time. Twice she dined with Carter at his exclusive hotel in Curzon Street. He had regained his good temper—which he lost frequently at rehearsals—and was again the completely charming host.

He said, "I stay here because they know me. They see that I'm lugged in and out without a dozen nit-wits standing round to murmur 'Pore feller'. It's old-fashioned and clean, and—well, I like it."

Genevra said, "Do you know, Melton, I think you make far too much of this disability of yours. I don't believe that people are half so sympathetic or half so interested as you believe. You imagine too much."

She watched his eyes narrow as if he were annoyed, then he suddenly smiled at her and said, "Dear Genevra, you don't happen to be me. If you were you'd know better than to make 'courageous' remarks of that kind. Incidentally, once we're launched I'm going to risk asking you to marry me, do you know that?"

Speaking gravely, she answered, "I hope that's not true—unless I'm so good that you think a proposal would be the best means of giving me a permanent contract!"

"Your mind runs on nothing except the stage!" He was half amused, half irritated.

"Isn't that a good thing, to be serious, absorbed in one's work?"

"Not to the exclusion of everything else, my dear. However, don't think about that threat—or promise—or what you will—let's get the play launched."

The play was launched. To Genevra the day passed in a kind of walking nightmare. The Smithsons were kind and attentive. Smithson said, "I can assure you, miss, that I have seen Mr. Lorimer in just the same state of nervous apprehension before one of his big dress shows! But they've always been most successful."

Genevra nodded. "I know, thank you, Smithson, but you should have seen what the dress rehearsal was like! Awful—simply awful! Everything went wrong, everyone *was* wrong. I was the worst of all."

She went down to the theatre, thinking, 'After all, I needn't go on! No one can kill me, arrest me, if I don't. Little Mattie is quite a good understudy. I can catch a train to Manchester and stay there with gran'ma'. And yet she was moving towards the stage door.

The stage-door keeper said, " 'Ole pile o' telegrams for you, Miss Menetti, an' some luverly flowers. The best of luck, miss, the very best of luck."

Genevra licked her dry lips and said, "Thank you, Gibbons."

Her dresser was waiting. "Something to tell you that should make you very pleased. Just as I walked in a little black kitten came up, crying pitifully. I took no notice, but it followed me—and look, there it is."

Curled up in a soft ball on one of the chairs was a minute coal-black kitten. Genevra stared at it. "Is that lucky?"

"Oh, miss!"—reproachfully. "Just about the luckiest thing that can happen!"

"Has it had anything to eat or drink?"

Her dresser nodded. "I sent out for a drop of milk from the dairy, and a bit of fried fish from the place round the corner. It ate the lot, must have been starving. Now, come along, miss. Do you want to look at your flowers and telegrams?"

The strength seemed to have left Genevra's limbs; she said weakly, "I will, after the first act."

She began to make up; Hubert Wright came. "Genevra, my dear, all the very best of luck. You're coming to Melton's party afterwards at the Dorchester, aren't you?"

"If I'm still alive."

He gave her a note, saying, "He'll be in a box. He can't get round very easily, but he sends you his love and all his good wishes. He told me to say, 'Tell her that I'm not afraid!' "

"Bless you—and him—Hubert."

Felix Manvers came with his good wishes, James Cowper and Nellie Gosforth, who said, in her fine resonant voice, "My dear, tell me—*why* do we do this, when we might be happy, healthy charwomen? Well, all the best!"

Jane Heriot, ready dressed and looking so beautiful in the dress which Henry had designed for her that Genevra was shaken out of her state of nerves into a sudden sense of jealousy. Jane was so tall, so elegant, so much mistress of herself. Genevra felt that she did not remember a single line, recall a single move.

The call boy knocked. "Half an hour, pleese!" It seemed to Genevra that within five minutes he was back, calling, "Quarter of an hour, pleese!"

The kitten woke, stretched out two paws with pink pads, yawned and stared at Genevra with milky blue eyes. She managed to whisper, "Kit, kit!" The kitten slid down from its chair, came forward, rubbed itself against her silk-stockinged leg, then returned to its chair and slept.

May said, "It's not worried, anyway—is it?"

"Overture and beginners, pleese."

Genevra said, "Give me my part, May dear, just for a second."

May Neville shook her well-dressed head. "Forgive me, but no, dear, definitely no! Just sit quite still, and try to relax for five minutes. Think of something right outside the theatre. Something lovely."

She waited. Think of something lovely—what? That the curtain had fallen, that the first performance was over, that she was going back to the flat to sleep. She could think of nothing more beautiful.

"Miss Menetti, pleese."

May said, "There we are. God bless and all the best."

At the side of the stage Charlie Tancroft whispered, "Good luck, my dear. Wonderful house. Nellie got a laugh on almost every line! Go on—show 'em!"

She listened for her cue, thinking, 'How cold my feet are—and my hands! They'll show scarlet through the wet white! Oh—it's me!'

The audience saw a slim young woman, with bright golden hair and a smile which was kind and friendly, as she went forward to greet Nellie Gosforth. She moved smoothly, and without affectation, and when she spoke her voice was deeper than they would have expected. Deeper, and full without being heavy or over-coloured.

She felt that the act was moving swiftly; their pace—that pace on which Carter had insisted so firmly—was right. There was no hurry, but the whole machinery fitted beautifully. She made her first exit; Jimmie Cowper was waiting in the entrance. He whispered, "They're eating it!" and made his entrance. She waited, still too occupied with her own part to pay attention to anyone. Once someone whispered, "Miss Menetti, the Guv'nor looks very pleased; he's in Box A on the prompt side."

She had no idea who spoke to her, but nodded mechanically and said, "Oh, that's splendid . . . splendid."

A rest at the first interval; Genevra felt like a boxer after the first round, thankful to lean back in her chair, her hands hanging loosely at her sides, conscious that May would give her until the last possible minute before she came forward with her second-act clothes.

Hubert Wright tapped on the door, entered and said, much as he might have spoken to a woman immediately after her successful confinement, "It's going very well, dear. Melton's very much pleased. Good luck."

She was dressed. May stood back, saying, "I thought that the first-act dress was lovely, but this is even lovelier. That Mr. Lorimer's a wizard."

The second act was easier; for the first time she had to display a certain amount of emotion, and even passion. Carter had said so often: "Make it real, but keep it restrained. Don't go—all out. Hold your horses, Genevra."

As she made her exit she heard the applause come over; she stood for a moment listening, the noise swelled like the sound of an incoming tide. They liked her! Nellie Gosforth, waiting to go on, caught her hand.

"That's lovely, darling. Oh, it's going wonderfully."

The third act. Genevra felt that the play had been going on for years, she could scarcely remember the time when she had not been on the stage at the Queensway. Years and years! When had she left Bury Street? It must have been somewhere in the Dark Ages. Hubert came round to speak to her at the side of the stage before her entrance.

He bent his narrow head with its smooth hair and spoke very softly.

"Melton says in this first scene—go all out. Later tone it down, but have that one big—burst! Nellie knows exactly how he wants her to play it with you. You're doing splendidly."

She felt her face stiff when she tried to smile, whispering, "Yes, yes." Her brain felt as if it were divided into two parts, the one dealing—and dealing adequately—with the immediate lines she must speak; the other darting ahead, concerning itself with lines which were still to come: moves, noting the positions of people, furniture—were they as she had known them at rehearsal, or had they been changed?

Her big emotional scene gained applause, wholehearted and unrestrained. She felt as a jockey who knows that he is 'into the straight'. Nearer and nearer—and at last . . . the final lines, the tag hitherto forbidden to be spoken.

In the wings a tall young man in evening clothes, with untidy hair and a dead-white face, caught her hand and said, "Thank you so much. I am grateful." Then noticing that she did not remember him, he said, "I'm Wilfred Mawson. I wrote the play."

Calls—calls—calls. Charles Tancroft calling, "Now—you, Nellie, and Harold." Later, "Jane and Felix—oh, for God's sake get on! Genevra, you and Nellie again. Get on—oh, get on! Now, all on! I said—all on, yes, you two as well. Damn it, we've rehearsed it. Not an idea! Off—Nellie alone. Genevra, by yourself! Do as you're told."

Applause, rolling over the footlights. The whole company on, with Mawson appearing with them in response to cries of 'Author'.

Tancroft hissed, "Say something! Oh God, say something."

Mawson, so white that Genevra thought that he was going to faint, took a step forward.

His voice was thin and flutey; he said, "Ladies and gentlemen, thank you, but the credit belongs to this wonderful company and their producer Melton Carter," and he motioned towards the box where Carter sat leaning forward, his face as pallid as Mawson's own.

The curtain fell for the last time. It was over. Tancroft said, his face beaming with delight, "Looks as if we've done it, eh?"

Back in her dressing-room Genevra really tasted the joys of success. Henry and Aunt Tilda, her grandparents—Lottie inclined to be a little tearful—people she scarcely knew crowded in to offer her their congratulations. She smiled; felt wildly happy and pointed to the tiny sleeping kitten.

"That brought us luck, didn't it, May?"

"I felt it would, Miss Menetti. Nothing like a black cat."

The call-boy knocked. "Everyone on the stage in ten minutes, pleese."

Henry waited until everyone drifted away, then came over to Genevra and took her hand, "You were quite right not to give it up. My dear, I am so proud of you."

CHAPTER EIGHTEEN

Playing Cards was a success; the company enjoyed packed houses, the Press had been enthusiastic, and the public took the play to their hearts. Not even the heat of summer could kill the play; when the chill nights of November came to follow dull days the play was still doing business which made Hubert Wright rub his hands with satisfaction.

"We shall get a year out of it," he told Genevra, "possibly more."

She grimaced. "Oh, Hubert, we're all getting rather tired of it!"

"If I tell Melton that he'll make you rehearse every day for a fortnight. He's going to redress the whole show for Christmas. Would you like a holiday, my dear? I think that it could be managed."

"A holiday! In November! Hubert, where on earth can one go for a holiday in November?"

"Plenty of places—Madeira, south of France, Italy."

She said doubtfully, "Oh, I don't know. . . ."

She saw very little of Melton Carter. Genevra reflected that his sudden burst of sentimentalism at Follingly must have been merely an impulse. Her sensation was one of relief, she did not want to be forced to make decisions. Her work absorbed her; she loved her success, enjoyed the small additional luxuries which her considerable cheques every Friday made possible. She liked Carter, admired him, but when she tried to imagine herself in love with him she knew that the very thought filled her with dismay.

Henry had been away often during the run of *Playing Cards*: he had gone to America and brought back stockings for Genevra, which were finer than any she had ever seen. He had been to Australia, and told her that he wanted to make the Australians 'clothes-conscious'. He went to South Africa on the same mission, and came back to complain that 'the wrong kind of people bought the right kind of clothes'.

His attitude towards Genevra was always studiously kind; he was adamant in his refusal to allow her to give up his flat and take a furnished one for herself. She told him that she believed he liked to keep her there 'under the eye of Mr. and Mrs. Smithson'. He smiled, and said that she might be speaking the truth.

"I can't be there to keep an eye—only I should assuredly keep both eyes—on you; I can't let you just run about London alone!"

She frowned. "Henry, this elder-brother attitude is something new."

"I don't think so. I've always felt protective towards you."

"How do you know that I want protection?"

He still smiled. "You may not *want* it, it's highly probable that you need it."

He made his sketches for the redressing of the play, and took them up to Follingly to show Carter, who was unable to leave the house after a long and serious attack of bronchitis. Henry found him looking thin and fine-drawn; his hands looked almost transparent as he held the sketches which Henry had brought, and his voice lacked its usual strength.

"They're beautiful. You've surpassed yourself, Henry."

"I thought, myself, that they were rather pleasant."

"I must get well," Carter said, almost peevishly. "I want to see the show redressed; we're having new scenery—oh, I forgot,

245

you know all about that. The doctors want me to take a holiday —Hubert suggests Madeira or the south of France."

"Hubert suggested both those places to Genevra when she complained of feeling tired," Henry said.

"You're not suggesting that I should ask Genevra to come with me!"

Henry said, rather stiffly, "It hadn't occurred to me to suggest it."

Carter twisted round in his chair, so that he faced Henry, and said, "Tell me, are you in love with her?"

"It would be more to the point to ask if she felt any such feeling for me, surely?"

Carter scowled. Henry thought how bad-tempered that scowl made him look. He was all right while he smiled, or even looked reasonably pleasant, but when he grew irritable you noticed those deep lines at the sides of his mouth, the single straight wrinkle between his eyebrows. Poor devil, it was scarcely to be wondered at if he allowed his temper to become frayed. He'd a lot to put up with.

He said, as if he challenged Henry to deny what he said, "Because I may tell you that I am. If I wasn't the miserable thing that I am, I'd ask her to marry me to-morrow! I'm not even certain that I shan't take a chance and ask her once I can get to town again! Damn it, I can help her in her work. I can give her everything she wants!"

Very quietly Henry said, "Can you? Do you believe that?"

Carter said sharply, "You mean children? My good chap, science makes all kinds of things possible! The main thing is that she's an actress. I can give her opportunities, put her on the map——"

"I had imagined her to be—on the map—already."

"On the strength of one performance! There have been too many 'one-part' actresses! In one rôle—magnificent; in everything else—unless they had proper direction—they were hopeless. You can think of at least half a dozen of them." He was talking excitedly now, the bad-tempered lines showed less plainly. "I believe that she likes me. I believe that she's ambitious, she wants success. Look here, Henry, it's obvious that you don't want to marry her. You've had plenty of chances, you've known her for years. All right, then give me a chance. I swear that I'll be good to her. She can have anything and everything that she wants. I'm a rich man; even I scarcely know how rich I am. I shan't make old bones. By the time I'm through she'll still be a young

woman. Blast it!"—with a sudden return to his former fury—
"I've had precious little out of life up to now."

Henry did not move. He sat very still, his face grave and
intent. He was repulsed by the very idea of Genevra—that lovely
thing—being married to Melton Carter. He admitted his brilliance, even a certain attraction, but as a prospective husband for
Genevra Menetti he knew that, mentally at least, he shuddered.

In his coldest and most impersonal manner, which women
found so fascinating and men so infuriating, he said, "Oh,
admitted. But remember, my dear fellow, that once you begin to
pity yourself, no one else has any pity to give you. Now, I think
that if I'm to catch that last train back to town I must begin to
move. Good night, and I'm delighted that you like the sketches.
I think that dinner dress for Nellie will come out magnificently."

Carter said, "Yes, I expect the car is waiting. Good night,
Henry, and give me a chance; that is if you've any feeling in that
direction yourself."

In the train which was carrying him to London Henry leaned
back in his corner and tried to drive away many of the thoughts
which came crowding into his brain. He had always liked Carter
moderately, but after his accident Henry had felt a surge of
admiration for him. The man had courage, and Henry rated
courage highly. He knew that he loved Genevra very deeply;
whether he could make her happy was a very different thing.
Although he had known her for so long, he realized that their
lives were essentially different, and in each of them there existed
that ambitious urge, the desire to attain something which should
set them apart, as it were, from other people. They were both
well on the way to realizing that ambition.

Married to Genevra, Henry wondered how she would accept
the necessity for him to meet, and meet fairly frequently, other
women, women who were as attractive as she was. He had built
up his reputation, and at the moment it was growing with every
month that passed, on a sort of 'personal interest' basis. Not that
he had ever indulged in actual affairs with his clients, although the
opportunities which had been offered to him were countless. He
had taken a pride in studying his clients, in watching their movements and planning their clothes so that they should be completely suitable as well as merely beautiful. It had been part of his
scheme to make use of his excellent education, his good looks—
for Henry had no illusions and no false modesty—to assist him
in his dealings with his clients.

He had told Levelle, "I can make a better, more individual

design for a woman if I have lunched or dined with her. It is not a matter of mere measurements, this dressmaking, it is a matter of understanding the character of the woman."

Levelle had nodded his head with its immense crown of snow-white hair and said, "R-right, r-right, my tear poy. Inteed how ver-ry r-right!"

Even if Genevra were content to make allowances, to accept his assurances—which would be the truth—that there was nothing in the least sentimental in his friendships with his clients, would he be able to accept her profession and all that went with it? On the first night of *Playing Cards* he remembered how deeply he had disliked watching Genevra clasped in the arms of Felix Manvers. There was nothing in it. She had more than once said that she disliked the man, but Henry knew that he had hated those scenes more than was actually reasonable.

He would like to have a home, a wife—and that thought caused him to sit erect, and frown. That was what it all amounted to. He did not love Genevra sufficiently to make any radical change in his life. If she loved him at all—and there were times when he thought that she did, others when he asked himself how he could have been such a conceited fool as to imagine any such thing—he doubted if she would be content to make adjustments.

'And after all, why should she?' he asked himself. 'She's young, very lovely, the critics hail her as something of a "white hope". Why should she make adjustments? On the other hand, do I want to give up my complete freedom? If I don't, then why the devil should she?' His face twisted a little, he looked older, tired, and the thought came to him, 'Really, I expect that we're both selfish. We want our cakes to eat and still to have. We can't see ourselves exchanging one type of life for another. If I can't imagine myself doing it, then why in Heaven's name should Genevra? Let Carter have a fair field and no favour!'

The following evening he dined with Clementina Gossage. He had seen a good deal of her since her husband's death, and George Gossage had appointed Henry as one of his executors. Henry liked Clementina, and found her not only essentially kind but restful. Her flat was beautifully run, and the meals which she ordered for him were invariably exquisite. Henry, who admitted that he was something of a sybarite, appreciated luxury.

He sat opposite to her, watching her ugly, attractive face and thought how, if he were married, this would be one of the friendships which would have to be curtailed.

She said, "Worried, Henry?"

"Not really. Puzzled, perhaps."

She shrugged her shoulders. "Life, I expect, puzzles most of us who take the trouble to think about it. You ought to marry, my dear. Marriage solves so many problems."

"And produces a complete crop of new ones," he said.

Clementina sighed. "I could cope with the complete new crop. God, Henry, it's so damned lonely without George."

He smiled. "Marry again, my dear!"

"Whom? You?"

Perhaps he felt reckless, perhaps the excellent wine which he had drunk had gone to his head. He was terribly tired. Levelle had been over in London and had almost driven him frantic—questions, questions, questions. He had talked about the inevitability of war. Germany was too strong. Germany wanted still more power. France—the old man shrugged his shoulders. "Fr-rance! Do you know, my 'Enry, what a 'medlar' is? It is a fr-fruit which is only fit to be eaten when it is ro-rotten. So will Fr-rance be ready for the Germans to eat! W'en? *Mon Dieu*, 'ow do I know w'en? But it is coming, every day, nearer and nearer."

He said, "Me? You're, I think, the only woman I could bear to marry."

"Your little Menetti?" she raised her eyebrows.

" 'My' Menetti—you used the word, I didn't—wouldn't marry me. We're too individual. I want to go my own way, and she apparently wants to go hers."

Clementina murmured, "Adjustments are always possible."

"They're difficult to people who are almost completely absorbed in their work."

"Then it's obvious that you're neither of you in love!"

He shrugged his shoulders. "You're probably right."

She said, half irritably, "You're tiresome, my dear. Completely absorbed in Levelle's! You've no actual life of your own."

Henry smiled. "I find that it takes up most of my time. Don't worry about me, Clementina. One day I shall suddenly realize what I want and go after it."

"By that time, whatever you decide that you really want may have been snapped up by someone else!"

"I'll take my chance."

He remained in town to see the redressing of *Playing Cards*, and then went off to Caux, where he acquired a splendid tan and returned feeling better than he had done for years. Back in London he was inundated with work, and among the women who came clamouring for 'something new', or 'one of your own special creations, Mr. Lorimer', was Charlotte Bennings.

Henry disliked her intensely. He distrusted her oversharp tongue; he disliked her almost insane love of malicious gossip, and the set in which she moved: irresponsible people who turned night into day to no great profit either to themselves or other people.

She said, "How was Caux?"

"Most enjoyable."

"I loathe it. Was Clementina Gossage there?"

"She was."

"Someone told me that you were going to marry her. I forget who it was. Someone who knows you both quite well."

Henry smiled coldly. "I haven't seen the announcement in *The Times*."

"But you don't deny the possibility!" She gave her unpleasant neighing laugh.

"I see no good reason for denying anything so preposterous."

"I believe you're a dark horse, Mr. Lorimer."

"I am flattered that you think about me at all. Now, do you think this design is what you would like? The lines are nice, I think—graceful. . . ." He felt almost unreasonably angry; true he and Clementina were very good friends, but he had no sentimental feeling regarding her. In the early days of 1938 Henry knew that he thought very often about Genevra. On many evenings, as he passed the Queensway, he would slip into the theatre and stand at the back of the pit to watch some scene in which she was concerned.

He thought that she was growing more and more attractive, that her voice was fuller, her movements more smooth and delightful. He actually met her very seldom, and then usually at week-ends when she came down to Barnet to stay with his mother.

It struck him towards the end of February that she looked paler than usual, seemed restless, a thing he had never known her to be. When they were sitting talking late on the Sunday evening she said suddenly, "I wish to-morrow wasn't Monday!"

He looked up startled. "But I thought you adored your part—loved playing it!"

"I do—oh, I do, but things are difficult. Henry, can I talk to you?"

"My dear, of course."

She sighed, as if to have the opportunity was a relief to her.

"At Christmas-time Melton asked me to marry him. I tried to be as kind as I could, but—oh, I couldn't marry him! I know that he's done so much for me, that he will do even more. No one could imagine a better producer—he's brilliant. But marriage!"

"You're not in love with him?"

"Henry, I'm certain that I'm not. I'm desperately sorry for him, but I couldn't face living with him for the rest of my life. I tried to be kind—as I said—but he refused to take no for an answer. He said that I was ambitious, that there was no one who understood me and my work and development as he did; that he was ready to give me everything I wanted and needed to make me a really great actress. I said, 'That isn't enough'. He asked if he was repulsive to me. Henry, what was I to say? He isn't entirely. I shudder when they bring him in, when I hear his foot dragging as he moves along. He could so easily be wheeled in, or find some other means of getting on to the stage. It's getting on my nerves. At first I was so desperately sorry for him, I felt that I must never look at him when he came in, must pretend to be absorbed in my mail, a newspaper, anything.

"Now, so much of that pity has gone, and there is something like disgust instead. I sometimes think—it seems so horrible even to think this—that he almost likes making other people feel uncomfortable. He was leaving for Follingly the next day, and since then he has been ill. He has sent me notes and flowers, and Hubert comes to town and sees me and watches me with grieved-looking eyes as if I were to blame for Melton's illness.

"He came to see me on Friday, and said that he wished to speak to me privately. So May went out, and he began. He enumerated all the things Melton had done for me—oh, I'm so tired of hearing that, and yet it's true—and said that he'd been so brave. I admit that he *is* brave, and how he—Hubert—so longed to see him have 'a little happiness'. He said that Melton was dreadfully unhappy, that his illness was aggravated by that depression, and wouldn't I reconsider my decision?"

Henry did not move, his face was impassive; he said, "And what did you say?"

"I said that I couldn't. He said would I give Melton some hope that in the future I might change my mind? It all upset me terribly. It's going to make everything so difficult! I can't face being in the new production if Melton is going to beg me to marry him continually, or allow Hubert to come and plead for him. I couldn't do my work—I couldn't, really."

She looked suddenly to Henry Lorimer very young and

appealing. In his heart he despised Melton for asking any girl to marry him. He had asked for a 'fair field' and—damn it, that was what he had had! The thought of Genevra, young, golden-haired, ready to love life, to enjoy her work, being married to Carter, crippled and distorted as he was, seemed incredible. Girls like Genevra Menetti did not marry a man because he was brilliant and could help them in their profession, they married because they wanted a man who loved them, whom they love in return; a man who would give them children, happiness and content.

He said, "I see how difficult it all is. Is there a part for you in *Skeleton Leaves*, or whatever the play's called?"

She nodded. "I've read it. It's a wonderful part for me. I think that I could play it now; I couldn't have done a year ago. Oh, Melton has helped me, I know—I admit it. . . . I'm grateful."

Henry remarked drily, "You haven't done so badly for Carter yourself. You've contributed quite an appreciable amount to the success of *Playing Cards*. All the gratitude need not come exclusively from you." He watched her and thought that she was ready to burst into tears. He wished that she would say, as if from a sudden impulse, "Why don't you marry me, Henry?" He wished equally that he could force himself to say, "Genevra, marry me, and put an end to that particular worry." Then he reflected that he did not actually want to say anything of the kind; he wanted to tell her that he loved her, always had and always would love her. Then he reflected that if he spoke now, no matter how carefully he chose his words, Genevra might feel that he was taking advantage of the present circumstances regarding Melton Carter, or she might accept him because he offered a way of escape.

Genevra sighed. "It's going to be difficult, isn't it?"

"I'm afraid so, my dear. Carter 'ud be a fool if he let you go."

She flashed suddenly, "Carter can't keep me, if I decide to go!"

Henry lay awake for a long time that night. He felt angry and disturbed. Of course he should have asked her to marry him! Why did he invariably allow doubts to beset him in his relations with Genevra? He could make rapid and invariably correct decisions in his business; only when it came to things on which his whole future happiness depended did he argue, debate and vacillate.

He drove her back to town on the Monday; when he left her at the entrance to his flat she said, a little wistfully, "You didn't give me much good advice, Henry, did you?"

Conscious that he spoke stiffly, he replied, "I don't like giving advice, my dear. Remember that people don't really like taking it." Then energetically, "I know one thing: I should loathe to see you married to Melton Carter—loathe it!"

All day Genevra could still hear that sudden intensity in Henry's voice; as she made up that evening she smiled at her reflection, and said very softly, "I should loathe it . . ." with a certain satisfaction.

Two days later Genevra was lunching with Jane Heriot. Jane and she lunched together periodically, though neither of them could have said precisely why. They were in no way friends. Genevra always felt that Jane's feeling for her savoured rather of subdued dislike than affection. Jane was a popular young woman, possessing a number of very wealthy friends, people whose chief mission in life was to 'have a good time'. They regarded Jane's anxiety to act as a slightly eccentric form of amusement. They visited the theatres where she might be playing, told her that she was 'divine' and sent her masses of expensive flowers. When she left London—where she had been playing small parts, and playing them with a certain sureness and distinction—to join Melton Carter's company they told each other that Jane was 'a darling, but crazy', that she would never be heard of again but lie buried in 'some awful little provincial town playing *East Lynne* or something too frightful'.

When Jane returned to play at the Queensway they rallied round her, screamed their admiration, and admitted her into their circle once again.

Genevra admired her, and was faintly envious of her. She 'went everywhere', which meant that she lunched, dined, supped and danced at whatever places were considered the right places for the moment. She was very good-looking, with a beautiful figure, and the ability to wear her clothes well. As an actress she was rather above the 'adequate' mark, her brains were not of the first quality, and she had no particular wish to achieve fame or a place among the front-rank actresses.

"I like acting," she told Genevra. "It amuses me. I've a good memory, and can learn any part easily. I like the life, now we've got away from that ghastly Follingly and that still more ghastly Lelton. I suppose that eventually Bill and I will get married; we're very fond of one another—really fond. But we want to have a good time first. Marriage is bound to tie you down, and of course Bill's people will want two or three sons. Family possessions, estates and so forth. Of course, you're different, Genevra. I believe that you put acting above everything else."

She laughed and said, "I believe, too, that you think of it as —My Art, all in large capital letters, don't you?"

Genevra said, "Well, acting is an art, isn't it?"

"You don't gallivant about a great deal, do you?"

"I'm generally fairly tired after the show. 'Susan' does demand a lot of energy."

"Oh, my dear, I can imagine it. I'm quite content to play small parts, wear those lovely clothes Henry Lorimer makes for us, and save my energy for when the show is over. Oh, that reminds me! Do you know Charlotte Bennings? Oh, you *must* know 'Charlie' Bennings! I meant to tell you this last night. I was lunching with her yesterday. She's great fun. What do you think she told me? Henry Lorimer's engaged!"

Genevra said, "Henry's engaged! How did she know? This Charlotte Bennings?" Her first sensation was one of sick dismay, then immediately followed a great wave of indignation. If this were true why had Henry not told her? He had allowed her to confide her worries to him, and had shown no confidence in her.

Jane laughed. "I believe you were attracted to Lorimer, Genevra!"

"Henry's rather like a very kind, elder brother. I've known him all my life. But tell me about this engagement. Who told your friend?"

"*Henry!* Yes, one morning last week when 'Charlie' was seeing him about a new design he's making for her. It's a dream. She says he gets better and better. Yes, he told her. Oh, it's no surprise. It's not actually announced yet, but he said that he certainly couldn't deny what 'Charlie' had heard. He hinted that they wanted it kept a secret for a time, because George hasn't been dead a year yet. Of course, it's been common knowledge that Clementina Gossage has been wildly attracted to Henry for ages! My dear, he was always visiting them, going cruises in their yacht, staying with them down at Ammerly Manor. I suppose that he'll leave Levelle's and open some smashing place of his own. Clementina's simply rolling! But what a dark horse, old Henry! Not saying a word to you! Are you surprised?"

Speaking very slowly, and choosing her words very carefully because she wanted to be certain that she could enunciate them without any hesitation, Genevra said, "No, not really, because I know him so well. If this engagement is a secret, then to Henry it would be a secret to *everyone*. I don't think that he has even told his mother; in fact, I am certain that he hasn't, because I was staying there last week-end."

She felt that her statement had taken hours to make, and that the effort had left her tired. Henry going to be married! No wonder he had apparently taken so little interest in Genevra and her worries. Then she remembered his sudden outburst, "I should loathe to see you married to Melton Carter—loathe it!"

She said to Jane, "Are you sure that Miss Bennings really did hear Henry say that? It's not just adding two and two and making them five?"

"No! Oh, no!" Jane was indignant at the idea. " 'Charlie' told me exactly what he said. 'I am most certainly not in a position to deny—what you have heard.' He then said, 'It's not announced yet, of course. It will be in *The Times* when it's made public'. He admitted that the lady was Clementina Gossage, and of course 'Charlie' understood that they won't make it public until her husband's been dead twelve months. Oh no, dear old 'Charlie' —she is a scream that woman!—wouldn't make a mistake about a thing like that."

Genevra returned to the flat; she found a note waiting for her from Henry. Old Levelle had been taken ill at Nice, and he was leaving immediately. He did not know how long he would be away; that depended upon Levelle's recovery. He begged her to keep on the flat, and added, "Don't do anything impulsive that you might be sorry for. I meant what I said when I left you the other morning." He was hers 'always affectionately, Henry'.

She sat staring at the letter, written in Henry's characteristic, and rather attractive hand. Henry, who had admitted to this woman—whoever she might be—that he was going to marry Mrs. Gossage! Genevra felt numb. She did not even ask herself if she felt so because she had realized how deeply she loved Henry. She was too stunned to argue anything out clearly. By to-night, if she knew Jane Heriot, the whole theatre would know about Henry. Henry, who was leaving for the south of France. She could imagine what hints would fly round that in all probability Mrs. Gossage was following him. One thing emerged from her distress, her pain that Henry should not have confided in her, and that was that she could never marry Melton Carter. At that moment she did not believe that she would ever want to marry anyone!

Genevra was not a woman who dramatized herself. She did not imagine that her heart was broken; she only knew that she loved Henry Lorimer, and that she was unable to imagine that any other man could ever mean so much to her. He had been so much part of her life; her childish admiration for him had developed and grown into something very deep and strong. With the exception of George Powell—it seemed strange now to realize that she had to think for a moment to remember his surname—she had never indulged in a love-affair. Filmer Turner had attracted her for a very brief time, George Mason she had liked because she had believed—as she had done with Turner—that he had a knowledge of acting greater than her own, but she had been in love with neither of them.

During her longest wait at the theatre that evening Hubert Wright asked if she would see him. He sat in her dressing-room, his long, thin face serious, looking, Genevra thought, immovable.

She asked after Melton Carter. Hubert shook his head.

"That's really what I wanted to talk to you about. You wouldn't come up to Follingly next week-end, would you, Genevra? It would do him so much good. I believe it would just put him right, to see you and talk to you. Could you manage it?"

"Hubert, it's no *use*," she said patiently. "I can't—and won't—marry Melton. To come to Follingly would only mean that he'd ask me again; want to know the reasons *why* I refuse him. That surely wouldn't do him good. I've said 'No' verbally, I've written to him. I've told you to tell him! I've tried to be kind about it. I've tried to make myself quite, quite clear. I can't do any more."

Hubert sighed, "It's desperately hard luck on him."

Her voice sharpened a little as she said, "My dear Hubert, I'm not a kind of matrimonial philanthropic society! I've got a right to think of my own happiness: you'll admit that?"

"He believes that you're in love with Lorimer."

"As I heard to-day that Henry is going to be married, you can disabuse Melton's mind on that point!"

"Really?" But he didn't sound interested, and continued, "You see, Genevra, my dear, it's going to be so difficult for him —Melton—and also for you when we put the new play into rehearsal. You must see that."

"Can't he keep his business affairs apart from his private ones?"

Hubert shook his head. "Difficult, when he'd see you every day, when he'd want to discuss the part with you, at length. Oh, very difficult. In fact, I don't know if he can face it. I don't really."

Genevra rose, and said, "Just call Mrs. Neville, will you? I ought to change. Don't go, Hubert, I've got the screen. Get me into the second-act dress, May dear, will you?"

Hubert droned on; his voice, Genevra thought, was singularly monotonous, lacking light and shade. She caught words and bits of sentences:

"Insuperably difficult . . . it's bad luck . . . hoped this association might have lasted for years . . . the poor fellow. . . ." Genevra heard Mrs. Neville make a little clicking noise, "Tech, tech!"; she knew that her own patience was wearing thin, she felt nervous, unstrung. She came out from behind the screen, and even Hubert, absorbed in his own and Melton Carter's problems, felt a momentary thrill of admiration. How lovely she was! If only she'd marry Melton and make him happy!

She said very crisply, "When does *Playing Cards* come off?"

"Probably at the end of March or beginning of April. A great deal depends on how well Melton is, of course."

"And the new play goes into rehearsal at once?"

"As I say, if Melton is——"

Her temper snapped. She felt that she had been hearing nothing except that one name for hours. Melton, Melton, Melton! She said, "I agree that it might be difficult. The solution is obvious. I leave at the end of this run. Don't be apprehensive, Hubert. Melton will get over this; he'll find someone who is a better actress than I am. I'll write my notice formally to-morrow."

Her announcement galvanized him into life, his pale face flushed painfully, he stared at her with his rather indeterminate grey eyes, his mouth a little open. Mrs. Neville said briskly, "You must go down, miss. He has called, you know."

Hubert said, "Genevra, you don't mean it! You can't mean it!"

She was moving towards the door. "I do mean it, indeed."

"I can't imagine what Melton will do!" Hubert almost wailed.

"If you mention Melton's name again I shall scream. Good night, Hubert," she said, and went out, leaving him to shake his head dolefully.

CHAPTER NINETEEN

THE result of Genevra's announcement that she was leaving the Carter management was to bring forth a storm of protests from Melton. He wrote, he telephoned, he bullied and besought. She remained adamant; not even the promise of a large increase of salary moved her in the least. Henry was still in the south of France. He sent her a brief note saying that Levelle was improving, but that the old man seemed opposed to his return, and the doctors threatened that to leave him might possibly aggravate his illness. Henry was working on fresh designs, sending them back by air, and was thus able to satisfy his clients.

Genevra felt frozen and unhappy. It was not only that Henry had become engaged to another woman, but that he should not have had sufficient faith to confide in her. That, she told herself, was what hurt her most, though there were times—times of almost complete revelation—when she knew that she loved Henry and that the thought of his marriage with Clementina Gossage hurt her unbearably.

She remained in Henry's flat, not particularly because she wished to, but because she felt too tired to look round for somewhere else in which to live. There, with the kitten which had arrived on the first night of *Playing Cards*, she spent most of her spare time. She was reading with avidity everything she could find which dealt with the stage. She sat for hours reading, the cat curled into a ball on her lap. She had not been down to Barnet since she had heard of Henry's engagement. Aunt Tilda had written several times expressing a rather hurt surprise, but Genevra continued to make excuses for remaining in London. She wished to go to some Sunday-night show; there was a special concert which she must attend; she had invitations which could not be refused.

Towards the end of February she caught a late train and went to Manchester to spend the week-end with her grandparents. There was something so reassuring about them both; something in the solidity of their house, which she felt stabilized her. She was tired of Carter's reproaches, of his pleadings; she longed for Lottie's sound common sense and Josh's sane kindliness.

Her first question was, "How is Haig?"

Josh said, "Now, Genevra, there's no call to go in off the deep. He's all right, but we've got to face it: he's getting no younger nor what we are. He sleeps a goodish lot. Doesn't want to walk far. Well, no more do I. Mind you, Haig has everything any dog can want, and will continue to have it. Come and 'ave a word with him."

The little dog was lying in his basket; at the sound of Genevra's voice he got to his feet. His skin, she thought, looked too big for his body; his eyes—those beautiful eyes which had always looked at her with such devotion—seemed to have a slight mist over them. His dark muzzle was almost completely grey. She knelt down beside him, her arms round his neck; he licked her cheek, and made small loving noises of welcome.

That night, when her grandparents had gone to bed, she sat,

her elbows on her knees, watching him, her eyes filled with anxiety and tenderness. She talked to him very softly, telling him of her personal worries, hoping that he would look up at her with the same expression of comprehension in his eyes as she had known. He moved his head once or twice, even thumped his stubby tail, but she knew that he was sleepy and that sleep had come to mean a great deal to him.

Lottie had said, "Nay, he sleeps a lot; well, sleep's as good as food." The noisy clock on the mantelpiece—Josh said that he liked a clock that told you it was a clock, and ticked to some purpose—showed that the time was half past two. Genevra stood up, looked down at Haig, then stooped and said, "Good night, my Haig, I'll still be here in the morning. Perhaps I can take you a nice drive in a car. You like driving in a car, don't you?"

He did not move; she knelt down and stroked him, saying urgently, "Haig dear, Haig—look at me!" He remained quite still; she saw that his eyes were closed, and that his mouth was very slightly open.

She knew that Haig had left her for the happy hunting-grounds of good dogs—and which dogs were not good? she thought. A great wave of desolation swept over her. Haig, who had been with her for so long, whose life had been so tangled with hers, who had never failed her, had gone.

Henry had gone; now Haig had left her also. She crouched beside his basket, with its gay, spotlessly clean blanket, covered her face with her hands and cried bitterly. Then she rose and went to the writing-desk where Lottie did her accounts, and which was always stuffed with papers that no one would ever want to look at, and wrote a note to tell her grandmother what had happ ned.

She finished the note, lifted the basket where the little dog had slept his life away, and whispered, "You always slept in my room when you were with me; I'll carry you there now."

She slipped the note under the door of the room where Josh and Lottie slept, then carried Haig into her own bedroom. Very gently she laid over him a large and beautiful silk scarf, which Henry had once brought her from Paris, saying, "Sleep well, darling, and thank you for all you've been to me. Good night."

They buried him in the sooty Manchester garden next morning, Lottie sobbing uncontrollably, while Josh muttered at intervals in a husky voice, "Nay, luvey, dean't carry on. It 'ul do no good, an' you're just upsetting Genevra."

When Genevra left to return to London, she said, "I've

always had some of my heart left here in Manchester with you both; now another piece is left here with Haig."

The houses were falling off a little. *Playing Cards* had skimmed the cream off the theatre-going public of London. True there were still houses which were satisfactory, and on certain nights of the week the 'house full' boards made their appearance. Charles Tancroft said that they'd run until the end of April; "we shall have had a full twelve months out of it."

Genevra went to see Miriam Warner, who exclaimed, "Child, what have you been doing to yourself? You look tired to death. Anything wrong?"

"I've had a rather difficult time. I think that I want a rest. I'm leaving Melton Carter at the end of the run."

"Ah? Difficult?"

Genevra nodded. "Yes, rather. I don't want to talk about it. In many ways he has been terribly good and kind. I think that a change will do me good. I must work, you know."

"Um—er." The agent nodded like a wise Buddha. "Ever thought that you'd like to go to America? Wait a minute, I'll get Roland Fleming. He's at the Savoy, and looking round for someone. You might be just his type." Genevra listened to the one-sided conversation, heard her name mentioned, and the question, "What—immediately? She's here now. Yes—you'll let me know? Good-bye."

"Go down to the Savoy, ask for Roland Fleming. Say that it's by appointment and that you've come from me. Good luck, you'll like Fleming."

She did 'like Fleming'. She found him to be a thin, young-elderly man, with beautifully white hair and a skin which looked rather like fine leather. His eyes, behind heavy tortoiseshell-rimmed spectacles, were both shrewd and kindly. He was excellently dressed, and his hand—which he offered to Genevra—was very large, bony and well kept.

He said, "Well, now, sit down. Remember I don't know a thing about you except that you give a very fine performance in *Playing Cards*. Yeh, I was in last night. For that matter everyone concerned was good, but you want to get that pace speeded up a bit. Maybe you've gotten a bit slow after a long run, eh? This your first show in London? Well, I'll say you oughter go a long way, properly handled. Pretty name you've got! Genevra Menetti—like something that might taste nice to eat." He laughed at his small joke, showing incredibly white even teeth.

"I think it is rather a nice name," Genevra admitted.

"Foreign blood somewhere, I figure—your father? Ah, well, he gave you a pretty nice name. Tell me about yourself, now, Genevra. I like to *know* about people before I try to talk business. Say, how about some cawfee? They don't make it so hot here— maybe you'd rather have tea. You all drink tea in this country, don't you? In America the tea's not so hot, but the cawfee's about as good as you can find." He telephoned for tea, keeping up his running commentary all the time. "Say, gi'me service, will you? Strange how things are different in different countries, phrases, things to eat and drink—— Is that service? Well, I want tea for two—that was the title of a song one time, I seem to recall, in a musical show—yeh, tea for two, one five three. Make it snappy. Now, that's done," he beamed at her, "we can get on with our business chat. I can't stand for interruptions, they make me wild. You're not married, Genevra? I always call people by their first names; in addition I get real pleasure out of saying yours! Not married? I'll say the men in this country must be slow, or you must be darned hard to please. I wonder which? Gosh, here's the waiter with that tea. Set it here—that's right. Thanks. Now, Genevra, would you like to pour it out? My old dad used to say that a pretty woman never looked so pretty as when she was either holding a baby or pouring out tea. So, as we're short of a baby, will you take the alternative?" Again he laughed delightedly.

She drank tea, poured Fleming two further cups, and listened to his chatter for nearly an hour. At the end of this time he knew, Genevra thought, scarcely more about her than when she had entered his room. Her name, her age and the fact that she was not married. She, on her side, knew many anecdotes concerning his grandfather, his father and a particularly admired brother named 'Silas H'—"to distinguish him from my grand-dad, who was Silas B".

At the end of the hour Fleming sprang to his feet, said, "Gosh, look at the time! I've gotter appointment with C. B. Cochran at twelve! See here, take the script—where the hell is the thing? That's right, I've got it. Read it—it's the part of 'Caroline'. Mind, I don't say you've got it. We've a lot to talk over yet. I'll want to hear you read it, want to discuss terms, and so forth. However, read it and can you come round the day after to-morrow? Yes, here. What time? Darn it, where's my engagement book? Here, got it! Eleven-thirty. Suit you? Then lunch with me. I'd like to have Harry Fossick know you. You'll like Harry, everyone likes him. Goo'bye, Genevra, and soak yourself in that play. It's good. I'll be seeing you!"

She emerged into the noise of the traffic in the Strand feeling dazed, and as if someone had battered her soundly. For the rest of the day she pored over the script. The play was good, witty and amusing. Her part was important; more, it gave almost unlimited opportunities. Genevra's content grew. If only she could get this part! America would put the Atlantic between herself and Melton Carter; also—she sighed—between herself and Henry, and Henry's personal affairs. She had always dreaded the thought that she might have to go overseas while Haig was alive. Now . . . she could leave the black kitten with Mrs. Neville. Her grandparents were 'pros', they thought nothing of people leaving for America, for Africa or Australia. To them these voyages were all part of the routine of the life of the theatre.

If Fleming and the unknown Harry Fossick gave her the part, if the play had a good run, by the time she returned Henry would be married to his Clementina, and Melton Carter might have forgotten about Genevra Menetti. If . . . If . . . If . . .! There might be a chance to work on a film, there might be—there might be—there might be . . .

Two days later she went to the Savoy and asked for Roland Fleming. He was sitting at his desk, but sprang up as she entered, saying, "Now isn't this nice?" as if she were paying an unexpected call. Another man rose, and Fleming said, "Genevra, I'd like you to meet Harry Fossick. Harry, this is Genevra Menetti. Remember, I told you about her."

Harry Fossick was a man of about middle height, with a strongly marked feature which proclaimed him to be a Jew. His hair was dark, and grew strongly. Genevra thought that it must be crisp to touch. His eyes were large and very bright, his nose inclined to be melancholy, his mouth sufficiently full and well shaped. When he spoke his voice was gentle, with what was not more than a faint indication of a lisp.

He did not actually say, 'T'is ith a great pleathure', but she felt that he might quite easily have done.

Fleming said, "Now you know each other. That's fine. Now, tell us, Genevra, what 'cher think of the play? How d'you like 'Caroline'? I'm going to be quite frank. Harry and I have seen five other young ladies, and mind, two of them were good. Eh, Harry?"

"Darn' good, Roland."

"Umpha, darn' good. We talked it over and finally came to see your play again. You were pretty good last night. Eh, Harry?"

"Darn' good, Roland, darn' good."

Fleming nodded; then, as if struck by a sudden brilliant idea, said, "Say, what about some tea? I'll say, Harry, Genevra pours tea out beautifully. My old dad used to say that a pretty woman never——"

Fossick said, "That's a swell idea, tea. I recall that you told me that crack of your dad's. I'll order it." He went to the telephone, ordered tea, then returned to his chair. Genevra saw that he moved very smoothly and easily, that his gestures were graceful, his hands surprisingly well shaped and beautiful. She wondered who he might be.

Fleming said, "Good, that's fine, thanks a lot, Harry. Now, what I'd like would be for you to read through certain passages of the play with Harry, Genevra. I'll tell you the pages—whatcher call 'em here? Sides? Gosh, here's the tea. Harry, watch Genevra pour out tea! I reckon we'll introduce a tea-party into the play if we engage Genevra, eh? Give a nice touch, don't you think? Now," he sipped his tea rather noisily, "now, what about——" he turned the pages of the manuscript which lay on his desk—"page twelve—y'know, Harry, where you come in and find her lying on the couch. Got it? Got it, Genevra? Then—shoot!"

Fossick began to read. His voice was, Genevra thought, extraordinarily pleasant; it held colour, and the inflections were beautifully modulated. Instinctively she felt, 'I should like to play with this man! He must be a lovely person to have in a play. He even looks different when he begins to slip into the part'.

His charm was infectious, she knew that she was reading well. The play was essentially modern, and more than once she found phrases which were unfamiliar to her. Fossick obviously noticed her hesitation, for he smiled at her—a very friendly smile—and said, "Never mind, Miss Menetti. You're an English character. If you play 'Caroline' I guess we'll have those phrases translated—" he laughed—"into your native language. What you say, Roland?"

Roland said, "Betcherlife, Harry."

When they finished the scene Fleming said, "Now, let's take that big scene in Act Two—where is the darn' thing?—got it! Page thirty-seven. Shoot!"

Fossick said softly, "Let yourself go, Miss Menetti."

For an hour they read, while Fleming's bright eyes watched Genevra intently. Her nervousness had left her. She felt that Fossick liked her voice, approved of her delivery, even enjoyed her enunciation. Her confidence grew, and when Fleming asked for a scene in the last act she was able to give her lines real weight and considerable emotion.

Fossick closed his script, and laid it carefully on a table by his side. "Fine," he said; "you're swell, Miss Menetti, just swell."

Fleming said, "I'll say she is! Was I right, Harry, or was I right?"

Genevra flushed with pleasure. "Does that mean that——"

"That you've got it! We've only to get down to cases—terms, and the rest. I reckon we'd better talk that over with Miriam; whatcher say, Harry? Right, I'll get on to her the minute we've had lunch."

"But just a minute, Roland. We've not asked Miss Menetti if she likes the part. She's got to have the last word."

"That's so; but, Harry, there's no sense in us asking her and then us saying—if she likes the part, 'Well, shucks to you, sister, it's all fixed with another young lady!' See my point? You remind me of my brother Ed; he always says, 'Now, folks, what I say is——' "

Fossick laughed, that low, warm laugh which Genevra liked so much. He said, "I reckon this calls for highballs. Could you manage a highball, Miss Menetti? Just to seal the bargain, always supposing that Miriam Warner doesn't want a million dollars a week for you!"

The whole atmosphere of the luxurious room was so friendly that Genevra knew that she felt suddenly happy, relieved and reassured. She had been through a great deal, she thought, recently; she had dreaded Carter's letters, Hubert's pleadings; Henry's reticence regarding his engagement had hurt her terribly, and then losing Haig had seemed to be the last straw. Now these two men, so good-humoured, essentially kindly, seemed to have filled her with new confidence. The thought of going to America gave her a sense of freedom.

She smiled easily at Fossick, saying, "I don't think that I'll have a highball, thank you——"

Fleming cried, "Say, who dragged you up, Harry! English young ladies don't drink highballs before luncheon. They have a cocktail or a sherry."

"I should like a sherry, please. Dry."

He exclaimed in delight, "Look, what did I tell you?"

They gave her a delicious luncheon. Fleming amused her, and Fossick was attentive and kind, his beautiful voice was a joy to her ear. He told her that he would be playing in *Sleeping Goddess* if she came to America. "I believe in the play, and Roland can tell you I've a kinder hunch about plays. I've just got some kind of magic power for spotting winners. I believe that together we could make New York talk about us in a big way. You'd have some lovely clothes, Miss Menetti, and Roland's scene designer is a marvel. It sure would be a great little show!"

Two days later Genevra signed her contract. Her salary was far in advance of any which she had hitherto received. *Playing Cards* was due to finish its run on March 25. Fleming would arrange for her to sail on April 5. They were leaving earlier, but before they sailed Genevra saw them several times.

The day before they left, Fossick asked her to have supper with him.

He called for her at the Queensway, and over supper talked to her in a more intimate way than he had ever done before.

"I've loved this stay in England. It's a great little old country, even if they do say 'I'll post it—' when they mean 'mail it', and talk about the 'pavement' when they mean the 'sidewalk'. Kind of quaint and old-fashioned. I shall look forward to meeting you there right on the docks at New York. I'll fix up an hotel for you; one that's all right. You can't stay just anywhere in New York. It's a queer, grand city, little old New York, but you've got to have someone show you the ropes. Now I know your boat I can check up on your arrival, and I'll have every single thing fixed up."

Genevra said, "You won't find something that will be too expensive for me, Mr. Fossick, will you?"

He replied, "Honey, trust me, and why 'Mr. Fossick'? Kinder unfriendly, don't you think?"

She laughed, watching his mobile features, so sensitive and fine, listening to the sound of his voice—rich and yet never over-coloured. She thought, 'If he and Fleming are typical of America, then I'm going to be happy.'

She said, "Harry, then, remember that I'm not seeing my name in lights in Broadway yet."

"Don't worry, honey, you'll see them there soon enough."

When he drove her back to the flat he held her hand just a little longer than was strictly necessary. Again she looked at him with attention, and thought that she could trust him, believe in him. Bury Street was very quiet, only in the distance she could hear the noise of the traffic in Piccadilly. At long intervals a taxi passed, once or twice a strain of music reached them from some restaurant or from a radio in an apartment. The night was very fine and clear, with that crisp radiance which sometimes imbues London nights, a kind of serene stillness. The words of a song came to her, 'London is going to sleep'.

Harry Fossick said, "Well, I won't be seeing you again, not until we're both in New York. Genevra, honey, remember that there isn't anything I won't do for you. The sky's the limit. There, time you were in bed. You go and hit the hay——"

She laughed. "My bed is stuffed with hair."

"If it's anything like yours, that's a sin. It ought to be sent to the Bank of England and melted down into gold! Good night, and take care of yourself—until you get to New York, then I'll take care of you. Bless you, sweetie."

For the first time since she heard of Henry's engagement Genevra went to bed and slept soundly and dreamlessly. In the morning she told herself that she was not in love with Harry Fossick; she liked him, she trusted him. She repeated that assurance many times during the days that followed.

She went to Manchester, said good-bye to her grandparents. Lottie repeated that she was certain that Genevra was overworking. Josh declared that hard work hurt no one, and that Genevra must make hay while the sun shone. Lottie snapped at him, "Oh, you and your old work! The girl wants a holiday. She's been working hard for years. Genevra, my luv, I wish that you'd get married!"

Genevra nodded. "Let me see my name in lights, Gran'ma, and maybe I will."

The day before she sailed she went to Barnet. If Henry was at home—and she believed that he was still nursing old Levelle —she wished the time she spent in the house which she knew so well to be as short as possible. Aunt Tilda reassured her. Henry was still in the south of France, the old man was very weak and could not bear to have Henry leave him.

She added, "Of course Henry's got plenty of friends there. Mrs. Gossage has her yacht in the Mediterranean. She's a good friend of Henry's."

Genevra, bracing herself as if she were about to take a plunge into deep water, said, "Someone told me that Henry and Mrs. Gossage were going to be married."

Aunt Tilda shook her head. "I've heard nothing, but after all it's not a year—or barely—since her husband died, and Henry can keep a very tight mouth when he thinks it's necessary. She's old for him, I think, but after all if she makes him happy . . . I often thought that he'd have married you, Genevra. I should have liked that."

Genevra shrugged her shoulders. "He asked me once. I refused and he has not asked me again."

The older woman's eyes widened. "You turned down Henry! Genevra, how *could* you! Plenty of girls would give their heads to marry my Henry!"

"Henry asked me," Genevra said. "He was very nice about it, but he made me feel that he was fulfilling a kind of duty, not asking me because he loved me."

For the first time in her life Genevra saw Aunt Tilda annoyed. Her rather heavy face flushed, her eyes hardened, she breathed heavily.

"Well!" she ejaculated. "My Henry's never been an actor, never studied parts and learned to say his speeches so that the audience would applaud him. He's a man of the world—no sense in denying it—but there's something simple and direct about him that prevents him going into ecstasies over things or people. You've known him long enough, you ought to know if Henry says a thing he means it. I must say that I'm surprised at you, Genevra."

Genevra often wondered if she was not surprised at herself. She had longed, in spite of whatever protests she might have made, whatever reasons she had given, to marry Henry Lorimer. She remembered a favourite expression of Lottie's, 'Mind, you can go over-far through the wood, and miss a lot!' Now, listening to Aunt Tilda, she told herself that she had been a fool. She ought to have accepted Henry, ought to have believed that her influence would have made him able to speak more easily. She saw now that for years Henry—young, attractive, and essentially personable—had studiously held himself in hand, rather than become entangled in some liaison which would only have served to hinder his progress. Then, when he had asked her to marry him, he found that he had lost the ability to speak easily. His attitude had chilled her, dismayed her. She had felt that he was speaking from a sense of duty, not because he was impelled by actual love.

Was that true or was she indulging in 'wishful thinking'? She knew that she was immersed in her work, as Henry was in his, but had he made his proposal in more ardent terms, might she not have forgotten her career and accepted Henry with complete content? She sat there, in the familiar room, the room which she had known since she was a child, and, frowning, listened to Aunt Tilda's reproaches, and let her own thoughts occupy her at the same time. It was too late now, to-morrow she was going to Southampton, and early the next morning she would be out at sea. There was no sense in looking back; all that she could do was to look forward, to determine that her work must absorb her; Henry belonged to the past and could, as the husband of Clementina Gossage, have no part in her life.

As she travelled back to London she thought again of Henry. She knew with a quiet certainty that he would always hold the greatest part of her love and admiration. There were times when, she thought, 'I could almost cheerfully have hit him—but I should have wanted to take him in my arms the moment I had done it'. There was no use in moaning, she had thrown away her opportunity, and now it was too late. She was cutting adrift from the London that meant Henry, she had replied for the last time to Melton Carter's letter appealing, promising and reproaching her for 'both ingratitude and heartlessness'. She was facing a new and strange country, and she must face it with her head up and her heart filled with courage.

'Had I been wiser, less self-centred', she thought, 'I might have acted differently. I made a mistake and I've got to pay for it. Still, even admitting everything, Henry could have come and told me—not as someone he once asked to marry him, but as someone he has known for so long'.

Her mood was regretful. Henry had meant so much, he had been the rule by which she measured other men. He had been 'in her life' for so long, even though at rare intervals; now he had gone, and she felt lonely and abandoned.

The passage to America gave her a chance to rest. She mixed very little with the other passengers, despite invitations and offers of friendship. She lay in her deck-chair, wrapped in rugs, and revelled in the luxury of complete relaxation. She had not known how utterly tired she was until she knew that there was, for the moment, no need to flog herself into activity. It seemed like being translated into a kind of heaven, to know that the whole day was hers to use as she pleased, that she might go to bed as early as she wished, and rise as late as she wanted, without the thought of a photograph call, an additional rehearsal or a matinée.

Fleming and Harry Fossick were waiting for her when the great ship came into New York. She was delighted to see them, and their efforts made her passage through the customs easy. Fossick's face had lost its melancholy; he beamed at her, his dark eyes shining with pleasure.

While Fleming was answering questions put to him by the officials, Fossick caught her hand and said softly, "Gee, I never knew I'd miss anyone like I have you, Genevra! It's heaven to see you again, honey."

She liked her hotel. The 'gadgets' delighted her; the stock of face tissues, the soaps, the hundred and one things 'presented by' this or that firm astonished her. Fleming and Fossick had arranged everything, and she stood at her window looking out on New York, filled with a sense of well-being, health, and content.

The rehearsals were long and difficult. Genevra had studied her part on the voyage over, and was word perfect when she attended the theatre for the first time. The rest of the company had been rehearsing for over a week. Roland Fleming was clever, sensitive and reasonably considerate. Her clothes were beautiful, and everything was done for her comfort. Harry Fossick was charming to work with, and often in the evening she dined with him in order to discuss the scenes which they played together. As always when she was intent on a part, that part absorbed Genevra to the exclusion of everything else. She ate mechanically, she slept the sleep of complete exhaustion, and woke filled with energy and the desire to get to the theatre and work at, polish and embellish her part.

Fleming said, "Genevra, you're doing fine. I'm happy about you."

Harry Fossick said, "I never knew anyone take so much correction and never get sore, never knew anyone quicker on the uptake, never knew anyone who made work so dead easy. You're God's gift to actors and producers."

Two nights before the opening of the play Fossick sat with Fleming in his apartment late at night. Fleming had worked with Harry again and again. They understood each other's methods, and their friendship was based on mutual respect. There were times when Fleming's long-winded and frequently repeated stories irritated Harry momentarily; but his essentially good qualities far outweighed trivial things, and he was so good-tempered that when Harry cut him short in the middle of some 'oft-told tale', he never showed the slightest resentment.

He had little education, and had, as he always said, educated himself "in the wide, wide world, just knocking about and keeping my eyes skinned". Fossick, on the other hand, had received the finest education that his father's money could buy, and he had profited by it. Old Josiah Fossick had never wished his son to be an actor, but when he realized that his mind was set on that profession to the exclusion of any other, he gave his assent and concentrated upon his younger son, Simon, who showed from the time he left college that his mind turned only to business, and 'big business' at that.

Now, in Fleming's apartment, which was furnished with a view to extreme comfort and the exclusion of all good taste, the two men lay back in the ultra-modern steel chairs upholstered in brilliant scarlet leather, each with a highball at his elbow, and in a desultory fashion talked of the play.

Fleming had a block and pencil on the small table at his side, and from time to time made a note for some detail which their talk suggested to him.

Fossick said, "It's going fine, Roland. Fine!"

Fleming frowned. "We'll hope so. Don't tempt Providence by being so darned sure. I don't like you lighting Genevra's cigarette. Better let her do it herself. You know, in Act Two."

"Umpha, as you like—yeh, maybe it's better. Damn it, it *is* better at that juncture. You're right!"

Fleming grinned. "I always am. She's doing well, that girl. I reckon she is going to make them sit up and take notice."

Fossick nodded. "She's made me take notice all right."

"I guessed it, Harry."

"Think I've got a chance?"

"Not until after the first night's behind us!" Fleming warned him. "I don't want her upsetting. The part's a tough proposition. She's only young, even if she has poise and intuition. Susan Carret may have the bigger part—more pages to it—but little Menetti's got the hardest row to hoe. Bett'cher she's in her room now, working at this and that. Gosh, what a worker!"

Fossick drank deeply, and sighed as he set down his empty glass. "She's some girl! I'm crazy about her. Not only because she's lovely to look at, but because she's—well, she's a real, genuine, nice girl."

Fleming refilled their glasses and handed one to Fossick. "I guess you're right. Only hold your hosses until we're launched. My uncle Roland—I'm called after him—always said, 'Don't hustle your horses. Take one fence at a time'."

Harry replied that Uncle Roland would have had to be a remarkably clever fellow to take two fences at a time.

Roland replied, "Oh, shucks! Clever bastard, ain't you?" They returned to talking of the play.

Genevra had worked hard; she had begun to learn that working alone was not enough, and to that end she had developed her power of concentration and her critical faculty. It was sufficiently easy to learn a part, but she realized that she must have the power to devote all her energy—when rehearsing alone—to certain passages which presented difficulties. She refused practically all invitations. After rehearsal she returned to her hotel, and in her very comfortable and ultra-modern bedroom she began to work. No inflection was too slight, no movement too small for her to devote time and intense concentration upon it. The part, she felt, was definitely shaping. She felt sometimes that she could actually see it growing, and note where in the future actual flowers might blossom.

The first night came; she forced herself to go out instead of poring over her part. Fleming held a short and almost informal rehearsal; after that she was free until the time came for the evening performance. She looked longingly at her part, then, with determination, dressed to go out. Whatever was wrong now, it was too late to change; the part must stand!

She did not feel any sense of actual nervousness. Rather it seemed that all her senses were sharpened, her appreciation, heightened. She noticed the colours of materials in the shops, stayed to look into a florist's, astonished that she had never before so completely realized the beauty of form which the various blossoms possessed. Each one, she thought, was a gem of shape, colour and beauty. She had ordered her bouquets, her various presents for the company, the day previously, and now she was able to stand and stare, feeling that she was drinking in beauty. The sight of the flowers, graceful plants, little formal posies refreshed and contented her. She walked back to her hotel, thinking, 'It's come! I'm here, going to open in New York to-night. To-morrow—I shall know what they think of me here! It's all like "dreams come true".'

At the theatre, in her dressing-room, which she thought far less comfortable than those in English theatres, she was calm and only conscious that she felt every nerve in her body tingling. She longed for Mrs. Neville, she longed for the black kitten; most of all she longed for Henry to be able to come in after the performance, and to hear him say, "I'm so proud of you."

Flowers, presents, telegrams and cables. Gram'pa and gran'-ma, Aunt Tilda—yes, even Melton Carter and Hubert Wright—had cabled. Jane Heriot and—she took the cable which her dresser handed to her—Henry.

There is some awful mistake (stop) For God's sake wait until I come over (stop) Levelle better (stop) Coming first boat (stop) Only you matters (stop) Explain everything (stop) Great success and my love Henry.

Genevra laid down the cable and said "Oh!" so suddenly that her dresser cried in real alarm, "Not bad noos, I hope?"

Genevra shook her head. "No, the best news in the world," then folded the cable and put it into her bag.

On her way down to the stage the stage manager spoke to her. "Good luck, Miss Menetti. Not noivous, are you?"

She smiled, "Of course——"

"For land's sake, what of?" he grinned.

Still smiling, she said, "Oh, just everything."

He laughed softly. "What-cher-know about it?"

Two and a half hours later she was back in her dressing-room, conscious that New York didn't like her. They had been attentive, polite, possibly even too polite; they had laughed in the right places, they had given her applause, but over and under it all Genevra had felt a chill. She had played well, she knew that, she was too good an actress not to know when her performance had been good or bad. The play itself had evidently been a success, but the completely unknown girl—Alice May—had walked away with the honours. From the moment she had set foot on the stage, the audience had been held spellbound by her. Her part was not very large, but it was highly effective and she had played it with great skill and understanding. Even the long-established Susan Carret had less applause than this tall, thin young woman with her strange voice and queer little mannerisms.

The dresser said, "I'll say it was lovely! My, how they applauded! I've been in stage business all my life and I never knoo a show go better."

Fleming came, his face wearing a puzzled expression. "Fine, Genevra, fine! It's a wow!"

She shook her lovely golden head. "Roland, be honest, they didn't really like me."

"Gee, I'll say they did! They fairly ate it all." His indignation, she knew, was overdone.

She laughed. "So long as I didn't let the show down, that's all right."

He echoed, "Let it down! You certainly did not let it down. You were fine, I tell you, just fine!"

Henry Fossick talked in the same fashion, and all the time Genevra knew that they were disappointed. They had believed that she was 'a find' and she had proved to be a competent actress, who might add a certain distinction to the play, but whom the audience had never taken to their hearts as they had done the lanky, brilliant, unknown Alice May.

"Honey," Fossick said. "I've never seen anyone look so

beautiful. It was like the moon and the stars all shining together when you came on."

"Not the stars, Harry; I shall never be a star in New York."

"I'll say that you will! Jeze, I'll make you a star! Not only here, but in Hollywood. Together, Genevra, you and I'll show them things!"

That night, as they sat at supper in the newest and smartest restaurant in New York, he asked her to marry him. His beautiful voice was low and filled with deep admiration and affection. She listened to him as she might have listened to an orchestra playing exquisite music. His words might be simple, but his sincerity and his voice were very moving.

He ended by asking again, "Genevra, darling, will you marry me? I swear there is nothing in the world I won't do to make you happy. Genevra, don't let to-night worry you. I've seen things like this happen before. It's happened to me. I've come off saying, 'That's me—just a flop!' The next night they're changed: everyone in the audience has been on my side."

She laid her hand on his—it felt cool and smooth under her fingers. "Harry, my dear, it's nothing to do with to-night that makes me have to say 'no'. I do like you so much . . . I think I like you better than any man I've ever met—except one. I've known him practically all my life. There has been some mistake. I thought that he was going to marry someone else. I knew that I loved him; I believed in my heart that he loved me. To-night he cabled me, and that cable crystallized everything for me. He's coming over here. He'll explain everything to me. . . ."

She saw his dark eyes narrow a little. "Just suppose that you didn't like the explanation, honey?"

"I don't think that it would make any difference," she said, "even if I couldn't marry him, even if he didn't really want to marry me, there can't be anyone else."

"What—never?"

Genevra shook her head. "I don't think—ever."

Harry nodded. "That's just too bad—for me. No use going on hoping?"

"I don't think so, my dear. Harry, I am so sorry."

"Never mind, sweetie, it's been good to just think about up to now. We'll still knock hell out of that darned play together, won't we?"

"Of course; you're an actor, and though I may not be a very good actress, we'll do our damnedest! I'll try not to let you down."

CHAPTER TWENTY

THAT night Genevra lay in bed staring into the darkness, conscious that in spite of the fact that she had not justified Fleming's hopes, and the belief which Fossick had placed in her, she was happy. She had read Henry's cable again and again, she had repeated the words softly, and felt her heart singing as she read or spoke them. How Henry had discovered this 'mistake' she did not trouble to imagine, it was sufficient that he had discovered it, that he was coming to explain everything to her.

She did not sleep very much, and towards morning her mind wandered back to Harry Fossick and the theatre. Poor Harry, and she liked him so much, admired him as an actor, and knew that in addition he was a good friend. Their scenes had gone well, the audience loved him, knew him, and were ready to admire his work again and again. The fault must have lain with her. Yet she knew too much about her work to believe that she had played badly. She knew that her work had been polished, smooth, easy; there were scenes in which she had risen to considerable emotional heights. The audience had recognized them, applauded them and, Genevra knew, had waited impatiently for Alice May's next entrance!

Fleming had called a rehearsal for eleven o'clock, and Genevra picked up her script and, sitting up in bed, went slowly through her part using every critical faculty she possessed. Finally she came to the end of the play, laid down the script, and decided what was wrong.

'Too much technique, too much polish, and not enough warmth. Alice May has scarcely any technique at all, she exploits her personality. I was too busy trying to "fit in", to have everything "dovetailed". I've got to play it much broader, warmer, even perhaps with less polish, and a greater sincerity.'

She rang for her morning tea and she thought again how badly they made tea! Those nasty little bags floating about at the end of a string in the teapot! She smiled at the thought of what her gran'ma would say to tea made so! It was easy to smile this morning, in spite of the fact that with her tea would come the morning papers, and in the morning papers would be the criticisms!

They came, an armful of them, every one containing more

pages than even the largest Sunday newspaper in England. Genevra poured out her tea, grimaced at the colour of it, and began to read what the critics had to say about the *Sleeping Goddess*.

To the play itself they were uniformly kind. Susan Carret was well known, much liked, and she received considerable praise. They grew eulogistic over Harry Fossick, and became positively delirious about Alice May. She was a discovery, a diamond of the first water, she had the power to laugh at herself, it was obvious that her work was a delight to her. As for Genevra, they admired her looks, declaring that she was 'an English type in spite of her foreign name'; her performance was, they complained, lacking in warmth. One critic said, 'I could not believe completely in the character which Genevra Menetti portrayed; I doubt if she fully believed in it herself'. They told her that she 'obviously suffered from that slightly superior air which so many English actors and actresses think it incumbent upon them to wear when they make their first appearance in New York'. Another judged 'that Miss Menetti is very young, probably almost as young as she looks. If this is so, time and experience will teach her that it is not sufficient to be friendly to other members of the cast, she must be friendly towards her audiences'.

She read them all gravely and attentively, then took out Henry's cable and read it again, as if she savoured each word.

Fleming was satisfied with the Press, he told them all at rehearsal. The advance bookings were good, and he predicted that the criticisms in the weekly and bi-weekly papers would strike a note of much warmer approval.

Fossick said to Genevra, "Those bums of Press men haven't scared you, have they, honey? Aw, take no notice, they've just gone crackers over Alice May. Mind, she's good, that girl. She's a lot smarter than you are. She exploits her personality, you sink yours in your part. Let it come right through. I'm looking forward to to-night!"

She smiled at him, her eyes suddenly moist. "Harry, what a generous person you are! I am so grateful."

"G'wan," he said, "I'm just a guy that's been in love. I've been given the air, but I'm still in love! That's all there is to it, sweetie."

Fleming's prophecy was correct and amply fulfilled. The Sunday Press were enchanted with the *Sleeping Goddess*, they flung complimentary adjectives at everyone in the cast, reserving their strongest and most eulogistic for Alice May. They said that Genevra Menetti had 'power', 'great distinction' and, 'for one who is obviously so young, she had a dignity far beyond her years'. One well-known journal went so far as to say that 'many of our younger actresses might well take a lesson from this beautiful young English actress. She might "tear passion to tatters"; instead she exercises great restraint. Again and again she proves that she has reserves of power and emotion on which she never draws, and, we admit, the part gains by her economy'.

Harry Fossick telephoned to her, "Good morning! Read the papers? Now, what do you know?"

Genevra replied, "Not much, I admit, only that you people in New York are terribly kind, and a certain Harry Fossick is the kindest of them all." He laughed. "Stop kidding and I'll call for you to come out to lunch some place, eh?"

Assuming a dreadfully overdone and theatrical American accent, she replied, "O.K. by me! I guess I'd like it a lot! S'long, Harry."

She had a second cable wirelessed from Henry the following morning.

Half-way over to you (stop) Thinking of you all the time (stop) If possible will you meet 'Mercuria' arriving Wednesday ten morning (stop) Preening myself at the thought of your success which was inevitable (stop) My love always Henry.

Again Genevra experienced that sense of stability, knew that her fears had vanished and that she was capable not only of waiting expectantly for Henry's arrival, but that she was prepared to extract all possible enjoyment out of life until he came. Life in New York amused her, excited her. The endless photographers, the constant demands for 'personal interviews'; the invitations— some, Fleming warned her, boring in the extreme; others, he said, would be 'real bright parties'.

On Wednesday she dressed with extreme care, and found that she was smiling at her reflection in the mirror as she brushed her hair. She thought, 'I'm twenty-three. I've got years and years in which to work, to enjoy myself and to be with Henry. Life's wonderful'.

There were many people waiting for the *Mercuria* to dock, and as Genevra stood, her eyes turned expectantly towards the slow-moving steamer, eyes watched her with not only interest, because so many photographs had been shown of her in the Press that she was familiar to hundreds, but because, as one man said to another, "That girl's happy and doesn't care who knows it."

The other replied, "If she's waiting for some guy from

England, and he doesn't know what a darned lucky fellow he is, someone ought to tell him."

The great steamer drew to the dock-side; Genevra heard the clatter of the gangways being lowered, raked the deck with her eyes and saw Henry. He stood very straight and slim, his face rather pale, his eyes searching anxiously. Suddenly he caught sight of her, and looked suddenly younger, even excited. Henry Lorimer—she had never seen him actually excited about anything! He snatched off his immaculate hat and waved it wildly. Genevra's smile widened. Henry, who hated demonstrations!

She knew that her heart was beating heavily, her cheeks burning with excitement. She found herself hearing an old pantomime song running through her brain—who had sung it? —was it lovely Dorothy Ward?

"When you come to the end of the journey . . ."

Henry was coming down the gangway, she heard herself call, "Henry, Henry," and a second later he was standing at her side. He kissed her as he had always done, on the cheek, holding her hand in his.

The two men who had watched her before noted the salutation.

One said, "Typically British. Cold-blooded guys! If I had a girl like that waiting for me she'd have had more than a peck on the cheek!"

The other answered, "They pride themselves on that darn' silly attitude. Call it—decent, and proper reserve! What d'you know!"

A small, very dapper little man rushed up to Henry. "Mr. Lorimer! Now, just tell me where you're staying, hand over any papers. I'll see your baggage through and be right along. Glad to see you! Fine to know that Mr. Levelle's throwing off his sickness."

Henry, still holding Genevra's hand, said, "Thanks, Scroby, I shall be obliged. Genevra, may I introduce Mr. Scroby, one of the leading lights of Cloutte? Scroby—let me introduce you to Miss Menetti."

Scroby swung off his hat. "Miss Menetti, glad to know you. Not that I really need an introduction. I've seen your picture in a dozen papers, and what's better still, I've seen you in the *Sleeping Goddess*. 'Roly' Fleming's certainly got something there. Keep New York audiences happy for a long time. S' long, Mr. Lorimer, I'll be right along."

In the taxi, where the wireless was playing some sentimental tune, and Henry, leaning forward said, "Would it be possible to do without that musical accompaniment?", and the taxi-driver replied, "Dook, I do'n see why not, done by the mere turnin' of a knob, your lordship," Henry twisted round and looked at Genevra; he smiled, and lifting her hand, kissed it.

"And you," he said, "are responsible for the only quarrel— well, scarcely a quarrel, rather an animated and heated discussion —my mother and I have ever had! I hope that you're ashamed of yourself, my child. Then, as the result of this discussion, I had to leave my business, my work, which is terribly in arrears owing to my having to stay with Levelle for so long, and come out here. I cannot afford to run about the world after you, something will have to be done. Genevra, will you marry me?"

She said, "I should like to, Henry, but that's the second time you've asked me and still you've said nothing about my loving you, or you loving me."

"Look here," he admonished her. "I've just come off that steamer, I've not even seen you for months, you can't expect me to have rehearsed the whole thing in the solitude of my state-room. I'll do better when we get to my hotel."

"Where are you staying?"

"The Waldorf Astoria."

Genevra giggled happily. "How typical of you, Henry! I can't come and sit in your bedroom, though. Americans are terribly proper."

"I knew that we should have various arguments and for that reason I have an apartment. Haven't you noticed how I've dressed myself for the part of a sober, honest and well-behaved man? Did you ever see clothes which breathed such respectability?"

She wanted to tell him that no man ever looked so distinguished, that she loved his lean, clever face, his firm mouth which could soften so when he smiled. His eyes met hers so directly, their expression was softer than she remembered ever to have seen it. Impulsively she laid her hand on his.

His eyes crinkled at the corners. "Yes——?"

"Nothing—just—oh, Henry!"

In his sitting-room he ordered drinks, a multitude of drinks, it seemed to Genevra—bottles of this, of that, soda-water, lime juice with dry biscuits, and the like. Only when the door closed on the waiter did he turn and take her in his arms, only to release her and say, "Oh, darling, take off that damned hat! It's lovely, but I want to kiss your beautiful hair."

She took off the hat, saying, "That cost me the best part of a week's salary!"

"I don't believe it! Remember I'm in the business, I know about these things. There—" as his arms went round her—"my Genevra, what a silly stupid muddle it's all been. What a fool I've been with my overdone reticence, and stiff-necked determination, my nonsense about my career! To hell with my career! All I want is you! You know that. Tell me you really do know that."

They sat together on the big overstuffed sofa, Genevra leaning against his shoulder, thinking how lovely it was to be with him again, how much she liked the faint smell of Russian leather which hung about him. How she admired his hands, and their long, slim fingers, how she loved everything about him, even his queer, half-pedantic remarks.

"Why did you say that you were going to marry Mrs. Gossage?" she asked suddenly.

Henry almost shouted, "I never said that I was going to marry her! I never asked her to marry me, or had the slightest actual intention of doing so. Anyway, who told you? It's a lie—a damned lie!"

"Jane Heriot told me, and someone called 'Charlie' Bennings told her that you had told this Bennings woman. That *you* had told her."

"A likely thing that if I had wanted to confide in anyone that I should have chosen Charlotte Bennings! A detestable woman, a bitch of the first water! Charlotte Bennings! Let me have a word with her when I see her!" Slowly and carefully he repeated the actual conversation with the imaginative Miss Bennings, then, "As for Clementina Gossage, she's one of the grandest women imaginable, but there has never, never been anyone except you. No matter how grand, or honest or kind they may be. Get that into your adorable golden head."

She nodded. "I think I've got it firmly in, Henry."

He continued, "Then you go and tell my mother! That's number one grievance—if I were engaged why had I not been 'open and above board' about it? If there is an expression I detest, it's 'open and above board'. I had not told my mother, I had not told you—'and she's like your own sister, too'. I never wanted you for a sister! Then, you told her that I had asked you to marry me, but—let me get this right—that I had been so stiff and formal that you felt I was speaking solely from a sense of duty. That really put me in the wrong! How dared I—'that lovely girl'—why didn't I have sufficient sense to know that a girl wants to be told a man loves her. Genevra, I had to listen to a monologue for hours. It will take a long, long time for you to atone for your mistakes!"

But he smiled as he said it, and she answered demurely, "I shall try to do my best, Henry."

That evening he came to watch the play, and later when he called for her to take her to supper in his sitting-room, he was silent. She wondered if her acting had disappointed him, and yet she knew that she had played well that evening.

'It's not only that I'm growing to understand the part better, to know exactly how and where to get my effects, it's because I'm happy. That's what the play turns on—happiness and the power it can give. Now, since Henry came back, I know that the author was right. I'm happy, and it's given me additional understanding, additional power.'

She plied Henry with questions. "Did you enjoy the play?"

"I thought it an excellent play, and quite admirably acted."

"Alice May is good, isn't she?"

"Quite. Possibly a little obvious, I felt."

"And I?" She could not resist asking that question. "Was I good?"

He leaned across the round table on which supper had been served, his face grave, his eyes thoughtful and serious.

"Once upon a time," he said, "I was fool enough to suggest that you left the stage and married me. I suppose in my innate conceit I imagined that I might be regarded as a consolation prize! Now, I still want you to marry me—it's the thing I want most in all the world—but I say, and mean it—you must go on. In many ways it will be very good for us—yes, both of us. We shall have separate lives, and yet we shall have our precious lives together. After all, I shall see more of you than the average business man sees of his wife, far more than a sailor; in fact, I shall begin each day by shaking hands with myself and offering Henry Lorimer my sincere congratulations."

He rose and came to where she sat, slipped his arm round her shoulders and said softly, "Tell me that you're happy, darling Genevra."

"So happy that I feel that I ought to pinch myself to prove that it's really true."

He drew her to the window and together they stood looking out at the miracle of the lights of New York. Henry said softly, "Artificial, no doubt, but it's lovely, and gay and—yes, and self-confident! Genevra, how long is this damned play going to run? I have to be back in London in just over a week. I can't spare more than four days here. You can't come back with me?"

"And leave the show! My dear!" The actress in her was shocked.

He laughed. "First, last and all the time—your duty as an actress?"

"You'd hate me to be different."

He nodded. "I know. Oh, you're right, but the moment the run ends——"

"I shall be on the first boat, even if I had to come as a stow-away."

He took her in his arms, kissed her repeatedly, then, letting her go as if he were reluctant to part with her, he sighed.

"I must take you home. . . ."

She nodded. "I know. Good night, darling. Early to-morrow, telephone to me. I can't believe it's true. I shall want reassuring many, many times a day. I've really been in love with you for so long. . . ."

"When," he asked eagerly, "when did it begin?"

"When a little girl came to your house with a dead monkey in her arms, and met you first in the evening. Poor little Monk——"

He said gravely, "I wish that when I'm dead someone would speak my epitaph so beautifully. Come, my dearest, we've both got work to do to-morrow."

"I know, but think of all the endless to-morrows that are waiting for us! That's something, isn't it?"

"All I know is that you—are everything!"

THE END